A MARKET IN
THE
MAELSTROM

A MARKET IN THE MAELSTROM

THE COZY ABYSS BOOK 3

HARMON COOPER

Podium

Cover design by Daniel Kamarudin

ISBN: 978-1-0394-5501-6

Published in 2025 by Podium Publishing
www.podiumentertainment.com

Podium

A MARKET IN
THE
MAELSTROM

CHAPTER ONE

A SPECIAL ANNOUNCEMENT

Sylas Runewulf spent most the day on his farm, preparing for another crop of corn. As he worked, Patches the pub cat watched from the farmhouse's porch, while Cornbread the farm dog patrolled the fields, pausing randomly to sniff at things and bark at the other dogs in the Seedlands.

"Enough," Sylas told the dog after she had barked for what seemed like an hour. She came running to him, her tail wagging hard enough to shake her whole body. "Just give me a little time." He reached down to scratch behind Cornbread's ears. "It shouldn't be much longer now, girl."

Sylas needed to clear his mind.

He hadn't planned to jump right into things upon returning from the Chasm, yet with everything that Nuno the manaseer had revealed, the last thing Sylas wanted to do was wait around.

Nuno's words came to Sylas as he worked through Mana Infusion:

"The Celestial Plains have spoken. And our reply will be shaped by how we interpret the invasion message. It will become our legend, forge our legacy, and if we're unlucky, herald our demise. I know this isn't the message any of us wanted to hear, but now that we understand what is happening, we can act."

The Underworld, the place that Sylas had grown to love in a relatively short amount of time, had just thirty-eight days before the Hexveil came down and the Underworld merged with the Chasm. This had been heaven's mandate, the Celestial Plains ordering the demise of Sylas's newfound home, at least in the way Nuno had interpreted it.

Gone would be the Hexveil, the protective barrier keeping hell itself from boiling over and Sylas's world would be plunged into depths of darkness never thought possible as demons charged forth into the villages, towns, and cities of the Underworld. Even worse, with its proximity to the Hexveil, Ember Hollow would be one of the first settlements to be invaded.

Towns like Cinderpeak would follow, taking with it the Seedlands and all of its farms. Douro, where Sylas got fireberries, would fall, as would all the smaller places, each with their own story to tell. Sylas didn't know what would happen to larger Underworld cities like Battersea, but he suspected all would suffer, especially as the Hexveil came down on all sides.

After all, the Underworld existed *within* the Chasm, the space carved out by the Celestial Plains to be a destination for those who didn't deserve to go to heaven but had somehow skipped out on instantly being deposited in hell.

Yet now, that was set to change.

The Plains had spoken, and through the message Sylas got every morning, an invasion was imminent. It would seem like this invasion came from the collapse of the Hexveil.

But Sylas and a few others would know the truth.

If an invasion happened, it might come from the Chasm, but it would be orchestrated by the Celestial Plains.

There were ways to send a message to the Celestial Plains, but according to a local farmer named Trampus, it took tens of thousands of Mana Lumens to do so. While Sylas could net quite a bit with his farm and pub, he didn't know how much the actual cost would be, nor did he think he had enough time to afford it because of a rule by which things became pricier after a person had more than twenty thousand Mana Lumens.

"And later," he reminded himself as Mana Infusion took place, his fields with a golden glow to them, "I'll have the market too."

The Ember Hollow market seemed to be the last thing on Sylas's mind. But it was the first thing on Mira's, the apothecary who had gone in on the purchase with him.

She had spoken excitedly about it earlier over breakfast: "If you're working on the farm, I'll be working on the market. As soon as we can get it set up for vendors, we can start renting out booths and you can sell more ale there. Double the brewing, if that's fine. This will create another channel of passive MLu income, but, and I hate to say it like this, we don't have much time."

"No, we do not," Sylas said to himself as he continued his work on the farm. "No, we do not."

Quinlan caught his attention. The former soldier exploded out of his hammock, startling Patches, who took off, the cat's belly causing him to slide to the side before he finally got control over himself. Patches scrambled to his feet and raised his tail in both alarm and annoyance.

"Mate!"

"What is it?" Sylas asked Quinlan as he approached.

"Nightmare, that's what it is." Quinlan squinted up at the sky, which was always golden because of the Plains. "Or 'daymare.' I was thinking about this time when I was a boy and I was peering down into this well. My brother shoved me by the shoulders but caught me just in time. I thought I would fall in. I didn't, but I did in the nightmare. Bloody hell. Then, we were climbing through a tunnel toward the Chasm—" He sucked in a deep breath through his nostrils. "I guess it doesn't matter. Are you almost finished up?"

"I would be finished by now if I had help," Sylas said, a lie.

"Help, yeah?" Quinlan laughed as he caught Patches glaring at him. "Scared him, didn't I? Sorry about that," he told the cat.

Cornbread woofed.

Sylas looked from the farm dog to Tilbud, who traveled quickly down the lane toward them, the archlumen hovering with a gust of wind at his feet. Dressed in a purple suit, one with yellow stitching on the lapel that matched the small hat on his head, Tilbud seemed to be moving in a panic.

"Speaking of kitties, look what the cat dragged in," Quinlan said, a joke that seemed to bring more ire from Patches, whose ears folded back. "Noted. I'll never wake you up from a nap again—"

"Ah, good. You're here! I'm here. We're all here," Tilbud said, a bit of panic in his eyes. "Ahem. There has been a development."

"What kind of development?" Sylas asked.

"The Hexveil. A few things have gotten through, and the Hexveilian Guard have dealt with them. For now. But it is rather shocking. Demons do make it through the Hexveil, as you know, but not a full-on force."

"A full-on force? What do you mean?" Quinlan asked, growing serious.

"I'm not one to understand the military parlance that may make more sense to a man of your rather checkered history. A squad? A battalion? A troupe? A baker's dozens of detestable demons is what I'm referring to. They were organized, led by a mage who was able to use mana. Quite shocking really, such a blatant attack."

"And it's taken care of now?" Sylas asked.

"It is, yes. But it might do us all good to see what that looks like."

"So we go to the Hexveil, easy," Quinlan told Tilbud. "It isn't too far from here anyway. We'll beat the bastards back."

"Yes, I'm sure you would. But as I already said, they have been handled."

"Did anything reach Ember Hollow?" Sylas asked Tilbud.

"No. And if it had, Nuno and I would have handled it. Ah, and there's another thing regarding our dear manaseer: he has since departed. And asked that you give him a day or so to speak with his contacts in Battersea. Nuno wants you to meet him there near his home, at some coffee or tea lounge. He said you knew where that was."

"So I should go tomorrow?"

"Best to go the following morning."

"And Raelis?" Quinlan asked Tilbud. "Did you check on him?"

"I did not, but Nelly and Karn have been alternating between looking after Raelis using some medicine given to them by Mira, and running the general store. He'll be better soon, I believe, I pray, even though I'm not the praying type."

Quinlan scratched the back of his head. "That reminds me. Kael. We need to get him from his retreat. He'll be able to help in some way, I just know it."

"Agreed," Sylas said as a plan quickly formed in his mind. "I've been thinking the same. How about this? We got to Battersea to meet Nuno and continue on from there for your brother."

"Or perhaps we see what we can get into in Battersea, I visit Geist, and we pull Kael out of his meditation hole later this week," Quinlan said. "It would be best to get my brother once we know more of what is happening."

"I can see that." Sylas turned back to Tilbud. "Another question. I heard that you could spend MLus to send a message to the Celestial Plains. How expensive is that?"

Tilbud considered this, his bushy eyebrows angling up as if he were counting numbers in his head. "It isn't cheap," he finally said. "But there may be a work-around. Let me have a think. In the meantime, perhaps you two would like to see what has happened at the Hexveil. Undoubtedly, it serves as a warning of what might happen if we don't take action."

<hr>

The Hexveil had indeed changed.

The magical barrier wall still stood just as Sylas had remembered it, mirrored in certain ways like a reflective fog that would never lift. There were cracks in it now, reminiscent of the stained glass in a destroyed cathedral in Riverpool. Sylas had once camped in that very cathedral during a long campaign to retake the city for the Aurum Kingdom. It was a very particular image that sat with him, namely because Sylas had seen it mere mere days before his death.

"Just like it," he muttered as archlumens beyond worked to seal up the magical barrier shielding the Underworld from calamity. Around them, the Hexveilian Guard stood at attention, the giant soldiers as intimidating as ever in their thick armor and the way they towered over everyone.

"Like what?" Quinlan asked.

"Riverpool. The glass at that cathedral," he told Quinlan as he pointed it out. "Right before I died. So much had been shattered at the cathedral aside from one portion at the top, of the sun. And then one of our archers fired a rock at it. The bloody moron."

"Eh, he was probably just blowing off steam. We all did stuff like that from time to time, you know."

"Still, not acceptable." Sylas stared out at the Hexveil and the signs of an epic fight that now lay before it. There were craters on the ground and patches of grass were singed. There were a few piles of debris that were still smoldering.

"Eh, it is what it is. But this . . ." Quinlan gestured to the site of the battle. "I think people need to know what all of this is about." He turned to Sylas and offered the man a grin that was partially covered by his scruffy beard. "I might be going out on a limb here, and maybe this isn't exactly the best idea considering how people are prone to panic, but maybe we tell everyone."

"Tell everyone?"

"Everyone. They deserve to know about the message you're receiving."

"Where? At the pub?"

"Why not? It isn't Wraithsday yet. You and Azor normally have a feast on Wraithsday, yeah? What better time to tell everyone that all hell is going to break lose—literally—in what? Thirty-something days?"

"Thirty-eight."

"Give or take a few, then, yeah?"

Sylas looked back up at the Hexveil. "I suppose that could be an option. Invite everyone we know."

"Bloody right. Get Tilbud involved. He knows loads of people. You could fill The Old Lamplighter with his lovers."

"I'd have to run it by Nuno as well."

"Easy peasy. We run it by anyone who wants to hear us out," Quinlan said. "We'll go to Battersea and see what the manaseer has to say."

Sylas considered Quinlan's suggestion. He had a feeling it would be Mira who went with him to Battersea, and while he didn't want to tell his friend not to tag along, he also wanted to tell him that he didn't need to come. "I can talk to Nuno. You should head on to Geist."

"Like that, is it?"

"Didn't you want to go to Geist?"

"Did I say that? I mean, maybe I should go to see Prissy, but I think I heard somewhere that absence makes the heart grow fonder. I don't know if I agree with that sentiment, though."

"Would it feel better if I told you I was planning to ask Mira to go with me?"

Quinlan laughed. "Now that makes more sense. Come on, mate. Let's get out of here. And let's pray that the Hexveil holds. Don't forget the Taurigraith, the nasty bugger."

Sylas thought about the Taurigraith that night as he poured up pints. He remembered the sheer size of the hellacious monster, its bovine horns, bull's body, and terrifying tiger face complete with razor-sharp teeth, and how his group had nearly been forced to fight it on their way back from the Chasm.

It made him shudder to think one could have gotten through the Hexveil, but they had no evidence that this had happened yet, only an offhand remark from Quinlan, who had decided to stay at the farm that night rather than visit The Old Lamplighter.

"That remains to be seen, or hopefully, not seen," he said under his breath as he polished a pint glass.

Godric the fireweave tailor and a few of the farmers were in the pub, the group taking most of Sylas's attention until they got distracted by Cornbread, who ran in playful circles in front of them yapping.

"She's really the cutest," Azor said in between serving pints. "Patches gets so jealous, which is also cute in its own way. I wish there were such things as little fire puppies and kittens. I would have so many."

"Ha!" Sylas looked over to the piebald pub cat, who sat on his perch in the window watching the farmers laugh at Cornbread. "As for Patches, I really wonder what he's thinking sometimes."

Azor grew a pair of fiery cat ears. "If I could talk to Patches, I have a feeling he'd be grumpy. So maybe he is thinking grumpy things. Hungry grumpy things."

"Hungry grumpy things, huh? Like what?"

"I don't know. I didn't really think that statement through." She laughed and a pair of fire whiskers formed on her face. "How's my cat costume?"

"Ask Patches."

They both looked over to the cat, who seemed to be raising an eyebrow at Azor, unsure if the fire spirit was mocking him or not. In the end, he turned his rump to them and stared out the window.

Later that evening, Mira came, as did some of Ember Hollow's militiamen, including Duncan, Cody, and Gary. Once Mira was seated with an ale in front of her, Sylas got everyone's attention by tapping on a glass with a butter knife. "Before the night goes any longer, I wanted to let you all know that we will have a special announcement at this week's Wraithsday Feast. You all should be there. And you should let your friends know."

"Yeah?" Godric called out. "Did you really think we had somewhere else to go?" A few of the people seated around him chuckled at this comment. One raised his pint and cheersed Sylas. Bart the bard said something and everyone laughed again.

"An important announcement?" Azor asked, the fire spirit nearly spilling her tray of pints. "Is this about the you-know-what? And less importantly, what should I cook?"

Mira looked at Sylas suspiciously. "What's this about?"

"Can I tell you later?"

"You can tell me now," she said as the crowd at the pub continued to murmur.

"Give me a moment." He cleared his throat. "Everyone, just be sure to be here for the Wraithsday Feast and invite anyone that you know. I'd appreciate it. Now, Azor."

"Yes?" she asked.

"Can you cover for a moment while I walk Mira home."

"I sure can!"

After a bit more banter, Sylas and Mira left the pub. As soon as they were out, Mira took his hand. "Really, Sylas. What is this about?"

"Quinlan and I were talking."

"Were you now? About what? Is it about Raelis? He's doing better, you know. He had a long conversation with Nelly this afternoon before falling back asleep. He seemed clearheaded. It's progress, that's for sure."

"That's wonderful to hear. I didn't want to bother him when I returned from the Hexveil."

"Ah, so you heard about the breach?" she asked, her brow furrowing. "Everyone was talking about it earlier, but it seems to have been patched up. It's not great, especially if we want to open soon. I would be lying if I said I wasn't worried about the market."

"How so?"

"For one, it doesn't have a name. A stupid worry in light of what is happening, I know," she told Sylas, "but giving it a name gives it life in certain ways."

"I agree. In that case, what would you like to name it?"

"I don't know. I thought we would come up with one together. I was hoping it would be a bit more original than something like 'The Ember Hollow Market.' Although, names like that work. I actually thought of a name, but it is a little redundant. I also realize that all of this is a distraction, but it is a much needed one."

"Well?" Sylas asked after she was quiet for a spell. "What's the name you came up with? And never mind the distraction. Sometimes, those are the little things that keep us going."

"Promise you won't laugh?"

"Cross my heart."

"Funny. The name I thought of was 'The Bargains Market.' You know, a market where there will be bargains. So it's not 'bargains plural', it's just a market where we hope there will be bargains."

Sylas grinned at her. "The name is a little on the head."

"I believe the phrase is 'on the nose.'"

"I would argue that the nose is on the head."

"I'm sure you would."

Sylas noticed movement beside them. He moved by Mira and placed his hand on her lower back. "Just Patches."

The cat became visible. He mewed and Mira scooped him up into her arms. "You really just wanted some attention, didn't you?" she asked as he purred even louder.

"He could get as much as he likes back at the pub."

Mira pressed her nose against Patches and the cat seemed to grin. "Is Cornbread getting all the love? And what do you think about the name? The Bargains Market? Do you like it?"

Patches mewed softly.

"Then I suppose that settles it," Sylas said as they neared her home. "The Bargains Market is a fine name. And don't worry about getting it set up. That is indeed our plan for the week. Or perhaps after we solve what needs to be solved. Which brings me to my next point. Quinlan suggested that it was time we tell people. That's what I was referring to when I said I'd have an important announcement at the Wraithsday Feast."

"You really think it is time to tell people about the invasion?"

"As risky as it may be, I do. They deserve to know."

Mira bit her lip as she considered this. "I don't know, but I agree with Quinlan, I think people deserve to know."

"Of course they do."

"It's hard to think about sometimes. We've made such great progress in Ember Hollow over the last two months or so. Even my ornery old uncle is behaving himself to some extent. By revealing this to everyone, things could change. We don't know how people will react. Are you sure you want that?"

"I'm not sure if it's up to me or not. But I think people need to know, and I want to confer with Nuno and Tilbud, who seems to have disappeared. I honestly thought he would come back here after he sent Quinlan and me to the Hexveil, but I haven't seen him."

"He stopped by the market actually and said he would return soon."

"Ah, I see. Presumably, he wants to head with us to Battersea."

"Presumably, yes." Mira's face hardened. "We'll get it sorted, Sylas. In the meantime, you should get back to the pub. I'm sure Azor needs your help." She placed Patches on the ground and surprised Sylas when she lifted onto the tips of her toes and kissed his cheek. "Bargains Market. Think about it."

Before he could say anything, she had stepped away.

———

What a fun night! Cornbread made a whining sound as she approached Patches, who stood near the cat door. *Fun! Fun!*

Stop your barking. You are too friendly, you know that?

Me? I guess I am friendly, Cornbread told Patches proudly as the cat licked his paws.

And you weren't paying attention.

Attention to what?

I noticed something strange when I went out with the big man earlier.

Cornbread sat, her tail still lightly tapping against the ground. *You did? Like what?*

A change in the air. You didn't sense it when we came from the farm?

Cornbread's right ear flopped to the left. *Now that you mention it, something was different out there. Shall we do some exploring?*

Patches stood. *I thought you would never ask.* He glanced over to the fire spirit, who was already resting near the fire, her flames flickering lightly. *Let's go.*

Soon, the two were exploring the shadows around the village of Ember Hollow, Patches leading their mission as best he could. *I know there are interesting smells,* he told the dog, *but we don't want to be seen by the militiamen. Keep quiet.*

Why not? Cornbread lifted her snout into the air and took in a deep whiff. *They're nice humans.*

It is best if we remain in the shadows. Earlier, I caught a whiff of something this way, toward the magic wall.

Cornbread turned her nose in the direction of Patches's snout. *Wait. You're right. Something has changed! I know exactly what it is. I'm surprised I didn't notice it.*

You were too busy running around and playing, Patches said. *I'm surprised you can still smell it. I can't smell anything.*

I certainly can. There has been a breach. But the wall is repaired. Temporarily. Her ears flattened. *This is bad.*

What's bad? Patches asked. *And that's my line!*

Something came through! Cornbread made like she was going to bark and caught herself. *Sorry. The monster from the other side. The one. Sort of like a bull and a tiger. It is here, it is near.*

No . . .

Come on! Cornbread took off and Patches tried to catch up with her. He eventually gave up and just waited for her barks to join the farm dog as she raced through the woods outside Ember Hollow. They came to the magical wall, which was still being seen to by humans and guarded by beings that made Patches shudder.

They certainly weren't human.

Have you found anything?

Cornbread sniffed at the ground. *It's so faint, the smell. It's like the beast appears and disappears. But I think it went . . .* She grew alert. *Toward the farms. Toward the Farmly Realm!*

We can't possibly go there tonight.

We could wake the big man?

How would we tell him what it is?

I don't know, Cornbread said as she began to circle nervously. *I really don't know.*

Stop being erratic. If there is something there, we will soon find out about it. You're sure of what you smell?

I am. But I'm also not as sure as I'd like to be, she admitted. *The scent is very faint.*

I can't smell it at all. But I do sense the magic. Patches sat and began licking his paw again. *I do this when I'm thinking,* he told Cornbread after feeling as if he were being judged. *And I think that we should go back to the Tavernly Realm. The Farmly Realm will be fine. The other man is there.*

Yes, him. He's very good at what he does, she told Patches, her tail wagging.

He is. And we will know more in the morning. Perhaps we can ask around the farms as well.

Cornbread nodded excitedly. *Yes, let's do that!* She took off toward the pub. *Race you there!*

CHAPTER TWO

FUZZY FEELING

The system information came to Sylas the next morning as it always did.

[You have 37 days until the invasion.]
[A loan payment of 80 has been deducted from your total Mana Lumens.
Your total loan balance is 24523 Mana Lumens.]

Name: Sylas Runewulf
Mana Lumens: 8128/8128
Class: Brewer
Secondary Class: Farmer
Tertiary Class: Landlord
[Lumen Abilities:]
Flight
Quill
Mana Infusion
Mana Saturation
Harvest Silos
Field Warden
Whimsical Drift
Soulfire
Bargain Binding
Ward of Welcome
Structural Reinforcement
Territorial Domain
Architect's Arsenal

Sylas groaned at the weight of the doomsday message, how at odds it was from the life that he had started for himself, one of cozy good times and a growing love interest.

As he lay there petting Patches, Sylas ran the numbers in his head to see that while he had spent a good amount on Mana Infusion, he had recouped it over what turned out to be a busy night at the pub. With his loan payment, he wasn't too far from where he expected to be. "Not bad," he said to himself as he continued to pet the purring pub cat. "Not bad at all."

"Happy—"

"Tombsday," he told Azor after she flashed into existence in a puff of flames. The fire spirit swooned forward, her flames all but disappearing until they reformed, first as scales, before finally smoothing out.

Sylas heard Cornbread barking as he raced up the stairs to join them. The dog burst into the room and launched herself onto the bed, startling Patches.

The cat yowled at her, Cornbread barked, and Patches finally gave in and let Cornbread lick his face.

"Happy Tombsday. Which means the Wraithsday Feast is in order," Azor said. "And look how cute your pets—our pets?—are. Awww. But back to the feast. And never mind the announcement you want to make. I'm thinking of this dish I was served on the ship when we sailed across Lake Seraphina. I want to make something similar for humans. I think it would be best to get some venison—I saw some for sale at the market in Cinderpeak, though it would probably be cheaper in Duskhaven at the Finmarket if you care to visit—and I was thinking that I would wrap strips of this venison in flour after blending it with wild mushrooms."

Sylas's stomach grumbled. "I'm listening. And I consider them our pets. Patches loves you like a mother."

"Ha! Hardly. And don't worry, Mister Tummy," she told Sylas's stomach as she produced a bulbous one of her own, "I have breakfast downstairs too, just need to warm it up, Mister Hungry Pub Man."

"I'm fine."

"Your stomach begs to differ. I think you licked your lips too, like this." Azor conjured a fiery blue tongue and licked her lips.

"I did? Are you sure that wasn't Cornbread?"

The dog barked and Patches swatted her snout with his paw.

Azor laughed. "You two, get along. Where was I? The feast. Here's what I'm thinking: the venison will be baked inside the flour so the outside is golden and flaky and the inside is perfectly moist. Actually, before I baked it all, I would sear the venison after a sprinkle of salt, pepper, and a bit of herbs. Then, the mushrooms and probably onions and a bit of garlic—one can never have too much garlic according to Quinlan—would be chopped finely and spread over it *before* I wrap up the cooled concoction, and spread some egg wash over it. I'll serve it with herbed butter. That's easy to make. You'll see, Sylas. It will be wonderfully delicious."

"I have no doubt at all. And it makes me want to get creative on the brewing front. It sounds like your"—he cleared his throat— "was there a name for it?"

"The elemental that served me on the ship was named Wellington. So let's call it a Wellington. How's that?"

"Okay. A Wellington. It sounds like your Wellington is quite layered. I'd want an appropriate ale to go with it, something that perhaps presented one flavor at first sip, then something else entirely as it goes down." Sylas thought of the special ales he had already tried, fireberry and flamefruit. "Something the opposite of what I've done thus far, that's what I'm saying. You know, I could probably find something to use in the Finmarket."

"You could! And we could go together." Azor's eyes nearly doubled in size. "Please? Can we go to the Finmarket?"

"Let me check my calendar." Sylas pretended to do just that and then smiled at the fire spirit. "Sure."

"Can't wait!"

Cornbread hopped off the bed and headed over to the door.

"I've got food for you too," Azor called after her. "Come on!"

The fire spirit bolted away and Cornbread took off after her.

Patches made what Sylas interpreted as an annoyed sound in his throat. He started petting the cat again, scratching behind his ears. "Don't let the dog bother you. She means well."

———

Before Sylas left for Duskhaven's Finmarket, he made a stop at his own market and found Mira hard at work. The apothecary had a bandana tied around her head and a nail sticking out of her mouth as she fixed a post that had partially split.

"What am I thinking?" Sylas asked aloud. He set down the packaged sandwich Azor had made for Quinlan and immediately moved to help Mira. "How can I be of assistance, milady?"

"It's fine. You already have two businesses you're running," Mira told him after she finished hammering. "I didn't mean for that to sound sarcastic, really."

"I'm part owner here, and I should be doing more. Sorry for that. My plan today was to check on the farm, loop back around here, and head to Duskhaven with Azor so she can get supplies for the Wraithsday Feast. Would you . . . care to come?"

"To Duskhaven?"

"Yes. And then we can work on the market until the pub opens."

"I wish I could go, really, but I need to do some things here, and I plan to be open for a few hours tonight." Mira squinted up at the golden sky. "That's right. I need to see Miss Barrowsly. But—"

"Miss Barrowsly? I've heard you mention her multiple times. She lives here in Ember Hollow, yes?"

"Near here. Closer to the woods beyond the portal. You actually pass her place if you walk to Cinderpeak. Why?"

"Interesting."

"Not really. She isn't very mobile, but if you want to visit her…" Mira seemed to consider what she was about to say. "Perhaps I shouldn't simply invite you."

Cornbread, who had joined Sylas, came tumbling out of a stack of wood. She got to her feet, wagged her tail, and acted as if nothing happened.

"How did you even get in there, girl?" Sylas asked as he examined the stack, the cleaning up of which was one of the tasks he planned to tackle that night. It was a mess of scrap wood that had no real purpose other than to take up space. Sylas planned to go through it, salvage anything of value, and let Azor handle the rest.

Mira crouched and Cornbread ran over to her. "It doesn't matter," she told the dog, who seemed embarrassed. Mira looked up at Sylas. "I probably shouldn't bring you by uninvited. Miss Barrowsly is a bit eccentric. She has been here forever."

"In Ember Hollow or the Underworld?"

"Both, I think. Her memory is a little off." Mira stood and Cornbread took off again. Sylas whistled after her and the dog returned.

"Anyway, I'm going to check on Quinlan and drop her off," he told Mira, gesturing to Cornbread. "I'll be back later. Anything you want me to do, just let me know. But I definitely plan to tackle this pile of wood."

"As long as you don't burst out of it like Cornbread did, that sounds fine to me."

"One more thing before I go," he said, remembering something. "I wanted to make an interesting ale for the feast, something different than what I have tried before. I figured if anyone knew of an herb I could use, it would be you."

"It would be me, yes." Mira adjusted her head bandana. "What kind of interesting ale do you want? Are we talking about effects, flavor, or perhaps appearance?"

"Effects are always nice. Obviously, flavor is important, but I could likely brew something up with barley, which will have a stronger flavor profile. So, give me, I don't know, some ideas. What would you do if you were trying to pair your ale with…" Sylas thought of how to describe the food Azor had suggested.

"It's like a meat pie, only better, elevated, and tasty. Herbaceous. She's calling it a Wellington, and it will be paired with butter and a garnish."

"Huh. Well, *Wellington*, you've done fiery ales so how about something cool and soothing?"

"Cool and soothing." Sylas pursed his lips and nodded as he thought of the taste. "I like that. The ale will already be slightly cold due to how I store it."

"I mean it will create an additional chill inside someone. If used properly, it might also give off a warm, fuzzy feeling. It could be quite nice."

"An ale that creates a chill and then a warm, fuzzy feeling?" Sylas ran his hand over his beard. "I'm in. That sounds fantastic. Tell me what I need to get."

———

Sylas had said goodbye to Mira and continued to the Seedlands, where he found Quinlan resting in the hammock on the front porch of his farmhouse.

Cornbread barked and jumped into his lap before the former soldier could get out of the hammock. "Now that's a good girl," he said as the dog squirmed playfully in his grip. "Sylas."

"Morning. Special delivery from Azor," Sylas said as he showed him the sandwiches.

Cornbread hopped out of Quinlan's lap and he took the sandwiches. "Not at all what I expected, breakfast delivery, but I'll take it. Have you eaten?"

"I'm fine," Sylas said.

"She made two."

"She thought you'd want two."

"Heh. She was right."

"How was it last night?" Sylas asked Quinlan as he looked out at the corn.

"Nothing to report, mate, but you should be here tonight just in case. As you know, it'll be tomorrow and the final night that things get a bit out of hand."

"Cody was here too, right?"

"Sure was. We talked a lot about where we came from. I like the lad. He's my kind of people. I'm starting to see why you like it here in Ember Hollow. It has quite the appeal. This is a comfortable little area of the Underworld."

"You still have Priscilla back in Geist."

"I know. I need to get back there. I really do. She's going to be royally—"

Cornbread barked and took off into the woods outside of the farm. Sylas and Quinlan exchanged glances.

"Should we follow her?" Sylas asked.

"Let's just see if she returns." Quinlan grinned at his old friend. "Besides, I have some sandwiches to eat. Cheers, mate. And tell Azor I said thanks."

———

The Finmarket was bustling with activity, which gave Sylas an idea as he waited for Azor to collect the things she needed to make her Wellington.

"I'm just going to do a bit of exploring, yeah?" he told her, still speaking in the way he would have likely spoken to Quinlan. It was amazing how much being around his old friend wore off on him.

"Don't worry, I'll find you." Azor laughed. "That's usually easy enough, even with all the people."

"You can always return here as well." Sylas tapped on the fire brand on his arm, which signified the bond he had formed with Azor.

"I certainly could. But I'll get these prices right first. I'm not opposed to a little haggling." She puffed up and someone moving toward them stepped around the fire spirit. Once they were gone, Azor deflated. "That's right, buddy. Now, back to these meats."

Sylas looked over at the butcher she had just spoken to. He stood behind a booth piled high with slabs of meat. There were carcasses hanging behind him near a woman who was grinding sausage, and she was surrounded by a stack of large bones that Sylas assumed could be used for broths.

"There's another butcher across the way," Azor explained. "I'm going to see if I can't get a little bidding war going. How do I look?" She smoothed her fiery hair back and laughed. "Kidding. I know I look good, especially in my fireweave gear."

"I'll be around," Sylas told her, secretly glad to see her feeling so confident.

He moved on, Sylas slipping around a pair carrying a large fish over their shoulders. From there, he went down a set of stairs to reach the vegetable market, where he found a woman selling various herbs. She was an older lady with a head that seemed twice as large as it should have been for her body, her eyes big and saucerlike, and her hair kept back by a blue beret.

"Can I help you?" she asked.

"I'm looking for something called athershade leaf."

The woman stared at Sylas for what felt like a full minute. "You mean aeferd shay leaf."

Sylas thought back to what Mira had told him. "Sure, does it give you a warm, fuzzy feeling?"

The woman cackled. "Who told you that?"

"An apothecary."

She quickly swallowed her laugh. "I know some about things like this, but I would trust the apothecary over someone like me. Could have double-classed, but being classed as a merchant works for me. I keep good company anyhow without adding a bunch of ailing old-timers to my list of customers."

Sylas raised an eyebrow at this statement. The woman had to be pushing eighty, at least at the time of her death. "I'm Sylas Runewulf," he finally said, "owner of The Old Lamplighter in Ember Hollow. I guess I didn't need to introduce myself like that."

"Where would we be as a species without bloated introductions? I'm Esta Lemtop, owner of this merchant stand that sells herbs. Now that the awkward introductions are out of the way, let's get down to business. You want aeferd shay leaf, and I just got a fresh stock in. It's not cheap, though. Five hundred MLus for a bundle."

"That isn't cheap."

"There's a reason for that. It's technically an illegal narcotic, that's why. Well, not illegal, but the powers that be—" She paused yet again to look Sylas up and down. "They don't like people having it."

"Why?"

"It makes them feel good, for one. The people, not the powers that be." She glanced skyward for a moment. "The bastards. They think control makes things more orderly, that this order will make them happier, but it only pushes them toward more order."

"I believe I'm aware of what you're speaking of."

"I've been here a long time, Sylas."

"I'll bet," he told the woman.

"But who am I to say things are changing?" Esta asked. "What do I know? I come to the same market every day and see most of the same people. Anyway, aeferd shay leaf. Let me find it." She puffed her cheeks out. "You did want to buy it, right?"

"I was planning on making an ale with it."

"Doesn't ale already give people a warm, fuzzy feeling."

"Not after a deep chill. That's how the apothecary described it. A deep chill followed by a warm, fuzzy feeling."

"Eh. I didn't know that part. I honestly never advertise that I have the stuff and haven't tried it myself. Occasionally, apothecaries come by to pick it up for medicinal purposes. As you can imagine, for soothing a wound, it does wonders. But a bundle, yeah? Is that what you'd like?"

"Sure."

[Transfer 500 MLus to Esta Lemtop? Y/N?]

Sylas selected "yes" and considered what the woman had said while she rummaged about her shop. He already knew about the Celestial Plains and the hold they had over the Underworld. Sylas was more interested in her statement about coming to the same market day in and day out.

"Let me ask you something," he said as Esta placed a bundle of dry leaves on a scale. The leaves were blue with green dots on them, outlined in black rings, and seemed brittle.

"Ask away."

"I'm opening a market."

"I thought you had a pub."

"I have a pub and a farm, actually."

"A man of many talents or a man that likes to keep himself distracted. What do you grow?"

"Corn."

Esta considered this. "Huh. A pub and a corn farm. Only in the Underworld would that make any sense."

"My businesses are wildly different from one another, I'm aware. But I classed as a landlord and bought a market with the apothecary I told you about."

"Who seems like a love interest."

Sylas stifled a laugh. "Maybe she is. In any event, The Bargains Market, as we have named it, will open next week, I believe. Or a bit sooner. And we're looking for vendors. If you could use a change of scenery, you're more than welcome."

"Bargains Market? What kind of name is that?"

"It's a name like all names."

"I suppose so. And what kind of market is it?"

"Maybe something like this?" Sylas gestured around to the Finmarket. "But less food. Relics, antiques, and food. So people can come to peruse the antiques and pick up food along the way. I think it will grow."

"In Ember Hollow."

"Why not?"

She cackled again. "Have you been to Ember Hollow? I'm kidding, I've been plenty of times. Well, before the village lost its luster. But it sounds like you are bringing that back. And it's a good location too. There is a market in Cinderpeak, but they don't have relics."

"There will be a branch of my brewery at the market as well."

"Drinking and shopping? Now I'm intrigued. You said you had a partner, an apothecary."

"I do."

"Is this apothecary running the show, or are you?"

"Actually, I think Mira will be running it more than me," Sylas told Esta. "I went in with her for a number of reasons. For one, I like Ember Hollow and I'd like to see it restored to its former glory. I also like her and it makes her happy. I guess there are also the MLus, but that's less of my interest at this point."

"And the relics?"

"I am interested in things that may appear at the market, sure. Things that were here before the Crafting Laws."

"I see," she said. "I'm even more intrigued now. I want to try this ale you plan to make. When will you serve it?"

"Wraithsday. We have a feast. It will be aeferd shay leaf ale and Wellington."

"Wellington?"

"It's food, a gourmet dish."

"You had me at food. You convinced me at gourmet. But we'll see if I actually make it."

"You should certainly try."

Esta beamed a smile at him. "In that case, I'll be there, and I'll bring a few who I know are also looking to expand. Now you should be careful," she said, growing serious. "The people that run the Finmarket wouldn't like to hear you're going around poaching their vendors."

"That wasn't my intention, honest. I came for the herbs, and I've left with so much more. But I'll let you talk to Mira when you visit the pub. I also don't see why someone couldn't be at both markets. I believe we'll only be open four days of the week, Wraithsday to Specterday."

"Intriguing. And I like the fact that it's only open half the week." Esta handed him the bundle of aeferd shay leaf. "I wrapped it so they won't know what it is at the front."

"I didn't see any security."

"Then they were doing their job."

"Is it really that illegal?" Sylas asked the older woman.

"Yes and no. There's always a gray zone and you'll stay in that gray zone by keeping this concealed. If someone does ask where you got it, don't say you got it from me. Say, um, say you got it from Hilda. Her booth is across from mine, the old hag, and we don't get along."

———

Patches watched the big man go about the market, moving things around and speaking to the medicine woman. *It seems like they are going to do something here.*

The big man hoisted a rotten board over his shoulder and took it to an increasingly large pile of debris. Near it, the fire spirit rubbed her hands together playfully as blue horns flared out of the sides of her head.

The fire spirit is such a devil. Ah! Patches jumped back as she torched the pile of rubbish, her fires burning bright and blue to the point that the pub cat decided to hide.

He took off and used an overturned crate to reach a beam above, where the pub cat was able to climb out of a hole in the shingles and escape.

Patches remained above them now, looking down, his ears flitted back.

The big man pointed him out to the medicine woman, the two laughed, and he went back to work. While the big man removed rotted wood, the medicine woman followed him with a piece of parchment where she occasionally jotted down information.

What are they discussing? Patches intuited that it was about the market, but were they really going to get it running again? He tried to think back to a time when the market was actually operating and couldn't.

This made him sad. It was brief, but in that moment Patches understood how much he had forgotten of the past people who lived in the Tavernly Realm.

It would be good if I could write something down too. Patches looked left, expecting to see Cornbread. *Right, she's in the Farmly Realm.* Patches's whiskers drooped. *It seems like I'm alone for now, watching the humans create yet another place I will have to defend.* This thought inspired him to some degree. *On the other paw, the realms grow . . .*

Patches stood, his ears perked up. He used the same hole in the roof to reach the rafters and crept along until he spotted some movement at the base of a post.

Rats.

Patches turned himself invisible.

He moved as quietly as possible, his belly rubbing against the wooden beam as he got into position.

Patches jumped, hit the base of the post, and grabbed the first rat while the second scampered. He ripped into the rodent, injured it to the point it wouldn't be able to escape, and raced after the second rat, which was heading toward a hole in the floorboards of one of the booths.

The rat reached the hole and shoved its large body in.

Not on my watch! Patches was on it in a matter of seconds, his claws digging into its back as he pulled it out.

Patches clamped down onto the rat's throat as it tried to scratch and nip at him. At this point, the big man came around, a surprised look on his face.

Why is he laughing? Patches thought as he finished with the rat. *I'm only trying to help!*

———

"He killed two of them," Sylas said, his hands on his hips. "*Two.* Patches is a serious hunter." He laughed again as Mira approached. "A real feline warrior."

"It's so gruesome. What's funny about this?"

Sylas's smile thinned. "I suppose nothing. I was just shocked to see Patches hunting and . . ." He scratched the back of his head. "I don't know why I laughed. But I guess I should add the rats to the burn pile. Unless Azor wants them for her Wraithsday Feast."

Mira tapped him on the arm playfully. "Don't give her any ideas."

"There are rats?" Azor said as she flashed into existence next to Sylas, the fire spirit carrying just a hint of brimstone with her.

"Two. Patches got them."

"I'll toss them in." She grabbed the first by its tail and rushed toward the fire. "Be right back."

Mira turned to Sylas. "I need to get going. As for what needs to happen here today; the roof clearly needs repairs, but I don't suppose that's something you will be able to do on your own."

"I can try."

"We'll hire Anders. He does good work."

"He does." Sylas had a history with Anders, the man who had once broken into his pub only to be attacked by Patches. Yet now they were friendly and the carpenter had done a lot of work for Sylas and Nelly over the last several weeks.

"As for Esta and other potential merchants, I'll try to meet with all of them tomorrow, if I can. Perhaps we will meet some others through the Merchant Guild when we go to Battersea. I'm going to assume that Tilbud knows some as well."

"He most certainly would," Sylas said.

"Then that settles it. And you're sure you don't mind?"

"I already told you I don't mind, Mira."

"I don't mind taking the lead on all of this, but you are the co-owner and what you think about the operation matters to me. I just don't want to be too forward."

"If I find something to be *too forward*, I will let you know. But I have enough to run on my own. And I'll need to get the market set up to have a brewery as well."

"Yes, I thought that section would be nice, near the entrance." Mira motioned closer to the main road, if it could be called that, which ran through Ember Hollow. "I figured someone could come in and grab a pint, or leave and do the same."

"Or, come in, peruse, decide not to buy, have a pint, and return to buy anyway."

"That's evil," Mira said with a grin, "but it could actually work. The other option would be to have it at the back. But I think the front of the market is better because of what we've already said, and the pub will be a bit lively, meaning it will attract people."

"Agreed. And I want to work something out with Bart and some of his musician friends to perform on Friday afternoons. They could later move the performance to the pub proper."

"Love it." Patches approached the apothecary and she nearly scooped him up into her arms. "Nope, he just bit a rat," Mira reminded Sylas as the cat purred and rubbed the side of his body against her leg. "No cuddles for you."

"I've got no problem with that." Sylas picked Patches up and kissed the cat's forehead.

"Ewww," Mira said as Patches purred even louder.

"I think he just wanted some attention." Sylas tucked the cat under his arm. Patches remained more or less happy as he stared back at Mira, his whiskers occasionally twitching. "And we need to get rid of all the rats we can. We don't want them chewing through things."

"You are suggesting we get more cats?"

"What do you think?" he asked Patches.

"They wouldn't be like Patches, you know."

"Aware. But he could be their commander of sorts. Not unlike your uncle and his militiamen."

"Please, Sylas."

Azor appeared again. "Did someone say we're getting more cats for Patches to boss around?"

"I'm just thinking out loud here," Sylas told the fire spirit as flames flickered off her shoulders and settled. "A few market cats would be nice. They could be an attraction themselves."

"That would be something possible in Battersea," Mira said. "They're the only city with an animal shelter."

"There's a shelter there?" Sylas asked.

"I went once when I was mad at my uncle. I nearly bought a goose."

"A goose?" he asked Mira.

"They can serve as guards, you know. The one they had there, in particular, was quite bossy. I was planning to use the goose to force my uncle to keep to his side of the yard, but then I gave up that fight. Pick your battles, you know."

"A goose or some more cats sounds about right. Or both."

"Not both," Mira said. "We're not running a zoo."

"A goose would be adorable." Azor morphed into a goose and waddled around.

Sylas pointed a sideways thumb at her. "Or Azor could do it . . ."

The three laughed and Patches purred even louder. Mira spoke again: "It would be nice to have something around here to keep guard. Patches might not get along with other cats, but a goose? Who knows? The only problem is a goose wouldn't actually hunt rats. Or would it?"

Sylas considered this. "It would keep them away and it could keep bigger things away as well. We'll have to see what is available in Battersea, but I like it."

"I do as well," Mira said. "I really wanted the goose they had at the shelter. My uncle would have hated it."

"Now I like it even better," Sylas told the apothecary. "Anyway, it's back to work for me. I'll see you at the pub tonight, yeah?"

"Sure. I can't wait to tell Nelly we're getting a goose!"

CHAPTER THREE

MAGICAL MISHAPS

After the pub closed, Sylas went to work crafting his newest brew. He did so as Azor hovered over him, the fire spirit quiet for once while he intuited what needed to happen next. By this point, Sylas was so attuned to his brewer class that he didn't need to experiment to make his newest concoction. And sure enough, it all fell perfectly into place. Upon finishing most of the steps, from malting to mashing, Sylas added the strange and possibly illegal herb that Mira had suggested at the hops phase, so it could be part of the flash fermentation and instant maturation part of magical brewing.

"I still don't know what this herb is called," he told Azor as he waited for the final processes to take effect. "Aeferd shay leaf or athershade leaf. I'll have to ask Mira. Let's hope it does something."

"To be honest with you, I haven't heard either name," the fire spirit said. "Do you think it would work as a garnish?"

Sylas smelled the leaf and shook his head. "Likely not, but you would know better than I."

"Ooo, but look at the color."

The mixture had turned blue with a light green foam on top. Patches, who had been hiding in a corner, hopped onto the table to examine it.

"Careful." Sylas placed the pub cat back onto the ground.

Patches mewed and looked up at him, his tail lashing against Sylas's leg.

"He's just curious."

"I can tell. But just in case—I don't know, it *explodes*—let's keep Patches away."

"We definitely don't want something like that. Shoo, Patches," Azor said as she waved him away. "Shoo, shoo, shoo." When that didn't work Azor flared up, causing the cat to hop away from the two and scatter toward the stairs. Azor and Sylas returned their attention to the brew as Patches headed up, tail raised in protest.

"He'll be fine," Sylas assured her as Azor started to fret over scaring him. "I'm taking him to the farm tonight."

"He likes it there. Patches loves lying on the porch back-to-back with Cornbread. It must be so nice for him!"

"Must be."

"As for the farm, were you planning to be gone the next three nights?"

"That's right," he told Azor. "But I suspect tonight won't be so eventful. And at that point, Quinlan and the militiamen will be around, and Raelis should be up tomorrow."

"I checked on him earlier, but he was sleeping."

"Mira says that he is doing much better, that he talked to her for a while. She gave Raelis something to keep him in bed another night. He wanted to come down." Sylas laughed as he thought of Raelis and his stubbornness. It had been that same stubbornness that had seen Raelis perform heroic, yet ultimately fatal acts on the Night of Raining Arrows. And likely the same stubbornness had inspired him to go on a Hallowed Pursuit. "Anyhow, the new brew."

"It's ready?"

"Just about. I'll taste a little and if it's good—and it looks like it will be good—I'll make another cask tonight. That will give us two for the Wraithsday Feast. We'll pair it with your Wellington and charge fifteen MLus. Sound fair?"

She gave him a fiery thumbs-up. "Sounds fair."

"I know we could charge more, but I'd rather people be fed, have a nice ale, and then stick around for more."

"And the announcement?" Azor asked a few moments later.

"Yes, that. I'll discuss it with Tilbud and Mira first. Perhaps it would be best to make the announcement after everyone is fed, especially after they have fuzzy feelings." Sylas looked at the slightly blue ale, the green foam on top thicker than it had been during the brewing process. "At least I can say that it looks interesting."

"But does it taste interesting?" Azor asked.

"Let's see." Sylas took a sip and immediately noticed that there were unexpected subtle blueberry undertones. The brew was cold, but only as it passed down his throat. "Oh, wow."

Sylas placed the ale onto the table as a new sense came over him. He felt calm to the point that he wanted to sit down. He did so on a stool that Anders had built and let out a deep breath, his troubles fading into the background.

Another sip of the ale came with the same strange coldness as it passed his throat, one that left his senses tingling.

"Warm, fuzzy feelings?" Azor asked.

"I think," Sylas sighed. "I think, yeah. I feel like I just got to the second day of a vacation and everything is going well. Huh. It's like Charm or something," he said, recalling the Lumen Ability that Tilbud had cast in Battersea that had Nelly, Sylas, and the archlumen fawning over one another. "It's so good. I feel absolutely wonderful."

"So a perfect time to break the bad news to people?"

Sylas considered this with a grunt. "Perhaps. If you told me some bad news now, I'd be in the mind to accept it more easily. Want to give it a try? Do you have any bad news?"

Azor brought a fiery finger to her lips, as if she needed to mull this over. "Aside from the fact that you keep getting an invasion message and the Hexveil is having issues? No. I don't have any bad news, sadly." She laughed. "I could go out there and make some bad news, but I suspect you don't want me burning something down."

"Let's not and say we did."

She playfully saluted him. "I'll be a good fire spirit."

"And I'll be a relatively good brewer." Sylas took another sip of the ale and basked in the warmth he felt. "Just give me a few minutes. I'll tidy up here, finish brewing, and then head to the farm."

———

Sylas arrived at the farm to the sound of barking. He set Patches on the ground and turned to the forest, where he heard rustling. Quinlan emerged from the trees, the man in his armor with his weapon resting on his shoulder. He seemed a bit ruffled, and there was a leaf attached to the bottom of his beard that he had to pry out.

"What is it?" Sylas asked as he noticed Quinlan's body language. Patches flitted around him and headed straight into the forest on a mission.

"Cornbread. She's caught the smell of something. I'm trying to get her out of the forest—too dangerous there, too many unknowns—but she keeps running back in and barking."

"Cornbread!" Sylas shouted. He did so again as he approached Quinlan. "Cornbread!"

"I tried that already, mate, but maybe she'll come to you. But I can tell you this: something is out there. Something big. I don't want to say it, but I saw the tracks."

"Tracks of what?"

"You aren't going to like this."

"Try me."

"A Taurigraith. I think it might have gotten through in the breach."

"Do you think?" Sylas recalled the towering monster, one that seemed to be the meeting ground between a tiger and a bull. They had encountered one in the Chasm and it was an absolute beast, two stories tall with the shadowy properties of a Voidslither, meaning it could become intangible. "Is there a bounty for it yet?"

"There isn't. Like the Mana Ghouls, this one is hard to pinpoint during the day. And it hasn't been registered in the system yet. It might not be. People like me are the ones who register it, but doing so, as you can imagine, will bring out a ton of hunters." Quinlan squinted into the woods. "I even tried your glasses, but I only caught a glimpse of something big."

The glasses were currently tucked behind Quinlan's ears, resting on his forehead.

"Let me take a look."

"By all means."

Sylas put on the glasses that allowed him to see spectral beings and scanned the forest. "Nothing."

"It moves in and out," Quinlan said, "and that forest is large. It presses all the way up to the Hexveil."

"A Taurigraith," Sylas said. "This is bad. Are you sure you don't want to register it with the guild? We're going to need more hunters."

"Yes, I'm sure, and yes, you're right. But we may be able to gather what we need in these parts. Raelis, if he's up to it. Tiberius and his lot. And the reward for a Taurigraith will absolutely be worth not registering the hunt *and* putting up with the Thorny bastard. Believe me there, mate."

"A grand hunt tomorrow works for me. As for staying back, Cody and Duncan, yeah?"

"Exactly. And we'll cut them in if we get the Taurigraith to make it fair. Raelis should be better by then. He was good tonight, but Mira wanted him to rest for a bit longer."

"Heh. I'll bet he didn't take that lightly."

"Not particularly, no. But then he drank the tea she made and didn't have much more to say. I checked on him before I came here. He was snoring."

"Ha! I remember him rarely sleeping, and to hear that he was snoring . . ." Quinlan scanned the forest again. "He'll be a massive help. But for now, I think it's best we just take shifts in the fields. If we did encounter the Taurigraith tonight, we will be wishing there were more of us. I can tell you that."

"What about Cornbread and Patches?"

As if he had summoned them, both of the animals came out of the forest, Patches leading the farm dog like he had successfully completed a rescue mission.

"Looks like that answers your question, mate," Quinlan said with a snort.

————

But it's out there! Cornbread told Patches as she followed him. *I can smell it!*

Relax. I can smell it too. And I would go after the beast if I thought it was a good idea. I can't believe I'm saying this.

Saying what? Cornbread asked as she caught up to Patches, who had just reached the start of the big man's cornfields. *What are you saying?*

I can't believe I'm saying that we need humans.

They are strong. When they work together, they're powerful. But we are strong too. And I can rally other dogs! Let me get the other dogs. Cornbread barked. *Hey, everyone—*

Quiet! I would prefer we do it ourselves. It is our duty to protect both the Tavernly and the Farmly Realms. We will soon have a new realm.

Wonder spread across Cornbread's face. *A new realm? What do you mean?*

I'll get to that. Patches sat and began licking his paw.

We could still round up some of the others!

You already suggested that, and I already told you no. Your dog friends are hardly strong enough to take on a creature of that size. Patches remembered what he had seen beyond the Hexveil. The pub cat was no coward, but he knew it would take more than one cat and a troupe of dogs to deal with the monster.

I want to go back to find it. I was so close.

Don't, he told the dog.

She started whining. *But it's out there. And we're here. What if it comes here?*

The big man and the warrior are here. That will help even the odds.

And I can bark and bring my friends. Maybe the mean dog will help.

Patches shrugged off the thought. He had little interest in the white farm dog he had once fought. *For now, let's just focus on the Farmly Realm. It needs protecting too.*

Cornbread's ears alerted to something. She turned to the south end of the field. *I'm hearing something there now.*

Let's deal with it while the humans talk on the porch.

Patches followed Cornbread through the field, the cat keeping low to the ground and watching with annoyance at how much sound Cornbread made. Cornbread grew quiet once she neared the anomaly, the dog stopping, making eye contact with Patches, and then nodding her chin forward.

You surprise it; I'll pounce.

Cornbread licked her lips, her carnivorous side showing as she bared her teeth. *An ambush.*

I like the sound of that.

At Patches's instruction, Cornbread took off. She barked and the Mana Ghoul came alive, the creature quickly moving away from her barks and right into their trap.

This was one of the more useful things Patches had learned of Cornbread's skills. If called upon, she could change the directional sound of her barks, which meant that to the creature, the barks came from *behind* it, even though the two of them were in front of it.

As it neared Patches, he tripled his size and came down hard with his claws. He quickly disposed of it, and only looked up at Cornbread once the mana in the area had faded away.

Good work, Cornbread told Patches. She licked his face. *Good, good job. You're good at—*

That's enough of that.

You like it. Admit that.

Patches grumbled. *I do not. I am clean. If I'm dirty, I'll take care of it. Not you.*

My tongue is clean too.

I'm not going to debate this with you.

Cornbread bumped her head into his and licked Patches one last time. *You're so grumpy sometimes,* she said, her tail wagging so hard that it caused her body to shake.

Patches didn't say anything. Instead, he hiked his tail up and trotted toward the porch, where he hoped that someone would soon rest in the hammock so he could cuddle with them.

————

[You have 36 days until the invasion.]
[A loan payment of 75 has been deducted from your total Mana Lumens. Your total loan balance is 24448 Mana Lumens.]

Sylas placed his hand on Patches and slowly shifted the cat to the side so he could push himself out of the hammock.

He found Quinlan standing at the edge of the porch, drinking from a cup of hot liquid. "Look who's up."

"Azor here?" Sylas asked with a yawn.

"Indeed. She's inside with Mira. And before you go in with our big announcement, I already told them a Taurigraith is out there. Cue Mira grumbling about visiting her uncle, but what I'm saying is they know."

Sylas laughed. "You'd think you could have woken me for the big announcement."

"Eh, it wasn't necessary. I'm told an old guy like you needs his beauty rest."

"Ha! You're older than me."

"Something like that," Quinlan said with a wink.

Sylas heard Raelis's voice inside. He turned back to Quinlan. "You didn't tell me . . ."

"Oh, him? Yeah, sorry, mate, that was supposed to be a surprise. Surprise."

Cornbread burst out of the home and barked happily upon seeing Sylas.

"Sylas!" Raelis followed the dog out with his arms spread wide. His long dark hair was swept back and it looked wet, as if he had just gotten out of the shower. He approached Sylas and offered him a firm hug. "You're getting one whether you like it or not."

"Thanks," Sylas said as Cornbread continued barking at the two hugging men. Patches, who had been in the hammock, slipped past them and hurried inside with an annoyed look on his face.

Raelis placed his hands on his waist and looked his old friend over. "So they tell me we have what, thirty-seven days until the invasion?"

"Thirty-six," Sylas told Raelis.

"And they tell me who the culprit is." Raelis squinted up at the sky. "After all we've done for them."

"Do what now?" Sylas asked.

"All the Hallowed Pursuits. Who do you think ultimately sponsors them? Representatives from the Celestial Plains. A bit fishy, yeah? They won't even let us into their Campaign Cities in the Chasm. They used to, apparently. But I tried. I bloody tried, Sylas."

"I know you did."

"And I got caught up in it. It's intoxicating, you know, trying to reach some goal that you know in your heart won't happen, yet you do everything you can just keep the flame alive, believing that you will get there. I did *not* get there. And then, well, you know how it played out," he said, referring to his recent demonic possession. He stared at Sylas, sorrow in his eyes.

"It's fine. You're fine. We all make mistakes. Quinlan, here, is about to make one by heading to Geist and reigniting an old flame." Sylas motioned to Quinlan, who was already laughing at this statement.

"Priscilla is more than an 'old flame,'" Quinlan said. "She's going to be a raging fire if I don't pop my head in soon."

"And your brother? When will we go for him?" Raelis asked Quinlan.

"We need to see what Nuno the manaseer says first. But I reckon soon. Kael can't sit there meditating while the world burns all around him. Or, he can. He's the type to do something like that."

"Aye, that he is," Raelis said. "So in that case, you'll head to Battersea and I'll hang out here on the farm."

"I'll need to handle Mana Saturation when I come back," Sylas said. "I planted on Moonsday, it's Wraithsday, and that's two days in my book."

"Little less than two days if we're being bloody honest, but you seem to have a system and it clearly works." Raelis offered Sylas a proud smile. "You've done well for yourself. The Old Lamplighter. The farm. Say, does your farm have a name?"

"No. Not everything needs a name."

"Mira said your market was going to have a name," Raelis said. "The Bargains Market. I'm going to register a complaint with someone if there aren't actual bargains there."

"I'm with you there," Quinlan told Raelis. "I'll be looking for that Aurumite discount."

"There won't be that, but there will be bargains. I'm going to head in." Sylas tipped a hat he wasn't wearing at the two and stepped inside to find Azor anxiously waiting for something to finish baking. Mira sat at the table, the apothecary privy to the conversation that Sylas had just had.

"Morning," Sylas told her as he sat. "You look lovely as always."

"I was telling her that too," Azor said.

Mira blushed. "Stop, both of you. Before we meet Nuno, I want to go to an animal shelter. It's in the Brenham District, on the outer edge.

"For a guard dog or a cat?" Azor asked.

"Perhaps a goose."

"A what?" Azor looked at Mira with surprise.

"You were serious about that?" Sylas asked the apothecary.

"Of course, I was. They make good guard animals. We will see if they have a goose or know where we can get one."

Sylas grinned. "I seriously thought you were joking."

"I can imagine a goose wearing a little hat," Azor said, flaring up. "So cute!"

"I don't think the goose will like that," Mira said, the apothecary a bit cautious of the fire that Azor had just released. Azor had been careful not to actually burn anyone but the flames did flash all around them.

"What about a bow tie?"

"Or a sweater," Mira said. "I could see something like that happening. But let's not dress the goose before we get the goose."

"I would still prefer a brigade of attack cats, but I suppose I'm in the minority there," Sylas said.

"A brigade of attack cats might not turn out the way you'd like," Mira said as Raelis and Quinlan came in.

The two former soldiers plopped down at the table and, for a brief moment, Sylas was transported back to his previous life, the way he'd seen them huddle in similar ways around a campfire or at the rare officer banquet that the best of his men attended.

Sylas had to shake his head to snap out of his memories. He had to remind himself they were here in eternal purgatory, and as strange as it was, eternal purgatory was a place worth protecting.

Quinlan raised the cup Azor placed in front of him. "Cheers. First a trip to Geist for me; then, a goose; then, some answers; then, a bloody Taurigraith; and then, well, let's just make it that far."

"You are really going to go to my uncle, then?" Mira asked Quinlan.

"We sure are," Quinlan told Mira. He winked at Raelis. "You'll like him. He's sort of like you. But meaner. Shorter. Angrier."

Mira let out a theatrical groan. "He wouldn't like to hear you saying that."

"You wouldn't tell him, now would you?" Quinlan asked her.

"I would not."

"It's ready!" Azor announced. The fire spirit popped the oven open to produce a quiche. After running a flaming hand along its outer surface, she cut it into slices and distributed it to the table. "I'll give some to Cornbread too, but first it needs to cool off." Patches peeked his head in. "Fine, you can have some."

Raelis and Sylas were the first to get their plates. "Oh, it's hot," Raelis said as he chewed his bite.

"I told you it would be hot!" Azor told him as she brought plates for Quinlan and Mira.

Cornbread woofed and Patches quickly left. Before digging in, Sylas took a look around and smiled. The only thing better than good company was great company.

————

Upon arriving in Battersea, Quinlan continued on to Geist, and Sylas and Mira headed straight to the Brenham District. They passed a place selling sweet cold cream on the way and opted to stop for the treat, which was served in a waffle bowl and sprinkled with bits of chocolate.

"We shouldn't," said Mira, who had already taken a bite.

"You just did." Sylas tried his. "Should the pub start serving ice cream?"

"Is it ever summer here?"

"Not to my knowledge, no."

"How would Azor serve ice cream?"

"I admit, I haven't thought this all the way through."

"Come on, then," Mira said, moving ahead, still eating her ice cream. "The shelter isn't far from here. I hope it's open."

"Why wouldn't it be open?"

"Well, if there are no animals to distribute, they don't open. I've spoken to the owners before, a couple named Jenny and Catherine. The two love traveling around the Underworld and collecting pets."

"And where do they get these animals?"

"I was just about to answer that. One way they get animals is through their travels. There are occasional strays, but often, places like your pub that have an animal attached to it and no deed owner get picked up by the banks. The bank has an auction for the pets, and they bid."

"Why didn't the bank ever pick up Patches from The Old Lamplighter? He's a great pet."

"You could ask Shamus or someone at the bank about that," Mira said, "but I can already tell you why. Ember Hollow was a dying village. It still is. Only now, you and I are breathing new life into it. Funny to consider something like that, new life in a place that should be dreadful, and will be more dreadful if the Hexveil falls."

"Let's hope not," Sylas said as they continued on. The two passed outdoor vendors selling everything from rugs to umbrellas, and a few invited them into their shops. They reached a woman selling herbs out of a pair of leather trunks and he remembered something. "Aeferd shay leaf or athershade leaf?" he asked Mira. "Because I've been told both now."

"Athershade leaf. Anyone telling you otherwise isn't an apothecary."

Sylas thought back to Esta and all the herbs she had on offer. She was classed as a merchant, so it made sense she might have gotten the information wrong. But it also made little sense because she would have been corrected by an apothecary at some point. Could it have been her accent? Or maybe it really was that rare of an herb. "Huh."

"You don't believe me?"

"It's illegal, right? Or frowned upon."

"Everything illegal is frowned upon."

"Clever," he told Mira.

"But for common usage, yes, athershade leaf could get you in trouble. However, if you're classed as an apothecary, it's fine. You're in the clear."

"What about what I'm doing, using it for ale? Last I checked, I'm still a brewer."

"Well, that is technically something that could get you in trouble, but who will know? Just don't call the brew something like, I don't know, athershade ale."

"I can't believe you'd send me down such a criminal path," Sylas teased her.

"A criminal brewer? I never thought I'd meet such a man." She smiled at him and ate more of her ice cream.

The pair came to a small building that was painted red in a way that reminded Sylas of the barns of an Aurumite city named Victoria. The region was known for these barns, which made him certain that the two proprietors of the shelter were Aurumites.

Sylas knocked and was met by a barrage of barks, yowls, and even what sounded like a goose's honk. "Don't get your hopes up," he told Mira.

"My hopes are rarely up. Try to knock again."

Sylas knocked louder this time and was met with the same chorus of animal sounds.

"Coming, coming," a woman called over the ruckus. She slid the door open and grinned at the two of them. "Well, hello there. Sorry, we're not open yet. Wait, Mira? Mira!"

"Hi, Jenny," Mira told the woman, who wore a pair of beige overalls tucked into leather boots that extended all the way up to her knees. She had a bucket filled with feed, which she quickly set on an old wooden stool.

"Please, please, come in," Jenny said, stepping aside. "Come to peruse again?"

Mira took a quick glance around. "I did, indeed. In fact—"

"Who is it?" another voice called out.

"It's Mira from Ember Hollow."

Another woman joined them, this one in a similar set of beige overalls, her hair braided back. She carried a baby goat under her arm, one that was currently chewing on a tuft of straw. "Mira!" the second woman said like she was calling out to a long-lost friend.

"Hi, Catherine. This is Sylas, owner of The Old Lamplighter, the new pub in Ember Hollow."

Catherine and Jenny exchanged glances. "Ember Hollow has a pub?" Catherine asked as the goat continued chewing the straw. "I didn't know about that."

"Nor did I," Jenny said. "It's on the up and up, then?"

"You could call it that. Actually, that's the reason we're here," Mira said.

"You want a pub cat. I get it," Jenny told Sylas, "but those things are rare these days. I have other cats, but not a pub cat, not one that thinks it's a bit of a guard dog."

"Actually, I have a pub cat named Patches," he told her.

Jenny seemed surprised by this revelation. "You do? Then congratulations are in order. Not all pubs come with them, you know."

"And he's apparently an old one," Sylas told her. "Leah the veterinarian confirmed it."

"Leah did? She knows her stuff," Jenny said.

"She's great," Catherine added. "Leah taught us a lot about our shared class when we first arrived."

"I can't believe you know her," Mira said.

Catherine grinned. "It's a small Underworld. Anyway, you have a pub, you have a cat."

"I also have a farm and a dog," Sylas said.

Once again, the two women looked at each other and back to Sylas and Mira. Jenny spoke this time: "Quite the entrepreneur, you are."

"He is. And that's why we're here," Mira said, a hint of pride in her voice. "I have joined him in the entrepreneurial spirit. We are now co-owners of the market in Ember Hollow, which we are hoping to open next week. Both his cat and dog are either busy guarding the pub or they are at the farm during Mana Saturation nights, which can get a little crazy. We need something to guard the market. And we were thinking—"

Yet again, Sylas heard a honk from one of the rooms in the back.

"Actually, that's exactly what we were thinking of. Or better, what I was hoping for. A goose." Mira smiled at the two animal caretakers. "You don't happen to have a goose, do you?"

"Do you want to tell her or should I?" Catherine asked Jenny.

"You can go ahead."

"We have a goose, yes, Mira, but she's not here at the moment."

"Not here? We can hear a goose." Sylas scratched the back of his head. "Unless that noise is coming from some other animal." He took an exaggerated look around.

"You won't find another animal that can make that noise, I assure you. *That* noise would be one of her spells gone awry," Catherine said. "So here's the thing. Gertrude—"

"Gertrude?" Mira asked Catherine.

"The goose. The goose is named Gertrude. From what we can tell, she has had a number of jobs over the years. We know that she has worked at a tannery and also at a mill. There was a small farm she worked at as well. But she has certainly had more jobs than that. The last place she worked was near the academy in Gloombra."

"Which is where she is now," Jenny chimed in. "At the academy."

Catherine continued: "Yes, you see, Gertrude picked up a few rather odd spells in Gloombra, or more like curses, so we have sent her back there to get checked. And that's where she is."

"In Gloombra," Mira said.

Jenny nodded. "At the Grace Academy."

Mira turned to Sylas and they both said a name at the same time. "Tilbud."

"Who is Tilbud?" Catherine asked Mira.

"An archlumen who somehow always seems to find his way into our business. We're meeting him later. We will speak to him about it," Mira said. "What is wrong with Gertrude exactly?"

"Well, for one, she can't stop honking," Catherine said as another goose sound accompanied her statement. "And she has left spectral honks behind, which never stop. Day and night, we get a honk every couple of minutes or so. An archlumen there is seeing to it, but she seems to think it would be best to deal with Gertrude first—fix her, if possible—and then deal with the sound remnant here."

"There's the Archlumenry here in Battersea," Sylas said. "Surely, they can help."

"They would help if we were part of their guild. Otherwise, there's a waiting list," Jenny said. "You'd be surprised how many magical mishaps plague our world."

An idea came to Sylas. "What about this? We use our connection with Tilbud to get the sound dealt with through the Archlumenry here. We'll also head to Gloombra to pick up the goose, if, of course, you agree that we can purchase her."

"If you can get the honking fixed, Gertrude is yours for free," Catherine told him. "We didn't pay anything for her. She was donated to us."

"We have to pay you something," Mira told the two animal caretakers.

"No, no you do not," Jenny said.

"At least come to our Wraithsday Feast tonight," Sylas said. "Drinks and a meal on me. And we are going to have a market, so if you ever wanted an additional place to sell some of your animals, you'd be more than welcome."

"We have enough going here, but as for a meal and some drinks, what do you say?" Catherine asked Jenny.

"That sounds like a date to me."

"Good. We'll return in the next few hours with Tilbud," Mira told them. "Who will likely have some solution. We'll cover the cost of that."

"You don't have to," Catherine told her.

"No, we do. A good familiar is expensive, especially one with experience like Gertrude seems to have. And as for the goose herself, with Tilbud, I can't believe I'm saying this," Mira told the two women, her statement meant mostly for Sylas, "but Tilbud will know what to do. Weirdly enough, he always does."

"In that case, we will work something out then." The hope that had started to form on Catherine's face faded to some degree. "It can be hard sometimes to find a qualified archlumen, you know, one with availability. I hope this Tilbud fellow is qualified."

"He's certainly something," Mira said.

CHAPTER FOUR

GOOD FOR THE GANDER

Sylas and Mira arrived at the meeting place in the Brenham District, where they found Nuno standing outside his favorite café, the young manaseer's hands behind his back as he looked out at the water.

Mira's heart sank.

It didn't seem like Tilbud was there yet, and she assumed they were going to have to deal with his antics, which would only complicate what needed to happen next. But just as she was about to say something, just as she was about to voice her concerns to Sylas, the door of the café swung open and Tilbud stepped out in a dapper, lime-green three-piece suit with matching green cravat and a silver tray in his hands.

"Ah, Mira and Sylas, just the two lovebirds I was hoping to find. I went ahead and ordered some egg tarts for the table." The archlumen showed them the egg tarts, each of which was crisped gold and about the size of a cork. "Drinks to come. I was hoping to order something for Nuno as well, but like an angsty teenager—which fits to some degree, considering how old he physically looks—our dear manaseer isn't too interested in anything like that. Alas! That, or, more likely, he already drank something. Anyhoo, come. Join me."

Tilbud led them over to a table. He sat before the two and smiled at them after adjusting his tiny hat.

"We sort of volunteered your services," Mira said, figuring she'd come right out with it.

Next to her, Sylas took a bite of the pastry and said: "This is amazing, Tilbud!"

"Indeed. And did you say my services, dear Mira?" the archlumen asked. "What services would those be, famed apothecary of Ember Hollow? I have numerous talents, many of which I've yet to reveal to you. Do tell me, and don't worry about how long it takes. I don't think Nuno will mind. I really don't know what has gotten into the young man. Or old man. He's been staring out at the water, brooding like a confused duck ever since I arrived. A moody fellow."

Mira waited for him to finish before continuing: "We wanted an animal to guard the market in the same way that Patches guards the pub and Cornbread guards the farm."

"Is that so?" Tilbud tried one of the pastries himself. "Aren't these delightful! You were right, Sylas, and I should add that I was right in selecting these particular tarts. There were other choices, you know. But please, Mira, go on. And no beating around the bush. Oi! Nuno! We are ready whenever you are," he called to the manaseer, "but do give us a moment, lad. In that regard, I suppose we *aren't* ready whenever you are." He finished the pastry. "My word. These really are flavorful. Should I order another round?"

"Later," Mira told him. "We found a guard goose we want named Gertrude. However, there are some complications, which is where your services come in."

Tilbud licked one of his fingers. "Did you say 'guard goose'?"

"I did. I have been visiting the animal shelter in the Brenham District for some time. Before you came along," she told Sylas, "I tried to visit every time I was able to make it here. I'm familiar with the owners, and we went there seeking a goose. We heard a goose's honk, but as it turns out, this is just an imprint."

"A goose's haunting, or should I say honking, imprint? Consider me intrigued," Tilbud said. "So the goose is at this animal shelter and it left an imprint?"

"No, the goose is in Gloombra at the academy being studied."

"I know some people there, you know. Or, at least, I used to."

"I was hoping you'd say that."

"Well, I can't say that we have a good relationship. But I know my way around the academy, and that is worth something. I believe."

"Right," Mira told Tilbud. "I also thought you may say something like that. Here's the thing: I have promised the two owners of the shelter that you will be able to help with the imprint. I also thought you would be willing to come with us to Gloombra to fetch this goose, and likely figure out what's wrong with it."

Tilbud wiped his mouth. He placed his napkin in his lap and stared at Mira for a moment. "I am honored to hear you think so highly of my powers and my influence. I too think I am immensely talented and easily capable of a task such as this."

Mira forced a grin. She certainly didn't want to tell Tilbud what she was really thinking: that this little case of goose shenanigans was right up his alley, just strange enough that she assumed it would pique his interest. So far, that part was working.

"We really could use your help," Sylas said, even though he didn't need to.

"I can tell. And as you very well know, this is the sort of case that interests me." The archlumen eyed Mira's pastry.

"Please, have it," she said.

"With pleasure! What kind of imprint are we talking about here? Or did you already tell me?" Tilbud asked after he had taken her egg tart. "Sorry, I'm scatterbrained sometimes, you know. If we're talking a physical haunting, that might be something out of my purview. There is a branch of the Archlumenry which studies the occult, but I never found much interest in ghosty things. Although, I suppose it should be evident that this has nothing to do with a ghost if Gertrude is indeed alive."

Nuno finally turned to their table. He placed his hands behind his back and just stared at the three of them. Mira decided to hurry things along: "Not a ghost, just a sound. A honking sound that won't go away. They think Gertrude may have had some issue and that's why they sent her to Gloombra, to be studied there."

"Yet her honk has remained here in Battersea. Huh. Huh, huh, huh." Tilbud twirled the end of his mustache and sat back. "Fascinating. Odd. Provocative. Intriguing. Dare I consider this a mystery? Truly, Mira. This is something I have to see."

"Do you think it's something you could help them with?" she asked.

"The removal of goose's honking remains? It's certainly something that I could look into. Meldon at the Archlumenry owes me a favor. Or he doesn't, but he can be charmed—"

"No Charm spells." Sylas turned to Mira. "Trust me, you don't want to be charmed. At least not this way."

"The Charm spell is absolutely a solution to dealing with Meldon, but I can save it for a last resort. Honestly, this case may interest the Archlumenry, but I must say, if that is indeed the situation, they will probably want to send their own expert in. That might cost something."

"Whatever it is, we'll cover it," Sylas said. "I will."

"You don't have to—" Mira was just about to check her stats when Sylas placed his hand on hers. "Really, Mira, let me. You've done so much for The Bargains Market."

"The what now?" Tilbud asked. "That's the name? No. That won't work. I don't want to be the one to tell you, but since no one has told you, I guess that task falls to me. Another name is in order. 'The Bargains Market' sounds like a place no better than the discount bin."

"It's our market," Mira told the archlumen.

"Indeed. And surely you have a better name in you than that. Remember your youth, my dear. Were there any markets in your village or city, or wherever you're from? I must say, I have lost track of place names in our former world. I only have so much space in the old noggin for details like that, especially with the pub quizzes. Speaking of which—"

"Petticoat Lane."

"The what now?" Tilbud asked Mira.

"The market when I was a girl," she said as the market formed in her mind's eye. Mira remembered going there with her cousin to fetch food for family meals. "It was on Petticoat Lane. People just called it the Petticoat Lane Market. It was later destroyed in the war."

Tilbud finished the pastry and wiped his hands on a napkin. "That's a wonderful name. If I may, there's a certain regality to it. I like that name. Really, I do, Mira. Do consider it."

"What do you think?" she asked Sylas. "The Petticoat Lane Market?"

"It works for me," he told her once he saw the slight desperation in her eyes. He knew she wanted to get this right, that Mira didn't want any mishaps along the way.

"I will consider it," Mira finally said. "Now, back to the goose. Can we visit the animal shelter and the Archlumenry after this?"

Tilbud puffed his cheeks out. "After this? Well, I did have a lunch planned with Rufus. But there may still be time for that. We could make it a double date. That would be a bit less awkward."

"You're back with Rufus now?" Sylas asked Tilbud.

"I'm not *with* anyone at the moment, sadly, or perhaps in my case, *justly*, but sometimes it's important to check on old flames and see if there's still a spark there. A little newfound warmth can go a long way. Visiting him and seeing to your hat the other week was good. It was nice. And I thought we would have lunch. It will be even better if you are there. So yes, lunch. And you can cover it for my services. How's that?" he asked Mira and Sylas.

"That's fine," Mira said.

Tilbud pressed back in his chair. "Even better. Now, about Gloombra. I don't want to get into details now, and I certainly don't want to get into details in front of Rufus, but there may or may not be an old flame of mine who now works at the academy. She would know about the goose. And you have the paperwork necessary to collect it?"

"Yes. They're going to give it to me when we return," Mira said.

"Because you'll need that. And hopefully, Gertrude's goose issues have been seen to at the academy and we don't need to wait around."

"I can't wait around," Sylas said. "I have things to do on the farm. And the feast is this evening."

"You should have done your farm work before you left," Tilbud told him.

"Agreed."

"But that's fine. We can make all of this work. Perhaps before lunch, you head back, do what must be done on the farm, and then we continue on from there. Or you do what must be done during lunch. We really don't want to have to leave the academy once we arrive in Gloombra, just in case we need to stand our ground."

"Stand our ground?" Mira asked Tilbud. "Why would we have to do that?"

"Ah, a good question. They train a particular kind of archlumen there, a kind that has double-classed as a demon hunter and is later used on border missions to protect portions of the Hexveil. What I'm saying is that there could be some action there. Likely not, but we may have to steal the goose and fight our way out."

"You're joking," Mira told the archlumen.

"Indeed I am. But what I can't say is if that action involves us or not. Probably not. But who knows. Either way, best to deal with fields and old flames beforehand!"

"I'm ready to speak," Nuno said.

"Then by all means, good man," Tilbud said as he motioned to the seat next to him. "Speak. You've kept us bloody waiting to the point that we have gorged ourselves on pastries and taken on an additional side quest regarding a goose named Gertrude and her enchanting, or should I say haunting, honk. Please, sit. And give us the bad news."

———

Rather than say anything to the others after he sat, the deceptively youthful manaseer called a waiter over and placed an order. Nuno then proceeded to wait until the coffee came, seemingly basking in the silence.

It was rare to see Tilbud so annoyed. Sylas couldn't remember ever seeing him this way, the archlumen shifting uncomfortably as Nuno added milk to his coffee, sipped it, added some more milk, sipped that, and then added a dash of cinnamon.

"Better. And I'm sorry to keep you waiting," Nuno finally said. "You did seem to be discussing something, though. Hopefully, your plans for the rest of the day won't be ruined by what I'm about to say." The manaseer placed both hands around the cup of coffee and sat there for a moment. He drank a little, and a frown formed on his face. "The Celestial Plains are coming. You all know that. Years ago, the Crafting Laws were signed to prevent the merger—"

"You're calling it what?" Mira asked Nuno. "A . . . merger?"

"I am only using their term for it. The powers at the time believed that the Underworld was no longer necessary, so they wanted to *merge* our realm with the Chasm. The Celestial Council currently in power believes the same thing, that a staging ground has muddied what it means to pass on, among other things."

Sylas swallowed the bitter taste in his mouth. After everything he had been through, to finally get to a place in his life where he was happy, only to see it on the verge of being upended roiled him to the very core. And for what? He squinted up at the sky. So they could live in glory, and those who had made errors must suffer eternally?

Sylas had voiced these concerns to Mira before. He didn't want to say them now. He knew she felt the same way. And he was certain Tilbud would agree. Instead, he focused on another option, even if he didn't know if it was possible or not: "Then we grow stronger. We deal with the Celestial Plains head-on. If they insist on ruining our way of life, we fight back."

Tilbud cleared his throat. "I don't think it will be as easy as that, my dear Sylas, but I do appreciate the fighting spirit. The Celestial Plains are the source of our mana, our lumen abilities. As legendary as it would be to band together with the best in the Underworld and fight them *head-on*, as you put it, that simply isn't possible. We are not going to be able to go to war with heaven itself."

"No, we are not," Nuno said. "One solution that has been discussed between myself and a few other manaseers I know is that we simply accept it. We brace for the invasion and shore up the larger cities, creating future Campaign Cities like they have in the Chasm."

Sylas couldn't believe what Nuno was saying. "But that would mean places like Ember Hollow and Cinderpeak would be lost. Geist, Duero, so many places are close to the border. Smaller settlements like mine would be the first to go. Ember Hollow is our home. You can't take our home—"

"I'm not the one that's trying to—"

"Anyone that suggests something like that is a fool," Sylas said, becoming increasingly agitated. He felt like he had been possessed by Quinlan. Even though he knew that it wasn't Nuno's fault directly, he started to feel a sense of disdain for the man.

Mira placed a hand on his arm. The tension didn't quite leave, but it did cool to some degree. She spoke diplomatically but in a firm tone: "You can rule that suggestion out, Nuno. I'm sure anyone in the Underworld that hails from a similarly sized village will feel the same way. And who decides what sights are worth protecting? We have recently returned from the Chasm. Is a city such as Wraithwick on the chopping block? Gloombra? Really, those in the larger places like Battersea must realize the way this will go."

Tilbud cleared his throat. "She does make a fair point. The agreement from your little coterie of manaseers tells me that there is more going on here than what might be evident on the surface."

"What are you implying?" Nuno asked.

"I'm implying exactly what it sounds like I'm implying. What is a manaseer such as yourself set to gain in a scenario like this? You will still have your power. Because mana is more corrupted in the Chasm, the more evil-minded of you would be able to wield it in certain ways. Stronger ways."

Something shifted on Nuno's face. At first, Sylas thought that he was going to be offended by what Tilbud had suggested. Instead, a smile formed. "That's an interesting point."

"I would say it's a fair point. A point that could use further discussion."

"I could see it that way," Nuno said.

Was this some sort of game? Sylas looked incredulously from Nuno to Tilbud. The way the two spoke to each other now was clearly coded. At least it felt that way. Normally, Sylas would have been at the point that he wanted to flip the table over, but something was happening here, something that told him that Tilbud had a trick up his sleeve, as he always did.

"Yes," Tilbud said, elaborating on what he had already said: "What's in it for them? What's in it for those that want the merger to happen? The manaseers you speak of are already using 'merger,' the Celestial Plains's term, for what is set to happen, yes? What is in it for them? And who else is involved? Surely, some wayward lumengineers want a cut of the action. I'm aware of the connection that your kind has with the Plains. Speak clearly, Nuno."

"I can tell you that you are correct, Tilbud."

"So perhaps that is one place we need to start. And that is considering we start at all, Nuno. I'm not convinced manaseers have the Underworld's best interests at heart. Perhaps some of you do, but others have their own motives. They also have a deep understanding of the source of our Mana Lumens."

"What would you suggest I do?" the manaseer asked.

Sylas exchanged glances with Mira as Nuno held Tilbud's gaze. Sylas wished at that moment that he could read her mind, that he could communicate with her in some quiet way and get a better understanding of what she was thinking. Her eyes bulged slightly but that was it.

"What would I suggest you do?" Tilbud leaned back slightly then came forward again and steepled his hands together. "Well for one, I suggest you choose a bloody side. That would be the first step. You don't have to do it right now. And it's not going to hurt our feelings either way. But you should choose a side, because clearly, this is a war on multiple fronts, with numerous solutions, good and bad. And what you have suggested, or what your peers have suggested, simply rolling over, my dear friend, is a terrible solution. I would say something like 'over my dead body,' but we have already passed that stage. Sylas, Mira." The archlumen stood and smoothed his hands over his jacket. "I do believe our work here is done. Let's go."

————

Tilbud said hardly a word as they traveled through the Brenham District. He wasn't the only one who was upset. Sylas felt desperate in knowing that they were getting into yet another side quest while the world seemed on the precipice of crumbling all around.

An idea floated to the forefront of his mind as they reached the animal shelter. He nearly cast it aside, but then realized that even the most ridiculous ideas were worthy of conversation. "Wait."

"Yes?" Tilbud asked as he turned back to Sylas.

"You have a plan, right?"

"For the goose's remnant of a honk? I haven't really thought about that, to be honest. You know me. I'll *wing* it until a solution presents itself, pun sort of intended."

"Not that. I mean about the invasion. The way you spoke back there made me feel like you had something up your sleeve."

"I always have something up my sleeve, dear man." Tilbud pulled his sleeve up to present a bejeweled bracelet. "Need more proof?"

Mira looked at Tilbud skeptically. "Be serious."

"I don't know how to say it other than this: manaseers can be nasty. But even if they are dead, and even if we are dead as well, they, and by that I mean *us*, or better, *we* are all human," Tilbud said. "And humans will do anything to survive. That's the point I was trying to make. Anything to survive. Even when we're dead. Wild, really. So in that regard, we really can't blame them. They see it as inevitable, and they're looking ahead to protect themselves."

"So you agree with them?" Sylas asked.

"It's much more nuanced than that. It is within their rights to want to survive the invasion. It is within our rights to do the same. Their solution is to let it happen and make plans for it. Ours is to stop it before it happens. What sounds easier? Accepting heaven's mandate or thumbing our noses at them?"

"Dammit, Tilbud," Mira said.

"I am right, yes? But that doesn't mean we have to give in so easily. It doesn't mean we let the weight of the Celestial Plains crush us. But something like an actual all-out war, or an invasion, will push us to the brink of what we are able to do. So we have to ask ourselves, what are our options?"

"I keep coming back to an idea that I just can't let go of," Sylas told the archlumen. "My father is in the Chasm as far as we know, likely at a Celestial

Campaign City or fighting the demon hordes. My mother, from what Catia said, is in the Celestial Plains. Maybe there is an angle there. Go ahead, call me crazy, but maybe there is a solution in reaching parents."

"An angle in reaching your mother, or your father?" Tilbud removed his tiny hat and scratched the back of his head. "Do they have some power title that you know of?"

"Not to my knowledge, no."

"I fail to see what you are suggesting."

"Are your parents in the Celestial Plains?" Sylas asked the archlumen.

"I really couldn't tell you," Tilbud said after a long pause. "I did not know my parents."

"Mine are," Mira said.

Sylas swept his hand toward the street. "Look around us. With all these people in the Underworld, surely there are enough with parents in the Celestial Plains that care for them to force a change, or at the very least, force a discussion."

"You are suggesting some sort of letter campaign?" Mira asked.

"I don't know exactly how it would work. I'm just saying we would do better to appeal to those in the Celestial Plains with loved ones here," Sylas said, inspired by his own idea. He had seen war. He had seen suffering and the anguish it brought. He had seen soldiers turn into animals, yet he had seen how the thought of their families could both soften their faces and strengthen their resolve to continue. But could it work? Could something as simple as his suggestion change heaven's mandate in such a short amount of time?

Tilbud brought his hand to his chin. "Huh."

"Nothing else?" Mira asked.

"Huh. Huh, huh, huh." Tilbud started pacing. "It costs a load of MLus to send messages to the Celestial Plains. Tens of thousands. It would be ludicrously expensive to fund such a campaign unless there were work-arounds. The only work-arounds may be through people who have maintained their powers after the Crafting Laws, but they are few and far between. It would take a team of Lumengineers to adjust costs, and they would be breaking every vow they have taken in the book to do it. It would take research, some exploitation. It may take being part of an envoy to the Plains, which we'd have to discuss with Catia and see what the lumengineer has to say, and in this instance, by *we* I mean *I*. I really should pay her a visit. But, I will say this," he told them as he paced even faster, "it's a wild solution."

"But it is a solution, yes?" Sylas asked. "You think it could actually work?"

Tilbud kept walking back and forth across the street, which annoyed a few people as he stepped right in front of them. Finally, he stopped, placed his hands on his hips, and offered Sylas and Mira a firm nod. "I absolutely think it is worth a shot. A parent's love knows no bounds. Or, at least, that should be the case."

"So . . . what do we do next?" Mira asked. "How do we tell everyone? How do we make this happen?"

Tilbud looked up at the animal shelter. "Next? Next, we deal with a guard goose. Later, we get the word out at the Feast. I tap some of my connections and you two go about doing exactly what you were going about doing—getting stronger, figuring out a way to net more MLus. I'll look into that as well. What we will likely do is highly illegal."

"It is?" she asked.

"When I'm finished wrapping my head around it, yes. Very likely."

"I forgot to tell you all something," Sylas said. "The Taurigraith that we encountered in the Chasm. It's loose in the forest near the Seedlands."

"My word!" Tilbud said.

"Quinlan saw it. The beast got through during the recent breach. Cornbread and Patches were tracking it last night. Quinlan and I figured it would be best to get Tiberius involved. So that's something else I need to do today, aside from the goose issue and my fields. Deal with the Taurigraith. And I guess lunch with you all."

"Yes, lunch with Rufus," Tilbud said, "such a busy day. In that case, perhaps we should go to Gloombra tomorrow, after we've dealt with the goose issue here. That should clear up some time. And we can start making a list of people we should talk to, starting with Catia. Probably best not to set up an afternoon coffee date with her considering all we have going on today, but it is an option."

Mira couldn't hide her disappointment. "So we're not going to Gloombra today?"

"Awww . . ." Sylas laughed at the way her face shifted. "I wasn't expecting that look."

"There's no look!"

"Let's just see how the day goes. But I suspect we will be dealing with the goose, and then the Archlumenry, for longer than we'd like," Tilbud told her. "And then there is the hunt and feast tonight."

"And I have work to do in my fields before that," Sylas said. "I'm pretty sure I've already made this joke before, but who would've thought a person would be even busier after they died?"

Tilbud roared with nervous laughter. "It really is like that, isn't it?"

Mira pushed ahead. "Let's get on with it, then."

"Yes," Tilbud said as he caught up with her. "The goose is out."

The three entered the animal shelter, where they were greeted by Jenny, who was crouched on the ground petting a puppy. Catherine came out soon after, moments before a loud honk filled the room, causing the woman to drop the pitcher she was carrying.

"Oh my," said Tilbud, who had jumped backward at the sound, which seemed to linger like a mournful wail.

Jenny laughed nervously. "It's bad. And it goes on all day and night. I don't know what Gertrude did or how this happened, but it has been terrorizing us for a week now."

Tilbud straightened up. "Well, in that case, we will see to this today. I'm aware that there is a waiting list at the Archlumenry for, well, spectral things like this."

"Spectral?" Catherine asked.

"What else would it be?" Tilbud asked the caretaker. "Gertrude has left behind an imprint. Generally, these are spectral in nature. The first thing we will need to do is analyze its frequency. Then, we will match it, and cancel out its frequency. But a counter-frequency is the easy part. The hard part will be setting up the tuning forks to create a lumen array. Because we don't want to just cancel out the sound, we want to completely eradicate it. But canceling it is the first step."

"And what is a lumen array?" Jenny asked, her face already showing signs of confusion.

"It is just a word I used to describe the special arrangement of tuning forks we will need in their location to make this work. I know, I know. It sounds impossible. Actually, it sounds ludicrous."

"I was going to say that," Mira told Tilbud.

"I figured you would. But we will both cancel out the sound, and then we will remove it from the premises. All for the low, low fee of—" He smiled at them. "Who am I kidding? I'm not going to charge for this. And if I did, I would charge Sylas by way of free pints of ale."

"Have you ever paid for a pint from me?" Sylas asked the archlumen.

"Not to my knowledge, no. But the day is still young. So, ladies, gentleman," he told them with a slight bow, "I have a lunch date I need to get to; before I do that, I will stop by the Archlumenry to arrange the objects I need. Expect to see me this afternoon and expect to sleep successfully through the night sans phantom honk."

"We can't thank you enough," Jenny said as Catherine nodded beside her.

"Don't thank me yet. But, if this is successful, then we can continue with the goose arrangement." Tilbud glanced over to Mira, who had since scooped the puppy in her arms. "I'm assuming you will help me with the tuning forks."

"Whatever you need."

"I would like to see how that works," Sylas said.

"Well, you can see part of it. You do need to deal with the farm." Tilbud checked his pocket watch. This time, Sylas was certain that the hands on the watch weren't moving. This reminded him of something he had pondered before. Sylas couldn't remember the last time he had seen a clock. And no one, other than Tilbud, wore a watch.

"We do have a little time. How about this?" Tilbud said. "You head to the farm now and meet us at a place called Kensington Kitchen once you finish. I will set a quest for you, so you know how to get there when you return to Battersea."

[New Quest Contract - Meet Mira and Tilbud at Kensington Kitchen in Battersea. Accept? Y/N?]

CHAPTER FIVE

MANA-SOUND WAVES

Sylas stood before his crops wearing his magical straw hat with its numerous dangling charms, which decreased yield times by two days and always created a legendary yield. As he was well aware, creating an item such as this was no longer possible because of the Crafting Laws, which he was increasingly starting to see as unwarranted Celestial interference.

[**Mana Saturation cost is 75 Mana Lumens per field. Would you like to begin the process? Y/N?**]

"Yes," he said, and with those words, mana poured forth from his palms.

A glowing radiance spread over the turned dirt. As more mana fizzled away, bolts of light connected all of the stalks. It had been the berry farmer named Trampus who had shown Sylas how to saturate his fields. Trampus had also pointed out that the process always drew attention from other beings, namely Mana Ghouls, which were able to avoid detection for half the day.

Sylas knew they would come that night, and he would be ready. He wasn't the only one.

Cornbread barked wildly as she ran through the fields. Patches tried to keep up with the farm dog, but he soon gave up and took a spot near Sylas, where he purred and weaved between his legs. Raelis and Quinlan eventually joined Sylas. He had already asked Quinlan what had happened with Priscilla and was simply told she wasn't available, whatever that meant.

If Quinlan was upset or anything, he wasn't showing it.

"Impressive," Raelis said, his face awash in a golden hue. "And here I thought being a demon hunter was rewarding."

"Nah, mate," Quinlan told him as he tapped one of his temples. "The real MLus are in the harvest."

The two laughed. Raelis clapped Sylas on the back. "I might need to become a farmer, then. Seems easier than running a campaign in the Chasm."

"I can promise it is. So how did your trip to the city go?" Quinlan asked Sylas. "You never said. You just showed up and started farming."

"It went well enough, and I showed up and started farming because I have to go back as soon as I can. Mira and I found a goose named Gertrude, but there are a few problems there."

"A goose? To do what?" Raelis asked. "I'd make a golden egg joke here, but I don't think that's what the goose is for."

"A goose to guard the market that Mira and I bought."

"Gertrude?" Quinlan smirked at his own cleverness. "Are you telling me that you all got a guard goose named Guard-trude? Heh, that's a good one."

"Oh, that's *terrible*," Sylas said, returning the man's grin. "I'll have to try that one on Mira."

"As long as I get credit, it's all yours. Now, tonight"—Quinlan rubbed his hands together—"the bloody monster has it coming. It will be worth a lot. Last I heard of a Taurigraith being bagged, it brought in a whopping forty thousand MLus. That's a serious load. Especially if we split it three ways."

"I like the sound of that," Raelis said.

"Other people are going to need MLus too, not just us," Sylas told them. He had yet to reveal the plan they had made in Battersea. There was more to discuss with Tilbud before he did so, and it still felt a little far-fetched. But his point remained. It was going to cost a lot of people a lot of MLus to send messages to the Celestial Plains, if that indeed was what they decided to do.

"Wanting to share, yeah? I figured you'd say that," Quinlan said, "but I told Raelis here we'd mention it anyway. So in that case, the sharing scenario: The way I see it, you, me, Rae, Tilbud, and Tiberius. A few of the militiamen—the good ones, Cody and Duncan—can stay back and guard the crops. Or, perhaps Mana Saturation will naturally lure the Taurigraith out."

"Azor? Cornbread? Patches?" Sylas asked. "They can take from my cut."

"Yeah, them too. It's not like we're going to be able to stop the dog and the cat from coming after us anyway, even if we tried to lock them inside. I suspect they would figure a way out. And Mira might want to come along," Quinlan said, "but, really, the team I mentioned is enough."

"Too bloody many if you ask me," Raelis told them, "but I'm not taking lead here. And as you know, if it was up to me, it would be the three of us, your dog, and your fire spirit. I've yet to see how this cat of yours operates, but I've heard good things."

"Patches?" Quinlan looked down at the cat, whose whiskers twitched slightly, as if he knew they were speaking about him. "He's the real hero around here."

"Really? An overweight pub cat?"

"Trust me on that one, mate," Quinlan told Raelis. "The cat will surprise you, overweight or not."

"But cats have a mind of their own. He's not going to listen to us like Cornbread will."

"True," Sylas told Raelis. "And that's both the disadvantage and what makes him unpredictable. But believe me and Quinlan, Patches is on our side. And he has a thing about tagging along with Cornbread, even though he probably wouldn't admit it if you could actually ask him. So if she comes, he comes. But we really have no control over that. Patches can turn invisible, you know."

"An invisible cat?" Raelis shook his head. "I guess I haven't given much thought about the animals here in the Underworld."

"Most of them are normal, but some have Mana Lumen abilities. Patches, for example, has been with the pub forever, his job being to protect it. Over the years he has grown his power and abilities with it. At least according to this veterinarian that visited."

"And Cornbread?" Raelis asked Sylas. She barked at the sound of her name.

"That's a good girl," Sylas said as the farm dog approached, her tail wagging. "She's younger, but also experienced. Any of the dogs that you might have heard barking in the Seedlands, all of them are similar. They are animals, but they have additional powers, and they have a purpose in regard to the locations that they found themselves."

"So they come attached to the real estate?"

"That's right."

"And this goose you want?" Raelis asked Sylas. "Where do you see Guardtrude fitting in?"

"That's more of an unknown, but she has performed guard duty in the past, and as far as I can tell, *Gertrude* will do the same at the Petticoat Lane Market."

"Didn't Mira call it 'The Bargains Market'?" Quinlan asked. "Something like that."

"Name change." Sylas looked out at his fields, which now glowed even brighter than they had before he started. "Saturation is done. I have to get back to Battersea for a lunch date and to see some magic."

"Yeah? I'd love to see some magic," Quinlan said. "But I'm guessing I shouldn't invite myself to this one. We do need to check on Kael, though, which means I'll need to head toward Geist again. Joy."

"Can't tomorrow. It looks like I'll be dealing with the goose even further," Sylas said. "Then there is the feast tonight. And don't worry, I'll catch you all up on everything that we have learned in Battersea before then. I'm just trying to get some clarity on it all now. And honestly, really, mates, I'm trying to wrap my brain around it."

"Huh," Raelis said, "is this something that needs clarifying?"

"Most certainly. Hopefully, this will all make sense soon."

Quinlan raised a hand in quick salute. "Then that's when we will go for Kael. Perfect time to visit Geist along the way too, see if Prissy will come out and play. Maybe we'll stay there that night? I'm thinking ahead. One day at a time, yeah?"

———

Lunch with Rufus turned out to be an awkward affair. It was clear that the haberdasher wasn't expecting any additional company. He was polite about it, but Sylas got the feeling that he wanted to be alone with Tilbud. So Sylas suggested he and Mira leave for a walk. "Mira and I can meet you at the animal shelter," he said just as they finished their toasted sandwiches.

"I think that's a grand idea." Mira wiped her mouth with a cotton napkin and pushed away from the table. "I wanted to check on some herbs anyway at the market here."

"I will see you there," Tilbud assured them. "You know, rather than go to the market and look at some boring herbs that you could probably pick up in Duskhaven at half the cost, there is an ice cream place just a stone's throw away from here. Perhaps the two of you would enjoy it."

"That sounds great," Sylas said.

"Didn't we already have ice cream today?" Mira asked once they left the restaurant. She took his arm.

"I can't seem to remember that one. Nope, no ice cream today to my knowledge."

"Normally, I wouldn't indulge myself this way, but perhaps that's fine. And anything to leave Rufus and Tilbud to work things out on their own. Did you see Rufus's face when you showed up?"

"I did."

"It was the same expression he had when he saw me."

"I suppose Tilbud will sort all that out now," Sylas said with a chuckle. "Or not."

"I'd say not."

Sylas and Mira found the ice cream place, which was called Bia's Cold Creams, and placed their orders. The apothecary chose a berry flavor and Sylas went with an ale-inspired ice cream. They continued on and found a bench that provided views of the city beyond, the homes tracing up and down the hills of Battersea.

"Well?" Mira asked after Sylas tried the ale-flavored ice cream. "How is it?"

"Remarkable. I wish I could serve something like this at the pub, but I would need to keep it cold in some way, and I'm sure there are other complications that I have yet to consider."

"There always are."

"Indeed. I suppose I'm in the market for an ice spirit."

"Don't tell Azor . . ."

"What could possibly go wrong there?" He laughed. "Relatedly, tonight, after the feast, the hunt is on. Once we are done at the animal shelter, we should likely return to Ember Hollow and speak with your uncle. We have arrangements to make."

"There are still some things we need to do at the market as well. I do intend to open this weekend, if at all possible. It would be nice to be done with this stage. I will say, however, I find it trying at times to be excited with the market considering what we know."

"But at least we have something worth trying now," Sylas said, referring to his idea to send messages to the Celestial Plains. "Between now and then, 'then' being the invasion, there's always the chance that something else will come to mind, some other way to make the best out of this. Because that's all I want."

Mira stared down at her ice cream. "That's all I want as well."

"Then eat your second ice cream for the day, be merry until there is reason not to be, and let's see about this goose."

"Gertrude better be worth it."

"If not, I'm sure Tiberius could always use *Guard-trude* at your home."

Mira moaned. "Really, Sylas. Did you come up with that joke yourself?"

He stuck his tongue out at her. "No, it was Quinlan. I told him I would give him credit."

"Good, because puns are, well, if there is any way to speed up the invasion message, it would probably be through bad puns. Just a theory, but let's tread lightly and not upset the powers that be."

"I will try not to *egg-splore* any other avenues."

Mira groaned in agony.

"Come on, Mira, that was good."

Once their ice creams were finished, Mira and Sylas took the long way back to the Brenham District, where they passed the same coffeehouse that they had met Nuno at earlier. Sylas expected to see the manaseer still standing there by the water, the strange man in deep contemplation. He thought back to what Nuno had said about the invasion, the conclusion other manaseers had come to: "We brace for and shore up the larger cities, creating future Campaign Cities like they have in the Chasm."

"What a load of rubbish," he whispered as they continued through the district.

Even if he didn't have the same understanding of Mana Lumens, even if Sylas had hardly been in the Underworld for two months, he knew that love, however corny it sounded, would ultimately triumph. A parent's love for their child, and vice versa, or any family member, really, would hold some sway in the Celestial Plains. He had to believe that. Sylas had to believe there was a chance.

They just had to figure out how to orchestrate such a connection between the people of the Underworld and their kin in the Celestial Plains, to inspire and afford for the entirety of the Underworld to reach out. Because sometimes, reaching out was the hardest thing for people to do, only made harder in the Underworld by the cost of sending such a message.

Sylas and Mira arrived at the animal shelter to find the door open and Tilbud already standing inside. He had already laid out gold tuning forks on a swath of leather and had instructed both Jenny and Catherine to sit on the stools. Jenny had a squirming puppy in her arms.

The puppy saw Mira, barked, and Jenny handed her over.

"Right, everyone is here," Tilbud said. "The first step will be to find the frequency. That is what this is for." He opened his hand and a crystal attached to a chain fell from it. "Now, we wait."

"How did it go with Rufus?" Mira asked.

"Ah, that." Tilbud furrowed his brow. "A discussion for another time. Sylas, Mira, please, in that corner there, if you will. It is best to stand out of the way so as *not* to disrupt the mana-sound waves."

"Mana-sound waves? Now you're just making things up," Mira told him.

"That's the best part of being a creative." Tilbud grinned at her. "Let's begin. And silence, please, while I get in tune with the honk. This should be exciting. And let's hope it works!"

Mira's jaw dropped. "You mean there's a chance that this won't work?"

"Heh, dearest apothecary. There's a chance that everything won't work, that's what makes trying so important. I would say you never know if you don't try, but sometimes you do know, yet you try anyway, so maybe there is more nuance to that phrase that should be worked out." Tilbud grew sad. "I hate it when I say something so profound that impacts my own thinking in ways I have yet to comprehend. Anyway. Enough of that melancholy, it really never helped anyone, and it is most certainly tied to the dreadful conversation I had with Rufus. Let's get to honking!"

Tilbud waited for a few minutes until Gertrude's timbre honk suddenly took shape, loud and random enough to make Catherine yelp. "Sorry," she said.

"That's quite all right. We will try the next time," Tilbud said. "If you think you are going to be surprised by it, you may step outside. But I think we can all handle it. After all, it's just a goose, well, a haunting goose honk, but a goose nonetheless, and we're all adults here. Dead adults, but adults nonetheless."

They waited again in silence. The honk happened again, and this time, Tilbud activated the crystal by touching it lightly with his finger. What followed was a wave of replicated sound, one that started as an echo but soon grew into a melodious noise that resembled a hum.

The archlumen conducted the sound with his other finger, which soon became a blip of swirling light, one that changed color from a melon yellow to a deep pink. It formed into an orb, which Tilbud carefully guided into the center of the room.

"Now, we will still hear the honk, but every time we do, this mana-sound orb will pulsate, absorbing its soundwaves. We are not finished yet, but I can tell you all that this has been a success thus far. So let's keep it that way. Mira, take one of the tuning forks and go to that corner of the room. Catherine, that corner," he told them as he pointed, "and Jenny, that corner. Sylas, take yours outside. We are going to capture the sound, and then send it outside to you. Once you receive it, you will bury it."

"You want me to bury it?" Sylas asked.

"No, I was joking. Once you receive it, you will now have the sound captured in the tuning fork. From there, I will take it to the Archlumenry for proper disposal. Unless it is something that you would like to keep?" he asked the two animal caretakers.

"What would a tuning fork with a goose's honk trapped in it do for us?" Jenny asked.

"The question should be what *wouldn't* it do for you," said Tilbud, who was still focused on the glowing orb. The women were already in position with their tuning forks, and there were two forks left. "But we can discuss disposal later, once the honk has been captured. Now, Sylas, outside, and I will get into position in here."

"Is there anything I should do once I'm out there?" Sylas asked as he took the tuning fork. The puppy that Mira had been petting rushed over to him. It sniffed Sylas and followed him to the door as Tilbud provided further instructions.

"Just stand in the direction of the back door, holding the tuning fork with both hands. Be ready to catch something. That's all. And keep the door open. Does it prop open?" he asked Jenny.

"It does. It's easier to let the animals out that way."

"Prop it open," Tilbud told Sylas.

"Got it. Catch the honk." Sylas propped open the door and got into position while the puppy sniffed around a large yard, which had a few kennels built into the back.

"Here?" he called to Tilbud.

"That's perfect." Tilbud took the final tuning fork. He stepped over to the only empty corner of the room and had everyone focus their instruments toward the glowing orb of honking sound at the center of the space.

Sylas felt a sudden tug at the tip of the tuning fork as he kept both hands on the instrument, pointing the thing forward like a wand.

"Steady does it," Tilbud said.

"This is vibrating our entire home; is this normal?" Jenny asked a few moments later.

"Nothing I do is normal," the archlumen told her, focused as ever. "But do not worry, it will work. If it doesn't, well, I'll bring in the experts."

"I thought you were the expert—"

Whoosh!

The honk exploded out the door, directly at Sylas.

Wham!

It hit him so hard that he flew backward and crushed one of the kennels. Everything went black for a moment, but then color returned. Sylas looked down at the tuning fork in his hand, which buzzed and eventually released a honk that sounded like a goose was directly in front of him.

Mira reached him. "Sylas! Are you . . . ?"

"I'm fine," he told her as he dusted himself off, the tuning fork still buzzing in his hand. "I wasn't expecting that, but who could expect something like that? I think it worked. Right?"

Mira helped him up. "You have clearly captured the honk, if that's what you mean. Now, it's a matter of what to do with it."

"I would hide it under your uncle's bed, but it might bother you as well."

"Funny," Mira said as Tilbud and the other two women approached.

"Ah, it worked," Tilbud said with delight. "Wonderful. Now, all we need to do is figure out what we should do with the goose-honk-laden tuning fork. We could keep it, you know. But the Archlumenry isn't opposed to rare items like this, even if they claim they are."

"Is there something we can do to silence it?" Sylas asked.

"Hmmm, I'll have to have a think about that. Actually, yes, that could work. For now, we can take it with us back to Ember Hollow and give it to Nelly, who will be able to store it due to the fact she's a merchant. She has that inventory list of hers, and that would keep it out of sight until we figure out exactly what needs to happen with it. But I do think it's worth keeping."

The tuning fork honked loudly.

Tilbud cracked a grin. "Even if it is a bit bothersome."

———

Once he got back to the pub, Sylas busied himself preparing the Wraithsday Feast. He had already helped out at the market, which was starting to shape up, especially now that Anders was doing some repairs. There was still one thing Sylas needed to handle personally before the opening, which he planned to do on his way to Geist the next day: stop by the Ale Alliance to finalize approval for kegs for the market's pub.

Everything was in order, everything aside from what he planned to reveal later that night.

"I'm going to head upstairs for a moment," he told Azor, who was busy in the basement with Quinlan working on the Wellingtons. "Make a few plans."

"A little late in the day for a nap, isn't it?" Quinlan asked.

"A nap isn't a bad idea with what we plan to do tonight and tomorrow."

"Heh. Bust Kael out. Deal with Prissy. Get some herbs for that goose. A loud one, that goose is, but I think she'll do just fine."

"As for the herbs, Mira knows what she's doing," Sylas told him as he headed up. He reached the stairs and Patches raced past his feet directly into the bedroom. Cornbread, who was resting near the back door, looked up at Sylas, yawned, and went back to sleep.

Once in his room, he got out a piece of parchment and sat down at the table. "What am I supposed to say?" he asked himself as Patches hopped into his lap, the cat instantly starting to purr. "I should just be honest with them. *Dear everyone, the Celestial Plains hates the Underworld and has decided to close it. They have deemed us redundant. Now we will all be part of the Chasm.* No, that won't do. Too blunt."

Patches mewed.

"I was just being sarcastic. I will get it summed up correctly without using the word 'redundant.' Maybe just some points will do. I will start with what is set to happen. Then, our plan. Then, ideas from the audience. We especially need to be able to afford to send all the messages up to the Plains. That is where others' ideas will come in handy. We'll need those MLus."

Patches continued to make noise, as if he were talking to Sylas.

"You are right. I should let them eat first. No sense in ruining a good time with the terrible announcement. Let the people eat and let them have their first ale, then after the second or third round, ding a pint glass, perhaps get on a table, and begin. I could also ask Tilbud to explain it."

Patches rolled onto his back and curled his front paws over his chest. Sylas reached over and scratched his belly and the pub cat instantly started purring. "You like that?" Patches purred even louder. "How am I supposed to get anything done with you around?"

A sound downstairs caught Patches's attention. He swatted at Sylas's hand, rolled over, and took off.

"I'll never understand the mind of a cat," Sylas mumbled as he went back to his points. There weren't many of them. But at least it would give him something to look down at later, if he got a little nervous while giving the speech. He didn't suspect he would, but it was always good to be prepared.

Before his death, Sylas had been asked to give rousing speeches several times.

He never really liked doing it, but it wasn't something that was alien to him. With the soldiers, he always themed his speeches around the same things: patriotism; fearlessness even when facing down death; support for their brothers-in-arms no matter what; pride in what they'd already accomplished; and a reminder that the future was much brighter than it seemed as long as they could hold the line, take the bridge, or drive back the Shadowthorne Empire.

Now that he thought about it, maybe he could stick to something like that.

They weren't yet on the front lines, and Sylas didn't know if it would come to that, or if there would be anything that resembled a front line, especially with their enemy both surrounding them and apparently above their heads. But there were ways he could give the speech that would fit into the parameters of the things he was used to saying in the past. So he decided to start there, jotting down everything he would say if he were saying this to soldiers in the field.

He finished, placed the piece of parchment in the front pocket of the vest he was wearing, and headed back downstairs.

Sylas got a chuckle out of the conversation that followed later that day between Tilbud, Nelly, and Nelly's husband, Karn. Always a showman, the archlumen produced the magic tuning fork several times, which drew stares from the other patrons at the pub as the space filled with Gertrude's ghostly honks. Eventually, Nelly agreed to hold on to it in the inventory list that came with her merchant class, as long as Tilbud would put it away.

"Phew, that's a relief," Mira said as she sat at the bar, watching Sylas pour up another pint. "I thought we were going to have to toss it in the well."

"You're not the only one. But it was an easier conversation than the one we had with your uncle earlier."

"Yes, to be expected."

That had been one for the ages.

The conversation had started between Sylas and Quinlan, with the two of them deciding that Raelis should stay behind, which turned out to be a good thing. Predictably, Tiberius's immediate reaction upon hearing there was a Taurigraith loose was to attempt to completely take over the hunt. He started barking orders revolving around how he would run it.

"That's not why we are bringing you in," Quinlan kept telling him. "I'm serious. We're not trying to get—"

"If we are going to do this, I'll manage it," Tiberius huffed with his usual defiance. "I will bring my men and—"

"I don't think you heard me, Tibby—"

"It's Tiberius, damn you! That's my bloody name, and it should be lord commander to an Aurumite such as yourself."

Quinlan stepped up to Tiberius at that point and the lord commander glared at him with his milky pale eye. He looked like a dwarf next to the hulking mass that was Quinlan, yet Tiberius never backed down, not even as Quinlan leaned over and poked his finger into Tiberius's chest. "This is our hunt, mate. We already told you what needs to happen."

Tiberius thrust his chest forward, which made it look like he was trying to bump Quinlan with his belly. "You come into my house—"

"We are *behind* your house."

"Both of you, enough," Sylas said after getting a look from Mira. He stepped over to them and squirmed his way in between the two. "You," he told Quinlan, "take five steps that way. You"—he pointed at Tiberius and gestured in the opposite direction—"five steps the other way. I will mediate this."

"Pfft!" Even though it was clear he wanted to protest Sylas's instructions, Tiberius did as he was told. "Well?" the lord commander asked once he was five paces away. "Are you happy now that you have separated us?"

"I am. And you two shouldn't be at each other's throats anyway. Didn't you all play nice after our trip to the Chasm?"

"Yes," Tiberius grumbled while Quinlan grunted in agreement.

"Then play nice again. This is what needs to happen: my farm needs guarding, which is where Cody and Duncan come into play. The three of us, alongside Raelis, who is classed as a demon hunter, and Tilbud—"

"I know who bloody Tilbud is and what the mad wizard is capable of!" Tiberius roared. "You act as if—"

"Don't you yell at him like that!" Quinlan shouted. The big man took yet another imposing step toward Tiberius, and once again had to be calmed down by Sylas.

"Let me handle it, mate," Sylas told him quietly before he turned back to Tiberius. "Now, I know you have your way of doing things, ahem, lord commander, and we have ours." Quinlan groaned at Sylas referring to Tiberius by his title, yet he continued as if he hadn't heard it. "But you need to remember an important factor: we are the ones that brought this hunt to you. It is worth quite a good many MLus, or so I've been told. Discretion is necessary."

"You won't know what it's fully worth until you turn it in to the guild. This is why we are going about this the wrong way." Tiberius threw his hands in the air in frustration. "If we inform the guild of it now, they will set a reward. Then we will know how much we are getting."

"How long have you been doing this, Tib? Are you really that mental?" Quinlan called over to them. He now stood about ten steps away, his back to Tiberius, arms crossed over his chest. "If we tell the guild, every hunter this side of Battersea will be in the forest tonight looking for the Taurigraith. We want the MLus, mate. We need them for what's about to happen. We don't want to share them with half the bloody Underworld."

"How am I supposed to know what is about to happen if you don't tell me?"

"We're getting to that," Sylas assured Tiberius. "But we have to get through this part first. So relax. Both of you, relax. Let's start here, and we'll end up there, yeah? Or we can talk about it tonight while we are hunting the Taurigraith."

Tiberius scoffed at this suggestion. "You aren't serious. Do you normally do a lot of talking while you are hunting an incredibly dangerous beast, one capable of mass slaughter? I think not!"

"Let's not get ahead of ourselves, mate," Quinlan called over to him.

Sylas turned to Mira. "Would you handle him?" he asked, motioning to Quinlan.

She stormed over, Quinlan instantly growing a bit sheepish as Mira quietly lit into him.

"Serves him right," Tiberius muttered.

"We have brought this to you," Sylas told the lord commander, his patience growing thin. "It is a good option, and it is something we can do together to net the rewards." It pained Sylas to say this. He didn't actually believe that they needed the lord commander's help, but he knew that Tiberius was experienced and that he would be an asset in a hunt like this. "We need your help."

The lord commander's eyes quivered. "You really need my help?"

Sylas was surprised that this had been the turning point in the argument. It was the point at which Tiberius finally softened, going from standoffish to open to the idea of the hunt.

"Yes, we do. We really do."

Now, as Sylas poured up some pints for a table of people from Cinderpeak, the feast about to begin, he thought about the moment the lord commander's tune had changed. For once, diplomacy had worked with Tiberius, and it started with calling him by his title and making it seem like they truly needed him for the hunt.

"I do hope you're careful tonight," Mira told him as she smiled at Sylas from across the bar. "My uncle has forbidden me to join you all. Normally, I wouldn't listen to him, but we do have a big trip to Gloombra planned for tomorrow for the goose. Plus, there are things I need to do at the market. So I figured some beauty rest would do me well."

"It would do us all well. But I'm not getting any tonight. And I'm fine with that," Sylas said as Azor appeared.

"Shamus is saying the next round is on him." She motioned over to the estate manager, who wore a plum-colored suit with a silver cravat.

"What's the catch?" Sylas asked.

"The catch? Ah. Shamus wants to announce an auction tomorrow for an abandoned café near the market." Mira turned to Azor. "There's a café? Where?"

"He said it is a yellow building near there."

Mira gawked at her statement. "That is supposed to be a café? I saw Shamus poking around it earlier, but I didn't know why."

"I'm just telling you what he said." Azor offered her best fiery shrug. "Yellow building, café."

"Absolutely not," Sylas playfully told Mira as she looked back at him. "I have too much under my belt as it is. We're *not* going in on a café. Sorry."

A wry smile traced across Mira's face. "Oh, please. I'm not saying that we should take out another loan, I'm saying this is a good sign. If real estate has become available, it means that people are starting to inquire about Ember Hollow, that more people will move here. Our village will be better off in the long run."

"I know what you mean," Sylas told Mira, "and sure, Azor, Shamus can buy everyone a round and make the announcement about the café, but after my speech. Let him know, will you?"

"Will do!" Azor flashed away and Patches hopped up onto the bar. The pudgy cat approached Mira and she placed her hand on his head. He started purring loudly.

"I don't want to come off as if I'm hoping for our demise," Mira said hastily, "but it's hard to plan for the future with this message of yours."

"I think we should continue to operate as normal here in the Underworld. We can't let the Celestial Plains get the best of us. Not today, not tomorrow, and not in thirty-six days."

"I am surprised my uncle agreed to that plan as well," Mira said, referring to the conversation they'd had after Tiberius reluctantly decided to join the hunt. "That was unexpected."

"It turns out you can teach an old dog new tricks," Sylas said. Patches turned back to him and mewed. "Maybe an old cat too."

————

The Wraithsday Feast officially started soon after and the crowd was larger than Sylas could ever remember having at the pub before. He was certain he would sell out of ale, especially after he made his announcement.

While everyone ate on the main floor, their voices loud and jovial, Sylas privately met with Tilbud in the cellar.

"Catia is here," Tilbud said, the first thing he had said to Sylas since arriving. The pub was packed and Sylas had barely been able to catch up with anyone in his rush to make sure there was enough ale available. "I have yet to brief her."

"You haven't? Why?"

"Well, for one, all of this is . . ." Tilbud's eyes darted left and right, which looked comical considering he was in a banana-yellow suit with a matching tie and a bucket hat made of yellow and green feathers that matched the color of his socks. "It is complicated, as you know."

"It is."

"And I didn't know how to bring it up. I suppose a person as garrulous as me should know how to bring it up, and really, I would gladly talk about it with anyone, but Catia is different."

"You're in love?"

Tilbud laughed. "Heavens no, Sylas. I'm in lust, as always. 'Love' is something I feel for many people, and love itself wouldn't dilute my ability to speak to them clearly. 'Lust,' on the other hand, makes me a bit nervous. It's messy. It's so bloody messy. And, if we're being honest, which I always am with you, I wanted to see how others reacted to your announcement first. So I will talk to her, and—"

"I decided to make part of my announcement a time where others could offer solutions."

"Well, that is always one way to do it, yet I would advise against not opening the floor to every single person. You have people upstairs who have been here for dozens of years and people who just showed up recently. We all have different ideas of how this works. Catia and her people will likely have the clearest understanding, one based in, well, not *science* because we don't have science here—at least not the same kind of alchemy we had back in our world—but based in reality, Underworldian reality. Likely, law. What an atrocious word, law. Ugh. You know how I feel about rules. Anyway—"

Azor rushed down with Tilbud's and Sylas's plates. "You two need to eat. Try this."

The archlumen's eyes lit up as he saw the food. "Ah, Azor, dear, I meant to take a bit down here with me. My apologies!" After a quick look around, he shrugged. "I suppose a dingy cellar is as good a place to eat as any." He took the plate from her and found a pair of forks. He handed one to Sylas and the two tried the Wellington.

"It's wonderful," Sylas told Azor, who had reached a point of anticipation at which she was entirely glowing. "I love the outer crust and the meat is done just right. And really, Azor, the flavor is fantastic."

"You think so?"

"Marvelous." Tilbud smacked his lips. "I'll have you know that I have eaten at some of the best gastro-dining establishments in all of the Underworld and none, well, a few, but mostly none, compares to The Old Lamplighter. In fact—"

"What about Horatio?" Azor asked. "Is he around?"

The water spirit appeared. "I'm here."

"I made something for you as well." Azor rushed to the other side of the kitchen and returned with a plate that had elemental-appropriate food on it. "Care to join me upstairs at the bar?"

"As a matter of fact, I think I will," the water spirit said. He headed up with Azor, leaving Tilbud and Sylas alone.

"Ah, I love to see that they're getting along," Tilbud said. "And, as you can imagine, I wish I could say the same for Rufus and me, but complicated things are complicated because they are complicated. I think that makes sense. And there might still be an angle there. If it doesn't—"

"Just eat," Sylas told the archlumen, "you don't need a pithy quote for everything."

Tilbud laughed. "Cheers, mate." He lifted an invisible pint glass. "We shouldn't have left our pints up there."

"I'll get them." Sylas took the stairs to the pub, the sound of the crowd louder with each step.

He grabbed the two pints and was just turning back down when Raelis called, "Oi, Sylas. You joining us or what? What are you doing down there in the basement anyway? Hiding from your adoring fans?" He burst out laughing and Quinlan did the same.

"I'll be back in a moment."

Sylas headed back down.

"So this is your new ale invention," Tilbud said a few moments later as he examined the slightly blue ale that Sylas had crafted. "It does have a unique color, I'll say that." He smelled it. "And it smells like ale, so I'll consider that a good thing as well." The archlumen took a sip. "My word."

"Right?" Sylas said as he took a drink. It instantly calmed his nerves, the cold ale giving him a quick shiver.

"You are very good at what you do, my friend. The Old Lamplighter has all the makings of a future landmark. I can see it now, people coming from all over to Ember Hollow to enjoy the unique ale and wonderful meals. Perhaps they will also come for a pub quiz."

"Perhaps," Sylas said.

"But to get to that point: to preserve our way of life, we have to stare boldly into the unknown and . . ." Tilbud sucked in a deep breath through his nostrils. "Once again, I'm at a loss for words. At least good words."

"Don't worry, I've done something like this before."

"Inspired people? Gave them hope in a hopeless situation?"

"Actually, yes," Sylas said, and while he didn't elaborate, the way he said this seemed to put Tilbud at ease. That, or his second sip of Sylas's new ale.

"Bloody marvelous," Tilbud said as he smacked his lips.

Either way, Sylas was ready to rally everyone behind what was increasingly becoming the most important thing he would ever do.

———

The time came once the crowd at The Old Lamplighter was satiated, some already working on their third round of ale, and everyone was good, tipsy, and merry. Sylas stepped around the bar with a fork and a clean pint glass. He took a deep breath in through his nostrils and dinged the glass three times.

Ding, ding, ding.

The crowd died down.

"What do you got for us?" Bart the bard asked. "Not a song, is it? Come on, good man, sing us a song. Isn't there one about a man who ran a pub on one side of town, where he lived with his wife, and a pub on the other side, where he often stayed with his mistress? I can't remember all the lyrics, but I remember the tune! I think it was called the 'Two-Sided Tavern.' Or maybe, 'A Tale of Two Taverns.'"

"No, that's not it," said Mr. Brassmere, who was there with his wife. "It's called 'Duel Ale and Hearts.'"

"Wait, that's right." Bart cleared his throat. "*In a town of cobblestone and cheer, lived a bold publican with secrets to revere. One pub on the east, and one on the west, he gave it his all, but he didn't give it his best!*"

Mary the lutist started playing along, her fingers moving rapidly as she found the chords.

"*In the east end near the docks, his wife waits while the gulls flock. And in the west, where the shadows play, his second wife sits by the window until the start of the day!*"

Next to him, Godric the fireweave tailor, clapped his hands together. "Enough, Bart, Sylas is trying to say something. Before you begin, and especially before Bart here tries any more singing, can I be the first to say that that was an absolutely incredible meal. Thank you, Azor. And thank you, Sylas, for

the positively wonderful blue ale. I never thought I'd say something like that."
He raised his pint glass to the fire spirit, who was near the bar next to Mira. "But
this has been bloody fantastic. Cheers, all."

This caused Sylas to look over at Mira and register the nervous look on her
face. He wiped his face with his hand and tried to begin again: "First, I would
also like to thank Azor for her wonderful meal."

"Hold on a minute, let's get back to this ale!" Iron Rose said. "It was great,
mate!"

"Hear! Hear!" some of the people at the back yelled.

Iron Rose continued, "If you don't share the recipe, I'm taking my swan
painting back *and* I'm asking Bart to continue his song."

"It's a bloody good song!" Bart roared.

Sylas pointed at Iron Rose. "That painting was a gift," he said in a playful
way. Several people burst out laughing. Mary brought her lute up and played a
quick number that had people clapping along.

"Please," Sylas said as he set his pint glass down. This was definitely not
the upbeat tone he wanted to start this talk with, so he tried again. He showed
everyone the palms of his hands. "Please, everyone. This is important. Let me
say my piece and then we can get back to our merriment."

With those words, the room changed.

There were a few whispers, but most were now listening intently to what
Sylas had to say. He scanned the crowd once more and caught thumbs-ups from
Quinlan and Raelis. Near them, Tilbud sat at a table with Catia the lumengineer and Meldon and Andrea from the Archlumenry. Like Mira, Tilbud had a
concerned look on his face, his mustache drooping slightly.

"I haven't been honest with you all," Sylas began, "but that's mostly because
I didn't know what this was, what I was experiencing. All of you know what it's
like to arrive here and be thrust into this new life of ours. But I'm going to go
out on a limb here and say that none of you arrived and then woke up the next
morning to receive a message."

"What kind of message?" Bart, who was clearly a little drunk, asked.

"Let him finish," Godric told him.

"Shhh!" Shamus the estate manager told the two.

"Don't you start shushing me—" Godric began.

"Relax, mates," said Raelis, the tone of his voice instantly quieting them.

"The message comes to me every morning. It started at eighty-nine, and
this morning it was at thirty-six. 'You have thirty-six days until the invasion,'
that's what it said this morning."

The crowd started to murmur. They were silenced by Quinlan, who clapped
his hands loudly. "Let the man finish, yeah?"

Sylas returned his focus to the people all seated around him. "So naturally, after receiving this message every morning, day in and day out, I looked into what this message could mean. It took some time, but I finally got confirmation from manaseers in Battersea. My initial thought was the invasion was coming from the Chasm. After all, there have been breaches before, one just recently. And, I guess in a way, the invasion will still come from the Chasm at some point, if that's what ends up happening here. But they aren't the ones who have called for the invasion."

"The bloody Celestial Plains," Iron Rose said. Sylas turned to her, surprised that she had so quickly come to that conclusion. Cinderpeak's reclusive brewer continued: "The Crafting Laws, and now this. Tell me I'm wrong, Sylas," she said, desperation in her voice. "Tell me I'm wrong and I'm not jumping to conclusions here."

"You *aren't* wrong. The Celestial Plains have decided that the Underworld should no longer exist. It is easy for them to simply *merge* the Chasm and the Underworld, rather than give everyone a new chance at life here. I don't fully know their intentions, but a few of us have come up with a solution."

Gasps filled the pub.

"We take the battle to them," said Nelly, who had been quiet up until this point. She said it again, louder, "We take the battle to them!" Beside her, her husband, Karn, gave Sylas a determined, yet slightly hesitant look.

"War against the Celestial Plains?" asked Anders the carpenter. "How would we even go about that? Even the highest flying archlumens can't reach there."

"We aren't going to battle anyone," Shamus said. "I do wonder what this will do to the real estate market, however. Ah, now that I somehow have the floor . . ." He took a quick look around. "The yellow café near the soon-to-be-market is still *on* the market, just so everyone knows. Doomsday message or not, if you're looking to buy, now would be the time."

"Really?" Mira asked Shamus.

"What? It is! Sorry, um—"

"Surely we can fight them off somehow," Duncan said. Next to him, Cody grunted in agreement. Both militiamen had frowns on their faces like they were hearing this for the first time, even though Sylas had already briefed them on it before.

"We're not going to be able to do that forever, though," Tilbud said. "Please, let Sylas continue."

Sylas did just that: "How can we appeal to an enemy that is stronger than us? That is the reason we are able to use these powers? We're not going to be able to to beat them in a battle. We can't even reach them. We're also not going to let some of the powers here in the Underworld divvy up the place in preparation for the inevitable. As all of you can imagine, there are those with access to influence who see an opportunity in this merger of the Chasm and the Underworld. They see this as something we cannot stop. They think of this as a chance for them to get ahead and get a nice chunk of what is to come. Personally, I see things differently. I see this as an opportunity for us to fight for what we love by appealing to those we love."

Cornbread, who had been at the back of the room, barked. Sylas couldn't tell if she was nervous or if it was too quiet for her. But Quinlan handled it by scooping her up into his arms. Sylas glanced over to Patches, who was in his place on the windowsill, quietly watching him.

"So that's what we're going to do," Sylas told those who had gathered in The Old Lamplighter. "We are going to use everything within our power to reach our parents, our extended family, past loved ones, anyone you can think of in the Celestial Plains. We will put everything we have into making sure everyone can send a message. We will pool our resources or use some exploit that we have yet to fully uncover but that I know will come. Because we are determined people. Our lives here aren't always perfect, but none of us—especially those of us who have been to the Chasm—want to invite that sort of chaos into the Underworld. We all deserve better, and we must use the power of our community to orchestrate change."

"Whatever it is, whatever we need to do, I'm in," Iron Rose said. "I never liked the Celestial Plains anyway."

"This isn't about liking," Tilbud told her. "They are the reason we can access Mana Lumens, the root of all of our powers. As far as we know, we would maintain our classes if the Hexveil were to fall, but we would also be inviting demons and endless conflicts that we don't currently have. Really, look around, how nice are our lives? If the Hexveil were to fall, many of us would survive, but that survival would look very different from how we live now."

"Then what?" Bart asked aloud. "We just hope that appealing to people above might help us?"

"If enough of us do it, yes. I know it is expensive to send a message that way. But that is why we brought you here," Sylas said, motioning to Tilbud's table, where he sat with Catia and the other archlumens. "It's also why you are here." He gestured to a man in the back who had kept his hood over his head.

The man pushed the hood back to reveal himself to be Nuno the manaseer. "It *is* why I'm here," Nuno said. "I thought about our conversation, what others are planning to do, and decided that this was worth it. That I agree with everything you've said. The Underworld *is* worth preserving. And I believe change is possible. It will start with what you have already proposed. Appealing to those above will have some effect. We will also need to visit."

Once again, the crowd grew quiet.

"Who will need to visit?" Mira asked Nuno.

"Sylas, for one. He is the only person, to my knowledge, who is receiving this message. Perhaps that means something. There are envoys, you know, ways to appeal to the Celestial Council. Most importantly, we need MLus. We need enough MLus for everyone in the Underworld who is willing and able to send a message, a request really, to preserve our way of life. We have less than thirty-five days, yet I suspect we have much less than that."

"That's already not a lot of time, mate," Quinlan told the manaseer.

"No, I'm afraid it's not. The Hexveil has started to fall. As more of it collapses, we can expect more breaches."

The front door of the pub swung open, and Tiberius entered. Mira immediately looked at her uncle skeptically. "Have you been outside listening to this the whole time?" she asked him.

"No."

"Lies."

He grew flustered. "The window was open, Mira. I merely happened to stroll by, considering all of my militiamen are here. And the manaseer is right. There are going to be more breaches. There have already been several smaller ones. I'm pretty sure I heard thirty-five days. I think we have less, much less."

Sylas watched as Tilbud and Catia had a brief, quiet conversation, the lumengineer clearly agitated. She finally relaxed to some degree and spoke. "Perhaps," she said, "perhaps there are some things that can be done now that we better understand the threat. Tomorrow, I will go to Battersea with you and Tilbud."

"We will get more done there," Tilbud told the former lord commander, "but I do not know if—"

"Nonsense. You need me. And I do have connections I'd like to share with you all. Plus, there is a rather good sauna in Battersea, another reason for visiting." Tiberius rubbed his hands together. "In that case, a plan is in order, everyone. Do not be scared. We will solve the invasion dilemma, and if we don't, I assure you all that we will shore up our defenses here. With some of the people who now call this village home, I have the utmost confidence that we will not only protect ourselves, but we will get to the bottom of this. For the Underworld!"

"Hear, hear!" Many of the patrons shouted.

Tiberius glanced over to Sylas, a proud smile on his face that said *That's how you do it.*

Normally, something like this would have gotten under Sylas's skin. But Tiberius, as cantankerous as he could be, was a natural leader, a former lord commander used to dealing with all sorts of people. He was just the ally Sylas was looking for, even if he could be a bit standoffish.

And Sylas had no doubt in his mind upon hearing the tone of Tiberius's voice that the older man would give his all to defend Ember Hollow, no matter what. Moreover, Sylas meant what he'd said about using the power of their community for change.

It would take all of them doing their own part to stop the invasion.

———

They are planning something, Patches told Cornbread later that night. *I know it!*

It has to be about the bull-tiger beast from the other side. Has to be, Cornbread said as she looked back and forth between the human's legs. *We're going to get it, aren't we?*

It appears so . . .

The big man had gathered several others at the pub, all of them wearing armor and now holding weapons, aside from the magic man, who kept twiddling with his fingers. Even the fire spirit was pumped up, her flames flickering blue and purple as she hovered anxiously near the door.

Patches's whiskers twitched. *In that case, we will go with them.*

And who will watch the Farmly Realm?

If someone has to stay back, I will. You are better at tracking than me. There, I said it.

Do you really think so? she asked Patches.

I wouldn't say it if I didn't think so.

You are a funny cat, you know that? Always so serious, but a good, loyal friend. And I think the farm will be fine. We should go for the bull-tiger beast together.

We are not friends. We are coprotectors. Never forget that, Patches said.

Protectors and defenders of the Farmly and Tavernly Realms, and the soon-to-be Marketly Realm! I'm aware. But that does mean we are friends, in my opinion.

That makes one of us. Even if he was being a little harsh, Patches approached Cornbread and lightly lashed his tail against the dog. Cornbread licked his face. *That's enough of that,* Patches said as the humans all headed out.

The cat quickly caught up with them, Cornbread doing the same. *Let's go! Let's go!*

She barked until Patches told her to keep quiet. *Hush!*

But I'm excited! We're going to slay that monster, I just know it. Let's go!

Don't get ahead of yourself, Patches said, but as he expected, Cornbread took off to the front of the group, leaving him at the back.

So Patches turned invisible.

Sometimes, he did it just because he liked the idea of disappearing. Patches couldn't remember a time when he couldn't simply vanish, and it was a power that he found most useful when tracking rats and other varmints.

Now, he would use his magical concealment to sneak around in the forest, allowing the humans to move ahead, Cornbread acting as a beacon once she started barking. Or he would use the power at the farm, stopping the Mana Ghouls from slurping up the crops.

I have to help the big man, he reminded himself as the group approached the portal. Patches hopped onto it just before they vanished, all of them reappearing in the Seedlands.

Their first stop was the farm, where two of the militiamen stayed behind after the short warrior with the strange eye shouted a few orders at them. The new man was with the group as well, the one with long dark hair who they had retrieved from the other side. He reminded Patches of the big man's warrior friend, only darker.

I will still need to keep an eye on him, Patches thought as the fire spirit did a quick check around the farm. *And you're being too bright!* he hissed at her, even though the fire spirit couldn't understand him.

The group continued onward, the warriors at the lead, the big man in the back, the fire spirit gone for the time being. Cornbread rushed to the front where she sniffed at the ground, her tail erect.

She is good at that, Patches thought as he maintained his position at the back. To give himself a better perspective, he decided to take to the trees. Patches quickly scaled up a trunk and out onto a tree's long, mangled branch.

He crouched there and waited for the group to pass below.

Then, Patches jumped to another branch and continued on in this manner, now above Cornbread and the humans.

The pub cat kept at it, moving rapidly and noticing as Cornbread became increasingly alarmed when the group reached a meadow. They paused here and the older, one-eyed man, cast something. The golden hue that Patches recognized as mana spread outward. With it came an incredible bellow that shook the ground.

The warriors got into position, and the one with long dark hair pointed for the big man to stand back. Cornbread couldn't help herself. She started barking ravenously as a terrifying, bull-like monster with the face of a tiger exploded out of the woods, a halo of gold repeatedly slashing at it.

The fire spirit came alive, scorching the ground, conjuring a wall of flames that the monster merely charged through. *Wham!* The hellacious beast struck a tree with its horns, which sent that tree into the same one in which Patches was currently crouched.

The pub cat made a frantic jump. *Here goes!*

He landed, bounced once, and quickly took his largest form. Coming out of his invisibility, Patches startled everyone as he swiped at the bull-tiger monster. He flashed invisible again, and bit onto the monster's tail, quickly incinerating it.

Cornbread's barks sent a wave of energy forward, which struck the monster hard enough that it staggered backward. Once Patches was grounded again, he used his supersonic purr power to disorient the monster as the men beat at it, and the magic man blasted it with bolts of mana. While they engaged it, the fire spirit spiraled around the creature to confuse it.

Cornbread bolted in, her jaw quadrupling in size as she bit down on one of the bull-tiger monster's legs, just above the hoof. She tore into it, holding tight as the creature tried to buck her off.

The warrior man with the long dark hair channeled something into his club, which he used to hit the beast hard enough to finally send it tumbling over to its side. Rallying, the humans all went to work, hacking away, the one-eyed man yelling, and ultimately summoning a bolt of mana that came down like lightning from the golden sky, piercing the monster's side and killing it.

Patches flashed visible again. *We did it!*

Cornbread looked over to him, the dog panting. *You flew down from the trees. I wish I could climb up there and jump down like that!*

It was a risk, but like most risks, it paid off.

Definitely, Cornbread said as she approached, her tail flapping back and forth. *Are you all right?*

Never been better. Patches offered Cornbread a rare, toothy cat smile. *Good job, back there. Your bark is clearly as bad as your bite.*

And your scratch is clearly as strong as your meow. That makes sense, right? Cornbread asked as the humans celebrated. *Right?*

CHAPTER SIX

GERTRUDE

The work on the farm wasn't over for Sylas, his companions, and his two pets. With Mana Saturation, they were kept up most of the night handling the ghouls that the unique power attracted.

"All in a day and night's work," Quinlan said once it became clear things were finally dying down, the fields quiet after a series of increasingly difficult battles. "Get some rest, Sylas. We've got it from here."

"You're certain?"

"Isn't that right, lads?" Quinlan asked Cody, Duncan, and Raelis.

"That's right," Raelis said as the two militiamen grunted beside him.

"What about me?" Azor asked, the intensity of her flames lowering.

"You're one of the lads in my book," Quinlan told her. "But really, Sylas. Head in. And by the time you wake up, we'll all be sitting down to a nice morning meal from Azor."

"That's right! I brought supplies from the pub this time," the fire spirit said with her usual fiery flourish.

Patches circled around Sylas's legs until he picked the cat up. "That's a good boy." He hugged the cat and brought him into the home.

Sylas fell asleep faster than usual. He woke to find Patches purring next to him and Cornbread resting at the foot of the bed as the prompts flooded in:

[You have 35 days until the invasion.]
[A loan payment of 681 has been deducted from your total Mana Lumens. Your total loan balance is 23767 Mana Lumens.]

Sylas and the team had each received 6,000 MLus from the hunt of the Taurigraith. They had given Cody and Duncan a cut, and had given as much as they could to Patches and Cornbread, which was something Tiberius had grumbled about, leading to an altercation with Quinlan.

"We wouldn't be here without those animals," Quinlan had told the lord commander. "They save our arses more often than not."

"That's not true."

"Easy, mate," Raelis said, which was the first he had spoken to Tiberius. "I think things are fair just how they are."

"Fine, be charitable," Tiberius said. "But next time, we're cutting my horses in!"

Now in bed, Sylas flicked through his own stats to see that all was looking well. After the harvest, he would be past the twenty thousand mark, after which things would become more expensive.

Name: Sylas Runewulf
MLus: 13286/13286
Class: Brewer
Secondary Class: Farmer
Tertiary Class: Landlord

After scratching Patches behind the ear, Sylas left the bedroom to find Raelis and Quinlan seated at the table, both shoveling quiche into their mouths. Cornbread barked and Azor immediately turned to him. "You're awake, good! Mira is outside. Happy—"

"She's here already?"

"With Tilbud, yes," the fire spirit said.

Quinlan swallowed a bite of quiche. "Your lady and that wild wizard friend of yours are walking around the fields and talking. Last I heard they were saying something about Gloombra. That's where *Guard-trude* is, right? Never been, myself. Heard it's interesting, though."

"That's right, Gloombra," Sylas said as he took a seat. Cornbread came to him and he petted the dog. By the time Sylas looked back up, a slice of quiche sat on a plate before him, a bit of steam wafting off it. Cornbread started to whine. "It's too hot for you, girl."

She whined even louder.

"He's right," Azor told the farm dog. "Right out of the oven is too hot for a sweet little pup like you."

"I'll give you some of mine," Quinlan said as he fed Cornbread a piece from his fork. "And you aren't sweet, you're ferocious."

Azor blinked quickly and changed subjects. "I really wish I could go to Gloombra with you all. Horatio was telling me about the place last night. He said it was interesting, but someone has to make these Wellingtons, and that someone is me!"

"I'm going to help you," Quinlan said as he gave Cornbread more of his quiche.

Raelis laughed. "Like hell you will. If you're downstairs at the pub grilling up Wellingtons—"

"Baking," Azor said.

"*Baking* up Wellingtons, who is going to watch the farm?"

Quinlan tapped his fork near Raelis's side of the table. "I don't know, mate, you?"

"Do you really need help in the kitchen?" Raelis asked Azor.

"I could always use help."

"And I fancy myself a bit of a chef," Quinlan said. "Who do you think made the stew during the Old Haven Campaign?"

Raelis barely hid a strained expression. "That was you? That was the worst bloody stew we had that year!"

Sylas laughed, remembering the strange concoction of bones, sour milk, and spotted leaves, which they had scraped together when rations were tough. "It wasn't that bad. Wasn't that good, either, but it also wasn't that bad."

Raelis curled his nose. "I was certain it had been flavored with rat."

"What?" Azor asked. "Is that even an option?"

Quinlan roared with laughter at Raelis's statement. "Flavored with rat? You would say something like that, you—"

"Now, I'm serious, Quin. There was a big hair in mine one night. I remember using it to make jewelry."

Azor flared with intensity. "You did what?"

"He's joking," Quinlan told her. "Raelis has a rather odd sense of humor. A bit macabre if we're being honest. And Azor, rest assured, I make a great chef's assistant. I'm a jack-of-all-trades, really."

"*Jackass*-of-all-trades," Realis said to another snort of laughter from Quinlan.

"And you promise not to fall asleep?" Azor asked Quinlan.

"When would I fall asleep?"

"You often sleep during the day."

"Pfft!" Quinlan waved her concern away. "I just like a good nap, that's all."

"If you're going to help me, someone needs to keep an eye on the Wellingtons as they bake."

"Can I keep an eye on them while I rest?" Quinlan grinned at her. "Kidding, and you're right. I probably shouldn't promise too much. Made that mistake with Priscilla."

"You're going back today, yeah?" Raelis asked.

"I am. Why? You coming?"

Raelis rubbed his hands together. "Perhaps. I always wondered what kind of woman would find you charming."

"Plenty of women have found me charming—"

As the two started in again, Sylas excused himself from the table and headed out to find Mira and Tilbud approaching. The archlumen wore a red suit and had a pink tie on, one with big stripes running diagonally over it. "Ah, Sylas."

"Ah, indeed," Sylas said as he looked out over his fields, which glittered with Mana Lumens.

"Quite the fight last night, right?" Tilbud grinned at his wordplay.

"Quite. So what's the plan?" Sylas asked as he joined them, the three standing around one of the scarecrows that Quinlan had previously erected. Cornbread came up barking, but was instantly soothed by Mira, who bent down to pet her.

"Well, since neither of you can portal to Gloombra, we will have to go by way of Battersea," Tilbud explained.

"So we head back to the pub and use my portal there," Sylas told Mira. "Easy peasy."

"Actually, that was something Tilbud and I had set up in Battersea yesterday while you were attending to your crops," Mira said. "There's a sigil in the Landlord Guild, one with direct access from Cinderpeak. What we learned was that as landlords, we are able to use it, and others like it in other cities, to portal anywhere without paying."

"It's free?"

"It is, because we might be showing a potential tenant the property."

"So we don't have to go to Battersea?"

"You always have to go there," Tilbud told Sylas. "This is the work-around. Rather than portal indirectly, you portal to the guild, and then go where you need to go from there. So it is a two-step process."

"We need one of those in Ember Hollow," he told Mira.

"Let's not get ahead of ourselves," Tilbud said. "You need to open the market first, and then we can petition for something like that. But I doubt it will be installed before, well, you know."

"The invasion."

"An invasion that we are seeing too," Tilbud reminded them. "Catia and I. And of course, you all."

"And Rufus?" Mira asked the archlumen. "How quickly we forget about him."

"He's not forgotten, just misunderstood. Or he doesn't understand me. Or perhaps one of us is incapable of understanding the other, and sadly, before you ask, Rufus doesn't respond well to flattery. He can see right through it, unfortunately. Alas, that is to be handled at a later day. But what's important is dealing with this invasion first. Then I can sort out my messy relationships and make a better man out of myself."

"No longer going where the breeze takes you?" Mira asked as they turned in the direction of the portal.

"Perhaps not as much. In my old age . . ." Tilbud started laughing. "I really shouldn't say it like that."

Cornbread woofed a few times as she beat her tail wildly.

"No, you need to go back to the farm," Sylas told her. The dog started to whine. He took a knee and scratched her head for a moment. Cornbread licked his face and he laughed. "We will be back later. Don't you worry."

After Sylas carried Cornbread back to the farm, he joined Mira and Tilbud at the Seedlands portal, where he was presented with numerous options:

Ember Hollow
Cinderpeak
Hexveil - Ember Hollow
Shadowstone Mountains
Duskhaven
Douro
Battersea
Everscene
Wraithwick
Geist
Ghostford

Rather than go directly to Battersea, they portaled to Cinderpeak, since the trip was free, and going directly to Battersea would be 300 MLus. The three briefly checked with Malcolm the grain supplier in the market and then headed toward the center of town, near Mr. and Mrs. Brassmere's tool supply shop. They saw John out front wearing a new pair of overalls and carrying supplies.

"Decided to visit the big city?" John jokingly called to them.

As if he had been summoned, Leowin, the constable of Cinderpeak, came around the corner thumbing the top of his truncheon. He spotted the group and eyed them suspiciously. He then swept his cape to the side, laughed, and turned in the opposite direction.

"I suppose that is a greeting somewhere," Mira said. "And if you're referring to a trip to Battersea," she finally called back to John, "then yes, that is exactly where we are going."

"In that case, have a good trip. Great work last night at the feast!"

The group pressed on, now going in the same direction of Iron Rose's The Ugly Duckling pub. There, they found the woman seated on a stool in the center of the pub, painting yet another portrait of a swan.

After a brief conversation, they came to a building that looked like a warehouse. Sure enough, there was a portal inside, along with loads of other supplies.

"You can have things shipped here as well," Tilbud said, almost as an afterthought.

"That would have been good to know over the last several days as we've been preparing the market with whatever we can find," Mira told him.

He laughed in his strange way. "I suppose it would have. Anyhow, come. We are almost there."

They stepped onto the portal and immediately appeared in Battersea. Instead of a warehouse, they were presented with a nice courtyard with numerous private gazebos and plush furniture. There was an expensive restaurant with tables under rows of pergolas, where people sat sipping on cold drinks.

"For negotiations," Tilbud said. "Just wait a moment and . . ."

A female voice spoke to them.

[Where would you like to travel?]

"Gloombra," Sylas and Mira both said.

[Your credentials have been authenticated. This will only take a moment.]

They portaled away again and appeared at the base of a large hill, which was hard to discern with all the housing that had been built across it. The roads that circled around the hill were lit by enchanted lanterns that added a mysterious glow to the entire city. As Sylas took it all in, he noticed that most of the homes were connected in some way, a patchwork of red brick and yellow roofs.

The portal was near a river where numerous boats were docked. Sylas spotted several people tying up boats as cats prowled about. Beyond the river was a dense forest, one that was filled with a mysterious, yellow-gray fog.

"Never would I have thought it would be that grand," Mira said as she looked up the steps to the academy. The cathedral-like structure had numerous spires that matched the pointed roofs of its towers.

"Yes, the Grace Academy." Tilbud admired it for a moment. "Grand as grand can be."

"Didn't you say something about us potentially fighting people?" Sylas asked. "Should I have brought my club?"

"No, there will be no fights. That was just to keep things interesting."

"So you made it up?" Mira asked him.

"Heavens no, Mira, I'm not the type of archlumen to make up stories. They do train here for certain types of excursions, but we should be fine." He swept the ends of his red jacket aside. "Come, we don't have all day. Or, we do have most of the day, but there is the feast and the big revelation. That should be a delight. I thought about perhaps hosting a pub quiz, but maybe that is inappropriate. Another thing, we're going to need some Charm here. Are you ready?"

"Wait just a minute," Sylas started to say.

"I'm kidding. Hopefully we *don't* need to use a Charm spell. And even if we did use it, they would likely have lumen detectors that would be able to discover it. No, I'm afraid we're going to have to go on with our own natural charm." He offered them a toothy grin. "So, best behavior—you especially, Mira—and hope that they haven't already dissected the goose."

"Dissected it?" Mira asked Tilbud. "And what did you just imply about my behavior?"

"Did I imply something? And regarding dissection, well, I hate to be grim, but what else will they do with it? That's what we're here to find out. I do still have the tuning fork, or Nelly does. But we can arrange for that to be delivered if that's what they would like."

"I hope you know what you're doing," Mira said as they started up the steps.

"I rarely do, yet I seem to survive. Or, I should say that I often do know what I'm doing, but there are variances at play that make it hard to both pinpoint and describe my motives, both clear and ulterior."

Sylas remained stunned by the grandeur of the location. It seemed like every street he looked down had some new mystery to uncover, like the homes themselves had been built into the side of the hill; or rather, the hill was wearing a cloak made of housing units. There was a splendor to it all that he enjoyed. Gloombra was bustling despite its strange name.

Sylas couldn't remember the last time he'd seen so many people relaxing in the Underworld, many sitting on balconies and having meals, others tending gardens, a few resting on the ground, their hands propping their heads up. It reminded him of Battersea.

"People that come here to the Grace Academy often stick around Gloombra," Tilbud told them. "So it makes sense that the women who run the animal shelter would bring it here. Gloombra does have the Underworld's highest concentration of archlumens aside from Battersea, and that's only because of all the guilds there."

"It sure is something," Sylas said as they neared the top of the stairs.

A huge pair of open doors revealed an inner courtyard that was filled with students in black capes practicing spells, some being observed by their professors. It didn't seem like the space could fit inside the academy and Sylas wondered if it had been worked in some way by magic. He stopped, looked back to the entrance, and then ahead, across the courtyard to the other side of the academy.

"Ah, yes," Tilbud said. "I see you are noticing that there is a bit of a spatial difference between how the academy looks outside versus how it looks from the interior. Interesting, hmmm? It is a type of understanding of Mana Lumens that I have not yet tapped into before with my Shrink spell. But that is neither here nor there. If you'd like a lecture, well, there are plenty going around." He motioned to some of the professors with their groups of students.

"Let's just get the goose," Mira said. "We still have a lot to do today."

"First, we have to find the goose. I have an idea." Tilbud glanced at a few students who were seated at a table, the group ranging in age from their early twenties to pushing seventy. He cleared his throat and they all turned to him. "Hello, I am Octavian Tilbud, A-Rank Sovereign of Arcane Mysteries and Paramount Luminary of the School of Echelons and Enchantments. Relatedly, I would like to show you something."

"School of Echelons and Enchantments?" a female student asked him. "I'm fairly certain that school has been disbanded."

"Disbanded and distributed to the other academies, I assure you. Not disbanded for any nefarious reasons, young lady. But that is neither here nor there. May I borrow a piece of parchment?" The woman hesitated at Tilbud's request. "I assure you, your parchment is in good hands."

"Fine." She tore off a single piece of parchment and handed it to Tilbud.

"Thank you, kindly. Now, let me see if I can make a goose. I'm pretty sure I can do a swan, but a goose may be a tad bit harder," he said as the woman gawked at him.

"Why do you want to do that?" Mira asked Tilbud.

"Because if I do this, we can find the goose we're looking for without having to search every nook and cranny of this academy, including its dangerous catacombs. They do exist, you know. Now, hold tight one moment, Mira." Tilbud worked meticulously with the piece of parchment, folding it and adjusting various portions until he made a goose with two legs. "Great. Stand back."

None of the students moved away from their table, but Sylas and Mira took a step back.

Both had seen what Tilbud was capable of.

"Are you ready? Then I say the magic word—kidding, there is no magic word. Just watch." The archlumen set the paper goose on the ground, and the creature came alive with a sparkle of gold. The paper goose waddled toward a door on the western end of the courtyard. "Follow that goose," Tilbud said. The archlumen tipped his hat at the students and quickly took off after his paper construct.

————

The paper goose created a little burst of golden residue with each step, which quickly drew the attention of other Grace Academy students in the area. Soon, a crowd was following behind Tilbud, Sylas, and Mira, which flustered Mira to the point that she reached out and grabbed Sylas's hand.

He squeezed it. "Nothing to worry about," he told her.

"Why does Tilbud always have to cause a scene?" she whispered to him.

"Because he's Tilbud. That's what he does. And you have to admit, this is rather fun."

"Is it, though?"

The paper goose headed up a short flight of stairs, Tilbud, Sylas, Mira, and several of the students following it. The archlumen turned and grinned at Mira. "If only I had brought the tuning fork. That would have made this more authentic. Actually, that wouldn't have been a bad idea. They may want to study something like that here. We will see. Onward!"

Onward it was, as they came to a foyer that featured a wraparound staircase that led up to a grand hallway. The paper goose waddled on. It circled around groups of students and reached another stairwell, forced to hop to make it to the next step.

"You really don't think this is a bit much?" Mira told Tilbud. "It feels like the whole academy is following us now. Weren't we trying to keep a low profile?"

"Who wouldn't want to follow us?" the archlumen asked. "A sight like this is rarer than you think. Sure, these students can fly, and they can do other interesting things, like make fireballs and perform basic spells. But animating an inanimate object is something only a master can do. Now, I'm not saying that is what I am, but it appears I'm not far off. Worthy of delivering a lecture on animating inanimate objects? Maybe. But I'll let the powers that be decide that at a later date. Come, our little paper goose will get away if we don't keep up with it!"

"I can't believe we're doing this," Mira said as they continued through another corridor, one lined with statues.

"Believe, Mira! And not to worry, we are getting closer," Tilbud said, his finger in the air. "I can sense these things, you know."

"How long can you keep it animated?" a student called to him.

"As long as it takes, my good sir," Tilbud said. Only when Mira was close did he tell her the truth. "Actually, if we're being honest, I can't animate the paper goose forever, but certainly for another few hours. The thing is, you don't want to let these young fledglings know that there are limitations. You want them to believe that the sky is the limit, literally, considering the Celestial Plains are above."

"Thank you for that explanation, professor," Mira said as the goose came to a large wooden door, one nearly twice a man's height and polished to a sheen. The goose hopped around and then pecked at the ground in front of the door.

"Good! I believe we have found it." Tilbud picked up the paper goose and turned to the group of students who had followed them. "How about you?" Tilbud said to the young man who had asked the question earlier.

"Me?"

"Here is your new pet. Treat him, or perhaps her, kindly, and maybe they will run around the academy for you one day." He handed the student the paper goose, which fell flat in the young man's hand.

"Um, thanks?"

"You're most welcome!" Tilbud swiveled, he knocked on the door, and it opened on its own. "Come," he told Sylas and Mira as they stepped into a new chamber that had classrooms on either side. The sound of a loud honk drew their attention. "That would be it."

"Her," Mira said. "Her name is Gertrude."

They stepped into the classroom to find a professor and what Sylas assumed was her assistant standing around a goose, who had been placed on the table. The professor, who had a shaved head of white hair and wore a pair of oval spectacles, looked up at them as they entered.

"May I help you?" she asked in a thin voice.

Her assistant, a man with a pointed goatee and a harsh look on his face, immediately approached as if he were going to usher the three out of the room.

"No need to approach us in such an aggressive manner, my good enough man," Tilbud told the assistant. "We are merely here to collect our goose."

"*Your* goose?" he scoffed.

"Mira, the paperwork, if you don't mind." Tilbud snapped his fingers.

"Don't do it like that," she said as she produced the document and handed it to the assistant, who walked it over to the professor. The goose, who seemed dizzy, honked loudly enough that it blew the professor backward. The woman caught herself with magic and landed on her feet.

"They are authentic ownership papers," the assistant called over to the professor after looking through them.

"Did you really think I'd bring you counterfeits? Perhaps we got off on the wrong foot." Tilbud stepped around the assistant and proceeded to make a wide berth around the goose. He offered the professor his hand. "Octavian Tilbud, A-Rank Sovereign of Arcane Mysteries and Paramount Luminary of the School of Echelons and Enchantments, at your service, Your Illuminance."

"The School of Echelons and Enchantments, huh? Octavian Tilbud. Octavian Tilbud. Nope. I can't say I've heard of you," the professor told him.

"Nor I you. Professor . . . ?"

"Archlumen Professor Arlayna Gwen of the Grace Academy's School of Ephemera and Arcanic Conundaries."

Tilbud squinted at her. "Arlayna Gwen. Ah, I have attended several of your lectures about Gloom Whispering and its origins through corrupted magical ledgers."

"I have been known to give those from time to time," she said, a bit flattered.

"Yes, about that lecture. I did have some notes. You know what? I will have them delivered. I would have brought them had I known you were here, or maybe I wouldn't have because they are quite extensive and my back isn't what it used to be."

The smile on her face flattened. "Notes on my . . . lecture?"

"It is our job to correct errors, especially dangerous ones, is it not? But that is neither here nor there, Your Illuminance. The goose. We will be taking Gertrude and anything you have on her condition that could help us"—Gertrude honked, startling all of them—"would be greatly appreciated. So please, hand over the goose."

Archlumen Professor Gwen made no attempt in hiding her desire to be rid of the goose. "I am actually glad that you've come to get it. Glad beyond words. I don't know what it is that is haunting this poor goose, but I have decided to call it Chaotic Honk Syndrome, or CHS, based on a condition found in other enchanted creatures that causes them to make noises repeatedly. It is believed to be linked to an overabundance of lumen aetherica discordia."

"Lumen aetherica discordia?" Tilbud used a handkerchief to wipe a bit of sweat off his brow. "Please, professor. You can do better than that."

"Excuse me?"

"Such a throwaway solution. Lumen aetherica discordia is only in the Chasm. Are you saying our dearest and most goosiest Gertrude is from the Chasm?" Tilbud asked.

Everyone in the room looked at the goose, who in turn looked back at them, her head cocked slightly. She was large and white, with black eyes and a golden-yellow beak. Mira had already whispered to Sylas that the goose was cute, but he couldn't see it. Gertrude just looked like a normal goose to him.

The professor continued: "We believe she has spent some time there, and more time here, yet in old age, the symptoms started. I have tried everything including casting Silence on her, but that doesn't seem to work."

"Interesting. Have you tried taking her to The Distinguished Society of Lumengineers and Etheric Constructs? Perhaps there is something that they can do there?" Tilbud asked.

She gawked at this suggestion. "What would a lumengineer do that I couldn't do?"

"There are a number of things, professor. If you would like me to list them, I most certainly could. But most I know would come up with a better solution than some barely understood Chasmic phenomena."

Archlumen Professor Gwen clenched her fists at her sides. Eventually, she crossed her arms over her chest. "You know what? Since the goose is yours, take it. I was tasked by the provost archlumen to oversee the study of its constant honk. I've taken the notes that I need, and I do not have a cure for it."

"Have you tried anything else?" Mira asked. "Perhaps something herbal?"

The professor looked at her incredulously. "Are you an apothecary?"

"I am, among other things, yes. Why does that matter?"

"Perfect, you can make one of your little ointments for the goose, then. I believe we are done here, Martin," she told her assistant. "There are other things to do, and I don't want to hold these people, not while they have the ownership papers for this wonderful goose that won't stop honking around the clock."

Gertrude made noise yet again.

"Is someone having a bad day?" Tilbud asked the professor. "Because if so, I do know of an ointment that apothecaries often carry with them that can cure bouts of grumpiness."

"Are you still bloody here? Please, take the goose and good luck."

The professor stormed off and left through the door in the back, her assistant racing after her. He reached the door, turned back to Sylas and the others, and shooed them away.

Tilbud started to laugh. "I really can't blame her. The poor woman has probably been without sleep for several days as she tried to figure out what was wrong with this goose. The professors here, they struggle to get tenure and will often go above and beyond just to be let down. After all, why do they deserve tenure when we have professors who have been teaching for hundreds of years?"

Gertrude honked. Mira approached the goose and gingerly took her into her arms. She seemed to like it there.

"As to your ointment suggestion," Tilbud told Mira as they turned to the exit, "it's not a bad idea at all. Let's head back to Battersea, to the great library there. They do have a nook on herbal medicines. I suppose we will leave you standing outside with the wild goose, Sylas. If you don't mind."

Sylas looked from Mira to the archlumen. "That's fine."

CHAPTER SEVEN

NEW ARRIVAL

Sylas likely wouldn't have stood outside of the Grand Library of Battersea for just anyone. But for Mira, he started to realize after an hour passed—and by extension Gertrude, who was in his arms honking sporadically and startling the locals—this was the least he would be willing to do.

"There, there," he told Gertrude as he patted the goose's neck. "Just try to relax."

For all he knew, the goose was relaxed. She was surprisingly friendly too, wagging her tail just about as soon as they took her away from the Grace Academy. Her honks seemed painful and they looked like they hurt her each time she released one. Sylas placed her down a few times, but every time he did, she flapped her wings and chased after anything she deemed suspicious. To passersby she would simply shake her whole body and approach them with the goose equivalent of a smile on her face.

"This is a library, you know," a man said in passing after one of her outbursts.

"Yeah?" Sylas asked him. "Should I bring the goose in?"

That shut the man up as he shuffled inside.

"Just you and me again," he told Gertrude. "A lovely goose and a pub owner in the big city. Imagine the stories they'll tell of us later."

Gertrude honked in response.

Sylas was relieved when Mira and Tilbud stepped out of the Grand Library, Mira with a few hastily written notes stuffed into the front of her purple apron.

"Any luck?" he asked the two as they approached.

"Something we can try, yes. I'll explain as we head back. We could hear Gertrude from inside, you know." Mira scooped the goose into her arms and Gertrude instantly relaxed. The goose placed her neck along Mira's shoulder and looked back at Sylas and Tilbud as the apothecary walked ahead of them.

Tilbud used a handkerchief to wipe a bit of sweat from his brow. "It was bloody warm in there, I'll have you know. All those books and the heated texts they contain. Ha! You are lucky to have stayed outside. How did it go?"

"It went. You would be surprised to know that people do not like a loud honking goose outside a library."

"Is that so? Well, I suppose you learn something new every day. This does make me want to fetch the tuning fork from Nelly and have a little fun with it." Tilbud beamed a mischievous grin at Sylas. "Anything to bring joy to peoples' lives."

"Maybe next time." Sylas caught up with Mira as they headed down an alley that fanned out onto a small courtyard overrun with flowerbeds. The tile here was a mixture of red and white stones, which he took to understand was a common feature in Battersea's Sigur District. Just as he was about to comment on it, Gertrude released an incredibly loud honk. "Your uncle isn't going to like that," Sylas told Mira.

"She won't be staying at my home tonight, if that was what you thought would happen. She'll stay at the market."

"Are you sure? I'm certain there's a nice place for her right under Tiberius's window. Then again, you'd have to hear it as well. I wouldn't wish that upon my worst enemy."

"Even a Thornian, as Quinlan likes to call us?"

"Even a Thornian."

"As for leaving Gertrude near my uncle's window, let's not and say we did. Although I agree, it would be funny. He would have a bloody fit. More likely, anyone living by the market will hate me in the morning. But all in due time. Tomorrow, we need to travel somewhere to get a pair of herbs that grow near each other. One is known as calmthistle and the other is called harmony dew. We'll have to go to Geist, and from there to the Cloud Forest."

"Got it, Geist for harmony dew and calmthistle," Sylas said. "Any particular reason it's known as the Cloud Forest? I have yet to hear that name."

"Don't answer that," Tilbud told Mira. "If he hasn't seen the Cloud Forest beyond Geist, then he's in for a treat." The archlumen rubbed his hands together. "It's a real delight. Spooky, yet cozy in its own way."

"I haven't seen it either, Tilbud," Mira said.

"Really? And how long have you been here in the Underworld? My dear, Mira, you need to get out more. Travel is important in this day and age, lest we remain trapped in our own little worlds to our own little detriments. But that's good, that's fine, that's well enough. In this case, you are both in for a surprise. How delightful!"

"And this will work?" Sylas asked her. "You're certain?"

"There isn't a guild for apothecaries anymore. But there is information that was written down before the Crafting Laws, which was where we found this potential cure. It isn't for a goose, exactly, but from what I know about calm-thistle, and how it could potentially combine with harmony dew, I think it could work. I really do."

"And you would just apply the ointment every day?"

"We'll have to test that. I suspect that I will have to apply the ointment for a few days. But after that, it should take hold and little miss Gertrude will be good to go." She hugged the goose. "At least that's the hope. Don't worry, deary, I'll handle that honk soon."

"Now that you mention Geist, I kind of need to head that way for a different reason," Sylas said. "Quinlan and I still need to visit with his brother, Kael. And Quinlan has another person he wants to visit there."

"Who exactly?"

"Priscilla."

Mira's eyes widened. "I did hear him talking about a Prissy one night over a pint. Could that be her?"

"That's her."

"And his brother, Kael, he's part of a meditation retreat, right?"

"Correct."

"Will Raelis join us?"

"Probably."

"And I need to do some more work on the market," she said. "And speak with Esta again."

"That's right. I should be there for that."

"You should. But your harvest is most important. I told you before, Sylas, I don't mind taking the lead with the market. It was sort of my idea."

Tilbud, who had listened to their entire conversation, sighed audibly once they reached the Ale Alliance, the guildhall with its famous cask shape and large sign out front with gilded letters and illustrations of hops and barley. After a short conversation with Greta, the pub inspector who kept asking about Corn-bread, and Marty, the sigilist, they prepared to take the portal back to Ember Hollow.

"I should probably stay here," Tilbud told them. "Someone has to tell every-body about tonight's big announcement. At least everyone that will see me at the moment. But expect the unexpected. Or, at the very least, expect the usual blokes from the Ale Alliance, the Archlumenry, Lumengineers, and anyone else I can round up. Make sure Azor has plenty of food. I don't want her stressing once she sees the crowd that I can conjure when I turn up the *Charm*."

"You aren't going to do that, are you?" Sylas asked.

"Why, of course, I am. And do not worry. By the time I arrive tonight, it will have worn off. Hopefully. If not, stay clear!" He laughed. "Kidding. Please don't look at me like that, Mira."

Gertrude honked loudly, startling a woman heading out of the Ale Alliance.

"And with that honk, I believe my departure is in order." Tilbud tipped his tiny hat at them. "I'll see you all back in the simply hollowest of embers. Cheers!"

———

Patches grew suspicious the moment the big man showed up on the farm with the medicine woman, who was carrying a plump goose in her arms.

Have they brought dinner? he asked, his whiskers suddenly alert.

Cornbread, who was just getting up to go greet them, laughed. *I don't think so. But maybe. I don't think I've had a bite of goose before.*

The pub cat remained on the porch as the big man's dark-haired friend came out to greet him. He eyed the goose, who now waddled on the ground and eventually released an absolutely ear-splitting honk that made Patches's hair stand at attention.

That can't be the noise it makes. How am I ever going to sneak up on anything with a beast like that?

Cornbread was investigating the goose. She looked back at Patches and barked. *Come over here and meet her!*

I'll come over when I'm good and ready. To illustrate his point, Patches took his time coming off the porch. He approached the goose to find Cornbread talking to her.

You're some kind of guard goose? Cornbread asked. *Neat!*

Gertrude tilted her beak skyward. *I suppose you could call me that, yes.*

What do you guard?

Whatever I'm told to guard.

This is the Farmly Realm. That's what the cat calls it. Cornbread pointed her snout at Patches. *We also have the Tavernly Realm. Both are well-guarded. And why are you making such a loud sound?*

The goose seemed embarrassed by Cornbread's question. *I don't know. It's been like this for a while. I can't make it stop. It's dreadful, really.*

The medicine woman will help you, Cornbread told Gertrude. *She knows these kinds of things.*

Ah, a medicine woman. Is that what she is? Gertrude asked. *I don't have the same sense of smell that you do. I thought she was just a nice woman. The man is nice too.*

Cornbread, who was panting a bit, offered a toothy grin. *The big man is the nicest.*

And the cat? Gertrude asked.

I am not the nicest, Patches said for himself.

He's nice. You need to get to know him. You'll see. Watch. Cornbread hopped over to Patches and licked his face. *A few licks and he softens up. Feel free to lick him—*

Hey!

Gertrude made a chuckling sound with her throat. *I don't believe I've ever met two animals like you.*

I don't see many birds myself, Cornbread told her. *And when I do see them, I usually chase them out of here. We can't have them bothering the crops.*

I'm not interested in the crops. Unless they need guarding. Gertrude straightened up. *Do they need guarding?*

They will tonight. But I think we will be able to handle it with the humans.

Gertrude looked around. *I see it now. There is energy in the crops.*

Yes, Cornbread said, excitedly. *They will be harvested tomorrow.*

So the medicine woman? You will be with her? Patches asked, wanting to get to the bottom of why the goose had interrupted his peaceful time on the front porch.

Gertrude honked loudly. *I'm so sorry! It just comes out that way.*

Patches scowled. *Warn us next time, please.*

I don't know when it's coming myself! As for who I will be with, I don't know. I think the woman. She seems to really like me. But the man held me for a while as well.

The big man has enough animals, Patches said with a slight growl.

Cornbread raised an ear at this remark. *I disagree. A human can never have enough animals. At least not dogs. Maybe cats. Too many cats is probably troublesome.*

Gertrude laughed. *If they're all grouchy, I can imagine that being the case.*

Patches started to back away. *Well, while the two of you laugh it up, I'm going to go rest and prepare for tonight.*

With that, Patches hiked his tail up in the air, turned slowly, and walked back to the porch.

CHAPTER EIGHT

GEIST

Gertrude didn't know what to make of her new home. She had already explored it, the booths of the market, and the seating area that looked like it would be a place for humans to gather.

Who am I supposed to protect it from? she asked herself, right before she let out a loud honk that caused her to hop backward. *Oh, blast.*

After gathering her wits, Gertrude waddled around to the front of the market, where she heard the sound of people. She spotted the big man heading toward the portal with a few men. The friendly dog and the grumpy cat were with them. The cat was currently invisible, yet Gertrude could still see him.

That cat.

Rather than stay at the market, Gertrude took off after the group, curious where they were headed. The dog rushed over to meet her.

Are you coming with us? Cornbread asked.

Am I invited?

Of course you are, the dog told the goose as her tail wagged left and right. *Everyone is invited. It's time to protect the farm—*

Farmly Realm, Patches said as he remained invisible. *And she's not going to help us if she's loud. We need stealth.*

I'm not loud.

Really? Was that you who made that noise just moments ago? Or was it another goose?

The big man approached. He picked Gertrude up and spoke to her for a moment. He then walked her back to the market and placed her there, where she released yet another honk.

Oh, blast! Gertrude said. *Sorry!*

The group was just starting off again when Gertrude approached again.

I think he wants you to stay here, Cornbread said. *But I don't know why. We could use your help. You can fight, right?*

I'm a very powerful goose. She waited for Patches to say something, but the cat remained quiet.

The big man conferred with the others who had joined him. There were some grunts and nods, and this time, he didn't take Gertrude back to the market. Instead, he let her follow along, until they all reached the portal. Once again, he scooped her into his arms and they moved somewhere else, to the land of farms that Gertrude had seen earlier that day.

I'm excited! Cornbread said as she continued to bark. She took off toward the fields of corn and Gertrude raced after her.

Soon, the dog and the goose came upon a pair of Mana Ghouls. Cornbread slammed into one of the monsters and brought it to the ground. Inspired by her actions, Gertrude did the same, only she downed hers with her wings, which grew to several times their normal size, the tips as sharp as knives.

Nice! Cornbread shouted, a portion of a ghoul in her mouth. She finished killing the Mana Ghoul and moved on.

Gertrude caught up with Cornbread, who was in rapid pursuit of a larger monster. It quickly became clear to the goose what they were doing on the farm. *The monsters are trying to absorb the energy! Not if we can help it!*

Flapping her wings again, Gertrude flashed over Cornbread and speared into a Mana Ghoul. She pinned it to the ground and quickly killed it.

Wow! she said as Patches rushed past, the cat several times his normal size. He clawed a Mana Ghoul, yowled, and brought it down. The two rolled on the ground for a moment until Patches was able to overpower the dark creature. He bit down on the spectral monster's neck.

Back on the attack, Gertrude chased after a Mana Ghoul, a smaller one that was quickly getting away. She snapped her wings in its direction and released a solid arc of energy that cut the fleeing monster down.

The goose jumped back as she came to an absolutely enormous Mana Ghoul, which had several heads sucking up the dormant mana. It batted at her with its claws, which sent Gertrude flying to the side.

Cornbread rushed in barking, each bark growing increasingly louder until her sound waves sliced into the large Mana Ghoul. Her actions also brought a chorus of barks from the other farms. Within moments, more dogs joined the fight, including a small one who didn't seem like it would be able to do much.

Let's get it! Cornbread shouted to the other dogs. *Follow my lead!*

They all moved on the mana-sucking amalgamation as a human entered the fray. One of the big man's warrior friends, the one with long dark hair, struck the Mana Ghoul with a blast of golden energy.

His attack disintegrated much of what was left of the creature, allowing Gertrude, the dogs, and Patches to move on to the next target. The three animals tore through several more Mana Ghouls until they came to a large one that the big man and his other warrior friend were defending against.

I've never seen one like this! Cornbread said as they circled around a tree-like monster that had taken root in the cornfield, its branches all mangled arms tipped with sharpened claws. The head, the eyes of which glowed with a muted gold, was positioned in the center of its body, and the monster's numerous limbs were making it hard to strike.

The dogs tried and were swatted away. The humans moved in next. One of them got close, but the monstrous ghoul managed to beat him back with a stray limb.

Seeing an opportunity, Gertrude drew her wings back, extended her neck forward, and fired through the air like a crossbow bolt, straight into the center of the monstrosity. Mana surged all around her as she drilled deeper into the creature, killing it.

Gertrude got to her feet, released another wayward honk—*Oh, blast!*—and shook her tail feathers.

The big man clapped his hands together in amusement. Patches, who had been seconds away from springing an attack, appeared next to Gertrude.

Not bad, he told her, his whiskers twitching.

I told you I could help.

I can see that now. In that case, welcome to the team. Patches lightly lashed his tail against the goose and moved on. *You did well.*

―――――

[You have 34 days until the invasion.]
[A loan payment of 199 has been deducted from your total Mana Lumens. Your total loan balance is 23568 Mana Lumens.]
[Your fields are ready to harvest.]

After a quick breakfast, Sylas donned his hat with the charms on it and moved into his fields.

[Your Harvest Silos are ready.]

The prompt came as the silos floated over the fields and the corn was sucked up while a hovering number tallied the yield. Cornbread raced through the fields as it happened, the farm dog barking gleefully as the corn was stripped from the stalks. After about ten minutes, Sylas received another prompt:

[You have yielded 15000 Mana Lumens' worth of corn. Pay tax now? Y/N?]

"Yes, that's fine."

[A payment of 1050 Mana Lumens has been deducted from your yield. Transfer to the guild now for distribution? Y/N?]

"Confirmed."

[You have received 13950 Mana Lumens.]

Once his taxes were paid, Sylas transferred Mana Lumens to everyone who had helped so the hunters could get their multipliers and his pets could receive some from the hard work they put in. He gave each of the pets a thousand MLus, and then gave the same payout to Raelis, Quinlan, Duncan, and Cody, which cost Sylas seven thousand.

He tried to give the two warriors more, but they both argued with him until he gave up and moved on.

"So I'll see you in Geist," he told Quinlan before he headed off back to Ember Hollow with Patches and Gertrude.

"Yeah, I'll be at the inn there trying to make nice with Priscilla. Story of my life at the moment."

"That's where I come in," Raelis said. "I've always been a matchmaker."

"Oh?" Sylas asked as he watched Cody and Duncan head off, the two militiamen waving goodbye.

"Right," Raelis said.

Quinlan looked at him skeptically.

"Really, mate. I'll be there to run interference. Make sure you don't say anything that you're going to regret. I might also tell her some of the things that you've done in the past, you know, sell you a bit better than you would on your own. Set you up in that way, yeah?"

"I definitely don't need that." Quinlan winced at Raelis's statement. "Definitely don't."

"Actually, you do, mate. There were a few times back in the day that you were a damn hero and no one knows about it but the few men who served with you."

"Sometimes that's the way it should be."

"Yeah, I've heard you say that before. But trust me, I'll put the word in her ear and sweeten her up a little bit."

Quinlan rolled his eyes but didn't seem disappointed with this prospect.

Gertrude honked loudly as they left, Patches following after. They reached the portal and appeared in Ember Hollow, where Sylas found Mira already working in the market.

"I brought your guard goose," he told the apothecary.

"Good. And she did well last night at the farm?"

"She did great. At one point, we were going up against this big treelike creature," Sylas explained. "Gertrude shot right into its center, spearing it with her beak. So that was unexpected."

"I'll bet." Mira ran the back of her hand across her brow. "I suppose we should get going because I need to meet Esta this afternoon to talk about her booth. Are you . . ."

"Am I what?" Sylas asked as he scooped Patches up.

"Are you certain we should be doing this? With everything that is about to happen, what does the Petticoat Lane Market matter in the grand scheme of things?"

Sylas shook his head. He knew that now wasn't the time to question something like that, to try to pick things apart. They had to keep pushing forward as if things weren't on the precipice of great change.

It wasn't about keeping up appearances or trying to convince himself that the inevitable wasn't inevitable. This was about the two of them, together, perhaps in the final days, or maybe at the start of a long partnership.

"It matters, Mira, it matters," he finally said. An idea came to Sylas, something they could do. He let the idea fade to the back of his mind as Gertrude honked, adding a strange touch to Sylas's statement.

The goose also had a way of breaking Mira's frown. "Right, well, I guess the goose is in charge while we try to find the herbs we need."

"And Quinlan is already in Geist."

"What a joy."

"Come on, you like him," Sylas told her. "A little rough around the edges, that's all."

"He does grow on you."

"And Raelis?"

"Are you fishing for compliments for your friends?"

"I believe I am."

"They're fine, Sylas. But I prefer *your* company. Anyhoo, I suppose we should get to it." She placed her hand on Gertrude's head. "You stay here and keep an eye on things."

The goose wagged her tail like a dog.

"I wonder where she learned to do that," Sylas said as they left the market. "Cornbread?"

"No, she was doing it yesterday before they met."

They were just turning onto Ember Hollow's main street when Henry approached them. Sylas had seen the older militiaman last night at the pub, but he didn't remember him saying anything about what they planned to do.

"You really think it's possible?" Henry asked instead of a greeting. "I'm not saying I don't think it's possible, I'm just hoping that we don't have to start contending with the Chasm. It won't be easy, especially living here. Tiberius thinks it's possible that we can change things. He's in Battersea this morning with that kooky archlumen and the other woman, said he'd manage everything."

"Did he?" Mira asked skeptically.

"We'll just have to see what Tilbud and Catia can uncover in Battersea," Sylas told him. "And, sure, Tiberius. But I can tell you this: We will figure out a way to accomplish this task without going to war with the Celestial Plains, and without kicking open the doors of the Chasm."

"Yeah? You really think so?"

"I do," Sylas told him, his voice filling with conviction. "I don't know about you, Henry, but I'm not the type to go down without a fight. That's the way I ended up here in the first place. Never backing down. Maybe it's hubris mixed with a bit of stupidity or maybe I'm just brainwashed enough to think that this sort of bravery can actually accomplish something, but it is who I am."

Henry cracked his knuckles. "Good to know, mate. That makes me feel a little better about all this, if we're being honest. Anyway, I won't hold you. I know you have something to do." He jumped at the sound of Gertrude's honk. Even though the market was practically on the other side of the village, all three could hear it.

"That's what we plan to handle today," Mira told the militiaman. "Rest assured."

"Yeah? That's your goose?" Henry scratched the back of his head. "I had my window open this morning and was wondering where that bloody ruckus was coming from. I certainly wasn't resting assured last night."

"That's our Gertrude." Sylas smirked at Henry. "And like Mira said, it's on the agenda for today."

"Three pets now?" Henry laughed. "Good on you, mate. I can barely take care of myself."

"To be fair," Sylas said, "Patches takes care of himself and Cornbread is pretty independent. And Gertrude is Mira's. We'll see how things shake out with the goose, but she is a hell of a fighter. We just need to see about her involuntary honk."

———

Sylas and Mira appeared in Geist, which was just as Sylas remembered it. The town was surrounded by black Geistian trees, which were as hard as stone. As often happens when someone visits a place more than once, Sylas noticed new details as they entered Geist, including the spire that pushed out of the forest that looked like it belonged to a temple. He also noticed that many of the homes had dried red berries pinned above the doors, which apparently came from the Geistian trees.

"What are those?"

"The Geistian redberries?" Mira asked as they headed toward Priscilla's inn. "They're thought to bring good luck. Medicinally, they don't really have any properties. They're quite sour, and I have heard of some people using them in pastries, but I haven't tried anything like that."

"I see. I should pick some up for Azor, then. She might think of something to do with them for next week's Wraithsday Feast."

"That shouldn't be hard," Mira said as they passed by a market. They found a vendor selling the berries and bought a bag for just a few MLus, which she placed in her bag.

They reached the inn to find Priscilla throwing Quinlan's things out while he begged her to stop. Raelis stood nearby, arms crossed over his chest, clearly trying not to laugh. A few people paused to watch the innkeeper toss Quinlan's things, but most moved on.

"You can't just bloody show up whenever you want!" Priscilla told Quinlan, the woman red in the face.

"It's not like that, darling, it's not—"

She grabbed some armor, which she had in a basket near the door, and tossed it out. "Gone. I want you gone!"

"Not my bloody armor! Pris, baby, please—"

"You can't stay here any longer, Quinlan. I already told you last time."

"Hello, everyone," Mira said as she stepped right into the fray. Sylas shot a wide-eyed glance over at Raelis, who also hadn't expected her to get involved.

"Who the hell is she?" Priscilla asked. "Is this another one of your—"

"No, nothing like that!" Quinlan cried. "She's Sylas's lady, not mine!"

Mira gave Quinlan a funny look. "Is *that* how you'd describe me?"

"Yeah? You two are going steady, right?"

Mira turned back to Priscilla. "Keep throwing his stuff."

"Hey!" Quinlan shouted.

Priscilla, who now had a couple of bundled up shirts in her hands, dropped them to her feet. The woman sniffled.

"Please stop, love," Quinlan said. "No need to—"

She started to sob. "You can't just show up when you'd bloody like and leave! You promised you'd stay here, that you'd help out. You can't just come and go like a wayward cat!"

Mira immediately moved to her. "Let's go inside, dear. You can talk to me about this."

"You? Who even are you?"

"Mira Ravenbane."

"You're a Thornian?"

"I was. That doesn't matter now. In fact, I might have something that can help relax you," she said as she patted her hand on her bag. "I'm an apothecary."

"Yeah?" Priscilla asked, the woman still sniffling. "A little drugs never hurt anyone, I suppose."

"Let's head in for a bit and leave the boys to themselves." Mira turned back to Sylas, Quinlan, and Raelis, and took on an authoritative tone. "Pick this stuff up and take it inside. Place it near the door so you can get it all later."

Sylas cleared his throat. "No problem, Mira."

Once she was gone, Raelis turned to him. "Mate."

"Don't say anything."

Raelis started to laugh. "I see Mira has taken a leadership role in your relationship. Maybe she's deserving of a title, something like lady commander."

"Watch it." Sylas grabbed some of the scattered armor. "What does Priscilla know about the invasion?"

"Nothing," Quinlan said, the big man still distraught. "I mean, I didn't want to bother her with it. And I didn't expect this, honest. I knew we were in a rough patch, but I didn't know—"

Raelis, who had picked up a pair of wooden blades, gave Quinlan an incredulous look. "Are you an idiot?"

"Oi, what's that supposed to mean?"

Sylas spoke again: "Let me try. Quin, mate. Maybe if you were clearer with Priscilla as to *why* you have been staying in Ember Hollow, she wouldn't have lashed out like she did. That could change things, you know."

"You mean the invasion? Eh, I was going to tell her, mate, really, I was. But then I showed up here and she already had my stuff ready to toss out. Never got a chance to get a word in, if we're being honest."

"You were here just a day ago," Sylas reminded him as he picked up more of the armor. "You were supposed to bring her to the Feast."

"I didn't get a chance to say anything then because—"

"Because?"

"Because, you know," Quinlan blushed. "That fight ended in passion is what I'm trying to say. I'll be honest, though. I hate all this. We used to get along so well. I lived at the inn, sure, but I was planning to add another class so I could go into business with her."

"You were?" Sylas asked.

"I was. So I wasn't just freeloading. I had other plans."

Raelis snorted. "You really are something."

"What's that supposed to mean?" Quinlan asked.

"Quin, mate, this isn't that complicated. All you had to do was tell her the truth. Then, you could have said something along the lines of, 'Prissy dearest, I got a mate that lives in Ember Hollow. It's a shabby little spot, but I like it, and I'm helping out around there for the time being, saving up so I can add an additional class by way of saving the Underworld. I'll be back here every other day, and when I do come, I'll bring you a little gift.'"

"What kind of gift?" Quinlan asked.

"Is that what you took from all that?" Sylas couldn't stop the laughter that flowed. "Quin, mate, you are as dense as they come."

"I'm trying!"

Sylas and Raelis both cracked up. Raelis finally got hold of himself. "You're a lost cause, and you know it, Quin. But that's fine. It seems to be a common thing here in the Underworld, a collection of lost causes that have somehow found their ways, or maybe their cause. Nothing wrong with that, really."

Mira stepped out of the inn. "Are you all ready to go?"

"What about my stuff?" Quinlan asked.

"Priscilla has agreed to let you keep it here until you return later, as long as you have a conversation with her about the invasion."

"So you told Prissy?"

"I did. I explained that you've been helping Sylas prepare for the invasion and that we have just now started telling others. I figured I'd let you discuss concrete plans."

"Letters to heaven, right? I mean, those are somewhat concrete."

"Do yourself a favor," Mira said as she approached Quinlan. "Sell yourself a little better, let her know you care, and, more importantly, that you care about the Underworld and the life you two will build here. Focus on that, and later classing up, and I think you'll be good to go."

"Yeah? That easy, huh?" Quinlan chuckled. "It's amazing what honesty can do."

"It's amazing what honesty can do and how often we disregard it," Mira said. "Let's head to the Cloud Forest for these herbs. But before we do, put your things inside. And one last thing?"

"Yeah?" Quinlan asked her.

"You can thank me later."

CHAPTER NINE

APOTHECARIES IN THE WOODS

The magnificent black trees of Geist continued along both sides of the road as Sylas, Mira, Quinlan, and Raelis took a carriage to the Cloud Forest, which Quinlan had arranged by calling in an old favor.

"It should get hilly any moment now," said Quinlan, who had already explained that he had spent a considerable amount of time around the forest on hunts. "But the portal doesn't work," he said for the second time. "No one out there to really maintain it, sadly enough. So we take carriages, which have their own issues."

"What kind of issues?" Mira said.

"The fact that the Cloud Forest is a hop, skip, or perhaps, a jump, away from Geist is the main one. You can fly back and forth, you know, but you have to go above the forest to do so, which makes finding the various established entrances hard."

"I was unaware that the portals needed maintenance," Sylas said.

"A sigilist handles them," Mira told Sylas as the carriage hit a series of small bumps. She waited until the path smoothed out to continue: "The person who does it for Ember Hollow is given MLus through taxes paid in Cinderpeak."

"And the Seedlands," Sylas said as he recalled the taxes he had paid earlier that day.

"Yes, there as well."

"So I'm paying for the sigilist. Nice."

Quinlan snorted with laughter. "You're one of the only blokes I know that's excited about paying taxes."

"As long as they serve their purpose, and having a portal in Ember Hollow is helpful. Otherwise, we'd have to walk to the Seedlands or Cinderpeak.

"There was a time when they were thinking of shutting the portal," Mira said. "But my uncle got involved and that thought disappeared."

"Tibby works in mysterious ways," Quinlan said.

"That, he does." Mira stared out the window of the carriage. "The Cloud Forest seems pretty far away."

"It's not too much longer," Quinlan told her. "Like I said, within flying distance of Geist, actually. I guess . . ."

"Yes?" she asked after he trailed off.

"I guess there's a reason that I wanted to take a moment here with you all. You in particular, Mira. Thank you for helping with Priscilla back there." Quinlan offered her a toothy grin. "Heh. I almost said 'handling' Priscilla. Glad I didn't."

"Yes, that wouldn't be the phrase I'd use. And she cares about you, Quinlan, she really does. I can tell."

"Yeah? You really think so?"

Raelis, who sat across from Sylas, slowly rolled his eyes. "Mate, I think there's a phrase about forests and trees that you might not have heard before."

"I know the bloody phrase."

"It applies," Raelis told him. "You got yourself a nice one there, mate, that Priscilla. Feisty, but you're the one that has set her on that path, yeah? But, really, I have to ask. I shouldn't ask, but I have to."

"Yeah?"

"What happened to her?" Raelis asked Quinlan. "Her face. She is pretty scarred up, not that she's not pretty or something. That's not what I meant. I hope I'm not being too forthright. I figured I'd ask you over asking her."

"Let's just say she had a hard time in our world."

"Ah, sorry to hear that," Raelis said.

Quinlan furrowed his brow. "She was an Aurumite who was taken prisoner. Prissy nearly escaped, twice. That was what happened after the first time. They did that to her. The Thorny bastards. No offense, Mira."

"I didn't say anything."

"The second time she tried to escape, Prissy actually managed to kill some of her captors, but they got her in the end."

Raelis patted him on the knee. "Sorry I asked."

"Nah, people should ask things when they're curious. Otherwise, they'll just keep staring and wondering what happened. People do that all the time about my missing hand," he said as he showed Raelis the stub of his left hand. "She would have told you if you poked her about it."

"See?" Mira told Quinlan. "It's things like that. You shouldn't tell Raelis to ask something like that. He can ask you, can't he? You have a particular relationship with Priscilla that doesn't extend to others. You should respect that."

Quinlan shrugged her off. "Eh. She's open about it. I've heard her explain it to customers before."

"Were they drunk?" Mira asked.

"Heh. Maybe. She often serves wine that she got from Douro. She gets it delivered. Bloody nice, that flameberry stuff. Turns people wild."

This comment reminded Sylas that he had been meaning to supply the Welcome Inn in the Shadowstone Mountains with ale but had never gotten around to it. Perhaps it would remain on the endless list of tasks he one day hoped to get to.

As Mira and Quinlan continued to debate asking Priscilla about her scars, Sylas's attention gravitated to the landscape unfolding outside the window of their carriage. Gone were the black Geistian trees, replaced by an increasingly thick fog that soon obscured their surroundings entirely. It was spooky.

"Would you look at that? We're getting close," Quinlan said.

"How are we supposed to see anything out here?" Raelis asked him.

"You can see a little, if we're being honest, but only the space directly in front of you. Sort of like the misty days in Joysville during the winter. Always with the fog, that place."

"Ah, Joysville, never got much joy there myself," Raelis said with a wink.

"I'll need to be able to find the herbs I'm looking for," Mira told Quinlan.

"You didn't let me finish. Normally, you can't see too much in the Cloud Forest, but I have special goggles for it, and Sylas, your sunglasses will help root out any monsters." Quinlan produced a pair of goggles from the front pocket of his vest. The goggles looked absolutely filthy, their leather strap frayed and tarnished. "For you, Mira. Meant to clean them up, but here you go."

He handed them to Mira and she examined them. "You meant to clean them up? These are absolutely filthy, Quinlan."

"Sorry about that. They'll still help you see, though, dirty or not. And we'll be able to protect you."

"Do we need protection that badly?" she asked.

"With an increasingly unstable Hexveil, yes, we might need the protection. You will be able to find the herbs, yeah?"

"Yes, that part isn't hard. My class comes with this instinctive nature when it comes to things like this. I'll be able to find them," Mira assured Quinlan, "I just need to be able to see to some degree."

"In that case, you worry about finding them and we'll worry about the monsters."

"I can handle myself."

"That's not how I meant it," he told her.

"And if we fly?" Sylas asked Quinlan. "Will we clear the fog?"

"You will, like I said earlier. Fly vertically and eventually the fog will dissipate. That's one of the best ways to get out if you lose your way," Quinlan explained. "Just head up through the trees and you'll move past the fog. Then, you'll see the Geist Tree Spire, the old temple in the city. In fact, that's something we should all be able to do. If things get bad, head up, and head there."

————

The carriage came to a grinding stop, the ground surprisingly hard even with all the fog. They got out, and as Quinlan spoke to the driver, Sylas took a quick look around the misty area. There was another carriage already present, the driver resting a club across her lap.

"How many are out there?" Sylas asked the woman as they made eye contact.

"Just a pair of apothecaries."

"Any protection?" asked Raelis.

"They seemed confident."

Quinlan approached and noticed the woman seated atop the carriage. "Jade, is that you?" he asked the driver.

"Quinlan," she said. "Look who it is. I didn't know you were back in Geist."

"Off and on, yeah? You know that about me."

She maintained a grin on her face. "I know more than I want to know about you."

"Heh." Quinlan straightened up. "You have guests out there?"

"Two apothecaries," Raelis said.

"Without protection?" Quinlan asked Jade.

"They said they could handle it. I tried to tell them to hire a demon hunter but they refused. It's not my job to babysit people, only to take them where they need to go."

"You do have a club," Raelis told her.

"That's for my own protection, yeah?"

"How long have they been out there?" Sylas asked her.

"A few hours now." The confident look on Jade's face started to fade. "Maybe it's been a bit longer than I expected."

"If we see them, we'll let you know," Quinlan said. "Better, we'll bring them back to you. It's not safe." He smirked at Mira, who had since put on the glasses he had given her. "You know, if someone hasn't already told you, you apothecaries are more trouble than you're worth."

"Oh, we're worth it," she said. "Trust me."

"Lads, lady," Raelis said, "let's get on with it."

Quinlan said goodbye to Jade the driver and the four moved into the Cloud Forest, Mira at the lead. The former Aurumite soldiers naturally shifted into a quiet pace. It reminded Sylas of one of the stranger occurrences he'd had as an Aurumite, the morning of the Battle of Graleta.

A great fog had settled over the battlefield outside of Graleta, much of which was forested. Sylas had gone out early with Raelis to look for a scout that never returned. They found the man pinned to a tree, whimpering, his tongue removed. There were marks covering his body, and it was amazing he was still alive.

While the Shadowthorne Empire was accustomed to cruelty—cruelty that, Sylas had to admit, also extended to his side of the border—this was something he had never seen before. There was a dark desperation in it that didn't match the normal Shadowthorne operating behavior. And sure enough, they soon learned, as they were surrounded by fur-clad men and women, Raelis and Sylas realized they had come across a group of cultists.

While the cultists had strength in numbers, they had little battle training, which gave Sylas and Raelis a slight advantage. The bloody fight that ensued, one marred by light cutting through the fog of the forest, was merely the start of an epically long day as they fought for control of the northern region of the forest, the Shadowthorne fire arrows making things that much worse, so bad, in fact, that Sylas had nearly forgotten of his early morning encounter by the time the day came to a close.

Now, as they traveled deeper into the Cloud Forest in search of herbs and a pair of apothecaries, it was fresh on his mind.

"Remember the cultists?" he asked as he stepped up to Raelis.

The dark-haired man didn't flinch as he scanned the mist ahead. "I do now. What a way to start your day, yeah?"

"What a way."

"Better here, yeah?"

"Eternally."

———

They came across signs of the two apothecaries at about the time Mira found the calmthistle, which had a green-silver shimmer to it. While she was packing the calmthistle up, Quinlan found one of their bags laying on the ground.

"Not good," he said as he examined the bag of herbs.

"I can track the person from here," Raelis said. "I bought this skill from an archlumen before I went on my Hallowed Pursuit." He took the bag from Quinlan. As he held it, a faint node of light formed. The node of light remained directly in front of him, just far enough away that if he approached it, the light would move, allowing him to follow it.

"We should go that way," Mira said. "I think the harmony dew is near as well."

"So you are saying we should be prepared for anything?" Sylas asked Quinlan.

"I believe so. I would shout for them, but that might attract unwanted attention. Honestly, we made a mistake not bringing Cornbread."

"I didn't even think about that," Sylas said. "I just thought it would be best to give her the day off after all the work she put in last night. The poor pup seemed exhausted."

"Quiet," Raelis said. "Did anyone hear that?"

Sylas had to truly listen in, but then he heard it, a whimper not far from their current location. He drew his club and turned to the sound.

Sylas had three mana attack spells at his disposal, if he needed to use them: Whimsical Drift could be used to create a gust of wind capable of blowing back an opponent; Field Warden allowed him to fire a horizontal blast of magic from the palm of his hand; and Soulfire, which paired better if Azor was in the vicinity.

Either way, he had options for what was to come.

The three warriors crept along, Mira a few steps behind them, though she reminded them that she was able to see farther ahead with Quinlan's goggles. This allowed her to tell them what was ahead, like the sudden ridgeline they came to, or the scree-filled creek bed that traveled down to a small stream.

It was here, pressed up against the embankment, that they found a woman lying on her side, her hand stretching toward the water.

"Please," the injured woman said as they approached, her voice quavering. She nursed her ankle, which looked badly bruised. "Please . . ."

Sylas immediately dropped in front of her. "Who else is here with you?"

"Percy. He . . . He . . ."

He looked north and returned his focus to the woman. "And you are?"

"Florence."

"She's saying they took the other apothecary, a man named Percy," Sylas called over to Quinlan as the other man searched along the shoreline for any tracks.

Raelis, who had already crossed the stream following the node of light, stopped. "Quin," he said. "Company, soon."

"Got it, mate."

"Mira, do you have anything that can help her?" Sylas asked, almost as an afterthought. Mira had already begun examining Florence, shaking her head as she saw her broken bones.

"She needs MLus." Mira reached into her pack and got out one of the mana-infused bread rolls she had given Sylas in their first interaction. "Eat this," she told the woman.

"Thank you," Florence said. She ate the bread, which gave her just enough energy to collect herself. "It was a kind of Manaboar, I know that much. Never seen one quite like that."

"Manaboar?" Sylas called over to Quinlan and Raelis. Quinlan looked back at him and brought a finger to his lips. "Sorry," Sylas whispered. "What is that?" he asked Mira.

"I wouldn't know, but we have to get her back to the carriage."

"What about Percy?" Florence asked.

"We will continue to look for him. Did the Manaboar take him?" Sylas asked her.

"I don't know. No, I don't think so. He chased off after it, once it attacked me. We were gathering harmony dew. There's a lot by the water." Florence's voice trembled yet again. "Oh, Percy."

Mira looked at Sylas and pointed at the shoreline, at the purple moss that he hadn't noticed before. "We need to get you to the carriages," she told Florence. "I'll take you there, and they will find your companion."

"Are you sure?" the woman asked as Sylas came to her again.

"Certain of it. Mira, get what you need."

"Will do," Mira said as she quickly gathered some of the purple moss. "This was what I came for anyway. And I'm sure they'll be able to find Percy," Mira assured Florence.

"We'll take care of everything," Sylas told them.

"Can you fly?" Mira asked Florence as the injured woman finished the piece of bread.

"I think so, yes."

Sylas turned to Mira. "Will you be able to find the carriages?"

"I have the goggles," she reminded him. "I'll find them."

Quinlan approached, the big man pressing out of the fog to find out what was going on. "Take her to the Geist Tree Spire, the big temple there, cathedral, whatever you want to call it. Let them know that there are Manaboars. They will round up the demon hunters in town. The reason I'm asking you to go is that we're going to need more, because Manaboars only come out when there's a break in the Hexveil."

"The Hexveil?" Florence asked. "What about Percy?"

"We will find him. That's his bag, right?" Quinlan gestured to Raelis, who still held the bag, the man just barely visible in the dark gray mist.

"It is," Florence said.

"Then we will find him and return him safely to Geist. But we need to focus now." Quinlan looked from the woman to Sylas. "Let's do this."

"What about your goggles?" Mira asked Quinlan.

"I should probably use them. Just head up, and when you're above the forest, you'll see the Geist Tree Spire due south of here. You can't miss it."

Mira took off with Florence the apothecary, flying first up above the clouds. Mira's arm rested around the other woman's waist as she scanned the horizon for the spire that Quinlan had mentioned. If they found the spire, they would get to Geist.

"I see it," Florence said, pointing ahead. She looked back down to the Cloud Forest. "I really hope Percy . . . I hope he didn't . . ."

"We'll know more later. But the best thing we can do . . ." Mira trailed off. She suddenly felt so overwhelmed by the moment that she lost her train of thought. It returned as she picked up her pace, wisps of fog blowing past her. "The best thing we can do is get you to Geist. I can go for help from there."

"You're right. Sorry."

"No need to apologize," Mira told her as she continued toward the spire. "These kinds of occurrences can be traumatic. I have certainly had my fair share in and around Ember Hollow."

"Ember Hollow? That's where you're from? I thought that was an abandoned village."

"Not any longer, it isn't. There's a pub there run by one of the men you just met. He and I also have a market that we have started, although it isn't open yet. There's a sundry store and an inn. I have an apothecary shop as well. It's quaint."

"Really? A market?"

"Yes, we're set to open it soon."

"Percy and I have been thinking about finding a market to sell things that we've collected over the years. We're collectors, you know. Relics."

"Legendary Locks?"

"If we can find them, yes, but they are hard to come by," Florence said. "But we do have a good amount of antiques and people seem to enjoy our collection. I certainly enjoy putting it together. We keep everything in a barn in Geist."

Even though she was flying over a blanket of fog, away from what she knew was likely to become a battle as she sought to round up demon hunters, Mira laughed at the irony of what Florence had just told her. "Then I suppose in a way that this was meant to be. I really don't know if there is a better time than now to tell you that we just so happen to be looking for tenants for our market."

"And we're looking for a market."

"A match made in . . ." Mira's eyes darted up to the Celestial Plains, which she had increasingly felt were mocking her with their golden hues and the secrets they held. The Plains were actively looking to dismantle the Underworld—her way of life, her new business, and the prospect of a peaceful future. "Never mind," she said under her breath as they neared the Geist Tree Spire.

She dropped down and landed in a courtyard, where a manaseer in robes spotted her. The manaseer, who had been pruning a tree, took the ladder down and immediately approached. "Whatever is the matter?" the older man asked, his voice raspy.

"Cloud Forest. There has been a breach in the Hexveil and Manaboars are on the loose," Mira said breathlessly.

"Oh my. Please," the monk told Florence as he motioned to a bench made of stone, "sit. I can help heal your wounds. You, what is your name?"

"Mira."

"Good. Mira, if you will, if you don't mind—"

"Anything," she told the monk.

"While I attend to her wounds, please head into the temple and ring the bell. Just pull the rope, that's all. Any demon hunter in Geist who is available will come running. We have a guild outpost here, you know, not that one would know if they spent a lot of time in the village because most of the demon hunters end up hanging out in various haunts and—"

"Ring the bell?" Mira asked with urgency.

"Yes, ahem, ring the bell, and I will see to your friend."

Mira raced inside the temple. She had been in a similar one before in Duskhaven, the temple clearly built before the Crafting Laws were erected. She wound her way up the path, its moss-covered stones forming a grand feeder to the entrance, where an enormous pair of intricately carved wooden doors welcomed visitors.

She rushed through the doors and found the rope hanging from the middle of the room, grabbed it, and rang the bell. "Just ring the bell, just ring the bell," she said as she put her whole body weight into it, jumping up and pulling the rope down. The sound was much louder than she expected, especially in the cavernous space. Mira clenched her eyelids shut, her head ringing a bit, and covered her ears with her hands. "Bloody loud, that was."

There was a commotion outside.

Mira moved back to the exit to find two demon hunters standing outside talking to the manaseer who took care of the temple, both in armor, clubs rested on their shoulders. They turned toward the Cloud Forest and took off.

"Should I go with them?" she asked, a question also meant for herself. Mira knew the demon hunters would be able to handle it, especially as several more arrived, the men and women all with massive clubs and wearing armor. Yet she asked the question anyway, and she knew as the words left her lips who they were actually for.

It was Sylas. That was why she wanted to go back.

And rather than waiting for an answer or checking on Florence's condition, Mira took to the sky. She followed the demon hunters, who seemed to know exactly where they were going, and eventually dipped back beneath the thick fog to find Raelis leaning against a fallen tree. She couldn't quite see them, but she could hear Quinlan and Sylas fighting the Manaboar nearby, the two now joined by an increasing number of demon hunters.

Mira landed and glanced at Raelis, who nodded at her to let her know he would recover. She raced toward Sylas, who jumped back to avoid a blast of mana that the Manaboar emitted from its nostrils.

Without thinking, she fired her own shot, which hit the beast square in the forehead, causing it to stagger.

"Mira!" Sylas shouted. "Be—"

A smaller Manaboar tore out of the fray and hit her, tossing Mira into a black Geistian tree. The speed in which Sylas moved into action was something she would never forget. It was as if Sylas had been possessed, the normally calm Aurumite enraged to the point that he let out a terrifying bellow as he beat the Manaboar away.

Still on the offensive, Sylas turned to the next monster and killed it with a single attack from his club. He reached Mira. "Are you—"

"I'm fine, Sylas," she said, warmth filling her heart as she looked up at the bearded man. Mira still had mana left. She still was able to fight, yet she also saw in Sylas his instinct to protect her, the volition in his eyes, how tense his arms were as he helped her up.

"I'll deal with them," he said.

"That's fine," she told him, just before Mira fired a bolt of energy at an approaching Manaboar, killing it.

"Or you can."

"No, go ahead," she said, a slight smile on her face. "Do what needs to be done."

Mira stepped aside and watched as Sylas did just that. He hit one of the Manaboars with Whimsical Drift, which sent it blasting in the air, directly into a group of more oncoming boars. Near him, Raelis and Quinlan beat at the boars, the two men practically back-to-back and enjoying themselves.

"Just like old times, eh!?" Quinlan shouted to Raelis over the squeal of pigs.

"Something like that, you cheeky sod!"

More demon hunters arrived on the scene, some of whom Quinlan apparently knew, as he called their names, the men and women cheering each other on as they continued to fight off the boars and reduce their numbers.

A few of the larger Manaboars had a power that allowed them to rip through the soil, which caused trees to collapse as their roots were severed. Using

Whimsical Drift, Sylas was able to blow some of these falling trees off course. Another demon hunter, a woman wearing a bear fur cap, blew several trees into blackened sawdust that gave the fight the scent of an old woodshop.

At least it seemed that way to Mira.

Because of her class, her senses were heightened. In times of stress, Mira noticed this heightening of her senses even more, which was something she'd never had to rely on.

Mira fired shots of mana if it seemed like a boar would break through their defenses. She did so as an absolutely massive Manaboar, which was able to take down trees with its tusks, appeared. Quinlan and Raelis both produced lances made of light, something Mira had seen her uncle do before, before spearing it from either side.

The mother boar, as one of the demon hunters called it, came crashing down, its tusks shredding the ground and filling the air with dust. The group rallied and the boars turned the other way, toward what Mira assumed was the Chasm.

"We can't let them retreat, lads!" Quinlan said. "Not on my bloody watch!"

Now regrouped, the demon hunters surged ahead, leaving Sylas with Mira.

"Are you good?" he asked her as he caught his breath.

"Are you?" came her reply.

He laughed. "That got a little out of hand, yeah?"

Sylas placed his hand around her waist, where it settled on her lower back. "You saved me back there."

"Are we still keeping track of who saves who?"

"I guess you're right. What about the apothecary? Did you all make it to Geist?"

"We did." The blood drained from Mira's face. "And Percy? Did you all find him?"

"Yeah, he's over here. Come on." Sylas led her around an embankment to an area that looked like a Manaboar den. He gestured to a man lying on the ground, nursing his knee. "Percy."

"Mate, I can't thank you enough," the young man said as he glanced up to Sylas. "I really thought I was done for. You and your men . . . I can't believe how many boars there were. I'm not ashamed to admit I was scared beyond belief. Wait. Where is she? You said—"

"Florence is in Geist, safe," Mira told Percy. "I'm the one that flew her there."

"Flo is safe? She's not hurt?"

"She's fine. Can you fly?"

"No, only Flo could," the man admitted. "That's why we were out here, gathering harmony dew so I could sell them to get the power. I'd have the MLus if we had a bloody place to sell our antiques—"

"In that case, hop on," Mira said as she motioned to Sylas.

"Hop on?" Percy asked, confused.

"Hop on him."

"You want me to carry him?" Sylas raised an eyebrow at Mira.

"Would you prefer I do it? You can tell him about the Petticoat Lane Market as we fly back to Geist."

Sylas considered this and shook his head. He approached Percy, helped him up, and turned his back to the man. "Get on, and no whispering in my ear or anything."

Mira laughed at the horror that traced across Percy's face at what was clearly a joke. "I wouldn't dare," he began to say.

"Let's get you back." Sylas locked eyes with Mira. "We can meet Quin and Rae in Geist. I already told them I'd likely head back with you to make sure Percy gets there safely." His stomach grumbled, loud enough for Mira to hear it. "I guess I'm hungry too. What are you waiting for?" he asked Percy, Sylas's back still to the man. "Let's get on with it, then, yeah?"

————

Upon arrival in Geist, Percy dismounted and limped to Florence, who came limping toward him with her arms outstretched. Sylas turned to Mira and grinned. "All in a day's work," he said as he jokingly dusted his hands. He wiped some invisible sweat from his brow.

"Look at you." Mira tapped his chest with a finger. "It's fun being the hero, isn't it?"

The grin on his face faded. "Only until it's not. Anyway, my stomach is talking and I have a feeling that Priscilla may have something for us to eat." He started walking.

"And you're sure your friends will go there once they finish?" Mira asked as she caught up with him. The two headed away from the cathedral as more demon hunters came onto the scene, the men and women joining together before taking off.

"With Quin, and if food is involved, I'm sure of it. Besides, Quin will want to do a bit of a victory lap for Priscilla. And good on him. He fought like hell back there," Sylas said as he recalled the early stages of the fight. The three had come across the first Manaboar, a medium-sized one, which would have been an easy kill had it not released a squealing shriek that called the others.

From there it became a chaotic fight in the misty woods with boars coming from every direction as if they were being fired by a teleporting archer. While Sylas likely wouldn't say anything about it, and he knew Quinlan and Raelis would also be too proud to admit it, Mira and the demon hunters' quick arrival had turned the tide of their battle.

It had been looking hairy there for a moment.

This also reminded him of a few skirmishes he had been in, ones in which backup finally arrived at the last moment, flanking their enemies and leading to victories that were too close to Pyrrhic for Sylas's taste. Still, there were celebrations to follow, especially in the lower ranks. While those at Sylas's level often shared nervous glances yet maintained the stoicism necessary for the job. That was why Quinlan deserved his victory lap, for then, and for now.

Lost in his thoughts, Sylas nearly tripped as he stepped on an uneven bit of pavement, which caused Mira to stop him from falling. "Sorry," he told her, "I was just having a moment."

"A memory?"

"That's right."

"Hold my hand, Sylas. I'll make sure you don't fall. And try to be present."

"In that order?"

"How about you start with holding my hand?"

"Don't have to ask me twice." Sylas took her hand and the two continued down the lane until they reached Priscilla's place, where they found the woman pacing nervously in front of the kitchen.

"Is he fine?" she asked, her eyes filling with dread upon seeing only two of them. The woman nervously brought her arms over her chest.

"You already know what happened?" Mira asked her.

"Of course, I know. They ring the bell anytime the demon hunters get called into action, and usually, if we're being honest, it's in the Cloud Forest."

"That was me that rang the bell."

"Wait, that was you who rang the bell?" Priscilla asked Mira. "You're really getting stuck in, aren't you? Been here, what, all of a few hours?"

Mira offered her a firm grin. "Something like that. I had to deliver an apothecary to the cathedral. Manaboar outbreak. I help when I can."

"Bloody right, you do. And that's terrible to hear about the Manaboars," Priscilla said. "They're pests. But Quinlan, is he? I don't mean to discredit your—"

"He's fine," Sylas assured Priscilla as he tried to ignore the smell of freshly baked bread in the air. "He's going to meet us back here with Raelis."

"And I'm guessing by the way you keep licking your lips that you're a bit hungry, yeah?" Priscilla asked Sylas.

"Am I that obvious?" Sylas asked.

"You are, mate." She motioned to a table behind her. "Take a seat. I've got some bread coming out of the oven, and I'll warm up some of Quinlan's favorite rabbit stew."

CHAPTER TEN

MIRA'S SCHOOL OF ETIQUETTE AND GRACE

While they waited for Quinlan and Raelis, Mira borrowed a pestle and mortar from Priscilla so she could prepare the calmthistle and harmony dew mixture that she would use to cure Gertrude's honking condition.

"You sure are thorough," Sylas told her as she continued grinding the ingredients together long after they had been mixed. It was fun watching her work. There was something cute about it, which was why he felt like teasing her for some reason.

"Is that your way of telling me you'd like to help? With those big arms of yours, I'm sure you could crush this even further."

"You think they're big?" he asked as he looked down at his forearms.

Mira rolled her eyes. "Are you going to help me or not?"

"Sure." Sylas took the pestle and mortar from Mira and continued mashing the ingredients together, the pub owner surprised at the thickness of the mixture. He also noticed a faint glow each time he pressed down, evidence of the inherent mana. "Could I do something like this?"

"You already are," she told him a bit wryly.

"No, I mean, if I just found the ingredients, would I simply be able to mix them together and form a medicine?"

"Ah, that. You could theoretically, yes, but it would lose almost all its potency. My apothecary class is what adds the potency to my creations, so while you could make this, it wouldn't have the same properties or strength."

"So you're saying there's a chance," he told her, a grin on his face.

"Sure, keep telling yourself that." The smile that formed on Mira's face was one that Sylas had grown used to seeing by this point, a smile that she couldn't contain even if she tried.

The door swung open, interrupting their moment as Quinlan and Raelis stepped in. Priscilla, who had been in the back room prepping vegetables for whatever meal she was planning that night, burst out of the kitchen and practically flew into Quinlan's arms.

"You bloody idiot," she said after pressing away. "You could have hurt yourself!"

Quinlan laughed her off. "A few little piggly wigglies? Hurt me? Pfft! Not happening, love. Not today, not tomorrow. Not alive and certainly not dead. Raelis and I probably could have taken down their entire flock—is that the right word for a bunch of pigs?—and still made it back in time for your lovely stew. Sylas too." He kissed her on the forehead. "Don't worry about me, love. I was in my element."

Priscilla beamed a smile up at the tall man. "So you're hungry, then, yeah?"

"We're beyond hungry, love; we're famished."

"Then you know how to help yourself." She stuck her tongue out at him and turned back to the kitchen. "Me? I have veggies to cut."

Quinlan watched her go with a toothy grin on his face. "Take a seat," he told Raelis, "I'll see about bringing out some stew."

It took Quinlan way longer than it should have to return with some stew, which had Raelis roaring with laughter upon seeing the big warrior step out of the kitchen.

"You make that stew yourself?" Raelis asked. "From scratch?"

Quinlan, whose hair was ruffled, his armor a bit off-center, winked at Raelis. "Never made a stew in my bloody life."

"What about that slop you used to make us on the front line?"

"Mate, if you call that a stew, then I have some oceanfront property in the Chasm I'd be willing to sell you for a good price," Quinlan told Raelis as he sat down in front of the other man and began shoveling stew into his mouth. "Good, yeah? I'd eat this stew every day of the week."

Sylas locked eyes with Mira and then looked down at his hand, which was on top of hers. He squeezed it and she blushed a little.

"Two lovebirds if I ever saw a pair," Raelis said as he saw their movement. "Two lovebirds."

"If you're looking to match up, Raelis," Quinlan told him, mouth full of stew, "Priscilla has a friend—"

"I'm quite all right, thank-you-very-much," Raelis told him. "We have other things to see about first."

"Kael," Sylas told them, growing serious. "We're here for Kael."

"That we are." Quinlan wiped his mouth on his arm and burped, ruining the serious look on Sylas's face. "Sorry, Mira."

"Manners would do you well."

"Would they?" Quinlan asked her. "In that case, I promise to learn some if we can save the Underworld, how's that? Mira's School of Etiquette and Grace. I like the sound of that."

"I'm sure you do." Mira stood. "I'm going to help Priscilla while you boys catch up. Call me when you're ready to go. Once we find your brother, we'll get back to Ember Hollow and see about Gertrude. We can't have her honking every couple of minutes, especially once the market opens."

———

The four took the portal to Wraithwick, where Sylas had once met Liza the haberdasher. Since they were in the area, he decided to stop by her mountain home to update the haberdasher on what had happened since they last spoke.

Yet upon arriving, they found her place empty, Liza nowhere to be found.

"She's the one that helped me with my Legendary Locks," Sylas told Quinlan once he asked for the second time why they were there.

"Right. Did you tell me that already?"

"I did. Your mind is somewhere else?"

"Maybe back with Priscilla," Raelis said.

"Heh. Maybe. Anyway." Quinlan pointed to the mountains beyond, which rose high into the sky yet still seemed leagues away from the Celestial Plains. "Kael is there."

"Is that right?" Raelis asked as he fiddled with his armor. He finally looked back toward the horizon. "And do you know where he is in the mountains, or are we going to have to find him? Some monks' retreat, yeah? Shouldn't be hard, Quin. Monks and nuns look similar here as they do in our world."

"They're not the same, I can tell you that. I'm the one who dropped him off, mind you. Do you all feel like doing a little more flying?" Quinlan didn't wait for an answer, he took off, the large man petering out for a moment before finding his stride.

"He's as graceful as a wounded bat," Raelis said before he took to the sky.

"Ready?" Sylas asked Mira.

"Yes. I've always wanted to explore this region. We do have a lack of mountains in Ember Hollow." She started to float. "The closest being the Shadowstone Mountains, or I guess the volcano around Cinderpeak."

"Is that something we could buy with MLus, a mountain?"

Mira flashed a teasing glance upward at Sylas's suggestion. "That would be a better question for Tilbud. Come. Let's find your friend, although, I must admit, I don't know how his presence will help us exactly."

"I don't either. But I do know if I'm going to have to go down fighting *again*, I'd like to do it surrounded by people I care for." Sylas joined Mira in the air. He moved just a few feet past her and she quickly caught up. "Want to race?"

"Last I checked, you don't know where we're going."

"To the mountains it is!" He sped ahead, just as Tilbud had shown him.

Sylas glanced back to see Mira trailing after him, the ends of her dark purple dress fluttering in the wind. He gave her a thumbs-up and then transitioned to his back, where he waited for her to catch up.

"You make it look so easy," she said with a huff. "Are you sure you weren't a bird in your previous life?"

He laughed. "Maybe I was." Sylas transitioned into a sideways position, one hand under his head, his elbow bent. "I make this look good, yeah?"

"You make it look ridiculous. And while you play around, your friends are getting too far ahead."

He glanced toward the mountains again to see Raelis and Quinlan barreling toward one of the slopes, the two men also racing one another. "Now that's a race I want to partake in. Come on, Mira!"

Sylas turned, extended his hand, and took hers. Together, they rocketed toward the two other men and blew right past them, startling Quinlan, who let out a little yelp.

Raelis burst out laughing. "What the hell was that?"

"That wasn't me," Quinlan said.

"Keep telling yourself that, Quin!"

The four finally reached one of the slopes. They hugged the mountain as they moved deeper into the range, Sylas yet again taken aback by the beauty of the Underworld. He could see himself having a small mountain retreat here, a place to get away from it all with a hut that could sleep a group of people and a big fire pit surrounded by seating. The slopes were too dramatic to host an actual village, but Sylas could imagine a place built on pillars to even everything out, with sweeping vistas from every window and brisk mountain breezes.

It would be serene, that was for sure. Sylas almost said something about it to Mira, but kept his mouth shut instead. Mentioning the future always carried with it an acknowledgment of the invasion, something he didn't want to think about just now.

Kael's retreat, which they finally reached after another thirty minutes of flying, wasn't anything like what Sylas had pictured. In his mind, the retreat would have been in a castle-like structure built into the side of the mountains, one carved of the land. There would have been spires, and perhaps stony paths for the attendees to wander upon.

But Kael's retreat was the exact opposite.

Instead, they came to a series of "cubbies," as Mira called them, which had been built into the natural rock formations of the mountain and shored up by bricks. They were all close to one another, forming a nest of sorts, each cubby with a small balcony and each part of a pulley system to carry supplies from a group of thatched homes at the base of the retreat.

As the four landed, three men with long, pikelike weapons appeared. Their armor reminded Sylas of the Hexveilian Guards, yet where they were broad-shouldered and thick with muscle, these ones were tall and rail thin, with sleek black gear that had a reflective sheen to it.

"Step aside, lads," Quinlan said as the three guards approached, "we're here for Kael."

"Kael Ashdown," said Raelis, who already had his club drawn. "And like my mate here said, the three of you can step aside, unless there is a more forceful way you would like us to make that happen."

"Let's not," Mira said as she pushed between the two of them. She smiled at the guards. "Good day, sirs. We are here for Kael Ashdown. Quinlan," she said, gesturing to her immediate left, "is his brother. We have an important message we need to deliver to him."

The three guards briefly turned to one another. They weren't Underworld-ians, that was certain. Sylas didn't quite understand Hexveilian Guards or how they were fueled by mana, and he knew that fighting them wouldn't be in their best interest, yet he couldn't deny there was a part of him that wanted to try.

Perhaps it had something to do with his friends or his anger with the Celestial Plains and their goal of destroying his way of life. Sylas couldn't shake it. He didn't like being held up by guards—what were they guarding, exactly?—especially with something that seemed arbitrary. Was it important to prevent people from reaching those who were on retreats? He understood that these sorts of rites likely had several initiation rituals, but what if there was an emergency? What if someone needed one of the future manaseers now?

"Kael Ashdown has not finished his retreat," one of the guards finally said, the man now holding his weapon in a menacing way. There was an other-worldly nature to his voice, as if it were being beamed into him. "You are to leave the premises now."

"I don't know if you need to take off your helmet and clean out your ears, mate, but we're not going anywhere," Raelis told the guards. "And really. Do you really think we're scared of a few lanky twigs? Best step aside now, mate, or—"

"He's right," Sylas said as he took over. "We will not leave until we speak with Kael Ashdown. Step aside, or better, point us in the right direction so we don't have to disturb everyone in the vicinity."

The guards bristled. They were about to say something when a monk with his skull wrapped in a white cloth appeared. From a distance, it looked as if the monk had a head injury, but as he grew closer it was clear that the wrapping was by design. His head wrap matched his clothing, which was clean and pressed, almost as if the man weren't living in a rural location.

"State your purpose," the monk said in a firm tone.

"We're here for Kael Ashdown, my brother. Have your guards stand down," Quinlan said.

"Kael is your brother?" The man fixed a scrutinizing stare at Quinlan. "Ah, yes. You were the one that dropped him off."

"That's right, and I'd appreciate it if we didn't have to do whatever this is. We have other things that need doing today. A goose comes to mind."

"A goose?" The monk creased his forehead at the statement. "Is this some sort of joke?"

"Look, mate, errr, your lordship, or whatever they call manaseers," Raelis said, "what I'm trying to tell you here is that time is of the essence. We're not crazy, but we can get that way if you push us."

"Oh?"

"It's like this," Quinlan said, a pleading look in his eyes, "I know my brother is supposed to be out in about thirty days, but we need to see him before then."

"And risk breaking his meditation?"

"He will understand," Sylas said. "Kael will understand."

The older manaseer considered this for a moment. He did so behind the three guards in their blackened armor, who still seemed poised to strike on command. "Kael may not like being awoken," he finally told Sylas and his companions.

"Awoken?" Raelis and Quinlan asked at the same time.

"My brother will be bloody happy to see me," Quinlan said. "You can count on that."

"You may think this is the case, and that could very well be true, but being awoken from one's meditation early can have terrifying mana results."

"Like what?" Mira asked. "And are these results you refer to in relation to him or to us?"

"*You.* He could become violent. You may have to stop him."

"From what?" Sylas asked the monk.

"It is inadvisable to wake someone when they are going through the manaseer ritual. During this time, a person is in very close contact with the Celestial Plains, which, if you didn't know, have their own forms of Celestial Beasts not unlike the Chasm. These can come through. They can be channeled through the seer. In fact, that is part of the ritual, channeling one of these creatures to harvest its mana. If you interrupt him, you might be forced to fight the creature in the same way that he is."

"Heaven has monsters?" Raelis asked.

"Indeed," the monk said. "And the guards you see here will do little to stop them."

"How's that again?" Raelis asked.

"They are mana constructs, and Celestial Beasts are able to tear through them with relative ease. I should clarify: their limitations are based in the Plains, not here. So if the beast came here, they could do something, but not there. As to why, well, you'd have to bring that up with someone who knows more about this subject than me."

Quinlan looked like he was a few seconds away from stomping his feet. "Kael never said anything—"

"Many do not know the rituals of a manaseer, nor the plight of the mana-soldier. I am only telling you about them now because you are insistent on meeting Brother Kael, or so it seems, and I would like for you to choose wisely. If you do go to him, we will not stop you. But we also will not come to your aid if necessary."

"So that's why the guards are here?" Sylas asked the monk, asking another question that had been at the back of his mind. "To protect from beasts that may come through the future manaseers?"

"Correct. Those in the Plains know that an operation such as this can create complications. It is a wonder they let us keep these retreats after the Crafting Laws, but I suspect there was a reason for that as well. And now, that doesn't matter."

"You know?" Quinlan asked.

"I am aware of the changes to come, yes. We manaseers have already discussed it, and while we don't welcome the change, we will adjust as we always have, especially since we will be granted special considerations, and we have already been assured our practices can continue."

Quinlan took a step closer and pointed a finger at the man. "Got yours, then, yeah? Figured you'd let the rest of us figure it out without your help, is it? Well, I'm here to tell you, mate, the word is out. We have a solution that we're working on. We will not go down without a fight."

"And you're making a mistake betting against all of us," Sylas said. "A mistake that won't be forgotten once we see this through."

The monk all but laughed, the delight on his face hard for him to maintain as he stood behind the guards. "You have . . . a solution? You think yourselves clever enough to go against heaven, the creators of the Underworld, *and* the Chasm? Do you think the Celestial Council would even hear you? Are you simpleminded enough that you cannot understand that their solution makes sense? That maintaining three realms is a drain on mana and that the people of the Underworld haven't been properly punished?"

Sylas placed a hand on Quinlan's shoulder. "This one isn't worth it," he said quickly, aware that while it seemed like Quinlan had a hot temper, he in fact had a *quick* temper, one that cooled off relatively quickly.

Raelis was the opposite. Once the man made up his mind to engage, he engaged. If Sylas didn't get control of the situation now, he would be forced to contend against three mana constructs and a high-powered head monk with unknown powers.

"We will see our friend and deal with the consequences," Sylas told the head monk, who continued to sneer at them. "No need to continue this conversation any longer. Our decision has been made."

———

Sylas, Mira, Raelis, and Quinlan followed the monk's directions as they took a set of thin stone steps leading up the face of a cliff. They reached the stone cubby in question and entered after pressing aside a swath of fabric covered in black beads. The interior was more cavernous than Sylas had expected, the walls covered in gold etchings that formed abstract petroglyphs.

Normally, it would have been something Sylas took in carefully, hoping to draw meaning from the carvings, yet in seeing Kael seated at the front of the room, Sylas's attention shifted solely to that of his friend.

"There he is," Quinlan whispered, in awe of his brother.

Deep in meditation, his head bent forward, Kael looked just as Sylas had remembered. He was much smaller than Quinlan, Kael's hair long, brow furrowed, and his beard thick.

The monk had told them what to do, but seeing him now, seeing how peaceful Kael looked, made Sylas wish that he didn't have to disturb the man and his meditation. He was also wary of what they had been told about Kael's potential awakening, how it could grow violent.

Sylas didn't want to fight him. There was little space for something like that in his meditation chamber, which was why he had already come up with a plan to deal with Kael as Raelis moved around to one side and Quinlan the other.

"Kael," Sylas said carefully. The man didn't move so Sylas tried again, louder this time. "Kael!"

"Just like the monk said," Quinlan told him. "You may have to shake him awake. Go easy."

"Be ready," Sylas told the two former soldiers.

"Always," Raelis growled.

"Please be careful," Mira said.

Quinlan smirked. "This one's a keeper."

"I'm right here," Mira reminded him.

"Yeah? And it's a bloody compliment," Quinlan whispered to her.

"How do you know I'm a keeper exactly?"

"Let's have this conversation later, yeah?" Raelis asked as Sylas took a step closer to Kael.

Sylas said Kael's name a few more times. When this didn't work, he reached out and touched Kael's shoulder.

Sylas stifled a shout as his spirit was stripped away from his body, everything moving skyward around him. He exploded through the golden clouds above and landed in a great arena crafted from slick white and black stone, where he saw a figure standing before him, his features obscured due to the low light hitting his back.

Raelis appeared next to him, followed by Quinlan, and finally Mira.

"What is this place?" Mira asked, her voice raising in alarm. "Are we—"

"Are we in the Celestial Plains?" Raelis looked down at his hand. He then touched his face and pulled at the front of his clothing. "This is real. Isn't it?" His voice quavered. "No, we're in the Chasm. This is the same thing that happened to me there. I was transported . . ." He shook his head to gather his wits. Raelis squinted ahead at the man standing before them. "Oi! Kael! That's him, all right!"

"Kael!" Quinlan called out to his brother, who remained before them, practically frozen in place. "What's with the posture? It's me. Get hold of yourself."

Kael lifted a few feet into the air as golden mana flowed down his shoulders. A sound trumpeted in the distance. Beyond, Sylas could see great towers and domed buildings. The sheer scale of it all, and the way that the buildings moved in an almost vertical way toward the horizon, told him that this was some sort of hallucination. It had to be. It couldn't be real. This couldn't actually be the Celestial Plains.

Yet they were somewhere, and it appeared, just as the monk had said, they were going to have to battle Kael.

It was instinct the way that Sylas brought his hand to his waist, as if he were about to pull his sword from its sheath. Much to his surprise, he actually gripped a blade and did just that as Aurumite armor formed on his body.

"I don't like this," Raelis said, yet he also drew a blade. "And what's with the armor?"

Quinlan drew his sword too. He turned it over in his hand, looking at it with a mixture of surprise and disgust. "That priest, or whatever, said we were going to have to fight Kael. He didn't say nothing about armor and swords. And didn't say anything about killing him either. We can't kill him here, right? We're not in the Underworld."

"Definitely not," Mira said.

"I really don't know," Sylas said. "We should try to subdue him. But that might not be—"

Kael fired a golden arc of energy at the four of them.

Quinlan dove to the right, while Sylas and Raelis brought up their swords to block it. It shouldn't have worked, yet none of this made any sense, and just as Sylas had hoped, they were both able to bat the arc of light away with their swords.

Kael touched down in front of them, one knee on the ground, his fist pressing into the stone.

He glanced up at Sylas and his companions, the man's eyes glowing with fury. He produced an explosion that turned much of the stone to ash as golden energy fanned out like that of a spiderweb.

Surprising all of them, it was Mira who got the opening shot as she fired at Kael with a bolt of mana from the palm of her hand. "We have to defend ourselves!" the apothecary said as she hovered into the air.

"That's the spirit!" Raelis cried.

"Kael, no!" Quinlan shouted as his brother drew a massive sword, much larger than any mortal should have been able to wield. Kael charged toward Sylas, who managed to block Kael's attack. He could feel the strength behind it and knew that just a few more strikes like that would stagger him.

"I've got you, mate!" Raelis jumped in from the side, which took much of Kael's attention as he beat the other man back.

Quinlan couldn't bring himself to fight his brother, so he remained on the sidelines shouting his name, yelling for Kael to snap out of it, cursing at him, and never joining the fray.

While Kael was distracted with Raelis, Sylas shouldered him and brought Kael to the ground. He managed to get Kael's sword out of his hand. Kael surged into action, delivering rapid punches to Sylas's neck and his face.

He spilled over to the left as Raelis tried to jump into Sylas's position. Kael bucked him off.

He turned on Raelis, grabbed his sword, and exploded into the air, where he did a quick arc downward, his blade pointed toward the ground. He drove it into the stone floor of the arena, which released bolts of golden mana-electricity that zipped around, seemingly connecting with invisible nodes and bouncing off them.

Mira came to the rescue yet again with a sizzling bolt of mana.

This stopped Kael from conjuring more of the mana lightning bolts, yet the ones he had already summoned continued to shift back and forth until they formed into a lion rimmed in sparking mana.

Even though he wished there was an easier way to do this, even if Azor wasn't there to aid in his flames, Sylas cast Soulfire. He placed a foot back to hold his weight as golden fire burst from the palm of his hand, where it broke into three chunks that all veered toward Kael.

Kael managed to bat the first one away with his enormous sword, but the other two landed, igniting his robes.

This drew Quinlan's ire. "Don't kill him—" he started to shout.

Kael moved back on the attack, even if his clothing burned bright. He rushed toward Mira, who blasted him again with mana, which Kael easily shrugged off.

Raelis rushed forward to intercept Kael. He brought his sword down and then swept it up, directly into Kael's chest. Quinlan yelped, yet there was no blood.

Instead, black particles poured out of Kael, the particles rimmed in a tarnished yellow-green. Kael looked up at them, light dripping from his eyes. He gasped, and they all vanished at the same time.

CHAPTER ELEVEN

ISSUE OF HEAVEN

Sylas and his companions reappeared inside Kael's chamber that was carved into the face of a mountain. The former soldier, who had been suspended in meditation when they arrived, lurched forward and exhaled. He coughed, tried to get control of himself, coughed again, and fell to his side.

"Kael!" Quinlan said as he rushed forward to help his brother up.

"Quin?"

"Yes, it's me, bloody hell, you were, we were—" Quinlan cupped his brother's cheeks and placed his forehead against Kael's.

"Kael, we're sorry to disturb you from your meditation," Raelis told him once Quinlan pulled away. "But there has been a development."

"What?" Kael's eyes bulged as they fell upon Sylas. "No. No, not you. Not you."

"It's me."

"Sylas? Good god, man. You died? How?"

"Stupidly, now that I look back at it," Sylas admitted to his old friend. "It was yet another fight to secure the border near Riverpool. We were overwhelmed. I should have tried to regroup, but something led me forward, right into the midst of it, where I was surrounded and quickly dealt with."

Kael clenched up and relaxed. "War is hell. I have come to truly understand that."

"Aye," Raelis whispered.

"Where were we just now?" Quinlan asked as he helped his brother back into a sitting position. "One moment we were here, the next we were gone. Were we in the Plains? It looked like the Plains. We exploded upward like a firework right after we touched you here, or Sylas did. But I wouldn't be surprised if it was some sort of mana-hallucination. Clearly, I don't know what I'm talking about, yeah?"

Kael collected himself by bringing his hands together. He gave a quick nod to let Quinlan know that he would be fine, that he was ready to speak. "Yes," he finally told them. "We were in the Celestial Plains, believe it or not. No mana-hallucination. We were in a space where manaseers who don't come classed that way go to train." His eyes focused on Mira. "And who might you be?"

"Mira Ravenbane. I'm—"

"She's my business partner," Sylas told Kael. "We both live in Ember Hollow and run a market there."

"Business partner and his girlfriend," Quinlan said under his breath.

Sylas glanced back to Mira, who blushed slightly, bit her lip, and nodded. "That too," he told Kael.

"How long have you been here?" Kael asked Sylas.

"We'll get to that, but not any longer than you've been here at this retreat. We disturbed you for a reason. I have been receiving messages every morning from the system telling me that there were a limited number of days left until an invasion. For the first month, I didn't know what that invasion could be. But now we know. We know what the message is in reference to. The Celestial Plains have plans to close the Underworld by merging it with the Chasm. That is set to happen in a little over a month, unless we do something."

"A month?" Kael said after a meditative pause. "Not a lot of time, really. That would explain why you came."

"Exactly," Raelis said. "Heh. We're getting the old crew back together, yeah?"

"And now that we know you were in the Plains, we should have just stayed there." Quinlan smiled at his brother. "Make it easy on us. Heh. I'm going to go out on a limb here and say things don't exactly work like that, do they?"

"No, they do not." Kael brought his hand to his chin. He stroked his beard, deep in thought. "And even if they did work like that, I was in a mana frenzy, one that was contained by an invisible dome that kept me pinned to that location. Had we somehow broken through that dome, the dormant mana in the air would have made me even stronger, especially near their Mana Fields."

"I saw something on the horizon, a city by the looks of it," Sylas said. "Domed buildings and towers. Maybe not a city? I don't know, but it was something. It looked quite large."

"Ah, yes, that would be Galataport," Kael said. "It is the Battersea of the Celestial Plains, the biggest city up there. It is the spawning location for the innocent, and it is often where people end up living. There are outer settlements as well, yet those are usually defensive posts to continue the battle against the Celestial Beasts, which are akin to the monsters of the Chasm, fueled by mana."

"Would that be one reason the Underworld is on the chopping block?" Sylas asked, the dots connecting in his head before he could truly think through the implications.

"It could, yes. Now that you say it aloud, yes, I believe that is a very real possibility."

Quinlan scratched the back of his head. "So it's not because they hate us? They are afraid of the power we are able to wield? Or maybe they want to keep it all to themselves?"

"I can't speak for the Plains," Kael said. "Their reasoning could be multifaceted, and the two guides I met there through the manaseer process made no mention of any power vacuums. But their fight against Celestial Beasts rages on. I do know that."

"Huh," Sylas said after a long pause. "The manaseers here seem to think the best way forward is to give in to the Plains and adapt."

This statement didn't seem to surprise Kael in the least. "They would think something like that. After all, they are in close communication with the Plains through rituals like this. They have more of a connection than your normal Underworld resident, and will benefit from any power the Plains have promised them. I am going to assume that by coming to get me, you don't feel this way, and that most in the Underworld wouldn't feel comfortable with the Hexveil coming down and the Chasm being unleashed."

"No, we don't, and no, they do not," Quinlan told his brother.

"Then what do you plan to do about it?" Kael asked. "Surely, you have a plan . . ."

———

Everyone traveled back to the pub in Ember Hollow together, where Azor entertained Raelis, Kael, and Quinlan, while Sylas and Mira went to the market.

"Gertrude!" Mira said as soon as she spotted the goose. Cornbread, who had tagged along as dogs often do, wagged her tail upon seeing everyone and woofed loudly. Her tail quickly went between her legs as Gertrude let out an ear-splitting honk. "She's all yours," Mira told Sylas. "I have to prepare the medicine and then meet Esta later."

"I'll take care of the goose. I've spent time with worse company." Sylas crouched and motioned for Gertrude to come to him. She rushed over to him and he ran his hand over her head. "We're going to get you fixed right up."

"We certainly are," Mira called over to them. She had her hand over the medicine they had ground earlier, charging the paste with mana. "The final step."

"And you just want to rub it on her throat?" Sylas asked as he carefully lifted Gertrude into his arms.

"That is the plan, yes."

Sylas brought the goose over to the table. "In that case, I'll hold her. It's not going to hurt her in any way, is it?"

"Heavens no," Mira said. "It's not that sort of medicine. See?" She wiped a small amount on Sylas's arm using something that looked like a butter knife. He could feel the paste instantly, and his nostrils twitched at its minty smell. Cornbread noticed this as well. The dog sneezed a few times and wagged her whole body.

"It must be a really strong smell to Cornbread," Sylas said after she backed away, still sneezing.

"Probably, but Gertrude will be fine. Hold her still."

"Whatever you say, boss."

"Please, just 'Mira' will do."

Because of Gertrude's size, and to make it easier for Mira to spread the medicine on her throat, Sylas placed the goose on the table and gently brought her head back.

"I'm surprised she's letting you do that," Mira told Sylas as she readied her medicine.

"I have a way with animals," Sylas said. "Patches sleeps with me every night, remember?"

"That's because you're warm and he thinks he is protecting you."

"He *is* protecting me."

"Ha." Mira used her hand to smooth the paste over Gertrude's throat. The goose relaxed even more and kept her head down as Mira massaged the paste in.

Cornbread barked nervously.

"Shhh," Sylas told the dog as Mira applied more of the medicine, which now had a slight golden glow to it. The goose made a sound like she had a hiccup trapped in her throat. She looked up at Mira with panic in her big black eyes, panic that quickly subsided as Mira applied a little more of her concoction.

"Just relax," she said in a soothing voice. "You're tired of making all that noise, aren't you?"

Cornbread stood nearby, curious as to what they were doing, and barked a few times.

"When one stops, the other begins," Sylas turned to the farm dog and picked her up. She instantly relaxed in his arms.

"We are so ridiculous." Mira placed Gertrude on the ground. "You should be fine for now. I will apply some more a bit later."

After the patrons cleared out of the pub that night and Sylas finished brewing, he brought several pints up to his friends, who were all seated around the bar waiting for him.

Quinlan belched. "Apologies, lads, I believe I've had too much. You know what? Hell, you're right, you're all right," he said with a big grin on his face. "What's one more?"

Kael laughed. For most of the night, he had only drunk water, but now that Sylas was having a pint, Kael decided to have one as well. Raelis, who sat at the end of the bar petting Patches, seemed a bit tipsy.

"Really, to think we were in heaven not so long ago. None of this really makes sense to me." Kael gestured to the ceiling and then in the direction of the Chasm. "What kind of afterlife is this, anyway? Wonky, yeah?"

"It's not so bad," Sylas told him.

"I wasn't implying that it was. It's just peculiar, that's all."

"Is anyone hungry?" Azor asked as little rows of concentrated flames trailed down her scalp. "I could fry up some chips. Who wants chips? Surely, one of you wants chips with your ale!"

Quinlan smacked his lips. "You wouldn't mind, would you?"

"No, it's fine," she said with her typical fiery flourish. "You all are old friends and there is nothing like the embrace of the familiar."

"The embrace of the familiar," Quinlan grinned at her. "Doesn't roll off the tongue, but it makes me feel nice saying it. It makes me want to get a hug from my brother."

Kael placed his arm around Quinlan and kissed his forehead. "How's that?"

"That's a little too close!"

The group roared with laughter as Raelis launched into a story about one of the men they had served with, who had been fond of switching out people's armor while they slept.

"The tricky devil," Raelis said. "But who am I kidding? It was funny. Especially if someone had already partially suited up. Watching them scramble around for armor in the wee hours. Not great in terms of battle preparedness, but a much-needed reprieve."

"Oof, I remember that." Sylas mimed what it had looked like when this happened. He called out one of the soldier's names in mock anger, and the four men grew louder and louder as they collectively recalled the past.

Since Sylas had emptied one of his casks to fully restock it, there was plenty of ale, so he kept drinking until things started to have a nice haze to them. "I don't think I've ever been hammered in my own pub before," he said, interrupting one of Quinlan's stories.

"Wait. You mean to tell us that you haven't enjoyed your pub for all it's worth?" Quinlan motioned to the seating against the wall, the built-ins that Anders had crafted as an apology for breaking into the pub. "It's a bloody fine place, mate. Relax and enjoy, yeah? See what it looks like from your customer's perspective, but don't get too comfortable." He shook his pint glass. "I'm almost out."

Sylas came around the bar and did just that. His friends joined him around the booth. As they got situated, Azor came up from the kitchen with a basket of fresh chips garnished with green onions and a side of Tartar's famous sauce.

"Extra crispy," she said, offering Quinlan a fiery wink. "Just like you like them."

"You remember," he told her. "Have a seat. Join us."

Azor did her best to appear as if she were seated. Cornbread came around, and climbed up onto a chair so she could get into Sylas's lap. Not to be left out, Patches hopped onto the table, where he sniffed at one of the chips.

"I think the cat likes it," Kael said after Patches took a single chip to the opposite side of the table, where he tried to eat it even though it was hot.

"You can have one too," Quinlan told Cornbread. He picked one of the chips out of the basket and gave it to her so she could lick some of the salt off it.

"This is nice," Raelis told the group. "I feel like it's been ages since we've done something like this."

"When was the last time the four of us had a drink?" Quinlan asked. "It must have been years ago."

"Well, I was the last to die," Sylas said. "As grim as that sounds. So it would've been before that. We really should have taken more moments to have a nice drink together. But there was never time."

"And we were always at war," Quinlan said. "Can't discount that."

"Actually, now that I think about it, I can comfortably say that I was the first," Raelis told them. "As grim as *that* sounds."

"Second," Kael said. "And there's nothing grim about it once the initial pain subsided."

"That would make me the third." Quinlan lifted his pint glass. "And I agree with my brother."

"Of course, you do," Raelis said. "You always agree with Kael."

"Flesh and blood, yeah? Better than arguing, agreeing. Right?" Quinlan smirked and continued, "Aside from the momentary sting of—what was it? A sword that ultimately struck me down? A war hammer? A bloke high and mighty on his steed with an extended reach? I can't remember—aside from *that,* and the flash of anger at dying by the hands of a filthy Thornian bastard who got in a lucky hit—the cheeky sod—it wasn't as bad as people make it out to be. Which . . ." He grew serious. "Is why we need to make sure the Celestial buggers above don't spoil it for all of us. We have a good thing going here, is what I'm saying."

Raelis snorted at the term "Celestial buggers." He said, "Maybe we shouldn't call them that, yeah? But you're right. This is the life. We have it good here."

"We do," Sylas told him as he took another sip from his pint.

Quinlan patted Sylas on the back. "And look at you, you've got a pub, a farm, and a market."

"The market is yet to open," Sylas reminded Quinlan.

"Didn't you have a meeting about it today?"

"I did. Mira handled most of the talking, but we're set to open this weekend. This woman I met at the Finmarket, Esta, she knows a load of folks looking for a new place to sell goods. Mira and her have set most of it up, and I just need to get the outdoor pub there up and running."

"So who is going to run that?" Raelis asked. "Don't tell me poor Azor is going to do it."

"No," Azor said, "I'm staying right here."

"As am I," Sylas said. "I'm actually looking for someone to manage it. We'll only be open Wraithsday, at night, to coincide with the feast, and then Specterday and Soulsday."

Quinlan popped another chip in his mouth. "So two and a half days a week."

"Correct. I'll have to figure out running both pubs, but—"

"Well, I certainly wouldn't mind doing something like that," Quinlan said, cutting Sylas off.

"Nor would I," Kael told him.

"I do have some experience running the commissary," Raelis said. "How much harder could handling a bunch of drunks be?"

Sylas placed his pint glass down and turned to the three of them. "You'd really want to do something like that?"

"Three of us. It's open two and a half days a week," Quinlan said. "Easy peasy lemon squeezy. And how hard could it be, anyway? You'd be doing the brewing, yeah?"

"Until one of you classed, or I should say, if one of you wanted to class, yes. Azor and I would be doing the brewing. You'd just be pouring up pints and keeping the crowd happy."

"A pint for them and a pint for me," Quinlan said. "Joking. You know we'd run a tight ship."

A vision of Quinlan pouring up pints flashed across Sylas's mind's eye. "I'm sure you would. But pints are always on the house for my mates, and you know that."

"Be careful what you promise," Quinlan said to a roar of laughter from Raelis.

"And since we'd be around the market," Raelis added once the laughter had subsided, "we could keep an eye on things there too."

"What about you?" Sylas asked Kael. "You really mean it? I figured you'd want to go back to the retreat if we're able to solve all of this."

Kael rocked his head back and forth. "Not certain. There are other things I can do in my free time for spiritual growth. If you couldn't already tell, manaseers aren't the most pleasant people. I learned that after deciding to become one. And now that I hear what the Plains are up to, it makes me very reluctant to go to manaseers for any sort of guidance. I find myself wondering what can be done here within the bounds of the system given to us? What can we do here? Really, it would be nice to have a better understanding of the Crafting Laws and their exploits."

"If it is exploits you are looking for, then you are going to love Tilbud," Sylas said.

"And who is he again?" Kael asked. "Someone mentioned that name tonight."

"Tilbud is an archlumen who's somehow at the center of all of this. We are waiting—"

"That's right!" Azor told Sylas. She did a fiery flip. "I'm so sorry. I totally forgot. He stopped by earlier and told me to tell you to meet him in Battersea tomorrow."

"Tilbud did? Where?"

Azor started to fret. "What was it? It was a guildhall with a long title, sorry, Sylas, I can't remember! I was so distracted when he came by. Nelly and Karn were doing repairs on something, and it was so loud—"

"The Distinguished Society of Lumengineers and Etheric Constructs? Does that ring a bell?"

"That's it," she told Sylas.

"That's a mouthful," Quinlan said.

"And Tilbud is doing what exactly?" Kael asked them.

Sylas answered, "He's working with a lumengineer to orchestrate our plan to appeal to the citizens of the Celestial Plains. Among other things. If there's one thing you should know about Tilbud it's this: he's always up to something."

"That he is," Quinlan told his brother. "And, related to what Sylas just said, if there is one man who might come up with a solution to our little conundrum, it's Tilbud. Do I trust the bloody archlumen? No. Do I like him? Somewhat, even if he seems a little off. But do I know he absolutely is the best man for the job? Yes. Remember Lhandon?"

"I do," Kael said, referring to a man they had served with who could be as unpredictable as he was reliable in a pinch.

"Tilbud is like him, only more colorful and with magic."

"Lhandon with magic. Noted," Kael told his brother.

"So you'll go there tomorrow?" Raelis asked Sylas. "Battersea."

"Apparently. I suppose I'll need to bring Mira with me."

Raelis laughed. "You two are attached at the hip."

"Oh, to be young and in love," Quinlan said. "I remember those days."

"Last I checked, you have Priscilla," Sylas told him.

"You're still seeing her?" Kael asked. "I would have thought by now that you would've shrugged her off as you do all the women you inevitably end up with."

"Nah, not this one," Quinlan said. "And you watch what you say around her. Don't go mentioning any of my old flames. She's special; I guess you could say I'm getting wiser in my old age." Cornbread barked. "See? The pooch gets it. Anyway, let's finish these pints, lads. I want to head back to the farm. And Sylas?"

"Yeah?"

"I mean it, mate. We mean it. When the market gets going, you've got yourself three loyal soldiers to man the Petticoat Pub, or whatever you call it. Now about our cut . . ." Quinlan laughed, and soon, they were working out numbers and enjoying the rest of Sylas's ale.

By the time he called it a night, Sylas could barely see straight. But he felt great. He had forgotten what it truly meant to unwind with old friends.

———

Patches watched the fire spirit finally relax into the fireplace. She seemed exhausted, especially after seeing two of the warrior men off, helping the big man up to his room, and then helping the warrior with the long dark hair to the other room upstairs.

They had been quite loud, the four men laughing and then even singing. But this didn't bother Patches. He had only become annoyed once Cornbread started howling. Even so, Patches could sense that there was something going on between everyone, something beneath the merriment, and he wanted them all to relax.

I wonder what it is, he said as he watched the fire spirit settle into her resting position, which wasn't unlike that of a cat.

Cornbread licked Patches's face. *What are we doing tonight? I think we should check on the goose. They did something to her earlier, you know. I wonder why she's not here.*

Probably because she's loud. Although, Patches said as his ears twitched, *I could sometimes hear her from here, and I've yet to hear anything tonight. Strange. What about you? Your hearing is better. Have you heard from her?*

My hearing is excellent, I agree. But to answer your question, no, I haven't heard anything from the goose. Which makes me wonder if we should go check. Her tail wagged. *We should, right? We should totally go check on her.*

I suppose so. But before we do that, I need to make my rounds. Things have been quiet in the Tavernly Realm as of late. But they won't always be like that.

Maybe they will. You have me now, Cornbread said proudly. *And creatures are afraid of dogs. We've a much nastier bite. You may have your claws, but—*

Let's not compare our lethal weapons. You will most assuredly lose. Patches headed downstairs, made his rounds, and then charged out the cat door onto the stoop, where he waited for Cornbread to join him.

The two circled around the Tavernly Realm and came to a pair of militiamen. One of them, a lanky fellow, spotted the dog and cat and approached. He spoke to Cornbread, who was friendly as always and let the man pet her head.

I don't know why you bother. We have important things to do.

You don't like being petted? Cornbread asked Patches after they moved on.

I do. But not while I'm busy. Humans always want to pet us. It's not like that's going to stop anytime soon. So I like to be more selective about when I allow them to touch me.

Should I be more selective? Is that what you're suggesting?

I am. You can be more graceful too.

Maybe I could become a cat.

Patches stopped to look at Cornbread, who did her version of a grin. *You are teasing me.*

You know you like it, Cornbread said as she licked his face yet again, her tail thumping.

Would you stop that!?

Sure. Cornbread licked his face one more time before she took off running toward the market.

That dog, Patches said as he picked up his pace. He reached the market to find Cornbread rushing into action.

Patches jumped backward as Gertrude burst into the air, the goose spiraling down onto a—

Rat! Patches quickly doubled the size and went for the first one that he saw, which was bigger than the rodents he had previously encountered in the Tavernly Realm. Patches landed on the rat and the pair tumbled into a wall.

As dust and debris fell from the rafters, the two continued their fight, Patches relentless with his claws until the rat eventually tried to flee. The pub cat dove for it but didn't go for its tail. Instead, he drove his claws into its rump, twisted it to the side, and smothered it with his weight in a final bite to its throat.

What is that?! Patches dodged left as a pair of phantom teeth flew forward and snapped onto one of the rats. He swiveled around just in time to see the teeth return to Cornbread's mouth, the rat in tow.

Before he could ask where she had learned to do that, Gertrude blasted a pair of fleeing rodents with a concentrated honk. It froze them in place. The goose flapped over to them and pecked one to death with her beak while the other was forced to watch helplessly. She slapped it with her webbed foot, hard enough that the rat tumbled to the side and rolled onto its back.

While the dog and the goose continued to fight, Patches rushed into the dark. He turned invisible, in search of something he'd seen before in a situation like this.

This is bad. Patches came upon a smokey being, one no larger than a child and demonic in nature. The Hellrift spotted him and hissed, baring its sharp teeth, the demon's face filling with fury as it exploded toward Patches.

Brave as ever, Patches stood his ground. He struck the demon with an expertly timed swat from his razor-sharp claws. Yowling, Patches hopped backward and split his form into two. The Hellrift went for the replica, giving Patches a moment to gather his power, which he transformed into a supersonic purr that pulled the Hellrift down.

Patches jumped over to it and incinerated the demon with an orb of mana that he produced from the back of his throat.

Cornbread came running. She found Patches breathing heavily, yet seated in a calm position, trying to make it seem as if he were casually licking his claws. *Are you all right?* she asked.

Never been better. What about the rats?

The goose just finished off the last of them.

As if on cue, Gertrude appeared, her feathers a little ruffled. *That was fun.* Gertrude threw her head back and let out a short honk as she flapped her wings. *Really fun!*

Cornbread sniffed the air. *What's that minty smell?* She turned to the goose. *It's coming from you.*

The medicine woman put something on my throat to quiet me down. I think it's working. I have more control than I used to have. I'm certain of it.

Patches looked up at her, his whiskers flickering. *So that's why I haven't been hearing your sounds.*

Precisely. Gertrude took a quick look around. *So this is what you all do? Run around the village hunting things? Fun!*

What we do is much more distinguished than that, Patches told her. *What we do is more important than life itself. I'm the protector of the Tavernly Realm. The dog is the protector of the Farmly Realm. We work together now.*

The goose cocked her head as she looked at the pub cat. *That would make me the protector of the . . . Marketly Realm?*

Patches and Cornbread exchanged glances. Cornbread spoke: *I guess that would. And you have your work cut out for you considering most of it is outside. We are close to the bad place.*

That we are. Gertrude threw her neck back and brought it back down with a short nod.

Which means we should work together, Cornbread said.

Patches sighed, even though he silently agreed with the farm dog.

Cornbread turned to him, approached, and licked his face.

What have I told you about doing that?

You know you like it, the dog said, her tail wagging with joy.

————

[You have 33 days until the invasion.]
[A loan payment of 1455 has been deducted from your total Mana Lumens. Your total loan balance is 22113 Mana Lumens.]

Groggy, but still happy that he was able to drink and have a good time with his friends, Sylas checked his stats.

Name: Sylas Runewulf
MLus: 18582/18582
Class: Brewer
Secondary Class: Farmer
Tertiary Class: Landlord

"How did you sleep?" he asked Patches as he scratched the back of the pub cat's head. "Heh. Look at you, just lying in bed and enjoying yourself. Did you get into anything last night? No?"

Patches responded with a purr, one that was quickly cut off as Cornbread exploded into the room and catapulted herself onto the bed. She got under the covers, at which point Patches hopped down to the ground and headed downstairs.

Cornbread licked Sylas's face.

"Easy, girl," he said as he cupped the dog's head and stared into her big eyes. "What's all the excitement about?" Sylas took a sniff of the air and smelled sizzling meat. "No wonder you're pumped." He heard some chatter downstairs. "Sounds like the boys are awake."

Sylas headed down, where he found Quinlan, Raelis, Kael, and Mira seated around the bar, the three soldiers shoveling food into their mouths as Azor brought another platter up from the kitchen. Mira smiled at him as Azor exploded with her typical morning enthusiasm.

"Happy Spectorday!" she said. "We decided to have a feast."

"I can see that. Can I help with anything?"

"Sure. Some pastries just came out of the oven. Put them on a tray and—"

"No, no, mate," Quinlan said as he pressed away from his stool. "Have a seat. I saved one next to your lady. I'll get some food for you."

"Please," Mira told Sylas in a more playful tone than he was used to hearing from her.

"No, no, it's not fair that we wake him up and expect him to get to serving us when we're here working on our second—"

"Third," Kael chimed in.

"Third plate," Quinlan said. "Have a seat, Sylas."

Sylas did just that. Mira reached out and squeezed his hand. "Are you excited to see what Tilbud has to say?"

"Excited and worried, if we're being honest."

"He left with such conviction the other day with your uncle."

"Tibby? Pfft. Tilbud wanted to spend time with Catia," Quinlan called just before he headed down the stairs. "He admitted that himself."

Mira made a face. "I would agree. And my uncle wasn't able to get anything from his contacts anyway. Believe me, I've already heard his spiel. And either way, I am less excited now. I can't imagine why we would be called to Battersea."

"Don't listen to my brother," Kael told her. "As to the type of news you are about to receive, I haven't a clue. But news is news nonetheless."

"And the market?" Raelis said. "You were telling us about the Petticoat Lane Market and its opening date."

"I wanted to wait until next Wraithsday," Mira said, "to coincide with the feast. But a soft opening is in order. A test opening. Esta has managed a lot of it, but I will be meeting with her after we go to Battersea to prepare the test opening."

"Exciting times," Kael said. "A test opening would be amazing."

"I believe so," Mira said.

Raelis took a bite of his eggs and chewed as he spoke: "I agree, and now it's time for the second part of the announcement."

"Second part?" Both Sylas and Mira asked him.

"Yeah, you already know this part, mate." Raelis swallowed. "Kael, Quin, and yours truly, we'll be running the pub. The Old Lamplighter Two. Or whatever you decide to call it."

"The Petticoat Lane Pub," Sylas said.

"The Petticoat Lane Pub and Grill?" Azor asked as she came up with the pastries. "Quinlan likes cooking. I like grilling meats. I will be able to work here and there, I think. It's only two days a week."

"Three," Sylas told her.

"Ah, right. In that case, the Wraithsday Feast will always take precedence over the grill. Anyone wanting food at that time can just head over here. In fact, we should only open the Petticoat Lane Pub after the feast. That makes it easy. As for grilled meats, as long as we get them grilling, I can check the fire periodically. We could smoke things back here."

"I like it," Raelis said, "but that's just because I'm hungry."

"How can you be hungry?" Mira asked him. "You have had two—"

"Three," Kael chimed in.

"Plates. Three plates."

"What did Quinlan say the other day? I remember. 'I'm a growing boy,'" Raelis told her with a laugh. "But back to the market. Yes, all of this will work. I'm excited to open, or soft open, and I think it will be an incredible success. But first. Before we count our successes, the two of you need to get to Battersea. So eat up, Sylas, and let's solve the issue of heaven."

———

Before they took Sylas's portal to the Ale Alliance, Sylas and Mira stopped by the Petticoat Lane Market to check on Gertrude.

"No," Mira said once she saw that a table had been knocked over and that there were big scratch marks on one of the walls. "What happened here?"

"That may be the culprit," Sylas said as Gertrude came waddling toward Mira, the goose sounding off with cute little honks.

"What did you do?" she asked as she brought the goose into her arms. "Bad goose!"

"Let me check around." Sylas moved through the market and noticed an overturned pail and a pair of stools that had been next to one another last he saw them. "Not too much damage," he told Mira upon his return. "And she was probably chasing something out. Rats, likely. We get those around here. Judging by those scratch marks, I'd say Patches was here as well."

"Which means Cornbread was here. Those two are inseparable these days." Mira placed Gertrude on a table and started applying medicine to the goose's throat. "I do hope they are careful once people start moving their stuff in."

"Today, yeah?" Sylas took another look at the market. "We're missing a sign."

"I was thinking that too. I was thinking we could either have one made from scrap, Anders said he could do that, or we could commission one in Battersea."

"Let's stay scrappy."

"That's what your gut is telling you?"

"I can't trust my gut at the moment," Sylas told her. "I just had breakfast."

"Funny."

"That wasn't even meant to be a joke, yet it came out that way."

After they checked the market one final time to make sure everything was in order, Sylas and Mira used the pub portal to go directly to the Ale Alliance, where Sylas had a brief discussion about the delivery of new kegs for the Petticoat Lane Pub and Grill and was told that he wouldn't have to pay for them, as he previously thought. As long as he had a separate pub. These would be delivered later that day as well, which meant Sylas would have to brew a lot that night in preparation for the soft opening. Marty, the Ale Alliance's sigilist, also reminded him that the casks were to remain at the market, that they couldn't be used at The Old Lamplighter.

"Not a problem," Sylas told Marty with a casual salute. "If we somehow ran out, I'd just lead everyone over to the market."

"Yes, smart," Marty said. "The Crafting Laws, like most laws, have loopholes."

From there, they went straight to The Distinguished Society of Lumengineers and Etheric Constructs, where Sylas hoped it would be easy to find Tilbud. As he stood before the white stone steps of the rather large building looking up at it, the guild framed by the golden sky, Sylas got the feeling that locating the archlumen would be more difficult than he originally anticipated.

But then, words took shape right in front of him: *Dearest Sylas and who I expect will be Mira because why would you miss the opportunity to travel to the big city with the budding love of your afterlife? It has come to my attention that you need to find me, and you are probably wondering where I am. Not a worry! I have used my mastery over the power known as Quill to lead you directly to me. Do you see the next message? You should by now.*

Another message materialized into existence at the top of the stairs.

Are you coming? it read.

Mira slowly turned away from the floating words. "What a bother, Tilbud."

A new message flashed into existence. *Come on, this will be fun.*

Sylas laughed. "He remains exceedingly eccentric. Let's just do what he has requested."

A few people gawked at them as another message appeared near the enormous open doorway: *You are getting closer. Careful of the marble. Catia tells me it was recently polished.*

Once inside, Sylas and Mira saw a message form at the top of one of the spiral staircases.

This way, lad and lady. And don't mind the paintings that line the wall. Everyone depicted is dead now. Ha!

Yet again, a distasteful look from a lumengineer passing by.

Upon reaching the top of the stairs, they came to another hallway where a new message took shape.

Ah, you are getting better at this. Truly. It has come to my attention that this would be an excellent way to trap someone in a dungeon, if that were my sort of thing. It isn't, I assure you. No wild goose chase—pun intended—even if it seems that way. But I do like having a little fun. Continue onward, then, and get your prize.

"Prize?" Mira asked as they reached a new hallway, one with a guard. The guard, who wore armor and had a club at his side barely noted their presence as a new message appeared.

Is there a guard? There was this morning when I set all of this up. In that case, greet the guard and continue down the hallway, to the third door on the right.

"Hello," Mira told the guard, who upon closer inspection was a large fellow in an outfit a size too small for his frame. He grunted a response. "May we pass?"

"You're already here, aren't you?" he asked.

Sylas stepped forward like he planned to say something but Mira put a hand on his chest. "Come, Sylas, let's be done with this little treasure hunt."

They reached the door in question and a new message appeared: *Not this door, the next one. Did I say the third door on the right? I meant fourth, but I didn't feel like going back and fixing my previous message. Rest assured: you are almost there.*

Mira and Sylas moved to the fourth door and yet again, another message. *Knock twice. Wait three seconds. Then knock twice again.*

"Tilbud, enough with the games!" Mira opened the door without knocking, and would have stepped into a great void had it not been for Sylas, who reached out and caught her. He pulled her back into the hallway.

"What was that?" she whispered.

"Let's just do what Tilbud suggested." Sylas knocked twice, waited three seconds, then knocked twice again.

He opened the door this time to find Tilbud and Catia resting on a couch, both in silk gowns. Tilbud had his head in her lap and Catia looked beyond embarrassed once she looked up to see Sylas and Mira.

"Apologies!" She hopped up, which caused Tilbud to fall off the couch. He got to his feet quickly and snapped his fingers, which changed his clothes from something that looked like his pajamas into a golden suit with sequined lapels, complete with a matching fedora that had a maroon feather sticking out of it.

"Finally," Tilbud said. "I really thought the two of you would never make it."

"What was that last room?" Mira asked Tilbud.

"Which one? Oh, you opened the door without knocking, didn't you? Ah, well, in that case, you should know that, not unlike the portal that brought you to Battersea, by not using the door's secret code, you opened a portal that would have cast you . . . somewhere. I really don't know where. I probably should have noted that in my message but it all seemed so fun and whimsical at the time. Believe me, it did."

"Fun and whimsical? Where would it have taken us?" Mira demanded.

"As I said, Mira, I do not know."

"It could have taken you anywhere," Catia said as she too changed her clothing with a quick snap, her outfit going from black robes to a black overcoat over a pair of high-waisted trousers and a ruffled gray shirt. "From Geist to Ember Hollow or somewhere in between. There's really no telling."

Mira crossed her arms over her chest.

"Relax," Tilbud told her. "You're here now and that's all that matters. Come, please." He motioned them to a table that started to arrange itself with tea and biscuits. "We will explain all we've learned since we last spoke. I hope one of you is ready for a little adventure . . ."

CHAPTER TWELVE

FORTUITOUS SERENDIPITY

Tilbud grinned for an excruciatingly long minute as Sylas and Mira sat before him and Catia. Mira was unable to hide the annoyed look on her face.

She didn't care if Tilbud had a thousand lovers or if his mustache was ruffled and his pupils seemed dilated; if he knew they were coming, the least he could have done, she thought, was greet them *outside* rather than leave a trail to a door that opened first into a void, and then into what was clearly a private moment between him and Catia.

For her part, Catia was harder to read than Mira would have been had she been in the same situation. She seemed embarrassed, but there was a hint of mischief on her face as well. The lumengineer sat next to Tilbud, her eyes darting between Sylas and Mira, never revealing anything like shame, concern, or even curiosity.

"And how is our dearest of geese?" Tilbud finally asked Mira.

"Gertrude is fine." Mira could have elaborated, but she didn't want to. Their world was at stake and she still had a lot to do in preparation for the Petticoat Lane Market's grand opening. Even though he wasn't necessarily projecting an air of smugness, Mira was annoyed as Tilbud scratched his mustache.

"I take it her honkings have subsided."

"They have."

"Wonderful. Absolutely wonderful." Tilbud folded his hands together. "And the pub, Sylas? How goes it? Anything I should be aware of?"

"The Old Lamplighter is doing just fine," Sylas told him. "We came to Battersea to discuss the Plains with you. What should we know?"

Mira nearly sighed with relief at the sound of Sylas getting right down to it.

"Right, the Plains. We should certainly discuss that. It is why you are here. But I must ask." Tilbud raised an eyebrow at them. "Quinlan's friend. No, his brother. I'm blanking on his name. Wasn't he named after a type of lettuce?"

"Kael," Mira said for Sylas, who groaned at what he had perceived as a joke from Tilbud.

"Yes, Kael. Is he . . . ?"

"He's fine. We got him out of his manaseer retreat," Sylas said, "which turned out to be a whole affair."

"Yes, tell us about that." Tilbud reached over and squeezed Catia's hand. "Tell us about this affair."

Mira tried not to roll her eyes. What was the archlumen getting at? Why beat around the bush in such a way? She wasn't normally this bothered by Tilbud, even if he had a way of getting under her skin from time to time. Could it be some enchantment? Had the archlumen cast something? Why did she feel trapped in her own skin at the moment?

Luckily, Sylas spoke again, "We were told that we would have to fight him. What we didn't expect was to be transported to the Celestial Plains—or at least some portal version of it; we're not sure of the mechanics of this—where the three of us had to nearly kill Kael to bring him back here. As soon as we beat him, we were transported back to the retreat, and we learned something . . . Actually, I wanted to ask you."

"Yes?" Tilbud asked. "Ask away."

"Are you familiar with Celestial Beasts?"

"I am." Tilbud squeezed Catia's hand again. "We are. Celestial Beasts are heaven's equivalent of the monsters from the Chasm. Celestians hunt them for sport, but some of these beasts can be quite destructive, and they have grown in power as of late. It is one of many reasons that we, and by 'we' I mean the entire Underworld, are on the chopping block. And to be clear: the reason I asked about Kael wasn't to annoy you, Mira."

"I never said it annoyed me," she told the archlumen.

"In that same spirit, the reason I asked about Gertrude *was* to annoy you. Because I wanted this conversation to be light as the news we have isn't great. Or it is. It really depends on your definition of fortuitous serendipity. Catia? Would you care to tell them?"

"Me?" Catia shot him a hesitant look. *They're your friends,* she mouthed to him.

"Yes, I suppose they are. Well, we already know one reason the Celestial Plains wants to merge the Chasm and the Underworld, and that's because there is a faction there that doesn't believe the Underworld should exist, that it has grown too powerful. Add to that the mana needed to maintain the Underworld and the growing threat of Celestial Beasts, not to mention the mana to maintain Celestial Campaign Cities in the Chasm, and you can see why they feel the way they do."

"So how do we fight back?" Sylas asked. "That's what you came here to understand better, right? We have our letter idea."

"Yes, that, the letter campaign," Catia said. She motioned for Tilbud to continue. "I'll let you explain."

"The letters are a last resort. To extract the mana that will be needed for us to circumvent the rules and the costs associated with sending a message is still something we are discussing privately. When you appeared earlier, that's what we had been doing."

Mira looked at the two of them skeptically. "Are you sure about that?"

"Well, things did get out of hand as they often do while having a heated discussion," Tilbud said, "but yes, that's what we were discussing. And we each have an opinion on how that may work. Catia is more of a fan of Clairvoice; I'm a fan of Lorewave. But we're at odds on how we could get the MLus needed to get the word to every inhabitant of the Underworld *and* transmit this message to the Celestial Plains. We do agree on one thing, though."

"What's that?" Mira asked, unfamiliar with either spell that he had mentioned.

"The envoy. I have it from here," Catia told them. "There is a lumengineer envoy leaving today for the Celestial Plains to meet with the Celestial Council. There will be several manaseers as part of the envoy, and we often bring people with other classes so our representatives in the Plains can get a better understanding of what is happening here, what it's like on the ground. We want to bring you both, but there's a cost."

Mira nearly gasped at the prospect of actually visiting the Celestial Plains. She brought her hand to her mouth to contain her shock.

"Yes, the price. It is steep," Tilbud said. "If it wasn't for my incredible talents and the customers I have cultivated over the years, I, myself, wouldn't be able to afford it. But I have always wanted to join a Celestial Envoy, and there just so happens to be a few spots that opened up recently. What do you say?"

"What's the cost?" Sylas asked.

"Fifteen thousand fixed MLus per person."

"That is steep," Sylas said.

"I can't possibly afford that," Mira said as she glanced at the brewer. "But you can, yes?"

"I can," Sylas said. "I can only afford for one of us to go. In that case, you—"

"No, Sylas. You go. I have things to deal with here at the market. You go to the Plains and . . ." Mira turned her focus back to Tilbud and Catia. "What then? Are you going to make some appeal? Is that what you intend to do?"

"That is the plan, yes," Catia told Mira. "Once we are able, we are going to execute Article 6196A of the Crafting Laws that allows representatives of the Underworld to challenge a Celestial Decision, as it is known, an article that can only be executed within the Plains themselves."

Sylas let out a startled laugh and shook his head in disbelief. "You mean they have a clause that allows us to dispute something, but it can only be done there?"

"I do. Care to read it?" Catia waved her hand and Article 6196A appeared:

Article 6196A of the Crafting Laws

Pursuant to the Celestial provisions set forth in Article 6196A of the Crafting Laws, representatives of the Underworld are hereby granted the authority to challenge a Celestial Decision.

This specific article, colloquially referred to as the "Challenge Provision," stipulates that such a challenge is permissible exclusively within the confines of the Celestial Plains themselves, in a Celestial Chamber, and not within the confines of the Underworld, the Chasm, Celestial Campaign Cities, or any pocket realm, such as an intermediary ground used by manaseers.

The execution of this article is subject to strict adherence to procedural mandates, as outlined within the broader framework of the Crafting Laws, and may only be initiated under conditions that ensure the equitable consideration of all involved parties.

Precedents and Citations:

Underworld v. The Celestial Council (5 B.C.L.): This landmark case established the foundational precedent for invoking Article 6196A to later be included in the Crafting Laws (C. L.), affirming that challenges must be presented within the Celestial Plains and underscoring the necessity for strict procedural compliance.

The Distinguished Society of Lumengineers and Etheric Constructs v. The Luminous Shields of the Western Hexveil (7 A.C.L.): This ruling elaborated on the procedural nuances required for a challenge, emphasizing that any deviation from the mandated process within the Celestial Plains would result in the automatic dismissal of the challenge.

The Archlumenry of the Grace Academy v. The Celestial Council (12 A.C.L.): In this case, the Celestial Plains were unequivocally determined as the sole venue for executing challenges under Article 6196A, with the court rejecting any alternative locations as invalid.

Citizens of Duskhaven v. The Celestial Council (72 A.C.L.): The tribunal reinforced that representatives of the Underworld possess the standing to initiate challenges under Article 6196A, provided that all conditions set forth by the Crafting Laws are meticulously observed.

"Wow," Mira said after scanning it. "That is a lot to take in."

"Yes, you are right," Tilbud told her. "But the point of the matter is this: the Plains hold all the cards, which means they make all the rules. So using their own rules against them may be an option here, and it may spare us from having to extract the mana necessary for our letter campaign, which won't be easy."

Mira smiled at Sylas. "You should go."

"Are you sure?"

"I'm serious. And in the meantime, I'll make sure everything is running smoothly here."

Tilbud clapped his hands together. "Good, good, great! In that case, get cleaned up, Sylas, we leave in an hour."

"Cleaned up?"

The archlumen winked at him. "Don't worry, I have a spell for that."

———

Even with his beard trimmed and his clothes magically washed and pressed, Sylas couldn't swallow the apprehension he felt upon stepping out of the lumengineer's guild. Mira turned to him, a sad look in her eyes that she quickly hid by forcing a smile.

"I look that good?" he asked.

"Please. And yes, you clean up nicely. That is some spell Tilbud has."

"He always has a trick up his sleeve."

"That he does." Mira moved a bit closer to him. "Anyway, good luck."

"I'll do my best," Sylas told her. "I'll be back tonight, right?" he asked Tilbud, who had just joined them. "You know what I mean. I mean, today."

"Because there is no night, right." Tilbud, who had his arm around Catia's waist, gave it a quick squeeze. "And yes, you will be back tonight. I know you have to brew."

"Brewing for the pub and the market," Sylas said. "We soft open tomorrow."

"Wonderful! I love a soft opening. Does this mean what I think it means?"

"What do you think it means?" Sylas asked Tilbud.

"I think it means a pub quiz. There's not a lot of time to get people excited, but we can get the word out. Or you can," he told Mira. "Yes, please, let people know there will be a pub quiz tomorrow night at The Old Lamplighter after the market closes for the evening. We can bring the people there with us. It really is a wonderful idea," he said, nodding excitedly. "Unless you all think . . ."

"Azor will want to cook, that's for sure," Sylas told him. "But let's wait until the Wraithsday Feast to celebrate the grand opening. It will be less hectic that way."

Tilbud's mustache drooped. "No pub quiz?"

"Let's save it for the feast next week. Since it is the Petticoat Lane Market's soft-opening night, we can have a free barbeque. A free plate per person."

"Yes," Tilbud said, and much to their surprise, Horatio the water spirit took shape beside him.

"I can help Azor," Horatio offered.

"Brilliant. This is all brilliant. I was disappointed moments ago, but now it is all lining up: the stars, our chances for success, and an absolutely stellar pub quiz," Tilbud said. "This means I can stay at the pub tonight. Or perhaps at Nelly and Karn's inn. We should stay there," he told Catia. "Yes, there, and leave Sylas's guest room for one of the lads."

"There are things that need to be done here," Catia said sharply.

"There are things that need to be done everywhere, love, but that should never stop us from taking a moment for ourselves. What I'm saying is if we always strived to complete all our tasks, we ourselves would never be complete. No? Let me try again—"

"We get it," Mira said, cutting him off. "Sylas, I'll stop by the pub and tell Azor what's happening. I'm assuming she will want to get meat for tomorrow. I can go with her if that's the case. I'll probably need to pick up a few things in Cinderpeak anyway."

"I should travel back with you, then," Sylas said. "We can use my portal. It's free."

Catia stepped between the two of them: "We should be joining the envoy. If it's travel costs you're worried about, you can use our portal here."

"You don't mind?" Mira asked her.

"No, I do not. Come. And Tilbud, please don't go anywhere. You know I hate looking for people. And no Quill messages. I believe we've had enough of that today."

He stifled a laugh. "Likely. In any case, I'll stay right here, love," Tilbud told Catia as he leaned forward and kissed her on the forehead.

"Good, I'll be back momentarily."

"She is a wonderful woman," Tilbud said as he watched Catia walk out of the room with Mira. "But I would be lying if I said I don't miss Rufus sometimes. And Elena, although she is a very feisty woman, and by feisty, I mean violent."

"You lead a strange life," Sylas told him as he remembered Elena, the MLR banker who had provided their loans to buy new classes and properties.

"Strange and wonderful, full of love only occasionally balanced out by heartbreak, as life should be. Too many societies have tried to strip color out of life so it better fits some social norm or expectation. It's one of the reasons I like the Underworld, you know. We're all dead. We have all learned the hard way that we are sinners, or that we were judged to be sinners enough not to be let into the Pearly Gates of the Celestial Plains. So people relax a little. Their expectations change. Their beliefs. It's rather nice, is it not? And without the threat of constant violence, like there was back in our world, it's even better."

"I haven't thought of it that way."

"Look around you, Sylas. Gone are the institutions that used to hold us back only to be replaced by new institutions, guilds, and the Celestial Council, their rules that are hoping to do the same. But it still feels different, and I would be lying to you if I didn't say I feel much freer here. I'm older than you, Sylas, or at least I died well before you. And during my time, the Aurum Kingdom was *still* at war with the Shadowthorne Empire."

"Which side did you live on? You never told me."

"That's because it doesn't matter. They are labels given in place of trying to understand our neighbors and better serve the entire world. What is the fight between the two kingdoms over anyway? Does anyone even know?"

"The border."

"And what about the border?"

"Where it starts and where it ends," Sylas told Tilbud.

"And to your knowledge, and as an Aurumite you clearly had knowledge, were there resources or something along the border, or in some border region, that it made it worth fighting over?"

"If there were, much of it was destroyed by the time I saw it." Sylas grimaced at the thoughts that followed. "Eh. The border was ravaged. Every town we visited or were stationed in was the same. It was repaired only for it to be destroyed in the following year or two as the line kept changing. It was like trying to catch the sun."

"It was the same when I was alive. And for what? You see now, as most do when they get here, that Aurumites and Shadowthornians want the same thing. That is something to keep in mind as we reach the Celestial Plains and invoke Article 6196A. We know what a border fight looks like. We know what will happen if the Hexveil comes down."

"I try not to think of it, but it's all I ever think about. There would be constant war."

"Right again, you are. Every time we made an advance against the Chasm, they would invade from a different angle or they would come at it a different way, like the tunnel they once used to your well. It would be a war that never ceased. A ten-thousand-years war." Tilbud grew serious for once. "And among the other reasons, reasons like that fact I truly enjoy my life, that is my biggest concern."

"Our new world becoming our old one."

"Yes. Only somehow worse. Much worse. More violence, demons, hell-spawns, crazed mages, corruption, and everything that would entail. It would thrust the Underworld into a sort of dark age, one that we would likely never recover from. I fear that places like Ember Hollow would be wiped off the map, that those of us who survived the initial onslaught would all move here to the center, to Battersea, where we would be refugees. That, as you have likely seen, would create more issues."

Sylas knew the plight of refugees. It still pained him to remember the way they were tasked with policing them, herding newcomers like cattle, and being very judicious in deciding if they were Aurumites, if they would be allowed into the kingdom, and what to do with them if they were rejected. Those had been difficult conversations, the results of which were likely why Sylas had ended up in the Underworld: for his murky history on the battlefield and behind the scenes as part of a decision-making team.

"It would be disastrous," Tilbud said with finality. "Battersea overrun with people from all the smaller villages. Perhaps some of the other cities would survive, some of the bigger ones like my home of Duskhaven. But we would need protection to do so. And that's another thing I wanted to talk to you about while we wait for Catia, who is taking longer than I thought she would."

"Yes?"

"Protection. It's not yet time to plan contingencies, but it is near that time. I don't want to ask the Celestial Plains for anything, cross my heart, I don't want what I'm about to tell you to even *be* an option. But if it comes down to it, we may need to ask the Celestial Council for protection. Surely, there's something that the Plains could do to protect our cities and villages if they close the Hexveil. I'm only telling you this so it is out there, Sylas, so it has been said so it can then be adequately processed. I absolutely do *not* want it to come to that."

"Nor do I."

"This would be something we could try, however, if our impending trip doesn't work. Just something to think about. I mean it when I say I do not want it to come to that. I'm not a darkly optimistic manaseer. I know what is to come, and I want to stand my ground alongside the people I care for." Tilbud changed his demeanor once he saw Catia, who stepped out onto the steps, her cheeks a bit red as if she'd been running around.

"Sorry. That took longer than I thought," she said. "The portal we have here has been temporarily moved to a subbasement. You'd think someone would have told me. But all is well, or well enough. Mira should be in Ember Hollow by now, and we still have time to get to the Celestial Summoning Grounds."

"Which are . . ." Sylas asked her.

"Just outside the city. I thought a nice, brisk walk would help all of us clear our minds."

"In that case," Tilbud said as he curtsied toward the woman, "lead the way."

CHAPTER THIRTEEN

INVOKE

As often happened in the Underworld, Sylas didn't know what to expect. From Battersea they headed into the mountains, where Sylas found himself wishing that Mira was there. Or Quinlan, or Raelis, or Kael. Someone else who he could share this experience with. Not that he minded Tilbud or Catia. They moved ahead of him, the two on-again, off-again lovebirds taking a lane that was lined with buildings that looked like churches.

"What is this place exactly?" Sylas asked. Every time he visited Battersea there was something new.

"Ah, the buildings." Catia motioned to the structures made of old gray stone. They looked ancient, many covered in withered vines. "Old ritual centers. The relationship between the Underworld and the Celestial Plains often changes, and has done so for a long time. Impossibly long for us to really consider. Which is why we never encounter people who have been here for more than several hundred years."

"I wondered about that."

"Eventually, they get sorted, up there or to the Chasm," Catia told Sylas ominously.

"So being here isn't a perpetual thing."

"Not quite," Catia explained. "I suppose in certain ways it is like our world. When you are there, it feels like you will be there forever. But then it ends."

"And you come here," Tilbud added, "or, if you're lucky, you go there." He squinted up at the Celestial Plains, which shone gold above, luminous. "Or so we are told."

The three started up a hill, one that exited onto what resembled a crater, the giant indentation not visible from the city below. It was here that they found a group of what Sylas assumed were lumengineers, considering they wore the same capes as Catia, black with gold stitching and a triangular emblem across their backs.

As soon as Sylas approached, a man with a long gray beard split at the end like a snake's tongue waved his hand. Initially, Sylas thought that the man was greeting them. But then the prompt came:

[Transfer 15000 fixed Mana Lumens to The Distinguished Society of Lumengineers and Etheric Constructs Celestial Envoy? Y/N?]

It pained him to do so, he even grumbled under his breath for a moment, but Sylas went ahead and gave the affirmation. "Sure."

"Ah, spending that kind of money never feels good," Tilbud said as he patted down a bit of sweat with a lime-green handkerchief. "Or at least, it doesn't feel good at the time. But later, once you have had the experience or purchased the home or whatever you decided to spend the numerical equivalent of your life's worth on, you do feel better. Or at least the damage is done. Or at least you're considered a functioning member of society, which does come with its advantages. Well, are you going to introduce us, Catia?" Tilbud asked the lumengineer as he nudged her.

She hesitated as the man with the beard approached.

"Catia," the man said in a deep, gruff voice. "I see you have decided to bring a brewer and an archlumen."

"Not any archlumen, my good man," Tilbud said as he extended a hand to the lumengineer.

The bearded lumengineer eyed him suspiciously.

"Really," Tilbud said, "must I mention I am very good friends with Lumengineer Sir Scott Reid, or that I graduated from the—"

"Sir Scott Reid? Is he the one who approved this?" the man asked Catia.

"Actually, yes. He mentioned there was an envoy, and we happened to have an acquaintance, Sylas, here, who was interested in visiting the Plains. Archlumen Octavian Tilbud," Catia said, gesturing to Tilbud, "has also expressed interest. I have yet to go to the Plains, so I thought now would be as good of a time as any."

"Did you?"

"Yes," Catia said, her voice thinning. "As is my right."

Tilbud shrugged off the bearded lumengineer's skepticism as he tipped his hat at the man. "Archlumen Octavian Tilbud, A-Rank Sovereign of Arcane Mysteries and Paramount Luminary of the School of Echelons and Enchantments, not at your service, nor at your disposal, not exactly ecstatic for the welcoming you have provided, but I will gladly answer any other questions you may have regarding my status, powers, or overall physiognomy."

Sylas stepped up, but didn't extend his hand or anything to the overbearing lumengineer. "We paid. So unless there is something else, we will join the others."

"Thank you, Sir Gregor," Catia told the lumengineer as they moved on.

It certainly wasn't the best of company. Sylas could tell they were being gawked at by the manaseers and lumengineers in attendance. That was until Tilbud used Quill to spell out the laws regarding an envoy, which eventually worked as people returned to their conversations.

"There, you are," Sir Gregor said to the person who Sylas assumed was the last they were waiting on to join their envoy.

Sylas was initially taken aback upon seeing Nuno, but recovered quickly.

"Ah, look who decided to join us," Tilbud said, a hint of disdain in his voice upon seeing the youthful manaseer.

"I'm surprised to see you," Nuno told them. "Sylas. I'm glad you are here."

Sylas didn't know Nuno's angle, and didn't have a chance to ask once Sir Gregor produced a staff of light. He drove it into the ground and it fired a bolt of mana up to the Celestial Plains like a lightning ball in reverse. The same golden lightning rippled across the bottom of the clouds, where it produced a cylindrical opening that soon formed into a long shaft willed with a fierce wind.

"Brace yourselves," Sir Gregor said as the shaft of wind barreled down upon them, Sylas feeling its force in his knees.

A sudden reversal exploded the power upward, firing all of them high into the sky. This was accompanied by a loud roar, like that of a thousand lions, which quickly dissipated into the silence of a vacuum as the group hovered above the glowing clouds.

They were deposited lightly into a circular courtyard with stonework painted in gold leaf, and Sylas was able to see the semblance of a city beyond. He recognized the structures from his experience with Kael: the domed roofs, the obelisks, the strange nature of it all.

It had to be Galataport.

Like Battersea, Galataport was built along the slopes of hills, yet the hills were made of clouds, and everything shone with a brightness that made it hard to take it all in, to comprehend it could even exist. There were certainly people moving about, but they were too far away for Sylas to make them out individually. He did notice that many of them wore flowing clothing with head coverings.

At least it looked that way from a distance.

Tilbud shifted behind Sylas, so he could stand next to Nuno, his mustache practically twitching. "May I ask why you have decided to come on this convoy?

Or is it an envoy? Eh, I suppose that part doesn't matter. Are you coming to reaffirm your commitment like the rest of the soulless manaseers around us? Or are you still playing for our team?"

Sylas was shocked at how blunt Tilbud was being, especially given how the archlumen usually danced around topics in his own style. Yet true to the Tilbud's nature, he asked these questions in a downright friendly way, his voice low enough that only Nuno and Sylas could hear him.

Unsurprisingly, Nuno never answered.

A couple of gasps from the crowd made it known that the representatives of the Celestial Council had appeared. They wore glittering robes that trailed past their feet, their heads were covered, their skin glowing beneath. Sylas counted six of them, and as they approached, he noticed that all of them were several heads taller than those from the Underworld.

Their leader, a woman in a gold crown, leaned over as if she were examining each of them. "Welcome," she finally said in a grandmotherly tone. "This is quite the envoy. More than usually visit. Yet you have all paid for your trip." She took her hand out of her robes and turned around. Golden Mana Lumens left Sir Gregor's hand and twisted into an orb above her palm, eventually fading away. "Good, now that that is squared away, follow us. And please, do not touch anything." She smiled at them. "I'm merely kidding. A little humor never hurt anyone."

"Actually—" Sylas stepped forward. He all but expected Tilbud or Nuno to stop him, yet they did not.

"Yes?" the crowned Celestial woman asked as she turned again to peer at him. "And you are?"

"Sylas Runewulf. Brewer from Ember Hollow. And a farmer. And I have a market."

"Well aren't you entrepreneurial? You may call me Vaire, Vaire of Izalith. Although my correct title would be High Seraph Vaire. But I don't expect you to remember all that."

"Is Izalith a part of the Celestial Plains?"

A few of the people behind her chuckled, but this didn't bother Sylas. He could barely contain his rage, the way she said *a little humor never hurt anyone.* He knew what they were planning. Sylas was being warned about it every morning, and he decided there in that moment to tell her exactly how he felt.

But then he stopped himself. He almost put his hand over his mouth so he wouldn't say anything. He wasn't Quinlan. There was an order here, and for him to deliver maximum impact, Sylas knew he needed to do this correctly.

A quick glance at Tilbud solidified this in his mind.

"Izalith is a part of the Plains," Vaire said. "You're from Ember Hollow, yes? Izalith is directly above you. I like it that way. Was there another question?"

"Not yet," Sylas said.

"And what do you mean by that?"

"Please," Sir Gregor told the Celestial woman, "let's continue. The brewer is new to this sort of attention. Don't mind him."

Sylas turned to Sir Gregor, locked eyes with him, and held his gaze for a full five seconds.

Yet again, he thought of Quinlan and how he was prone to outbursts. Sylas decided to react differently, as much as it pained him to let the rude lumengineer speak of him in this way. "I'll ask my question later," Sylas told Vaire. "My apologies."

"None needed." The crowned woman floated ahead, her robes grazing against the ground as her retinue fanned out to create parallel lines around her and let the Underworldians to pass through them. The Celestians rejoined at the back, which rubbed Sylas the wrong way as he kept getting the feeling that someone would spring an attack on him.

Vaire of Izalith swept her hands behind her as they entered a great hall, one capped by a domed ceiling covered in relief paintings. They were all golden the paintings exhibiting epic battles between what Sylas assumed were Celestial warriors and incredible monsters. At the core of one piece was a ghastly woman, her arms spread out, holding everything together or perhaps preventing some convergence.

A huge pillar stood in the center of the long room. There was a redheaded man in an elaborate crown seated atop it, his sparkling robes draping all the way to the ground. As they stopped before him, a marble platform pressed out of the floor, which brought the group up to the man, yet he remained a few feet above them so he could look down at the envoy.

"No need for introductions," the man said as a second pillar rose from the ground next to him with a chair on top. Sylas noted that, even though it should have been accompanied by the sound of stone grinding on stone, it was completely silent, which made it a little unsettling.

Vaire floated over to the second chair and took a seat. Once she was settled, the ends of her robes draped to the ground just like those of the man seated next to her. "This is Wigmund, the divine arbiter of Galataport," she said as she gestured to the man with red hair. "He likes to greet all envoys that come to the Celestial Plains."

"I absolutely do not," Wigmund said, yet there was a hint of humor in his voice. "Luckily for us, it is exorbitantly expensive to come here. I do hope you enjoy your tour. Where are you taking them today, high seraph?"

"I thought I would take them to a Celestial Market and the Lumenflow Rooms along the way. Perhaps by one of the Celestial Chambers."

"Is this not one of the Celestial Chambers?" Tilbud asked, which drew gawking stares from some of the Underworldians. "No, it's a legitimate question. This room and the art on the ceiling is depicted in the Book of Celestes. I recognize it."

Sir Gregor, who stood to Tilbud's right, spoke harshly under his breath, "You haven't seen the Book of Celestes."

Tilbud shrugged him off. "My good man, I just so happened to have a copy of it at my home in Duskhaven. It makes for a light reading on a dark day."

"How?"

"Why, I had a version I borrowed from a friend copied, that's how."

"The Crafting Laws should prevent that sort of thing," Sir Gregor said, embarrassment on his face.

"A law that can't be exploited by those with a little creativity is hardly a law," Tilbud said, which brought a surprise laugh from Wigmund, who continued looking down at them from his pillar.

"The archlumen is clever, I'll give him that," Wigmund finally said. "And it is wonderful art, is it not?" He slowly glanced up to the domed ceiling. "Why do you think my chair is so high up? It is a reminder of the power and prestige of my office, yes, but it is also so I can view *The Great Calamity*, as it is known. And to answer your question, yes, this is one of many Celestial Council rooms. It is my favorite, if we're being honest, but that is because I took part in commissioning it. A lot of Mana Lumens went into the creation of this place. Anyway, it was nice to meet all of you. May you continue on your tour and may you do so with the utmost joy. Who knows, one day, you may sit here beside me overseeing Celestial tasks."

"What's your title again?" Sylas asked.

"Excuse me?" Wigmund peered at him.

"She said it earlier, but I was distracted by the room. Actually, with all due respect, what are both of your titles?" he asked both Wigmund and Vaire. "If you're seated here, you must be on the Council."

"We are on the Council, yes," Wigmund said, a twinkle in his eye. "I am the divine arbiter and Vaire is a high seraph. This is indeed one of many Celestial Chambers, which are noted for their domed roofs, and for the fact they are meeting grounds for the Council. You will see another as you head to the market—"

"I think this is as good of a place as any," Sylas told Tilbud. "I don't care about their market, and it is one of the chambers used by the Council."

"Excuse me," Wigmund said, offended that Sylas cut him off.

"Agreed. Catia," Tilbud said with a nod. "Let's do it."

"Ahem. My lords, my ladyships, we hereby invoke Article 6196A of the Crafting Laws," Catia said in a shaky voice, which brought gasps from the lumengineers around her. The manaseers didn't seem to know exactly what she was referring to, but they took it from the way the lumengineers had started to murmur that something was afoot.

"Article 6196A," Wigmund said. "Not familiar with that one." He winked at the horror that spread across Catia's face. "I'm joking, of course, I'm familiar with the article that allows the Underworld to challenge a decision made by the Celestial Plains. I'm the one that helped write it. It is smart of you to invoke it here with witnesses. There are those on the Council that may ignore something like this."

"This is hardly the place," Vaire started to say before Wigmund cut her off.

"Really, high seraph, there is no better place. You and I both know that. The law was designed to be very hard to invoke—that was not my design, mind you—and just about the only way to do it would be in an envoy because the Celestial Chambers in the Underworld were abandoned ages ago as a result of this law. But there's one little problem."

"Yes?" Tilbud asked, his bushy eyebrows the most alert Sylas had ever seen them.

"There has been a change to Article 6196A. An unfortunate one, really." Wigmund sighed. Sylas couldn't tell if it was genuine or not. "I suppose there is a lesson here about enacting a law and making it hard for people to actually use, especially when you provide said people with an older version of a law that has yet to be contested." The divine arbiter waved his hand and words took shape:

<u>*Updated Article 6196A of the Crafting Laws*</u>

Pursuant to the Celestial provisions set forth in Article 6196A of the Crafting Laws, representatives of the Underworld are hereby granted the authority to challenge a Celestial Decision.

This specific article, colloquially referred to as the "Challenge Provision," stipulates that such a challenge is permissible exclusively within the confines of the Celestial Plains themselves, in a Celestial Chamber, and not within the confines of the Underworld, the Chasm, Celestial Campaign Cities, or any pocket realm, such as an intermediary ground used by manaseers.

The execution of this article is subject to strict adherence to procedural mandates, as outlined within the broader framework of the Crafting Laws, and may only be initiated under conditions that ensure the equitable consideration of all involved parties.

The execution of this article may only be invoked by a manaseer.

"When was that last part added?" Catia asked. "The part about the manaseer?"

"Not so long ago," Wigmund told her. "It's not my favorite clause, if we're being honest, it's a little deceptive. As any lumengineer worth their weight in Mana Lumens may know, the articles in the Crafting Laws, and any other laws passed by the Celestial Council, change frequently. By the same rules set out when we enacted these laws, we only send down updates when we deem necessary."

"And you didn't think changing a clause in the article that deals with who may invoke it was necessary?" Tilbud asked with disgust. "Sorry if I sound a little incensed, your most arbiterest, but really, that is predatory. It eliminates the need to have the Crafting Laws, or whatever rules you plan to use to govern us. If you can simply change them on a whim and not tell us, nor give us an option, why have the laws to begin with?"

Wigmund grimaced. "These are all good points, all points that I raised as divine arbiter. But the Council voted. And they had their debates before they did that. So while you can invoke Article 6196A, you would need a manaseer to do so."

"Manaseers who are already working with the Plains," grumbled Sylas, the brewer so upset that he was oblivious to the fact that Nuno had stepped forward.

"In that case, I invoke Article 6196A," Nuno said, his focus remaining on the two Celestial leaders seated before them.

"You what?" Sir Gregor's face flashed red. "You aren't serious."

"I am serious," Nuno told the lumengineer. "As per the regulations of Article 6196A of the Crafting Laws, I, Nuno Landling, manaseer, call for the execution of the article."

Wigmund grinned, even as Vaire buried her head in her hand. "Yes," he told Nuno, "good. You may invoke the article and we look forward to hearing your argument." The space around the divine arbiter began to sparkle with golden bits of mana. "The rest of the Council will be here shortly. I'm sure they will be excited."

———

More pillared seats rose from the marble floor below. They appeared one at a time until they were able to form a full circle around Sylas and the rest of the envoy. Numerous Celestial Council members blurred into existence, the group running the gamut from all the young, annoyed to curious as to why they had been summoned. There were even a pair of children on the Council, who wore the same flowing golden robes as the others, yet cast in miniature sizes.

Wigmund spoke, "Wonderful, everyone is here. If you are wondering why you have been summoned, well, that would be because Nuno Landling, manaseer of the highest of order, I've been assured, has invoked Article 6196A of the Crafting Laws."

"Why would he do that?" the male child seated to Sylas's immediate left asked. He had a hooked nose and he wore a golden crown encrusted with black jewels.

"I do not know why, Nylus. He has yet to tell us, nor has the appointed representative."

"I've got this," Sylas told Nuno as he placed a hand on his shoulder. "Let me explain it to them. Give me a shot at doing it."

The manaseer stepped aside without a word, indicating that he fully trusted Sylas.

"Ah, yes, you," Wigmund said from his perch. "The brewer. Go on."

"I, Sylas Runewulf, brewer, farmer, and landlord from Ember Hollow, will address the Council."

Nylus scoffed. "A brewer is speaking for them? Am I imagining this? You called me away from a wine tasting for this?"

Tilbud squeezed up next to Sylas. "I'm here for support," he whispered to him quickly. "But I say, bloody give it to them. We have made it this far, best not tiptoe around the issue any longer."

Sylas steadied his breath and let the intimidation he felt roll away. This was his chance.

He had, perhaps stupidly, spent an enormous sum to come here. Not only was he doing this for himself, for the things that he was trying to accomplish in the afterlife, he was doing this for everyone around him. And not for the Council, not those who sat on seats much higher than he. The common man, the Underworldian who didn't deserve to be pushed around in such a way by a seemingly unknown entity.

Sylas looked from Vaire, the high seraph, to Nylus. The youth's gold and black crown had slunk forward due to the way he scowled at Sylas. Finally, Sylas returned his gaze to Wigmund, the divine arbiter, and spoke.

"It has come to my attention, most notably through the alarming message that I get every morning—and have since I appeared in the Underworld—that an invasion is imminent," he began. "Upon further research, it is now clear to us that this invasion will come from the Chasm, yet the invasion itself will be orchestrated by the Celestial Plains for numerous reasons. The reason we know of thus far is that there are those on this Council who disagree with the very existence of the Underworld due to the Mana Lumens it uses. I also have reason to believe that the Celestial Beasts of your realm have become quite powerful, and some may feel that the mana would be better used here."

Sylas paused, expecting someone to take issue with what he was saying. When no one spoke and only a few Underworldians murmured around him, he continued: "We have asked Nuno, manaseer, to invoke the article of the

Crafting Laws that allows the Underworld to register concern and create a deeper discussion about what it is you plan to do. I'm going to stop talking this way now and be as honest with you as I can. The Underworld means everything to me. It means everything to the people that I know. It has given me a second chance at life, and it is a place that isn't built around war, unlike my world was.

"It is true that people from the Underworld can eventually take a place in the Celestial Plains. It is also true that some remain there, and others eventually move on to the Chasm. Yet the importance of my home—from the ale I serve at my pub to the corn I grow at my farm and the new market set to open in Ember Hollow—*cannot* be understated. All of you have people there. Surely, this is the case. At some point, all of you were part of our former world, all of you know what it means to struggle. Why bring calamity to us, then?

"Unleashing the Chasm will destroy people's lives in the Underworld. It will uproot so many things that people have worked for. You will destroy future chances for people to atone for their sins. It will create monsters of many of us, perhaps myself included." Sylas tapped his hand against his chest. "Because none of you know me. None of you know what I'm capable of. But I can tell you right now, I will leave a wall of bodies in my wake if it means protecting the things that I have worked for here in the afterlife. I don't mean this as a threat. But there are more like me in the Underworld, those who know and understand what is at stake, and those who may fall to dark paths if the Hexveil comes down.

"You may sit up here and wonder, 'What does it have to do with me? I am in the Celestial Plains. Heaven is my playground.' But I will remind each and every one of you that someone you care for lives in the Underworld, that this third place, this region between heaven and hell, this Underworld you have devised, is an integral part of the balance between our three realms. If this is about Mana Lumens, perhaps there are other ways to redistribute power. If it is about Celestial Beasts, maybe you would do well to call upon some of the best demon hunters from the Underworld to see to your pest problems. If it is about something else, well, then I look at this Council and I say to myself, 'All of you got here for some reason, in some way, and surely, working together, you can find a better solution than total annihilation.' So I am asking this: I'm asking you to reconsider."

Sylas stepped back and lowered his head.

"Well said," Wigmund told Sylas, enthusiasm in his voice. "Much better than I expected. Vaire?"

"It was a speech, yes, perhaps a bit long, not entirely unwarranted, but tedious," Nylus sneered.

"Your feelings are noted," Wigmund told the youth. "At this point, it becomes our duty to consider what they have asked of us. We can do that by breaking into subcommittees and discussing various parts, or we can simply have a vote right now. All in favor of subcommittees?"

There were a few *ayes*, but not many.

"I see," Wigmund said. "And those in favor of a simple vote?"

A loud *aye* filled the chamber as a majority of the Celestial Council decided to cast their vote now.

"I suppose, then, that we have debated this topic enough, but I do think that subcommittees are an important way to better understand the more nuanced subjects of this decision, ones that our dear brewer here may not fully understand." Wigmund rubbed his throat and looked up at the painting above. "I must say, I do like the suggestion of bringing some of the stronger demon hunters to deal with our Celestial Beasts. That is not a solution I have not considered. They would need to be outfitted correctly, but—"

"Our warriors are just as strong as theirs," Nylus said.

"Perhaps. But some of ours haven't been at war for hundreds, if not thousands of years, aside from those who visit Celestial Campaign Cities, and they have their own agendas. Look at the man standing before you. Not one hundred days ago he was engaged in fights that most of us could hardly fathom. A person like him would do well in our Celestial skirmishes, perhaps even better than one of ours, depending on how he is outfitted. But I digress," Wigmund said, "if it is a vote that this Council wants, then it is a vote we shall have. And it is a simple one. Well, the first vote is a simple one. Depending on how this question does, the follow-up may be a little more complicated. Do we open the Chasm in thirty-three days' time, or do we not? It's really as simple as that. All in favor, say 'aye.'"

The room filled at once with their affirmations. *Aye, aye, aye.*

Sylas's heart sank.

It was clear what they felt, even if a few voted against the proposal, the overwhelming majority were *nays*.

"In that case, the motion has failed," Wigmund told Sylas and those gathered. "My apologies. And since this went a bit longer than it normally does, your tour of the Celestial Plains will have to be cut short. Sadly. None of this is fair, I'm aware of that, but the afterlife rarely is, at least at your level. Thank you for coming," he said once some of the Council members faded away. "And Sylas, please stay here so I may speak to you privately." The divine arbiter turned to the high seraph. "Vaire, will you see the rest back to the portal that will return them to the Underworld? I will deal with the brewer."

CHAPTER FOURTEEN

A CELESTIAL DISPATCH

Once everyone was gone, Wigmund, the divine arbiter, met Sylas on the ground level, his robes now twisted around his body and bunched in his arms. "I'm sorry that your appeal didn't work the way you would have liked," he said, his gaze revealing a fleeting moment of understanding. "But surely, you knew that would be the case, did you not?"

Sylas swallowed a flash of disappointment and anger. Rather than answer, he crossed his arms over his chest. "Is that why you asked me to stay back so you could say?"

"No, not exactly. I asked you to stay behind for a different reason. Come. this might interest you." Wigmund turned, and with his next step the two were standing in an enormous archive with floor-to-ceiling bookshelves filled with countless manuscripts bound in brittle leather. The divine arbiter took a seat on a chair and moved the books on the armrests aside. He gestured for Sylas to grab a stool and join him. "I'm sorry I don't have better seating here."

"Is this something I need to sit for?"

"Not necessarily. You can stand if you would like. I can tell you're upset."

"Upset doesn't begin to describe—"

Wigmund waved his protest away. "And I can tell that you aren't going to go down without a fight. You likely spent almost everything you had to come here and deliver that statement, one that you hadn't previously written."

"You are right."

"You spent it all to deliver a statement meant to save your world, yet one that you put together on the spot. Not that there is anything wrong with that. It just shows me that you're the type to adjust to things as they happen, a man who can pivot quickly. And why? Why would you be like that? Is it because of your past?" Something flashed across his eyes and Wigmund's bushy red eyebrows responded as they lifted slightly. "I see. I understand now."

"You can see everything?"

"A gift and a curse. It does make one empathetic, much more so than your average Celestian. I knew taking on the role of divine arbiter so many years ago would come with its ups and downs. There is a lot that we deal with here, and it saddens me that those recently elected to the Council are so determined to demolish the work our forefathers put into this realm when they developed the Underworld. Namely, Nylus, whom you are lucky to *not* have the pleasure of knowing. But you don't care about local politics. What I'm trying to tell you is I personally believe the Underworld has its purpose, that it shouldn't be erased."

Sylas could only shake his head at the statement. "Then you should have done something."

"It is simply my job to hold the vote and cast my opinion. There isn't much else I can do from that point forward. I do wish they had broken into subcommittees. Alas, I cannot make them do so. But that is not why I brought you here. I'm generally not one to apologize. I brought you here because of something you said."

"What's that?"

"You mentioned our problem with Celestial Beasts. How did you come to know about that, hmmm?"

"Recently, a couple of old friends and I retrieved a manaseer-in-training. I learned about it then."

"And were you successful in retrieving your friend?"

"I was. Can't you see everything?"

"There is a lag when it comes to the current past," Wigmund admitted. "This is also a reason for bringing you here, because of some of the things you did before you passed. Something you said piqued my interest. We do have a problem as it stands, and perhaps a solution would be people like you."

"People like me?"

"Former warriors. Fresh ones. Ours have grown tired. They are capable, as you can imagine, capable beyond our wildest dreams with the mana they wield. But this is also a problem for them. Not only do they not have the same drive that someone like you would have, they react to the dormant mana differently. Years of living in splendor can do that," Wigmund said with distaste. "It is something that I despise about my countrymen. Between you and me, of course."

"Are you recruiting me?"

"In a way, I am. I'm offering you an opportunity, Sylas Runewulf, brewer of Ember Hollow. So many of our best warriors are wasted on campaigns in the Chasm that they forget we have problems here at home. I would like to propose a test, to see how strong you and your companions would be against one of our unique subsets of monsters."

"And what would be in it for me?"

"What do you want?" Wigmund grinned. "Think very carefully before you answer that."

"Do you mind if I sit?"

"By all means."

Sylas took a seat before Wigmund. He stared at the ground for a moment as he decided if it was worth it to reveal Plan B, the letter campaign they had devised. In the end, he decided to seek more information on the divine arbiter's intentions before doing so.

"Do you truly agree that there needs to be an Underworld?"

"Why, of course I do. I am one of the authors of the Crafting Laws, which we used to circumvent closing the Underworld well before your time. The Chasm is a terrible place. Dark Mana Lumens are something that we have studied for ages, yet cannot wield. Only one of ours was able to, and she was the one who created the seed that spawned the Underworld."

"I've never heard that before. What happened to her?"

"The combination of Mana Lumens and Dark Mana Lumens completely destroyed Fayeth the Raised. But I can tell you what she did was remarkable. And I don't think that it should go, no. I think the Underworld is integral to the sanctity of everything we do. I think that it would do well to last into eternity. So I ask you again, what is it that you would like?"

"What is it that you are able to provide?"

"Well, for one, I could provide you and people you care for, let's say up to seven or eight, instant approval for citizenship in the Celestial Plains. This would extend to any pets and spirits you may have. I know how people love their pets and spirits; I'm not a monster, you know. So that is one thing I could provide. A fairly good offer, if you ask me."

Sylas bit his lip as he considered what Wigmund had just said. The man had been so casual about it, that Sylas had the impression it was an offer on the lower end of the spectrum.

"It is quite the offer," Wigmund said when he didn't respond. "People spend the equivalent of several lifetimes to come here. I would offer you additional citizenships here, with the agreement that you would start, and maintain, a new school of Celestial Beast hunters. As I have alluded, we don't have as many good warriors as there may be in the Underworld. Our better ones are in the Chasm. I think there's an opportunity here for a program such as this, and I do have the power, based on a few favors owed to me, to start one."

"And you can't use that power to help the Underworld?"

"Different powers work differently. This is merely a power of *finance*. I have a fund that I haven't touched in a millennia or three. It has enough Mana Lumens to buy the passage of you and your friends, which, if you didn't know, is a substantial sum."

"How substantial are we talking here?" Sylas asked.

"Whatever the largest number you can think of, double that."

"And the other Council members can't be paid off with it?"

"Heavens, no." He grinned at his own cleverness. "They're already beyond wealthy. How do you think they got their positions?"

"Even the kid?"

"Ah, like your world, or perhaps your manaseer if that hits a bit closer to home, age isn't really the consideration here. We have loads of children. Most children go to heaven, you know. Even the naughty-ish ones."

"More Mana Lumens than I can imagine, right?"

"Correct."

Sylas ran his hand over his chin. "How long do I have to decide or to make a counteroffer?"

"You are bold to take as long as you have," Wigmund told him with a chuckle. "But it is something I can tell I will appreciate about you. How about this? Return to the Underworld and I will visit you in Ember Hollow tomorrow. At your pub, correct?"

"That's right. The Old Lamplighter."

"Good. A fitting name for a pub. And one more thing before I send you back."

"Yes?"

"I will, of course, be in disguise. But you will know it's me. In that case, bye for now." Wigmund snapped his fingers and Sylas vanished before he was able to respond.

———

Sylas didn't have much to say at the pub that night. Even as Tilbud and Catia prodded him to tell them why Wigmund had held Sylas back, he remained silent. He wanted to speak to everyone at once, so he asked that several key people in his journey through the Underworld thus far stay behind after the pub closed. This included his three soldier friends, Raelis, Kael, and Quinlan; Mira, Nelly, and Karn; Tilbud and Catia; and, of course, Azor and Sylas's pets, except Gertrude, who was at the market. The only one missing was Nuno, who had disappeared after his return to Battersea.

Before speaking to them, Sylas first brewed the casks needed, including the eight additional casks he would need for the market's opening the following day. The basement of The Old Lamplighter was cluttered with the additional casks and the meat that Azor planned to grill up the following day, but Sylas knew this was temporary, and it didn't really bother him as he thought about the conversation that continued to weigh on his mind.

"That should do it," Sylas said as he rubbed his hands together. "Are you coming?" he asked the fire spirit, who was preparing the meats.

"Sure," she said.

Together, they headed up to find everyone seated at the back of the pub. Quinlan was still nursing a half-empty pint. Patches was on the table, lying on his side, tail lightly lashing against the wood. Cornbread was cuddled in Nelly's lap.

"There he is," Raelis said. "I was starting to get worried that you had fallen asleep down there. We need to get back to the farm, mate, not trying to rush you or anything." He yawned. "Maybe I'm a bit tired as well."

"Let him speak," Tilbud said, a measure of severity to his voice.

Sylas took a seat at the front of the table. He leaned forward on his elbows. "So, as you all know, Wigmund, the divine arbiter of the Celestial Council—"

Quinlan snorted at the title. "That's a name, yeah? Sorry, Sylas. Continue."

"Well, I should back up a bit," he said as he looked over to Nelly and Karn. "I had a chance to go to the Celestial Plains as part of an envoy. We invoked an article of the Crafting Laws that allows us to protest and were told that a manaseer had to be the one to invoke it. Luckily, Nuno was there to do that. But I never got his reasoning or his intentions. Anyway. That failed. The Council voted and it failed. Then Wigmund kept me behind, and that's what I want to discuss with you all now."

"Well, go on, then," Quinlan said as he pressed back and folded his arms over his chest. "Sorry, mate, I just get the feeling that this isn't going to be one of those good discussions, if you know what I mean."

"It's a complicated one but let me get to the end of it and I'll tell you what I think. Wigmund made me an offer. He asked that I move to the Celestial Plains with seven or eight people who mean something to me—which would be you all—and that in exchange, I hunt Celestial Beasts."

Tilbud's little green hat nearly blew off his head. "He offered you citizenship? You and several others?"

"He did."

"And what did you tell him?" Quinlan asked carefully.

"I told him I would think about it. There's more." Sylas showed them his hands. "Before you comment again, there's more. I asked how Wigmund would do that, and he said he had Mana Lumens in, what I'm going to assume, are the millions. Or more. He claims to have a fund of them that he hasn't used for a long time. I don't know how long, but he didn't blink an eye at the cost, which I'm assuming is exorbitant."

"It is," Catia said. "You can buy citizenship to the Celestial Plains, but it takes, as you mentioned, millions of Mana Lumens to do so. The other way would be through good deeds, but there's a whole process with that, which can take the equivalent of several lifetimes to get the paperwork completed. It is something lumengineers help with."

"I figured," Sylas said. "And he made this offer almost as an afterthought. It didn't seem to mean much to him is what I'm saying."

"I find it incredibly discerning that the Celestial Plains may be having Mana Lumen shortages, hence the need to close our realm," Tilbud said, "yet they have access to incredible funds like this."

"They're the ones who make the Mana Lumens," Catia told him. "They extract and circulate them."

Sylas continued after their chatter died down: "Then I asked him if he could pay off the other Council members. I figured it was worth a try, yeah? I mean, if it is power they want and he has a huge amount simply stored up and ready to be used at his disposal, surely he could give some of his MLus to the others. But they're rich as well."

Quinlan grunted: "This world is starting to look more like ours by the minute."

"Aye," Kael said next to him.

"So he's offered you—and by you, us—a chance to just wash our hands of all of this," Raelis said. "All we have to do is become his little pet hunters, and then the Underworld can fall, and it won't affect us. Playing this out, we could simply become like them, just like these Council members you met. We could have a vast amount of MLus, yet not enough to really help anyone who actually needs it. We could sit on our lofty perches and watch the Underworld descend into chaos as the Hexveil comes down." Bitterness filled his voice. "Wouldn't that be fun? Watching the place turn to hell and reaping the benefits?"

"What did you say after that?" Nelly asked Sylas. "Was that the end of the conversation?"

"I'm curious too," Azor said, the tips of her flames now purple.

Mira, who sat next to Sylas, placed her hand on top of his. He looked from the apothecary, the first person he'd met in the Underworld, to the others seated before him. "I told him I'd think about it, like I said. But I already have the solution in my head. Or, at least, a solution. And I wanted to run that by you all."

"Do you, now?" Tilbud asked.

"Actually, I wanted to check it with you and Catia because I'm not sure how this could work. It might not even be possible. But it was the first thing that came to mind when Wigmund said he had access to an untold amount of MLus. I should say that he's receptive, as well. He isn't like the others. He thinks the Underworld has a place."

"Yet he can't do anything?" Quinlan asked. "That seems a bit suspicious if you ask me."

"I believe him, and I believe he may have given us a solution to enact our plan. What did you say the spells were called, the ones that could spread the information of the appeal to the Celestials?" Sylas asked Catia and Tilbud.

Catia responded first: "Clairvoice and Lorewave."

"And to send messages would cost us more MLus than we could easily come up with on our own, right?"

"That's right," Tilbud told Sylas, "well, at least without a work-around. Which is something I've been considering but haven't quite stumbled upon yet. What are you thinking? Come out with it, then."

"What if instead of citizenship to the Celestial Plains, we ask for those MLus to be used to spread the message around the Underworld and to fund sending the messages to loved ones in the Celestial Plains? Is that even something that would be possible? Assuming Wigmund would agree, and I believe he might. He might even help."

Tilbud stood. He began pacing back and forth, rubbing his chin with a hand. "Give me a moment," he told Quinlan as the man started to suggest something. "Catia?"

"Yes?"

"Please join me outside."

"Certainly."

The two stepped out back and Sylas returned his focus to his other companions. Mira spoke: "You would give up an opportunity to be in the Celestial Plains on the off chance that our plan could work? Are you crazy?"

Sylas smirked at her. "Maybe?"

"It's the boldest thing I can think of anyone ever doing," Karn said as Nelly nodded alongside him. "And if it were up to me, mate, I don't know if I could make the same choice. I really don't."

"If they say it will work, or at least they think it will work, it could be a brilliant solution," Raelis said. Near him, Kael grunted in agreement as Raelis continued: "But Karn is right. It is quite the risk. I'm not saying we could all be living in heaven and fattening up like a bunch of cherubs, but that would probably be how it went."

"That, and hunting Celestial Beasts," Quinlan said.

"Which would only keep us fit," Raelis told him. "You said Wigmund was receptive. How receptive are we talking here? Do you think you could have negotiated for higher?"

"I do. He didn't seem to care about the MLus."

"Bloody rich is what he is," Quinlan said.

"There's not a problem with that if we can use it to our advantage," said Raelis. "Sylas, I don't know what is going to come of this, but—"

"A little premature to congratulate him on a deal well bargained, yeah?" Quinlan said. "And I'm not trying to be salty here. I just have my doubts about this sudden angle, not that, if I'm being honest, our previous solution didn't have a few holes in it."

Tilbud and Catia entered before Quinlan could ramble on any further. "We think there's a chance," the archlumen said excitedly. "But only if you're sure. Only if it's a risk you are willing to take, Sylas."

"It's a big ask," Catia said. "You have a free ticket to the Celestial Plains more or less, and if you use it in this way, we may all be stuck here forever. And by forever, I mean until it all becomes the Chasm. I can't say how this will go, but I can tell you that Tilbud and I—"

"Certainly me," Tilbud said, finger in the air. "You know I love a good exploit."

"Will do what we can with our shared knowledge to make it work. It's really up to you, Sylas," Catia told him. "Perhaps you should think on it overnight."

————

[You have 32 days until the invasion.]
[A loan payment of 45 has been deducted from your total Mana Lumens. Your total loan balance is 22068 Mana Lumens.]

Sylas briefly scanned his MLus:

Name: Sylas Runewulf
MLus: 2707/2707
Class: Brewer
Secondary Class: Farmer
Tertiary Class: Landlord

"Ugh." He groaned as he scratched the back of Patches's head. "If you didn't know, it costs quite a bit to go to heaven."

Patches mewed in a sweet way. The pub cat rolled onto his side and eventually showed Sylas his belly. As Sylas scratched his stomach, Azor burst into the room, followed by Cornbread.

"Happy Soulsday!" She rushed around, flames flickering off her and leaving firework-like sparks around the space, enough that Patches yowled, Cornbread barked, and Patches ran out the room. "Too much?"

"Nah," Sylas said with a laugh. "It's Soulsday. Might as well start it with a bang. Or better, get up with a bang. How's the meat situation?"

"The meat situation? Right, the grills! Yes, I was able to rent some at the Finmarket. Super cheap. And they were delivered an hour ago with charcoal. I told them not to worry about the fire starter," she said as horns sprouted out of her head. "Actually, I should try something different." Azor grew a pair of antlers instead. "Not the same, right?"

"Not really."

"Your friends are here, by the way." She dropped to the ground in a fiery puddle. "They eat so much. But at least Quinlan is helping with the meats."

"And Kael and Raelis will run The Petticoat Lamplighter," Sylas said as the final name for the pub's offshoot came to him.

"Ooo, I like the sound of that."

"I thought of it just now. The Petticoat Lamplighter. Nice. What do you think, Cornbread?"

Rather than answer with a bark, the dog hopped onto the bed and buried herself under the blanket. She exploded toward the top, near Sylas's face, and licked his nose a few times before he gently nudged her aside.

Azor burst out laughing. "Safe to say she likes that one too."

"I guess I should see how everything is going. Has Mira been by?" Sylas asked as he got out of the bed.

"She has not. But I've been pretty busy dealing with your friends— Did I tell you Tilbud is here too? And Catia?"

"I assumed they would be."

"I didn't. When I was watching them set up the grills this morning, I spoke to Nelly. She said that the two were up late."

"Yeah?"

"That's what she said. I didn't ask what they were doing, but they both look a little dazed."

"I'll keep that in mind," Sylas said as he headed downstairs. He found the back door open and his friends outside, while Tilbud and Catia sat around the bar, Catia dressed in one of Tilbud's colorful overcoats.

"Really?" Sylas asked the two.

"It's not what it looks like," Catia said. "Well, it might be a little of what it looks like. We went back to Battersea last night to check on something and got back very late."

"Too late," Tilbud said. "Then . . ."

"Then," Catia said, ending any explanation of what may have happened next.

"What was going on in Battersea?"

"A dressing down, that's what," Catia told him as she forked through some cold scrambled eggs. "From Sir Gregor."

"I can warm those for you!" Azor offered the lumengineer.

"No, it's fine. Really," Catia said as Azor approached. "You've done enough."

"I'm not even done yet. Sylas needs a breakfast too—"

"Don't worry about me. I can whip something up," Sylas told the fire spirit. "I have to get to the market anyway. Can't let Mira have all the fun."

"Only if you're certain."

"I'm certain."

With a sigh of relief, Azor dashed out the door, where she immediately started with the grills. Sylas watched for a moment as she gave instructions to Quinlan, who did what he could while Raelis and Kael snickered at the way she was ordering him around.

"So, back to Battersea," Sylas told Catia and Tilbud. "Was it bad?"

"It wasn't good," Tilbud said. "Let's just say poor Catia here has been demoted. But in a way, she's not poor, because she learned a valuable lesson that no matter the life or afterlife, there will always be someone terrible above you that is too petty for words and deserves, if I may, to be boiled in a cauldron for the rest of eternity."

"Don't say that about Sir Gregor," Catia told Tilbud with a playful fist on his shoulder. "And I didn't learn a valuable lesson. I already knew that to be the case."

"Well, then I learned one. I always thought there could one day be equanimity here in the Underworld and it turns out that I was wrong, dead wrong. I won't say what I'm thinking about your fellow lumengineers, but know I'm thinking it."

"I know."

"And know that we will have the last laugh once we enact our plan. I'm just upset they called you to The Distinguished Society of Lumengineers and Etheric Constructs to be stripped of your title. At night. After you were prepared to go to bed—with me, mind you—"

She gasped. "Tilbud!"

"It's just a detail I thought worth adding to illustrate how late it was when they called you there to unceremoniously—well, I suppose there was a bit of a ceremony—strip you of your title."

"It's fine. The Groundwing Archives isn't a bad place to be."

"I've been there before. It's a dusty collection of information that might be . . ." Tilbud's eyes lit up. "My word, we've been blessed, haven't we?"

"How?" Both Sylas and Catia asked.

"The Groundwing Archives have details, or so I'm told, of past treaties and old spells. It might prove helpful to us as we look to execute our plan."

Catia slowly put her fork down. "Tilbud."

"Yes, love?"

She grabbed him by the back of the head and leaned in to kiss him. "You are brilliant. That's a brilliant idea. I didn't even think of that."

"I didn't either. It makes me wonder if, and I know I'm going out on a limb here, Sir Gregor was perhaps trying to help us."

"That's a stretch," she said. "Anyway." Catia smiled at Sylas. "I know you have to get going. Don't mind us. We will stop by the market later. And once you speak to Wigmund, please let us know."

"Actually," Tilbud said with a wink, "I had an idea about that."

"Yes?" Sylas asked the archlumen, who was now buzzing with excitement at his idea.

"Shrink."

"Your spell, Shrink," Sylas said. "I am familiar with it."

"Today, I believe I will Shrink myself and stay with you so I can be privy to this conversation with Wigmund."

"No," Sylas said.

"No? Why, yes. Yes! It's an incredible idea, if you ask me."

"Is it, though? What if he finds out?" Sylas asked Tilbud.

"He'll certainly find out. I'm going to be right there in your vest pocket. How couldn't he know?"

"That sounds like a terrible idea."

"A terribly *good* idea," Tilbud told Sylas. "I want to make sure you aren't duped. And I have an idea in mind of the number of MLus we would need for our little operation to work. That is, of course, if we don't find something in the Groundwing Archives. But we shouldn't bet on that. Only bet on a sure thing, and that's far from a sure thing. Actually, regarding gambling—"

"Tilbud," Sylas said, cutting him off. "If you're going to tell me shrinking yourself down and stashing yourself somewhere in my clothing"—

"Your vest pocket. Not just anywhere."

"Okay, my vest pocket. If you're going to tell me that's *not* a gamble . . ."

"It does sound like one, doesn't it?" Tilbud asked as he leaned back in his chair. "But it's a good one. A worthwhile one. I'll see Catia off and then I'll join you at the market. You did say that Wigmund could appear at any time, did you not?"

"Correct."

"Then we should be ready, Sylas. This does mean you'll have to put up with me most of the day, but that's fine. Or at least I assume it's fine. I won't interject too much. Or at least I'll try not to. Also, it will take a lot less pints to get me nice and buzzed, so you'll be saving MLus there."

"You're *not* shrinking yourself and drinking," Catia said.

Tilbud laughed. "It was a joke, love. I have no desire to be drunk in a shrunken state. But do keep Cornbread away from me. Patches, I trust. But the dog might eat me if I'm not careful. I suppose that leaves Gertrude as well, who may be less than enthused by my presence. Don't pick her up or anything while I'm in your pocket."

Sylas brought his hand to his face.

"What?" Tilbud asked. "It's a bloody good idea. Admit that."

"It's an idea, I'll admit that. But Wigmund didn't say anything about conversing with him alone, so I suppose if you're there, it could help in case I'm not clear on something. But you shouldn't be small when you speak to him. At least change back to your normal size."

"We'll see how it goes. What about my Charm spell? That could be a way to really—"

"*No*," Sylas and Catia said at the same time.

CHAPTER FIFTEEN

ORANGE TABBY

The Petticoat Lane Market was already bustling by the time Sylas arrived, the merchants mostly set up. Mira moved about with a bit of folded parchment, checking in with everyone and making sure they were ready for the market to open. Something else caught his attention, spoiling Sylas's initial view of the market.

"That can't be," Sylas said as he stood there, hands on his waist, looking at the yellow café that Shamus had announced was for sale a few days earlier.

Now, Ember Hollow's militiamen busied themselves around the café. Duncan and Cody were applying fresh paint while the others did minor repairs. At the core of the activity surrounding the café was Tiberius, who, like his niece, had a folded piece of parchment in his hands.

"Ah, Sylas!" Tiberius said as he waved him over. "Surprise." He beamed a smile up at the roof of the café.

"You bought the café?"

"I did. Me and the boys," he said proudly. But Tiberius couldn't contain himself as he burst out laughing. "You actually believe that?" he asked as Sylas gaped at him. The man's distaste for loans and banks was well known.

"I have no idea what to believe any longer."

"No, it wasn't me who bought it. Heh. wouldn't that be something? It was Duncan and Cody who went in on it together."

Sylas looked at the two militiamen, who were so focused on painting the café's trim that they had not noticed him. "Really? I did not see that coming."

"Why would I lie?" Tiberius asked with a chuckle. "I thought that they were going to double-class as demon hunters, it would have been smart, but they decided otherwise. They are a bit wayward in that way."

"Even with the invasion announcement I made?"

"Indeed. Because men like them, and guys like you and me," Tiberius said, growing serious as he struck his fist against his chest, "are not going to go down without a fight. If we want to run a café in the middle of the apocalypse, or a market in the maelstrom, or, hell, a farm in the afterlife, a pub in the Underworld—you get the picture—then so be it. That's who we are. Heaven will not stand in our way. Heaven be damned. Relatedly, Mira tells me that you are still going with the plan, the dispatch messages."

"We are."

"She didn't tell me much else." Tiberius took a step closer to them. "And it goes without saying, but really, Sylas, I'm here to help. I know we may have had our differences in the past, but I'm like anyone in Ember Hollow. If hell spills over, I will do everything to defend this place for however long it takes."

"Hopefully, it won't come to that. But I wanted to ask you something, now that I have you."

"I'm all ears. One working eye, but all ears," Tiberius joked.

"There may be an opportunity coming up."

"Oh?"

"Actually, let's go over there." He led Tiberius away from the café and the market to a quiet spot. As much as Sylas wanted to check the market and catch up with Mira, he knew it was best to deal with this now.

"Really, Sylas?" Tilbud asked as he popped out of the pocket of Sylas's vest.

Tiberius jumped back and grabbed for a weapon he didn't have, his hand going to where the hilt of his sword would have been. "What the devil? Is that the wizard?"

"Since when have you called me that?" Tilbud asked him. "You know I'm an archlumen."

"The term 'wizard' suits your kookiness better." Tiberius leaned forward and squinted at Tilbud. "Why are you there? What's your angle?"

"Don't worry about that. Continue your conversation."

"It is sort of hard with a tiny and extremely colorful man staring up at me."

"I would turn around," Tilbud said, "but that would put me in an awkward position."

"Tiberius," Sylas said, interrupting the two of them. "We may have an opportunity to do some hunting."

"I'm listening," the lord commander said.

"I will find out more about it today. And believe me, it's not what you're thinking."

"Another bloody Taurigraith isn't loose, is it?"

"Hardly."

"Then what? A Gorgon?"

"No."

"A Blight? Maybe Mana Ghouls? Perhaps a Hellhound or a Harpy? A . . . Nox?"

"Nope," Sylas assured him. "But it will be worth your time to hear us out if you're interested. Hear *me* out. Tilbud might not be part of that conversation."

"But I will try to be," the archlumen said from within Sylas's vest pocket.

"Well, if it's a hunt and there's an opportunity, you know I'm willing and able. If it has anything to do with the Chasm or the invasion, doubly so," Tiberius told Sylas as he puffed his chest out. "Like I said before, I know that we have had our differences. But this is big. And so is the market. Mira did well." He stood at attention. "I probably shouldn't hold you any longer."

"Probably not."

"Mira is the happiest I've ever seen her. So . . ." Tiberius let out a soft, hesitant cough. "I know it is not exactly you who made that possible, but you have played your part, and for that, and mostly for her because I want her to be happy, thank you. Thank you, Sylas. Now get out there and see your new market." As he said this, Raelis and Kael walked by, the two men pulling a cart of casks for the outdoor pub.

"Will do, lord commander," Sylas told Mira's uncle.

————

Mira had spoken to Esta. She had run everything by the merchants Glenn, Luke Phillip, Lorne, and Grant Sontag, a relic dealer who showed up at the last moment and set up in one of the final booths. She'd also talked with Percy and Florence, the apothecaries they had met in the Cloud Forest, who had set up a great little antiques booth.

Mira told them all that she wouldn't collect rent for this first weekend or the next Wraithsday Feast. This was something she had decided since it was a soft opening and she wanted her merchants to get settled in, for word of the market to spread.

As much as Mira wanted to think that by the following weekend she would be able to start collecting rent, she really didn't know what to expect.

She wasn't afraid of what Sylas was planning to do. She knew that the even-keeled Aurumite who had appeared in her life would do everything he could to keep the Underworld safe, yet she didn't know what the results would be. And without knowing that, she wasn't sure how the market would do.

So Mira had decided to treat this weekend as if it were the last. She wanted the opening of the market to be a success, even if she wasn't going to make any Mana Lumens from it.

The people of Ember Hollow knew about Sylas's doomsday message, but not everyone who came to the market would know. And even if the locals knew of the impending invasion, not many spoke about it. It was one of those things that was better left unsaid.

She wondered if Sylas's plan would actually work, if he would be able to get the divine arbiter to agree to giving them an untold number of Mana Lumens.

But instead of focusing on that, instead of worrying about the future, which she knew would only lead to anxiety, which would in turn force her to make up a concoction of muddleberries and loungebark to ease her nerves, Mira made her rounds. Gertrude the goose followed after her, and Mira tried her best to maintain a smile.

It was easy once she saw him. There he was, hands on his hips as he talked to her uncle.

Sylas made eye contact with Mira once, winked, and then turned back to the conversation. As usual, her uncle was enthused about something, but she also thought it had been nice of him to help Duncan and Cody with the café they had purchased.

That had come as quite the shocker as well. Mira had only found out about their purchase earlier that morning when she came to the market to prepare for the vendors and set up her own shop.

"I hope we didn't make a mistake," Cody had said as he scratched the back of his head. He turned to Duncan, his counterpart who was nearly twice the size.

"I always wanted to own a café," Duncan had finally said. "Ever since I was a wee little lad."

"Did you, now?" Mira had laughed. She had never picked up anything really from Duncan, aside from the fact that he was one of those men who kept to himself, was perhaps stupidly loyal, but had a good heart. She also couldn't imagine him as a child.

If the fact they had purchased the café came as a surprise, Duncan's next statement had solidified Mira's shock: "We will repaint the place an even brighter yellow, and we will get yellow aprons. Maybe we can wear little yellow hats, you know, something Tilbud would have."

"While he may have a fashion sense," Mira had told the militiaman carefully, "it is rather eccentric, and it is uniquely his own. I'm sure he would be flattered, and I'm sure he would point you to the best haberdasher in the Underworld— hopefully one that he hasn't already had an affair with—but you should think carefully about that."

"What about the yellow apron?" Cody had asked. "I sort of like that idea."

"Yellow aprons I could see," had been Mira's final words to the two men as she returned her focus to the market.

It was quite the bustling affair. As she stood waiting for Sylas to join her, she watched as Raelis and Kael brought casks to the outdoor pub. Mira wanted to pat herself on the back. She couldn't remember the last time she'd been so proud of herself, and she was unable to hide her smile as Sylas finally approached her, free of her uncle at last.

"You did great," Sylas said, his arms spread wide. She fell into them as she often did, and he gave her a strong hug. "And I'm sorry. I should have been here earlier."

"No, it's fine."

"Really, Mira."

"Sylas, I said it was fine. Everything is going according to plan. How about your pub? I saw your men with the casks."

"The Petticoat Lamplighter should be up and running any moment now. I was planning to head over there to make sure everything is connected properly. And Azor has been grilling all morning, so I suspect the food will hit just around lunchtime. I see you have done a good job with the vendors."

"A lot of that was Esta," Mira said as she led Sylas over to the woman. After a quick conversation with Esta about the herb's proper name—"Athershade leaf," Mira kept saying—they made their rounds together. Sylas was most interested in Grant Sontag's wares. There were just a few items there now, but the relic dealer promised that he had more on the way.

"But does he have a tuning fork that carries the honk of a goose?" Sylas teased her.

"I don't know, I'll have to ask him," Mira said as she slid her hand down his back.

"You seem extra friendly today." As quickly as ever, Sylas leaned in and kissed her forehead. "I hope that's okay."

"It's perfectly fine, and I am extra friendly today, as you say. Everything is working out. We have a solution on the horizon, the market is open, and Ember Hollow is buzzing with activity."

"We sure do!" Tilbud said from Sylas's pocket.

Mira jumped back. "Sylas, you should have said something!"

He burst out laughing. "He told me not to."

"Hello, Mira." Tilbud tipped his hat to her. "And if I may comment, the only thing missing from your sentence about how well everything is going is the classic line: 'What could possibly go wrong?' Care to make an addition?"

"Please, don't be morose," she told the archlumen.

Cornbread came racing around one of the corners, barking excitedly. She was joined by Quinlan, who carried some of the barbecued meats that Azor had grilled up on a plank of wood. He placed it on the bar of the pub and Kael took it.

Cornbread continued to bark loudly until someone gave her a piece of the meat. She wolfed it down and quickly gnawed on the bone, wagging her tail contentedly.

"I have to get to the farm. It's Mana Saturation day," Sylas told Mira.

"How's that going to work if you also need to be here?"

"I was planning to hire Cody and Duncan to watch the fields while I'm here, but that was before I knew they purchased the café, so I guess they're not available. But I will figure something out. Perhaps I can talk to some of the other farmers, Trampus or Sterling."

An idea came to Mira. "What about my uncle?"

"Actually, that's not a bad idea. Sure, I'll give him a shot." Sylas ran his hand over his beard stubble. "What's the worst he can say, no?"

———

Tiberius gladly joined Sylas, the lord commander surprisingly talkative as they took the portal to the Seedlands. Cornbread went with them, and she would stick around once Mana Saturation was completed, which Tiberius didn't seem to have a problem with.

"She's a pretty fierce attack dog," he said as he crouched to pet her. She licked his hand. "Friendly too."

"That she is," Sylas said as he went inside his farmhouse and put on his magical farming hat. Tiberius laughed at the way it looked, but he didn't say anything else as Sylas started Mana Saturation. Tilbud was still in his pocket and the archlumen occasionally commented on the process.

The lord commander kept quiet as the fields filled with golden light, all of Sylas's plants looking robust in a way that a farmer back in his world could only have dreamed of. He waited for the process to finish and then walked back to the porch, where Tiberius eyed the hammock.

"You can use it, you know," Sylas said. "Cornbread will alert you if there is any activity."

"I'm supposed to be on guard."

Sylas gave him a sly grin. "Half the time Quinlan is on guard, he's resting in the hammock, enjoying his life, and waiting for Cornbread to bark. I suggest you do the same, but it's up to you. It's quite comfortable."

"Yes, it does look like it would be a nice place to relax on a warm day."

Sylas dusted his hands together. "That's it. I should get back to the market. I'm sure there's something to eat inside if you get hungry. Azor always keep the place well stocked."

"I'll be fine," Tiberius said as he remained there, awkward as ever, still considering the hammock.

Sylas turned away and only looked back at his farmhouse once he was nearly to the end of the lane. Tiberius still stood on the porch, yet the lord commander had inched closer to the hammock.

"I'm sure you'll enjoy it," Sylas said to himself as he continued on.

He reached the Seedlands portal and selected Ember Hollow.

Sylas flashed away, and as he appeared, more people formed into existence behind him, stepping past Sylas as they headed to the market.

One of those people happened to be Iron Rose, who, as usual, wore all black and was carrying several swan paintings with her. She was assisted by John, the man who often helped Mr. and Mrs. Brassmere, the pair that owned the shop in Cinderpeak.

"Sylas," Rose said as John moved on with the bulk of her paintings. "Someone told me there would be a market and that I could just show up and sell some things. I'm kidding. Mira actually invited me, believe it or not. I'm a little late, but I told her that may be the case. We've been open the last several nights, you know. The popularity of your pub has reached Cinderpeak, and people keep bugging me to open after-hours."

"You mean after I close?"

"Precisely. And I must say, business at The Ugly Duckling has been good. I like to paint during the day and I don't want to open in the early evening. But later at night, I usually grow bored and have found that opening the pub later suits my lifestyle. Very much a win-win, dare I say, a joint venture between Ember Hollow and Cinderpeak. People trickle back from your pub, and what do you know, The Ugly Duckling is open and serving fresh pints for anyone that needs a nightcap."

"Do you mind if I spread the word?"

"Actually, that would be great of you. You don't have to. I didn't tell you that looking for any—"

"It's fine," he assured her.

"Are you certain?"

"Why would I not be? I'll be closed at that time."

"Right." Iron Rose beamed a smile at him. "But just during the week. On the weekends, I plan to sell my paintings here. People always ask about them when they come into my pub. That's another reason I like to open; it doesn't happen every day, but there are times that I sell some art as well. So this gives me a proper outlet for that so I can sling pints early into the morning."

"I might stop by one night on my way to the Seedlands."

"Your farm, yeah?"

"My farm."

"You experiment with any corn-based ales?" she asked.

"Now, I feel like that would be more of a spirits sort of thing. I did do something recently with athershade leaf."

"The blue one, I remember that. You might have to share that recipe with me. It seems like a great nightcap, a way to put people at ease."

"Now that you mention it, I think it would be." Sylas said, the two taking their time on the route toward the market. It was bustling as ever, and there was little time to continue the conversation with Iron Rose as Sylas hopped behind the bar of The Petticoat Lamplighter and started engaging with customers and pouring drinks.

"The musicians are fed," Bart the bard told him at one point. He burped and covered his mouth. "Sorry, mate. As I was saying, we're good to go. Ready for some music?"

"Certainly," Sylas said as he immediately poured the bard a pint.

"How did you know I needed something to wet my whistle?" Bart asked with a laugh.

"Brewer's intuition."

After a bit more chatter, Bart stepped up, placed a hand on his stomach, and waited for Mary the lutist to join him. She started a soft melody, and quickly picked up her pace as Bart sang words to a song Sylas hadn't heard before: "*Oh Luminae, the Dreaming, in your slumber the stars are weeping, rest in twilight's gaze until the time comes for you to wake. Rest now, Dreaming, in the sky, with Fayeth's light that never dies . . .*"

Mira stopped by, said a few quick things, paused long enough for Sylas to come around the bar and kiss her on the cheek, and then continued making her rounds. She was so happy. Sylas couldn't remember a time that she had seemed as happy as she checked in on vendors, and eventually helped Iron Rose get set up to sell her swan paintings.

It reminded him that people liked to be useful.

This was something Sylas had seen before, when he had finally organized his units correctly, and tasked the right people with the right jobs. That sense of purpose was contagious. Even in the face of an endless war, having a duty made a real difference.

The conversations continued in the afternoon as the market buzzed with activity. Azor brought more barbecue, which seemed to calm the masses for a while. The shopping picked up as all sorts of things were sold, from herbs to swan paintings, old chests to construction equipment.

It was incredible and as the afternoon slowly melted into a golden Underworldian evening, it came time for Sylas to head back to The Old Lamplighter and open the pub.

Raelis and Kael, who had gotten better at pouring pints relatively quickly, made the announcement to anyone in the vicinity that the pub would soon be changing venues. "We've got it from here," Raelis assured Sylas. "We'll see you back there in a bit."

———

"Still no sign of Wigmund," Tilbud said from Sylas's pocket once they reached The Old Lamplighter. "Boo. I've spent the whole bloody day in here, you know."

"I'm well aware."

"But there were a few good conversations. And you have truly tamed Tiberius. So kudos there."

"Have I?" Sylas asked as he opened the door of his pub to find *two* cats.

There was Patches, who was resting on his window perch, and there was an orange tabby seated on a table. If Patches minded that another cat was around, he wasn't making his feelings known. Patches merely yawned when Sylas entered.

"A new cat," Tilbud said as Sylas approached the tabby. "How odd."

"Hey there." Sylas reached his hand to the orange cat, assuming that it would want to sniff them.

The orange tabby batted Sylas's hand away and spoke: "Ah, Sylas and apparently that archlumen friend of yours. Good day to you both. I'm glad the two of you could make it. Let's chat."

Sylas yanked his arm back in surprise. "By the fates, Wigmund, you didn't say you would come as a cat!"

"It's one of my favorite forms to take when I come to the Underworld, particularly to Draugr," Wigmund said as he moved about the table. He hopped onto the ground and transitioned to a bar stool, before finally taking a spot on the bar itself. "Please, sit. Come on, then. I don't have all day, even if I technically do."

Sylas did as instructed. Once he was settled, Tilbud leaned forward, resting his arms across the edge of Sylas's pocket.

"You could have come in your normal size," Wigmund told the archlumen. "This isn't a secret meeting or anything of the sort."

"True, but it has been a blast being small for the day. Transformations are fun. People don't transform enough."

"I would agree with you there. I'll be the first to admit that there have been times in my life when I would have seen things differently, but look at me." To illustrate his point, Wigmund licked one of his paws. "The things we eternals do to entertain ourselves. I see the market is going splendidly."

"It was supposed to be a soft opening," Sylas said.

"All good signs."

Sylas couldn't help himself: "All good signs *if* the Underworld were to remain intact. But according to the Celestial Council—the Council you oversee, if I'm not mistaken—we don't deserve that right."

Wigmund didn't seem phased by the direct statement. "That is exactly what we decided upon, the right for you to exist. But, as you know, I'm on your side. Believe me. I find it lovely here, really. And the Hexveil is an important barrier, even if my colleagues don't quite see it that way. Yet I'm not here to discuss the benefits of the Underworld with you. That conversation is closed, I'm afraid."

"Actually, we'd like to reopen it in a different way," Tilbud said.

"Oh? Go on . . ."

"You have offered Sylas citizenship in the Celestial Plains in exchange for becoming heaven's newest hunter." Tilbud shook his head. "That sounded better in my mind than it did out loud. Let me try again. Ahem. You have offered Sylas citizenship in the Celestial Plains in exchange for his services. Not only that, this offer extends to his closest friends, which, I daresay, includes me."

"That's correct," Sylas said. He'd never really thought of Tilbud as a friend, but hearing the archlumen mention it made it seem right. Of course he was. While Tilbud could be a strange fellow, and he was a far cry from the men Sylas had served with, Tilbud was someone he could trust, someone he could confide in, and someone he knew wouldn't betray him, all traits of a true friendship.

Tilbud continued, "And I know because of my relationship with a certain lumengineer, and, if we're being honest, the fact that I've been around enough MLus to know their value, that citizenship, even if you *are* the divine arbiter, is expensive."

Wigmund's whiskers twitched. "What's your point, archlumen?"

"You say you are a champion of the Underworld, yes? You don't see us as some arbitrary gray zone. You realize that there are people here who are kindhearted, with a variety of skills and experiences that meant they went here instead of the Chasm."

"Yes . . ."

"Then what I'm saying, if I may be so bold, kind sir, kind Celestial sir, is that you could, and dare I say *should*, put your money where your mouth is. In this case, your MLus. We have another plan to sway our Celestial audiences. And we are willing to exchange Sylas's services, and the services of those that he deems worthy to bring with him on his expedition, for the MLus necessary to enact our plan."

The cat offered an uncertain grin. "And what would that plan be? You have piqued my interest."

"I have been called an orator before, but that was after a long monologue following a long night of debauchery that I'm neither ashamed nor proud of. Where was I?"

"Our proposal," Sylas told Tilbud quickly.

"Ah, yes! A good proposal indeed. First, and I say this with the utmost sincerity, divine arbiter, we don't want your citizenship. We will earn it, whenever that time may come," Tilbud said in just about the most casual manner possible. It was clear from his tone, however, that he wasn't being disrespectful.

He merely wanted to make his point known that Wigmund wasn't going to be able to bribe them into leaving their lives in the Underworld behind. "What we want is cold, hard MLus. Enough to fund what I would like to call the Celestial Dispatch."

"You're going to make me wait for you to get to the point, aren't you?"

"Would I be a good orator if I gave it away too quickly?" Tilbud asked.

"I would tell you that my patience is wearing thin, but I shouldn't have to. Besides," Wigmund said as his cat ears twitched, "people are finally starting to make their way to the pub. So you best be getting on with it, is what I'm saying."

"We need as many MLus as you can possibly provide so we can use either Clairvoice, my choice, or Lorewave, to spread the message all around the Underworld that the Celestial Plains are coming for us. I'm not finished," Tilbud said as he showed the divine arbiter the palm of his hand. "We would also use those MLus to dispatch messages from Underworldians to the Plains, messages to loved ones, of what the Council has decided to do. Our approach is this: we will appeal to parents, brothers, sisters, friends, and other relatives. Whoever knows someone that they can write to, we will help them get that letter written. And we will use the MLus to send those messages skyward."

"A letter campaign?" Wigmund's tail, which had been flopping against the wood of the bar, settled.

"A Celestial Dispatch, yes," Tilbud told him.

"And your plan would be to appeal to the commoners of the Celestial Plains in hopes that they would use their influence over the Celestial Council to convince them to have another vote? How did you know that they would be able to do that? You shouldn't be familiar with the Celestial Bylaws. None of those are available here."

"I have my ways—"

"It was my idea," Sylas said, interrupting Tilbud. "A hunch. And even if there wasn't some bylaw, public opinion can do quite a bit. It can turn a country to war, but it can equally foster a new peace."

Wigmund's whiskers drooped. They drooped until they started to turn upward as the cat burst out laughing. "Brilliant!" he finally said. "It's a brilliant plan, one that may actually work."

"You jest," Tilbud said.

"No, it really could work. But before I can distribute the MLus, you will still have to go on your hunt. You may have to go on several hunts because I have to be able to show the Council that this was your idea, that I merely provided funding as payment for the hunt. That remains to be seen. There is some risk there, but not much, and with my role, I should be able to smooth things over."

"So that's a yes?" Tilbud asked Wigmund. "You agree?"

The divine arbiter's tail swished back and forth. "I do, conditionally. Let me see how many MLus I will be able to muster up. You will be hearing from me soon. In the meantime, continue your research into how you will get the information out there, and try to enjoy yourself as if these were your last days in the Underworld. Remember, nothing is ever assured. Nothing."

———

Patches stretched his paws out before him and thrust his rear even higher into the air before finally coming out of the position. His ears twitched as he heard Cornbread's nails on the stairs.

The dog trotted down with the big man, who now stood in the militia armor he occasionally wore, a club resting over his shoulder. He said something to the fire spirit, who had just finished up downstairs. From there, the big man stepped outside with Cornbread, where they met the warrior with long dark hair.

I suppose I should go as well, Patches said as he watched them leave.

Rather than try to race to the front door before the fire spirit could close it, he headed out the back, circling the well once before moving to the fence, and then the yard beyond, where the woman who lived next door had recently planted flowers. He weaved in and out of some bushes, slipped under a fence that had recently been erected, and came onto the main road just behind Cornbread, who was so busy running around the big man that she didn't notice Patches.

The group passed by the Petticoat Lane Market. As they neared the portal, the goose charged toward them, flapping her wings and honking. *I want to go with you all!*

You are supposed to guard the Marketly Realm, Patches hissed.

But I've been guarding it all day.

The big man scooped the goose up into his arms and held her there for a moment as he spoke to the other man.

This drew Cornbread's interest. *Is she coming with us?*

No, someone has to stay here, Patches told her.

But she came last time.

It's the big man's choice.

Cornbread licked Patches's face.

Hey! What did I tell you about that?

You should stay here too, Cornbread told Patches. *I can handle the Farmly Realm with the humans. Besides, there are four warriors now. Not to mention the militiamen.*

Stay here? At first, Patches was a bit offended. But then he remembered something. He didn't have the same hearing as Cornbread, so he couldn't tell for certain, but Patches was fairly certain he had sensed a dark presence earlier, just before the strange cat had visited . . .

The appearance of the cat had been quite an experience as well. And what was with that other one, anyway? How was he able to speak to humans? The tabby had never said anything to Patches. He just sat there on a table waiting for the humans. Then, Patches heard speaking, like they were actually talking to the cat and he was replying.

Now that he thought about it, Patches was certain something foul was afoot. Before the people started arriving at the pub, and just as Patches had been getting comfortable in preparation for a long nap, he had sensed it.

A presence.

So maybe it's good if I stick around, he thought as he looked from Cornbread to Gertrude, whom the big man had just placed on the ground.

They aren't going to let me go with them, are they? Gertrude asked Patches.

No, but you and I have other plans. Come on.

Patches bid farewell to Cornbread by hiking his tail up and moving on. He turned back toward the market. He picked up his pace, the goose just behind him.

I already checked the place, she told him as Patches came to a large carving resting against one of the walls. At first he thought it was a shield, but it turned out to be a grotesque mask, one with horns carved on it like the fire spirit sometimes produced on her forehead.

What's this?

It's just something that someone brought earlier, Gertrude told Patches.

I don't like the way it looks.

You don't have to look at it.

I suppose I don't, he said as he moved on.

There were some rats earlier, but I handled them. They think that I don't see them while the humans are here.

Yes, that sounds like a rat to me. They think they're so smart. Patches sat and began licking one of his paws. *But they are loud and frantic. They can't stop themselves from succumbing to their nervous energy.*

And that's how you hear them, right? Gertrude asked.

It is. But my hearing isn't as good as the dog's. It's my eyes and my grace that are my real powers.

I don't know what I would do if I had a tail like yours, Gertrude said as she turned around to look at her own tail feathers. She shook her rump. *Mine works well enough, but yours is long and furry.*

If I had a beak like yours, I would use it to crush my enemies.

A wicked yet playful grin formed on Gertrude's face. *It is an advantage, I agree.*

Earlier today, a strange cat visited. I already told the dog about it, but she didn't seem concerned.

Do strange cats normally visit?

No. And this one spoke to the big man. I'm certain of it.

The cat could speak the human tongue?

I believe so, Patches told her as he swished his tail left and right. *And if he could communicate with me, he didn't try. Which I find a little rude.*

I would find that rude as well, if another goose showed up and didn't say anything. Huh. That's odd. I can't ever remember seeing an animal speak to a human.

Something is off. Everything is off.

You are so optimistic.

Patches's whiskers quivered. *I can't quite remember a time when it wasn't my job to protect the Tavernly Realm and the rest of the village. At that time, the rest of the world didn't really matter. But that has changed since the big man came into my life.*

Personally, I am happy to know him and the medicine woman. She fixed my involuntary sounds. Those were so painful.

And loud.

Movement beyond caught Patches's attention. *Come on.* He took off toward the far end of the market, closer to the yellow café that Patches hadn't really noticed before until tonight. He stopped in front of it and looked up at an open window. *The demon is in there.*

Do you think you can make the jump?

This is nothing. Watch.

Not if I can get there first! Gertrude charged forward, the goose flapping her wings as she flew through the open window. *Get in here,* she called out before Patches could say anything about the way she had blown right past him.

Patches hopped to the ledge and jumped inside just as a wisp of darkened mana trailed out of the back door of the yellow café. He was just about to chase after it when Gertrude extended one of her wings and whisked it forward, which caused several feathers to fly out, each of them forming daggers.

It seemed like they would cut into the wall, but then the feathered daggers took on a trajectory of their own as they exploded into the next room.

Patches rushed ahead, hitting his top speed in a matter of seconds as he reached the following space, where he found a creature that looked like a blanket blowing in the wind, spikes lining its body as the feathered daggers swarmed around it.

Patches thought he was going to be able to engage the demonic being, yet Gertrude's attack brought it down as the daggers continued to dive-bomb the creature, ripped at its form, and came in again.

You didn't say you could do that, he told Gertrude.

You never asked me what I could do. I know that you think of yourself as a loner, but you have companions now. The dog, me, even the big man and his friends.

What does that have to do with your powers?

It has everything to do with my powers. Did you hear what I just told you? Gertrude stepped up next to him and rubbed the side of her body against his. *Well?*

You want me to talk more?

No, I want you to trust more. You didn't need to stick around at the Marketly Realm.

I sensed something.

And that something is now dead.

The monster fluttered to the ground. *Not dead enough,* Patches said as he approached it and released a scorching beam of mana from his mouth that completely disintegrated it. *Now it is dead.* He hiked his tail up to solidify his point.

Where were they going anyway? Gertrude asked, changing subjects.

To the Farmly Realm. It is nearly harvest time and monsters are always afoot.

Gertrude laughed. *The way you say things sometimes is so ridiculous.*

What? What did I say?

The monsters are afoot.

I said they were always afoot.

I've never heard that phrase in my life.

Maybe I've been alive longer than you.

Maybe. But that doesn't mean anything. Although, I can say that I feel a little envious now. If there are monsters afoot, as you call them, what are we doing here?

We just dealt with something, didn't we? That thing could have come to the Tavernly Realm eventually.

Maybe, Gertrude said, and she nudged him again.

Would you stop doing that?

I think you like the affection. To illustrate her point, Gertrude draped her long neck over Patches.

He exhaled audibly. *You know, creatures like me sometimes eat creatures like you.*

Please. You couldn't eat me. I would have you running for cover in a matter of seconds.

I have claws, you know.

I see how you are with the dog. You let her lick your face. Why would you do that if you didn't like it?

I don't know why she licks my face. I don't necessarily like it. I'm clean. I can lick myself.

Gertrude moved away from Patches and started to laugh. *You are too much sometimes. Come on, we have a Marketly Realm to patrol.*

[You have 31 days until the invasion.]
**[A loan payment of 220 has been deducted from your total Mana
Lumens. Your total loan balance is 21848 Mana Lumens.]**

Sylas didn't know how Patches had made it to the farm, but there he was, as always, purring softly next to him. "Did Azor bring you?"

He continued to pet the cat for several minutes until he heard the sizzle of bacon in the other room. This was followed by several men speaking in low voices and a few loud woofs from Cornbread, who sounded hungry. Sylas came out of his bedroom with Patches in his arms. "Who brought the cat?"

"That would be Duncan," Quinlan said from his place at the table. "He stopped by late last night and said he found Patches rummaging around the market."

Behind him, Kael and Raelis were working on breakfast, Raelis manning the pans and Kael slicing bread. "Morning, Sylas," Kael said.

"Morning. What a night, yeah?" Sylas said as he sat at the table.

"Indeed. I thought we were in the clear, but I forget how much Mana Saturation brings out the buggers," Quinlan said as he massaged the bridge of his nose with his fingers. "Anyway, I should head out. I promised Azor I'd help her with the meats."

"At least eat something first," Kael told his brother as he brought some bread over to the table. "And don't say *I sound like our mother.*"

"You do, in a way. Heh." Quinlan popped a piece of bread in his mouth. "She's up there in the Celestial Plains."

"Mine is too," Sylas told him. "And to be honest, I haven't thought of that part much. I never really met her."

"Raised by your father, yeah?" Quinlan nodded over to Raelis. "What about you? Any relatives up there?"

"Both my parents, to my knowledge. They were saints." Raelis flipped some of the strips of bacon and Cornbread barked. "You'll get yours, girl. Just let me finish up here."

"Maybe we can slip away on one of these proposed hunts and find our mom," Kael said.

"That would be something. But we still don't know if this divine guy is going to actually give us the funds," Quinlan said.

Sylas had caught the three of them up while they guarded the cornfield last night. They were aware that Wigmund would be back soon with an answer. Sylas only hoped it was with enough time to make a difference before the invasion.

"Look at us, becoming mercenaries," Raelis said as he set the bacon down on the table. He sat, and Kael did the same across from him. "I never liked mercenaries."

"They have their purpose," Sylas said, "but generally, they get in the way. We won't be those kinds of mercenaries, though. We are simply there to get the MLus necessary for the Celestial Dispatch."

"I find it strange that they have come to us, or he has come to us," Quinlan said as he stabbed a piece of bacon with his fork, "to hunt something that they should clearly be able to handle. Why us? Don't tell me that we are more skilled in some way. There have been incredible warriors before us, on both sides. Surely they aren't just lounging around on a cloud being fed grapes by a beautiful woman."

Raelis cracked up. "It sounds like you're projecting there a little, mate."

"I mean, we did have the option to become heaven's goodest boys, but no, Sylas here decided to buck the system." Quinlan winked at Sylas. "And it was a good decision. One I would've made? Maybe not. But as they say, you won't know how the cat jumps until you rattle the cage. No offense, Patches."

Sylas glanced back at his bedroom to see if the cat was going to make an appearance or not.

As if he had been summoned, Patches sashayed through the door and yawned as he looked at the four men. Normally, Cornbread would have raced over to lick his face, but the farm dog was too focused on the bacon, her eyes tracking every time someone ate a piece or took one off the plate. She continuously licked her lips.

"Sorry, girl," Kael said as he noticed how patient she was being. He gave her a piece and she ate it quickly even though it was still hot.

Quinlan smiled at her. "Isn't she cute?" He fed Cornbread a piece of bacon as well. "If we have time, and I suppose we will come harvest, maybe we should head into Battersea and check the archives at the guild. Maybe they will have something on Celestial Beasts."

"Perhaps," Raelis said. "But it might take some digging. Kael? He always struck me as the scholarly type."

"Why is that?" Kael asked.

"Because you meditate? No, I'm joking. Well, I suppose I'm not," Raelis said. "You would be the man on the ground, as it were, to figure out the information we need."

"I could see myself doing that."

"See?" Quinlan clapped his hands together. "Then that settles it. We will continue on with the market today because Azor needs help, and Sylas can't run a pub without his bestest of mates. Tonight, this lot knows the drill: Defend the corn. Defend the corn!" He pointed at Cornbread and she barked. "Heh. She gets it. And tomorrow, the hunters will *dispatch* to the big city and see what we can find out. I love a good plan. Perhaps we will be able to visit Prissy in Geist as well. She would like that."

"She isn't the only one, right?" Sylas asked Quinlan.

"No, I'd like it too. Happy? Let's finish up here and get to the market."

———

As it had been the day before, the Petticoat Lane Market was brimming with activity.

The market was even busier than it had been on Soulsday and Sylas was surprised by the crowd and the excitement that seemed to spread through Ember Hollow. He had already stopped by The Old Lamplighter, where he had caught Azor just as she was finishing up some of the meat. The fire spirit was relieved to see Sylas and his friends.

He noticed that Nelly's General Store just next door was busy as well, which answered a question Sylas had had since the start of all this: What would the true effect of the market be on the rest of Ember Hollow? Thus far, the signs were good. The village was lively and he was increasingly certain that going in on it with Mira was the right move, even though they had yet to see any profit from the endeavor.

That was fine. He had expected it would be slow in the beginning. And with the threat of the invasion, Sylas was more worried about staying alive and retaining what he could than he was about making MLus.

After making his rounds and checking on Duncan and Cody's café, Sylas joined Mira at the back of the market, where she was speaking with a vendor who had shown up unannounced and was asking if he could sell his homemade pottery.

"We do have a booth still available, but it is a little smaller than the others," she told the pottery man. "I hope that will work for you."

The man examined the space. "This is fine, perfectly fine. Esta said that this was the place to sell my pottery, and here I am."

"Did you say you have pottery?" Sylas asked the man after he had scrutinized the shorter fellow.

"I sure do, an old hobby of mine. I actually run a general store in Lilihammer that caters to people venturing into the mountains."

"Ah, north. I keep hearing of Lilihammer but I've never been there," Sylas said.

"It is a popular destination here in the Underworld, and as a landlord, you should be able to travel there if you'd like without incurring any of the vacation destination tax they have there. I recommend it. Anyway, I could talk about Lilihammer all day, and I certainly would if you stop by my new booth later.

But, speaking of which, Esta said the booth was free for the weekend? Sorry to be so forthright about it."

"It is," Mira said.

"I don't mind paying. With this kind of foot traffic, I'll happily be here every weekend," the pottery man told Mira as he once again examined the booth. It was sandwiched between an antiques booth and a place that sold tools, yet it turned out to be the perfect space for the man as he summoned numerous pots, all of which had small plants in them that looked like miniature trees.

"These are so cute," Mira told him.

"You think? The plant is called—"

"Silver Thread. I'm an apothecary."

"Ah, then you know." He laughed nervously. "This plant makes a person feel calm if it's around. It's quite remarkable in the fact that it grows underwater. They grow wild in Lilihammer."

"They do? I was unaware of that. I knew they had a property that helps one focus, but that's only if it's ingested." Mira turned to Sylas. "What do you think?"

"About what?"

"Close the pub tomorrow and let's spend a day and night in Lilihammer. I'll gather some Silver Thread for our trip."

"*Our* trip. If I go there, you'll go with me."

"You are certain?"

"I am," Sylas said. He didn't want to go to the Celestial Plains again without her. "But yes, together, a day away."

As she looked at him, something Tilbud had once said came to Sylas: *There are things that need to be done everywhere, but that should never stop us from taking a moment for ourselves.*

"What do you think?" she asked.

"I'm all for it," he told Mira, unable to hide his grin.

"Yeah?" she asked as she moved just a bit closer to him.

"Sure. Let's do it. Let's go to Lilihammer tomorrow and get some of this Silver Thread. That sounds like a great plan, especially with all we have going on."

"Right," Mira said. "And there's little we can do until Wigmund returns anyway."

"Should I go somewhere else?" the pottery man asked. "I can give you two a little privacy, if you'd like. I'm not one to interrupt a moment if I don't have to."

Sylas kissed Mira on the forehead and moved on. "It's fine. I need to get to The Petticoat Lamplighter anyway."

CHAPTER SIXTEEN

A DAY AWAY

The doomsday message never ceased to send a brief chill down Sylas's spine, even though he had come to expect it.

[**You have 30 days until the invasion.**]
[**A loan payment of 215 has been deducted from your total Mana Lumens. Your total loan balance is 21633 Mana Lumens.**]

He waved the message away and didn't bother to check his Mana Lumens as he headed into the kitchen to find Azor cooking, Kael and Raelis seated at the table.

"Morning," Kael said.

"Where's Quinlan?" Sylas asked.

"Happy Tombsday!" Azor told him as she flipped a pair of sausages. She quickly transitioned to another pair resting on a cutting board, where she used a cleaver to cut the links in half. "It's harvest time!"

Her sudden movement startled Raelis, who nearly jumped out of his chair.

"Sorry," Azor said, her flames retreating. "I dealt with so much meat yesterday that I'm a little angry at it."

"Not a worry," he told her. "As long as the sausages are coming."

"Should be soon!" she told him as she went back to work.

"Quin is outside," Kael said, answering Sylas's earlier question. "In the hammock with Cornbread."

Sylas stepped onto the porch and found Quinlan sleeping in the hammock, one foot on the ground, Cornbread snuggled up with him. Rather than wake the resting warrior, he headed back inside and took a seat at the table.

"So no pub tonight?" Raelis asked as Azor brought sausages over.

"Not tonight, no. I'll deal with the harvest and be done with the day. We haven't had a night off in a while," Sylas said.

"I don't know what I'm going to do with myself," Azor said.

"I'm sure you'll figure something out."

She pouted. "Wish I could just cuddle up with Cornbread or Patches and sleep all day."

"I'm just ready for the hunt, myself," Realis said. "Not going to lie and say I'm not interested in seeing what the Celestial Plains has to offer, and why they asked us to do their dirty work in the first place."

"I've been thinking about that as well," Kael said. "We'll need actual weapons, I suspect. But I assume they will provide something like that."

"So what you are trying to say is the clubs aren't going to *cut* it." Raelis laughed at his own joke. "That was funny, right? Admit that was funny."

Azor paused, the fires on her face smoothing out as she gave the three men a serious look. "I didn't want it to come to this, but I think it's time: we may need to make a rule about puns. Quinlan seems to like them as well. They are affecting my way of being."

Azor's statement caused the three men to roar with laughter, and she eventually joined them, the four loud enough that they woke Quinlan, who stumbled in and found a seat at the table. "What's all the bloody commotion about?"

"Nothing," Sylas said. "Just eat your breakfast and enjoy your day off. And careful with puns around Azor, yeah?"

He flashed the fire spirit a toothy smile. "I'm a real *pun*-dit when it comes to wordplay."

Azor flared up and everyone burst out laughing again.

Once he was finished with breakfast, Sylas donned his magical hat and headed out to his fields. They looked glorious at the moment, the wind slightly twisting through them, the corn as gold as the Celestial Plains above.

He used his Harvest Silos power and the corn was sucked up into the magical silos, numbers flashing in the air as they were tallied. Cornbread came to him and sat directly beside Sylas.

"Good girl," he told the farm dog who barked once at him as the prompt came.

[You have yielded 15000 Mana Lumens' worth of corn. Pay tax now? Y/N?]

"Gladly. Well, not gladly, but that's fine."

[A payment of 1050 Mana Lumens has been deducted from your yield. Transfer to the guild now for distribution? Y/N?]

"Do it."

[You have received 13950 Mana Lumens.]

Sylas distributed MLus to his pets, Kael, Quinlan, and gave extra to Raelis, who would later give Duncan and Cody their cuts.

Sylas smiled. It felt good to check another thing off his eternal to-do list.

———

Not long after harvesting, Sylas joined Mira in Cinderpeak, where they took the landlord portal to Battersea. Rather than immediately continuing on, Sylas suggested they explore the grounds of the Landlord Guild. He was glad to have made this suggestion after they found a nice, cozy little coffee shop called Bennu Austin, where they were able to have scones and coffee before officially heading out.

[Where would you like to travel?]

"Lilihammer," Sylas and Mira both said, the two now holding hands.

[Your credentials have been authenticated. This will only take a moment.]

The two Ember Hollow natives appeared on a boardwalk, one that cut through an expansive, sandy beach that had several long piers that stretched out into the water. Waves sloshed at the pilings, and Sylas counted a half dozen fishermen with lines cast into a breathtakingly beautiful lake at the foot of a massive mountain.

"I didn't think it would be that large," Mira said as she looked up at the mountain, the peak of which was obscured by the gold-hued clouds of the Celestial Plains. "They say it reaches all the way up there."

"To the Plains?" Sylas glanced back at Lilihammer, which was built along the slope of the mountain.

Like other cities in the Underworld, the buildings in Lilihammer had a distinctive architecture unlike the various places Sylas had visited. They rose like pillars, the buildings all thin and rectangular in shape with roofs that offered views of both the lake and the slopes of the mountain.

"Mount Lili," Mira said. "Gorgeous, isn't it?"

"Stunning, really. I can't believe something like this exists here in the Underworld."

"I thought you knew about Mount Lili."

"How would I? I've only been here about two months," he reminded Mira as they strolled out onto one of the piers. Sylas saw a large fish jump out of the water, catch something, and dip back beneath the waves. "And you didn't tell me there was good fishing here."

"Now that's something I didn't know. Whenever anyone talks about Lili-hammer, they speak of the mountain, not the lake. I've always wanted to come. My uncle had a friend that came around when I was first here, a man named Lionel. He still lives here, I believe."

"Did they have a falling out or something?" Sylas asked.

"You know Tiberius."

"Indeed, I do. But we're getting along well enough lately, the lord commander and me. He seemed to enjoy himself on the hammock, judging by how comfortable he looked when I saw him later."

"I'll bet he didn't let you see him resting, though. Not my uncle."

"Certainly not. But I know he did. Look at that lake." Sylas stared out at the water. "It makes you want to go swimming. You don't happen to have a swimsuit, do you?"

"On me?" Mira asked as she placed her hand on the bag she brought.

"Yes. Did you bring one?"

"I didn't. Remember, I'm just now learning that there is a lake here."

"Then let me buy you one in town. I should probably get myself one as well. What I'm saying here is that we should go swimming."

"You think?"

Sylas spread his arms out wide. "Am I being too dramatic if I say this might be it?"

"It as in *it*? Yes, but maybe you're right. Let's see what we can find in town. But before we head in, can we stay here for another moment? It's amazing."

Sylas took in a deep breath through his nostrils. "It really is." After relaxing at the pier for a little longer, both leaning on the railing, Mira and Sylas turned in the direction of the city.

They passed a small, waterside market that sold trinkets on one side and fishing supplies on the other. "This is quaint," Mira said. "Really, Sylas. I'm so glad we came."

"Definitely not as bustling as our market."

"Yes, that has turned out rather well. It's almost as if we had planned it."

"Well, in a way we did plan it. Or you did. You did a wonderful job, is what I'm saying. A job deserving of a vacation."

"A one-day vacation."

"Sometimes that's all it takes," Sylas said.

Mira laughed. "Are you trying to be pithy like Tilbud?"

"That wasn't the plan, no." The two reached a shop that sold clothing, where Mira picked out a striped bathing suit. "Is that what we're going for?" Sylas asked her as he found a matching pair of trunks.

"Stripes? Sure, why not?"

"Then stripes it is." Sylas paid a hundred Mana Lumens for the set, and they left.

"And you're sure you don't have to go back to the farm tonight?"

"It will be fine. I'm not planning to do Mana Infusion today. Or tomorrow, if we're being honest. I just have this feeling, you know."

Her gaze shifted downward. "That everything's coming to an end soon?"

"That's the feeling. And it's dark, but I'm doing my best to embrace it. Now, where are we staying tonight?"

"We should have asked the cashier back there," she said as they started off down a street that had been paved with small white stones. Occasionally, the pristine white rocks were interrupted by black stones carved with intricate designs ranging from crabs to stars. The distinctive stones added a unique charm to the path, a quaint appeal that made Lilihammer seem like a great place to unwind.

"I'm sure we will find a place," Sylas said. "And maybe I will strike up a deal with them to sell ale. I still need to visit that inn back in the Shadowstone Mountains. But it's hard to focus."

"It can be, yes. And put a pin in your inability to focus." Mira lowered her hand and Sylas took it. They continued their stroll up a winding street, where tall buildings cast rectangular shadows across their path. They saw numerous shops and boutiques as they passed a small city center, as well as a pub called Lilihammer's Finest that Sylas planned to visit later.

After exploring some of the boutiques and having a quick bite at a small restaurant with outdoor seating, Mira and Sylas found an inn called The Northern Nook. The woman who ran the place, who wore a beige bonnet, smiled at the two as they entered. "Welcome."

"Two rooms, please," Sylas told the proprietor as he tapped his fist on the desk.

"No," Mira said as she squeezed his hand. "Just one will do."

"Well, the two of you are in luck," the woman said with a cackle, "because all I have is one room. And it's the suite. On the top floor, and you have private access to the rooftop balcony that overlooks Lake Silver."

"Is that what it's called?" Mira asked as she approached the woman.

Behind her, Sylas stood silent, still processing the fact that he would be sharing a room with Mira. It made sense, the two were close, but he hadn't been expecting that. It hadn't even crossed his mind before she said it, yet now it made sense. As much as he had going on, and with the weight of the Underworld on his shoulders, Sylas couldn't help that he was falling in love in the afterlife.

He couldn't shake this notion of love, even a few minutes later as they were led to the suite, which had a large bed, a cushioned seating area covered in cozy throws, and a balcony with sweeping views of Lake Silver. Sylas stepped out onto the balcony and stood there for a moment, dumbfounded by how amazing it all was coupled with his sheer luck.

"Some people are really living it up in the Underworld," he said, though he also liked the quaintness of Ember Hollow and how being there made him feel. It wasn't beautiful like this, yet there was a charm to it, one that was growing as the village became more popular.

Something shifted to his right.

Sylas turned just as a bird landed, a magpie with a shiny white breast. The sudden movement made him think it was Patches. He took another look around, half expecting to see the cat step out of his invisible mode, but this didn't happen. Soon, he took a seat on the deck and placed his hands behind his head as he stared up at the Celestial Plains.

He was startled when Mira came out and lightly grazed her fingers against his shoulder.

"What do you think?" she asked as she showed him the bathing suit she'd changed into. Aside from the striped suit, she also wore a short white robe provided by the inn.

"Looks great."

"Why am I the only one wearing a swimsuit? Is this some clever ploy of yours?"

Sylas laughed. "Wish I could say I was that clever. Give me a minute. Let me get changed and we will head out. And thanks for suggesting this trip, really."

"Everyone needs a break, even people who are trying to save the world."

"You mean the Underworld, right?"

Mira lightly tapped him on the rear as he passed. "Get changed."

————

Sylas stared up at the Celestial Plains as he floated in Lake Silver. Even while his attention sometimes drifted to Mira, who mostly kept to the shore, half submerged, he couldn't help but stare up at the shimmering sky and think of what was to come. The view was so at odds with his soon-to-be reality.

So, he went under. Sylas dove deeper and deeper, noticing that he didn't feel the same kind of pressure he would have back in his world. How long could he stay underwater here? While Sylas felt as if he breathed normally in the Underworld, this was something else, something different.

It seemed like he could be under there forever. This made him want to explore, but before he did so he surfaced and called to Mira: "Come swimming with me."

She obliged, wading in the water until she came into Sylas's arms. "Hey. You didn't tell me we didn't have to worry about breathing underwater."

"What do you mean?" she asked.

"We don't have to come up for air."

"Interesting. And with that in mind, I'll bet this is where we could find some Silver Thread. Ben said it grew wild here."

"Ben the pottery guy, right?"

"Correct."

"But he didn't mention the lake?"

"Actually, now that you say it, he may have. I was quite distracted, you know, with the market and all."

"What do you say, then? Shall we see how far down we can go?"

"Why not?" Mira took Sylas's hand and they both dove beneath the surface of the lake.

They held hands as they swam deeper into the abyss, the gold of the Celestial Plains lighting their way. Sylas saw numerous fish, their bodies with shocks of yellow and green running through them. He also saw the hulls of boats that had sunk long ago.

He moved closer to one of these boats and reached out to it. As he did, a school of bright orange fish raced out of an opening, all moving past him.

Mira seemed to laugh, but there were no bubbles associated with the humor she felt in seeing Sylas rush back, putting himself between Mira and the fish. She placed a hand on his shoulder and squeezed it. Her eyes lit up and she pointed ahead.

Sylas spotted the silver plants. He swam toward them, Mira joining him. They collected a good many before finally swimming back up to the surface.

"I hope that's enough," he said, Sylas now with an armful of the plants as he floated closer toward the center of the lake.

"It should be plenty. I can use one of my powers to dry them and grind them up into pills. They will help us focus in the Plains. We will need them, I think."

"Everyone could use a little more focus," he said as he looked back to the shore.

There were a few sailboats out, but they were farther away, along an outer perimeter. Sylas and Mira weren't the only ones swimming, either. There were numerous people in the water, everyone enjoying themselves. They also weren't the only ones collecting the Silver Threads. Sylas spotted another pair of divers, who wore blue suits and matching caps.

Together, Mira and Sylas swam to the shore and dried themselves off in the towels they had borrowed from the inn.

Sylas sat. "Maybe we should talk about what's about to happen."

"Maybe we shouldn't."

He considered this. "You are probably right. A day away, yeah?"

"Or we just relax a little longer here and discuss it on our way to the inn. After that, let's go back to pretending our world isn't about to end."

He shook her hand. "You strike a hard bargain, but deal." Sylas moved a bit closer to her. "Let's just relax for the time being.

Later, on the long and winding walk back to the inn, the two discussed what they already knew. But as they approached the door, they came to a subject that they hadn't really been explored in their planning, one Sylas had been holding off on. "Do we evacuate Ember Hollow, or not?" Mira asked.

"I don't know. Before talking in terms of defending a location, Ember Hollow isn't the ideal place to try to secure. It is surrounded by forests, the Hexveil is nearby, it's not sitting on a hill or anything, for such a small village it's a bit sprawling, and, aside from the core around the pub, there's no way we'd be able to maintain a perimeter."

"I was afraid you'd say that."

"There are some things we can start working on when we get back to make it better. Watchtowers. We can go around and move anyone that lives on the outskirts to the center. People like . . . What was her name? The woman you always take care of?"

"Miss Barrowsly."

"People like her. We're going to need to move them closer to the village's center. I'm going to assume those that live in Ember Hollow don't want to head to Battersea or something. I know your uncle won't have that."

"He will have a plan. I can assure you of that," Mira told Sylas. "He has been quiet lately, which tells me he is up to something. I've seen it happen before, you know. He gets to scheming, and sometimes it's not all that bad. Don't tell him I said that."

"I wondered what had happened since his failed trip to Battersea with Tilbud and Catia."

"Not failed. Those connections just didn't work out the way that my uncle wanted them to and he was embarrassed. That might be one of the reasons he readily jumped at helping you with your farm the other day. I know my uncle. He wants to be helpful enough that he can take charge."

"I don't even care who is in charge of this as long as it gets solved. That's my biggest concern," Sylas said as they neared the inn. "And it won't be solved until I speak to Wigmund again, and then, it's not actually being solved, it will just be us reaching the next step."

"Yes, the next step. You get to become a hunter. But this will help," she said as she patted her bag, where she kept the Silver Thread.

"You really think we need to focus that much?"

"I certainly do. I believe there are other properties as well."

"What kind of properties?"

"It strengthens your natural resistance, at least the Bronze Silver Thread does. And I think this is pure. But let me worry about that. Let's get inside and clean up. You are taking me to dinner, right?"

————

Sylas wished that he had brought better clothing. Then he remembered that he often wore the same thing and shrugged it off. It didn't matter, really.

Now in a brown waistcoat over a pair of dark trousers, Sylas looked himself over in the mirror of their room at the inn. He ran his hand through his dark hair, and leaned in close to notice that a few of his beard hairs were longer than he would have liked. "No scissors . . ." he said as he took a quick look around. He rummaged through a drawer and found a pair of tweezers, which worked well enough, but stung.

"What's taking so long in there?" Mira asked after he had started working on his eyebrows.

"Sorry." Sylas stepped out into the main space, where he found Mira dressed up. He wanted to ask her how. How had she gone from the modest clothes she was wearing earlier to something that looked like she had spent some time putting together?

"What's that look?" she asked.

"There's no look. Shall we?" He offered Mira his arm and strolled to the door. It was only after reaching the door and realizing they both weren't going to be able to go through the door together that he stepped aside and gestured for her to go first. "After you, your ladyship."

"Thank you, kind sir."

Sylas noticed a faint smell of vanilla and cinnamon as she passed. He practically leaned forward to take a bigger whiff of it. She smelled wonderful.

And for once, he didn't let the voice at the back of his head remind him that this was one of the reasons he was going to fight for the Underworld. He didn't want to think about that right now. He only wanted to enjoy the night.

They had dinner at the Lili Mountain Restaurant, which served fresh bass caught from Lake Silver, alongside herbs that grew high up the mountain and were thick and chewy. Over the course of their meal, Sylas and Mira spoke of everything—their pasts, the people they knew—but the one thing they didn't touch on was the future.

They spoke of Duncan and Cody's new café; of Tilbud's numerous love affairs and how they both thought their knowledge of his relations with people in the Underworld was only scratching the surface; of Quinlan and Priscilla; of how quiet Kael was; of how cute Patches, Cornbread, and Gertrude were when they hung out together. They briefly touched on her uncle again but left the rest of that conversation for another day.

"And what about Azor and Horatio?" Mira asked as after-dinner tea was served.

"They do seem to be fond of one another. It is a bit ironic, a fire spirit and a water spirit, or maybe ironic isn't the right word. Maybe we should all just leave love where it is and let it do what it wants."

"Maybe. Speaking of love, are you going to miss Patches tonight?" she asked.

"I will, sure."

"Did you forget you had me?"

"Are you going to purr and refill my MLus? Will you let me scratch your belly and rub you behind the ears?"

Mira clenched her eyes shut as she tried to contain laughter. "You're ridiculous."

"That's no way to talk to your favorite person."

"Oh? You're my favorite now?"

"I hope. You want to get out of here?" he asked a few minutes later, after they had finished their tea. "I wanted to check out that other pub."

"I did not come all the way to Lilihammer to spend the night in a pub with you. I think a better idea would be to see if we can't find a bottle of that local lakeberry wine they were selling closer to the shore and enjoy it on our rooftop balcony. What do you think?"

"I like it."

"I thought you might. Let's get the bill."

"I will get the bill."

"Sylas."

"Mira."

"Really, Sylas."

"Really, Mira."

She crossed her arms over her chest. "Stop copying me."

Sylas wanted to continue, and knew it would've been funny, but he leaned back instead. "How about this: you can get dessert later."

"Who said anything about dessert?"

"I did. There were ice cream places closer to the water, and little cafés that served cakes. You remember."

"I was eyeing one of those cakes."

"Which one?"

"It was round and had berries on it."

"Then a round cake with berries you will get," Sylas said as he called the waiter over.

He transferred the Mana Lumens and they left, following the roads until they were closer to the shoreline, where they shared a berry cake and found a bottle of wine. They returned to the inn, got a pair of wineglasses from reception, and enjoyed each other's company for the rest of the night as they sat on the rooftop looking out at the water and the radiant clouds reflected off the waves.

[You have 29 days until the invasion.]
[A loan payment of 1395 has been deducted from your total Mana Lumens. Your total loan balance is 20238 Mana Lumens.]

Sylas, who had his arm wrapped around Mira, leaned forward and kissed the side of her head.

"Just five more minutes," she said.

"How about an hour instead?"

"Works for me."

The two fell back asleep, and Sylas later woke to the sound of birds outside. He kept his arm around Mira for another couple of minutes. Sylas kissed her again. "I'll be right back."

As quietly as he could, Sylas grabbed a set of robes and stepped out onto the balcony.

For a moment, he just stood there taking in the view.

Lake Silver gleamed in the distance as birds hovered over its waters, occasionally dipping in and coming back out. Below, the town was just waking up, and Sylas could smell the scent of baked bread in the vicinity. He walked to the edge of the balcony and looked down to see a bakery across the street, one that he hadn't noticed before since it was tucked away at the start of an alley.

Soon, Sylas sat in that very bakery with Mira, savoring egg tarts and enjoying cups of tea. The tea, adorned with floating flowers on the surface, was especially good, each sip relaxing him even further. "Before we go back, I should probably stop by Geist," he said almost as an afterthought.

"Yes? What were you needing there?"

"Berries. Do you remember the ones that Priscilla had? I thought Azor could use them for the feast."

"It's Wraithsday, right. How could I forget?" Mira said. "You did buy Azor some to experiment with, but she might need more."

"I thought so. And I have decided something else as well. I think we should postpone the Feast by a day."

"A Thornsday Feast?"

"Why not?"

"Well, I would need to speak to the vendors, but I think that's fine."

"It means we won't have to rush around today, which I like. Tilbud should have a pub quiz as well. Normalcy. It's important to maintain some in times like this."

"Then Geist it is." Mira pushed away from the table. "After, I'll speak to the vendors."

"Just like that?" he asked, half an egg tart in his mouth.

"Well, if you want to switch days for the feast, we need to get a move on." A smirk formed on her face. "Did you want to stay and have another pastry?"

"Of course I did. This might be the last time."

Mira sat down and got comfortable again. "The last time? Please, Sylas. You are not usually the one who's dramatic."

"I didn't mean it like that. I meant I don't think we're coming back to Lili-hammer anytime soon. In fact—" Sylas glanced at a second exit in the bakery, one that opened onto a balcony looking out onto the mountain. "I say we take this pastry outside."

They did just that, enjoying themselves for just a little longer until Sylas could no longer swallow the itch to get back on task.

As they portaled to the Landlord's Guild in Battersea, Sylas made plans to get the berries for Azor and then head back to his fields. He wasn't sure if he would be doing any more planting.

After all, Wigmund could show up at any moment and he didn't want the farm to go unprotected.

They arrived in Geist and headed straight to Priscilla's inn, where they found the woman sweeping. Quinlan was also there, the big man helping her by moving some wooden boxes around in the kitchen.

"Look what the cat dragged in," Quinlan said in lieu of a greeting.

"I swear I've heard you say that a couple times now," Sylas told him.

"And I'll say it plenty more. I mostly say it for Patches, even though he isn't here. The cute little guy."

"Patches, Patches, Patches," Priscilla said. "You have mentioned the cat, some dog named Cornbread, and was it a goose named Guardtrude, or am I getting the name wrong?"

"You would know if you joined me there, love," Quinlan told her.

"Gertrude," Mira said as she leaned against one of the tables. "The goose is mine; the dog and cat belong to Sylas."

"And you two are together, yeah?" Priscilla asked as she motioned between the two of them. "Ha! That means they're your children."

"Is that what that means?" Sylas asked. "Well, I actually don't know what to say to that, so, I will tell you why we came. Berries. The berries you spoke to us about last time. We would like some of them. Or I would, so I can give them to my bonded fire spirit. We picked some up last time, but I figured you'd know the best place to grab them."

"Geistian redberries?" Priscilla wiped her hands on the front of her apron. "Sure. You can get them at the market, but the cheapest place to buy them is at a little shop near the Geist Tree Spire. Mira should know her way there. After all," Priscilla said playfully, "she rang the bell."

"Maybe I will ring it again."

The group laughed at Mira's comment. Quinlan could hardly contain himself. "And force every demon hunter in Geist to come running? Please don't, Mira. That won't be good for any of us."

"You have my word, Quinlan."

"Another thing," Sylas said. "Tomorrow. Thornsday Feast. We normally have it on Wraithsday, but after my relaxing day in Lilihammer, I feel like postponing the feast by a day. You should come, Priscilla, really. You haven't visited Ember Hollow yet."

"I have not," she said as she held her nose up to some degree as she turned to Quinlan. "But that's mainly because someone has failed to invite me."

"What are you talking about, love? I have cordially invited you a half dozen times now. I think I invited you this morning," Quinlan said.

"And where would I stay if I went there?" Priscilla asked him. "Hmmm? He never mentioned that."

"There's an inn there now, run by Nelly and Karn. I told you about them."

"Did you?"

"I think?" He scratched the back of his head. "Anyway, we can stay there. I'm sure I can get a discount."

"Or the two of you can stay at my farmhouse," Sylas offered. "It's quaint. And I'm not planning on starting another harvest at least for another day or so. I want to see how things shake out."

"Yeah, maybe we could do that," Quinlan said, and by the way he looked at Sylas, Sylas knew that he too was thinking about what they may have to do once Wigmund returned. It wasn't like they weren't up for the challenge, it was just the stakes of it all. Looking around, both of them happy with their significant others, these stakes seemed even more real than they had been back in their world when they were fighting for their country.

Here, they were fighting for their way of life.

———

Pandemonium wasn't what Sylas expected as they portaled into Ember Hollow. For once, he just stood there, shocked, as they found the town at war with Manaboars.

"Sylas!" Mira said, snapping him out of it.

"Head back to Geist, tell Quinlan," he said quickly as he gave her the Geistian redberries they had procured from Priscilla's recommended shop.

And with that, he was off running at top speed toward the center of the village.

He heard shouting, barking, and an incredibly loud goose honk and saw blasts of mana. He reached the dead tree in the middle of the village, not far from The Old Lamplighter, and spotted Raelis and Kael battling the boars. Tiberius was leading the charge from the opposite direction, his militiamen in tow.

Patches jumped from a rooftop onto a Manaboar. The cat drove his claws into its back and piloted it toward the wall of Nelly's General Store. He jumped back just in time for Karn to come charging off the porch to whack the boar with a club.

The cat flashed invisible, before reappearing, three times his normal size, in the middle of the fight and stopped a boar from charging directly into the pub.

"About time you showed up!" Raelis called to him. "Bloody breach in the Hexveil. Did you check the market?"

Sylas had run right past the market on his way toward the commotion. Now, he had a sinking feeling in his stomach that passing it would be something he regretted. "I've got to go back."

"I'm coming with you," Raelis said hurriedly. "Kael, mate, finish it up. And mind the cat, yeah? He'll be in and out of the fight!"

"You go ahead, I'll stay here!" Kael said.

"Come on, Cornbread!" Sylas called to the farm dog, who had just taken down one of the boars.

Cornbread quickly joined him as he charged toward the market, where he found Manaboars rummaging through the stalls.

"Bloody boars!" Raelis said as he used a bolt of mana to pin one to the ground. He proceeded to beat it while Sylas hit another with Whimsical Drift.

"Where's Azor?"

"I'm here!" the fire spirit told Sylas she came alive at the far end of the market, flames gushing forward.

Now that she was there, Sylas was able to use Soulfire in its full extent, which allowed him to ignite several of the Manaboars. They ran around the market, mana flames rising from their forms as they were chased by Gertrude and Cornbread.

The goose threw her wings back and fired knifelike feathers at one of the boars. She took to the air several times and came down like a drill on another, losing a few big white feathers in the process.

Raelis burst out laughing. "Don't see that every day!"

"What about the Hexveil?" Sylas asked as Raelis clubbed a boar that was running around squealing as fire engulfed its body.

Raelis finished and shook his head as the creature pixelated into tiny motes of mana. "I haven't been there."

"Should we go?"

"Not really our role considering the guards there, but of course, we should go. Rally the troops and seal the wall ourselves, yeah?"

"I can go check on it," Azor told Sylas. "You might not need to go. This is going to ruin the feast tonight!"

"We'll do it tomorrow night. I was hoping to cancel it anyway."

"You were? Then . . ." Her eyebrows flared. "Then that actually works! How did you know?"

"I didn't. But if it makes sense to tell people I did, do that." Sylas took a look around and saw that while the market was damaged, most of the boars had been handled. There was one trying to run away, but Cornbread and Gertrude were on its tail and the boar was nearly dead. "Yeah, you do that. Let me check everything here," Sylas told her.

"I'll be back. Don't burn anything down before I get back here!" Azor zoomed away, a flicker of flame left in her wake.

Sylas and Raelis exchanged glances. Sylas spoke again: "Let me fully check the market. There better not be any damage."

But he knew damage was inevitable. As he walked through the stalls, he could see signs of the boars all over, plus burn marks from his Soulfire power.

"Not looking great. Rest of the village is a little beat up too," Raelis said as Sylas returned to him.

"We will see what Azor says, check in with Tiberius, and if we're cleared, head to Duskhaven."

"Duskhaven? Why there?" Raelis asked as Quinlan and Mira appeared on the scene, the two fresh from the portal.

Priscilla quickly joined them, the woman holding her broomstick like a weapon. "Where are the Manaboars?"

"Easy, love," Quinlan told her.

"Tilbud. I need to speak to Tilbud and he's in Duskhaven." Sylas's attention shifted to Mira, the way her eyes filled with sadness when she saw the market. "I'm sorry . . ."

"It's . . . it's not your fault. And we have bigger problems at the moment. Come on!" Mira hiked up her skirt and took off toward the center of the village, following the noise of battle.

"Last one there is a rotten egg!" said Quinlan.

The group ran toward the commotion and were quickly passed by Cornbread, who raced around them, her tongue flapping out of her mouth as she charged at her top speed.

Rather than try to keep up with them, Gertrude burst into the air before landing right in front of them as they reached The Old Lamplighter. The only demon left was an enormous Manaboar, one that had taken out the building that belonged to Henry, a member of the militia.

Zap!

Tiberius killed the massive creature using a lightning bolt of mana. He stumbled and fell to his knees. Quinlan quickly approached and clapped him on the back. "You good there, lord commander?"

"I will be fine. And where the bloody hell were you?" Tiberius asked, but his heart wasn't in it. It was clear that he was completely broken by the fact that the village had been attacked. It was like everything he had always expected to happen *finally* took place and he wasn't prepared for the aftermath.

"Look at my home," Henry said as he paced back and forth, his club over his shoulder. Cody and Duncan tried to comfort the older militiaman, but he shoved them aside.

"Everything will be repaired," Sylas said.

"What's the bloody point?" Henry asked, his eyes suddenly wet. "How many days do we have left? Thirty? Less?"

"Less," Sylas said solemnly as Mira and Priscilla moved around to check on the other buildings.

"We can't keep defending against this," Henry said. "I'm no coward, you know that. But this is just the start. Soon, there will be bigger things."

"No, there won't," Tiberius said as he got to his feet. "We have to believe our strategy will work. In the meantime, we will deal with the repairs and shore up our defenses."

"I've sent Azor to the Hexveil to check on it," Sylas said, in a tone that he would have used with a higher-ranking officer.

"Good, good, that's smart." Tiberius turned to his niece. "Mira, check to make sure no one is injured. Boys," he told the rest of the militiamen, "divide yourselves and start the cleanup. We'll begin repairs on Henry's home tomorrow."

"I'll join them," Raelis volunteered.

Kael, who stood off to the side, tucked a piece of wood he had just picked up under his arm. "I will as well."

"Count me in," Quinlan said as he shrugged at Priscilla.

"I'll get some food made," Nelly said. "I was already working on some cress sandwiches."

"Good, we could all use a bite," Tiberius said.

"In that case, I'll head to Duskhaven," Sylas said. "Tilbud will have an idea of what we can do."

Tiberius paused for a moment as he considered this. "Yes, fetch the wizard, but wait until Azor returns. I want to know what we can expect next."

———

Sylas appeared in Duskhaven completely frazzled. To go from the beautiful Lake Silver of Lilihammer to Geist and finally home to Ember Hollow where they found the village overrun by creatures from the Chasm was a lot to process. But at least the breach in the Hexveil had been contained.

He barely paid attention to his surroundings as he turned toward the enormous citadel at the center of the city, passed the MLR Bank, and found Tilbud's spherical home. He knocked on the large circular door of polished black iron. When no one replied, he knocked again, louder this time.

"Come on," Sylas said to himself, all but expecting the door to pop open to reveal any number of situations, from the archlumen mid-coitus to a magical happenstance that would need some serious explanation.

Not one to disappoint, Tilbud finally opened the door. He was wearing satin green robes, his hair was a mess, and his cheeks were red. "Sylas?"

"Who is it?" called a male voice from inside, one that Sylas recognized as belonging to Rufus the haberdasher.

"Really?" Sylas asked.

Tilbud stepped out of the house, a bit of embarrassment on his face. "He's not the only one in there, ahem, heh, that doesn't matter now. Really, Sylas, you expected me to behave when doomsday could be just around the corner? Please, let it be! If I'd known there were guests coming, I would have wrapped things up."

Sylas showed him the palms of his hands.

Tilbud, whose eyebrows were ruffled, squinted at him. "To what do I owe the pleasure? Have you heard from Wigmund? How was Lilihammer? Did you come to visit the Finmarket on Azor's behalf? If something else is in it? What about the feast tonight?"

"Tilbud."

"Sylas?"

"There has been another breach of the Hexveil. I came back from Lilihammer to find that Manaboars had overrun the village. We chased them off. Azor checked the border and it seems like everything has been contained. Tiberius is setting up patrols now and managing the rebuild. The feast has been postponed until tomorrow."

Tilbud had a hand to his chest, barely able to contain his shock. "I'm sorry."

"For what?"

"For being here. I thought we were all taking the day off, so I arranged a tryst."

"We took the day off *yesterday*."

Tilbud looked at Sylas like he was stupid. "Yes, and the tryst carried over to today, as good trysts often do. Really, Sylas, how did you expect this to end?"

"Is that a trick question?"

"I suppose given the circumstances, it could be a confusing one. I'm assuming you are in need of my services, yes? Even if you weren't, I would be in Ember Hollow in a heartbeat."

"With Rufus?"

"Likely not. But I'll grab Catia."

"Wait. She's in there too?" Sylas asked, an eyebrow raised.

"Sylas, dear man." The archlumen steepled his hands together. "Love is complicated. Now, I'm sure you're worried about the village. Head back, and I'll be there shortly."

"One more thing."

"Yes?" Tilbud asked just as he was starting to swivel.

"Tomorrow night. A rare Thornsday Feast. A pub quiz. A pub quiz to raise MLus to rebuild Henry's home."

"Henry . . . ?"

"The militiaman."

"The large one?"

"No, that's Duncan."

"His friend?"

"No, that's Cody."

Tilbud pressed tongue against the inside of his cheek. "Was there one named Gary? I remember him being part of the Ember Maces quiz team. Odd fellow."

"Yes, but that's not him."

"Ah, the older fellow who has a bit of a cackle. Limps. I want to say his home has a blue door? Wiry, thin fellow."

"Yes, Henry. You remember him well, it seems."

"My memory serves me at the strangest of times. Well, before we launch into another conversation, yes, of course I will host a quiz tomorrow, I will host a quiz at any time and at any point as long as I am given twelve hours' notice. It will be one for the ages. Hopefully by then, we will have heard from Wigmund." He dramatically glared up at the Celestial Plains. "Is anyone listening to us? I would hope so. Now, as for the feast, go, gather something at the market for Azor. Surprise her. Horatio and I will be around soon after I clear up my little situation here. And Sylas?"

"Yes?"

"Let's keep this between us." He made a sideways gesture with his thumb. "I don't want people to think I'm not taking the invasion message seriously, I am. Really, I am. I just have my own ways of coping."

————

Sylas returned to Ember Hollow and called Azor to him by touching the flame tattoo on his arm.

"You're back!" she said as she appeared in a flash of fiery purple.

"I tried."

"You what?"

"I tried to figure out what you could use at the market for tomorrow's Thornsday Feast, and I came up empty-handed. There were some sales in the meat department. I even stopped by Corlin Tartar's place to see he had a bunch of ugly black fish. Did Mira at least give you the berries?"

"She did, and it's fine. What about if we go back to the Finmarket together?" Azor gave him a reluctant grin. "We could go there now."

"I should get started around here. I wanted to surprise you."

"You don't have to surprise me, Sylas," she said. "And the village is fine. It's not as good as it could be, but nothing ever is. Everyone is busy doing something." Her flames flared up and smoothed out. "I really could use a little break, is what I'm saying."

"I know, this has been a tough day for everyone."

"Let's just head back to the Duskhaven quickly, I'll make arrangements, and we can get started here. Beef, yes?"

"Correct." Sylas, who still stood on the portal, motioned for Azor to join him. He didn't even need to skim the list of options given to him. Duskhaven was close to the top.

Sylas and Azor appeared in the city and the two quickly arrived at the Finmarket. Along the way, Sylas overheard people discussing the latest breach in the Hexveil. He wondered how it was possible for news to travel that quickly, but he assumed that there had been people in Ember Hollow who had already gone out for supplies.

He confirmed this as he saw Cody and Duncan carrying slats of wood.

"Mates," Sylas called over to them.

"Oi, Sylas!" Duncan came forward with an expression on his face that changed from one of happiness to hesitation. "Not looking so good, Ember Hollow. Our café wasn't hit too bad, but there is some damage to the counter we just built."

"And the door," Cody said.

"We're going back now. You?" Duncan asked.

"I'll be there in the hour. Azor and I need to get food for tomorrow's Thornsday Feast."

"Still doing one of those?"

"I am," Sylas said. "To benefit Ember Hollow, specifically Henry."

"A benefit feast?" Cody asked as he exchanged quick glances with Duncan. "Will there be a quiz?"

"There will. That's part of it." Sylas tried to keep a jovial tone, but it was hard. It absolutely crushed him to see Ember Hollow after the Manaboars had done their damage. This was mostly because he knew it was a taste of what was to come. He knew that it was only the start of the chaos if he couldn't do something. "Well, we better get going. We need to get back to Ember Hollow soon."

"See you there," Duncan said. "We'll get everything solved."

While Sylas waited nervously by the exit, Azor arranged for the delivery of beef, mushrooms, potatoes, and everything she would need to make a pastry. "I'm thinking a braised beef and ale pie. I probably should think of something for dessert. But we'll see. I'd rather under promise and over deliver. How about ale?"

"What about it?" Sylas asked as they passed the herb section, where he saw Esta with a customer.

"Aren't you going to do something?"

"You know what? I should. I really should. But I might not. We'll see how I feel later. But one thing is for certain, there will be drinks on the house. For everyone. I'm sick of this grind for MLus. Either our strategy is going to work or it isn't."

"You aren't giving up, are you?" Azor asked as she retreated somewhat into herself.

"No, nothing like that," Sylas assured her. "I'm just anxious for Wigmund to return and get on with it."

CHAPTER SEVENTEEN

THE RIVER MUST FLOW

Patches paced back and forth in front of the orange tabby, who was perched on the windowsill where Patches normally stayed.

Do we wake the fire spirit? Cornbread asked him for a second time.

Patches finally responded. *No. The last thing we want is her involvement.* He glared up at the other cat. *You're just a few seconds away from finding out what happens to intruders in the Tavernly Realm. Be gone!*

What about the goose?

She's at the market, Patches told Cornbread, now beside himself with the anger he was feeling for the other cat and how little the dog seemed to pick up on this.

But she could help us. Or we could go help her. What if there's an issue?

I don't know. We have an intruder right here and I'm not worried about the goose.

I'll go get her, then. You stay here.

But—

Cornbread took off, the dog bursting through the cat door.

Patches wanted to run after the dog, but decided it was more important to protect the Tavernly Realm. The orange cat had *spoken* in the human tongue to the big man the last time he was here. Patches was certain of it. Even though he didn't know what the orange cat had said, he knew what the human language sounded like.

What to do, what do to? Patches wondered as he paced back and forth in front of the yawning tabby. He could always wake the big man. It wouldn't be that hard. Or the fire spirit was right there, resting in her usual spot in the hearth.

But part of him wanted to handle this on his own. Patches was always independent, always did his best to take care of everything on his own, and it was only recently that the big man and the dog, as well as the goose and some of the others, had come into his life. For as long as he could remember, it had been Patches, Guardian of the Tavernly Realm.

How would he handle the tabby if it were a rat? Or some other hellacious being from the other side of the border?

Patches hissed at the orange cat. *I should attack you. You have infiltrated the Tavernly Realm and trespassers must perish!*

The orange cat finally shifted his gaze to Patches.

You heard me, you are not supposed to be here!

The other cat yawned.

Patches doubled in size. *You think you can mock me?*

His whiskers flattened. He was on the verge. Patches knew it. All he would have to do was jump onto the windowsill and knock the orange tabby aside. He was fairly certain he could take out the other cat, even if the tabby had a golden glow about him.

I can use powers as well, Patches warned the other cat. *You'll be sorry.* He thought about splitting his form in two, using one as a decoy. *I can wake the fire spirit. She will cook you like the meat she grilled the other day.*

Yet something made him hold back, and he knew what it was when a bark sounded off in the distance. Cornbread would return soon, likely with the goose. It would be better for Patches to defend the Tavernly Realm with the other animals. That was without question. There was something off about this cat, and, even if Patches would never have admitted it in front of the dog or the goose, he liked the idea of them being around as backup.

You showed up. You spoke to the big man. You think you own the place, he said as he continued to scowl at the tabby. *But you don't. This is my realm.*

He heard the sound of Cornbread's nails on the back porch. Patches knew that the dog wanted to explode inside, yet was aware that the fire spirit was sleeping so she carefully came in through the cat door.

Cornbread immediately joined Patches and bared her teeth as she peered up at the tabby. *Am I doing this right?*

Hello! Gertrude peeked her head in. The goose tried to come through the cat door, but her rear end was too big. At least it seemed that way until she managed to thrust herself forward, to the point that she was almost stuck.

It took a little wiggling, but soon, Gertrude's webbed feet touched down on the wooden floorboards of the Tavernly Realm. *There, that does it! I don't think I've been in here yet,* she said as she took a quick look around. *Wow. So this is where the big man hangs out with all of his friends.*

I was telling you it's nice and cozy, Cornbread said through gritted teeth. *I like to sleep right there.* She nodded her head to a particular corner. *And the cat likes to sleep right there.*

And the big man is upstairs?

We can have this conversation later, Patches told the two of them. *We have an intruder. Now that you are both here, I say we do something about it.*

Gertrude looked up at the orange tabby. *I don't know. It looks just like you.*

I am very different from this cat.

You are a lot fatter, Cornbread said as she relaxed her growl, *I agree. And your fur is black and white. Everything is black and white. But he's a lighter dark and white than you are.*

Patches shook with agitation. *He's orange. Can't you see orange?*

Or-ran-ge? Is that a shade of black or white?

Never mind. Patches gathered his wits. *That's not what we're here for, anyway. We are not here to talk about appearances. We are here because of him!*

The other cat came to the end of the windowsill. He approached the edge and rested his head on his two front paws as he looked down at the three of them. "Relax, Patches," he finally said.

Patches's hair stood at attention upon hearing the tabby's voice. *Patches? What are you saying? And could you talk this entire time?*

"I'm talking to you now, am I not?" the orange cat asked. "And that's your name. That's what they call you, the humans."

Patches was abhorred by the revelation. *Why do they call me Patches?*

"Because your fur is black and white, Patches. Humans are simple in that way. Do you have a name for yourself?"

Why would I need a name?

"So, you don't. Well, in that case . . ." The orange cat yawned. "You are Patches and you," he told the dog, "are Cornbread."

Cornbread started laughing. *I get it. It's because I guard the corn on the Farmly Realm. Although I don't think I've ever tasted cornbread. Is it delicious? I do like bread, you know. I didn't know you could make bread of corn. Or did I? Maybe the fire spirit did that one time. I wouldn't know. I usually just eat what's in front of me. What about the goose? Does she have a name?*

"Gertrude," the tabby said.

Is that a pretty name in the human language? Gertrude asked.

"It's an old name. I wouldn't say it is pretty, but it suits a goose. Patches, Cornbread, and Gertrude."

They seriously call me Patches? The pub cat looked at his own rear. *It's so insulting!*

No, it's not, Cornbread told him as she licked his face. *It fits you, just like the not-dark cat said. Wait, if we all have names, then you have a name. What's your name?*

"Wigmund."

Huh, I don't think I've ever heard that name before, Cornbread told the tabby, *but I'm no expert on names. Although, now that you have told me what my name is, I believe I've heard the humans call me something else. Yes. The big man calls me a different name. It sounds like "ur-ll." "Urr-ll."*

"He probably says something along the lines of 'Good girl.'"

Does he? That suits me well. I am a good girl! Cornbread said, the dog seconds away from barking when Patches swatted at her. *Hey!*

We don't want to wake the fire spirit.

"Dogs often have other names aside from their main name," Wigmund explained.

What about cats? Patches asked, curious again.

"Perhaps not as much, no. Cats aren't known to be as friendly as dogs."

Patches hiked his tail up. *We are plenty friendly. You, yourself, are a cat. Wait, why should we listen to you? How do we know you're not some crazy cat that has just come in here to lie to us?*

"I can show you if you'd like, but maybe we shouldn't do this here with the fire spirit, as you call her," Wigmund said.

Then where?

"Downstairs."

Fine. I'll lead the way. Patches turned to the cellar. He stopped to make sure the others were following him, but did so as casually as possible, as if he didn't care if they were or not. Luckily, they were, Gertrude behind Cornbread and Wigmund.

The four headed down into the cellar, where Wigmund hopped up onto a stool.

Why must you always be above us? Patches asked the orange cat.

"I jumped up here for a reason," Wigmund told them. "Watch."

Patches nearly took his largest size again in fright as the orange tabby morphed into a man with orange hair, his fur replaced by flowing robes that seem to drape past the legs of the stool.

Cornbread's wagging tail came to a sudden stop.

You're . . . human? Gertrude asked.

"I am. Have you ever looked up at the sky and wondered what was up there? Why it glows with a golden hue? Or why it is never night here? I am from there. The Celestial Plains, heaven."

Cornbread took a cautious step forward, her tail now tucked between her legs. *If you are from there, then why are you here?*

"I am here to help Sylas."

Who is that? Patches asked.

The brewer.

Cornbread and Patches exchanged glances. Cornbread spoke: *His name is Sylas?*

"It is, yes."

Sy-las, Cornbread said as if she were tasting the word.

And the medicine woman? Gertrude asked, her tail feathers wagging with excitement.

"That is Mira. The fire spirit sleeping above, that's Azor."

Who is the man without the hand? Cornbread asked. *He's a good fighter.*

"That would be Quinlan."

Quin-lan . . . Sy-las . . . Mi-ra, Cornbread said.

And the one missing an eye? Patches asked almost reluctantly. He didn't like everything he was hearing, yet was now moved by curiosity.

That would be Mira's uncle, Tiberius.

That's a harder name to say, Cornbread told Wigmund. *Ti-ber-i-us. Pfft. Too hard.*

Who is the funny man that performs magic? Gertrude asked. *He was there when they rescued me from that terrible academy.*

You never told me about that, Cornbread said.

I'm still trying to forget it. They tortured me at the academy, poking and prodding me. It was because of my sound. The entire experience was dreadful!

I'm so glad you don't make that sound anymore, Patches told her.

It was involuntary, Patches.

He scowled at her. *That's not my name.*

Gertrude nodded her beak at the man seated on the stool. *He just said it was it was your name.*

Why does someone else get to decide my name and not me? the pub cat asked as he swished his tail.

Wigmund took this answer. "That's just the way things are. Any other questions about names? And the magic man, as you call him, he is Tilbud. Other questions?"

What about the human with long dark hair? And the other warrior, the one that just showed up? Cornbread asked.

"That would be Raelis and Kael. Kael is Quinlan's brother."

I knew it! Cornbread said. *I could tell by their scents they were related.*

"I'm sure you could. Those three men were friends with Sylas before he died."

Patches nearly headed back upstairs. He had heard enough. *Now, you are telling us that the big man—*

Sylas, Cornbread said.

I don't know if I want to call him that. Now, you are saying that he is dead?

"Everyone here is dead," Wigmund told Patches. "This is the Underworld. Above is heaven, the Celestial Plains. Beyond the wall, which is known as the Hexveil, is the Chasm. Hell."

We're all dead? Patches asked.

"Correct, you have been for a long time. But it's not so bad, is it? Being dead is something people should try more often."

So why are we here, then? Gertrude asked. *This is a lot of information to process. Why are you telling us this?*

"Well, for one, Patches wouldn't stop challenging me to a fight. And I'm not here to fight him. I'm actually here to speak to Sylas in the morning. I figured I would let him rest. Things are changing tomorrow, you know."

How so?

"Everything will be frozen soon. By everything, I mean Mana Lumens. It will not change until this is resolved. So wherever they are now—"

Cornbread woofed. *Wait! What are Mana Lumens? Did you already cover that? I might have missed something.*

"No, you didn't miss anything. You're being a good girl."

I'm always a good girl!

"Mana Lumens are your magic power. Your life force is fueled by Mana Lumens. I've tried what I can in the Plains to set things on the right course, but that has come at some costs. Let's just say it is the price of what is about to happen. After all, the river must flow."

You mean the information listed in the text we can see? Patches asked. *I don't understand it.*

"Yes, that would be it. And you don't have to worry too much about it because you will be going with them."

With who?

"Sylas and whomever he brings. But I suspect it will be the warriors, the archlumen, Azor, and perhaps Mira, although I do not know for sure. We will have to see what he decides."

Where will we be going exactly? Gertrude asked Wigmund.

"As part of the exchange, you will journey to the Celestial Plains to hunt for something."

I'm good at hunting, Cornbread said. *The cat is better.*

Patches, my name isn't . . . Patches grew flustered. *No, I like it better when you call me cat.*

I like being called Cornbread, the dog said as she wagged her tail. *It reminds me of where I'm from.*

Patches gave her a funny look. *You aren't from corn nor are you from bread.*

I know. I'm from the corn farm, though.

I like my name as well, Gertrude said. *I always wondered what they called me, the humans.* She returned her focus to Wigmund. *So you're telling us that we will go with them?*

"Yes, they will want you to come. I don't know if he will bring all of you, but I'm certain he will bring at least one of you."

Who will protect the Tavernly, Farmly, and Marketly Realms? Patches asked.

"The humans will, or at least they'll try," Wigmund said. "I'm referring to the ones who will stay behind."

And how long will we be gone? Cornbread asked as her tail continued to thump against the ground.

"Now that remains to be seen. Are there any other questions you may have? I can tell that this is a lot to learn in one night, and that's without getting into *why* the humans need to visit my realm."

I have another question, Cornbread said as her tail wagged back and forth nervously. *Does he like us?*

"Does who like you?" Wigmund asked.

The big man. Does he? I think he does.

Wigmund smiled. "Of course, he likes you. Sylas loves you all."

Cornbread moved her throat back like she was going to bark, but she didn't. *That's good to know. And the fire spirit?*

"Yes, Azor thinks you are adorable. She likes Patches, but thinks Patches likes her. She has no opinion on the goose because they haven't really had a chance to bond."

Do you like her? Cornbread asked Patches.

Does this matter right now? came the cat's rebuttal.

I'm just asking.

I think the fire spirit is fine, Patched told Cornbread. *Sometimes, she's annoying, that's all. Azor is her name, yes? That's a strange name as well.*

Wigmund rubbed his hands together. "Are we finished here? I would like to return to my cat form."

Wait, what about Mi-ra, Gertrude asked, taking care with her name. *Does she like me?*

Oh, bother, Patches said as he turned to the stairs that led up to the pub. *You are both so vain.*

"Mira cares for you immensely," Wigmund told Gertrude.

Good. The goose held her head high. *It's nice to be cared for.*

————

[You have 28 days until the invasion.]

Sylas was rubbing the sleep out of his eyes when a realization hit him. Where was the rest of the information? The part about his loan payment and what he owed?

He accessed his stats.

Name: Sylas Runewulf
Mana Lumens are currently locked.
Class: Brewer
Secondary Class: Farmer
Tertiary Class: Landlord

He sat up and was alarmed to find the orange tabby at the foot of the bed.

"Hello, Sylas," Wigmund told him.

"What does it mean?" Sylas asked as he tried to make sense of his status. "Locked? What about my loan payment?"

Wigmund stopped licking his paw and started laughing. "The first thing of concern is your loan payment? You are a better citizen than I would have thought! Not that I ever thought poorly of you. Let's just say your loan payment is in forbearance. Everyone's loan payments are suspended for the time being. It is going to take a lot of mana. More than I can actively gather. One of the main issues is that by gathering said mana, I will alert the governing body that oversees mana distribution."

"So you can actually get what is needed?"

Patches, who had been under the covers this entire time, pushed his head out. He locked eyes with Wigmund, mewed, and headed back under.

"That is why everything is frozen. I'm more clever than I may look," the orange tabby told him. "And I know people that have access to high levels of system management. There is a way to orchestrate a complete reset. That is not what this is. But it is one step before, which I've already approved with the Council. You didn't really think I was simply basking in the glow of the Celestial Plains up there, did you? No, my good man, I have been busy."

Sylas looked out the window as if he could see the village coming awake, knowing the confusion that would set in. "Everyone is going to be asking about this change in the system."

"They are. The Underworld is about to come awake to something that many have never experienced before. But some have. Those who were alive during the time of the Crafting Laws will help alleviate some concern. They will tell people that the Celestial Plains are working on a change. Some will rejoice, others will be less happy."

"And what about mana? I mean, can I brew tonight?" he asked.

"You can, yes. The mana you are able to spend normally will still work, at least for class-based things. But that's not going to concern you very much because by the time you return, this will all be resolved."

Sylas blinked a few times as he considered what the divine arbiter just told him. "How so?"

"I should clarify: by the time you return, we will hopefully know if this is possible or not. Or, better, we will be on the precipice of whatever is about to happen. Tomorrow morning—and notice that I'm giving you a day because I am aware that the Thornsday Feast is important to you—tomorrow morning, you and the people and pets you select will head to the Celestial Plains, to the staging ground."

"Why do I feel like this is a suicide mission?"

"What makes you say that?"

"A hunch."

"You have good instincts, but this isn't exactly that. You shouldn't worry about that now, Sylas. Just worry about putting your team together. I should say, as well, that your fire spirit won't be able to join you. If you took citizenship, I would be able to offer her a path as well, but for this mission, Azor will need to remain here. Again, not a worry."

"You know by telling me not to worry about it that I will worry about it, right?"

Wigmund yawned, his cat tongue curling out of his mouth. "Sorry, it's been a long night. I had a nice conversation with your pets, you know. They are very friendly creatures. Well, two of them are."

Sylas looked down as Patches swished his body beneath the blanket. "Can he really understand you?"

"He can, yes. Well, when I speak in his language. Right now I'm speaking in your tongue, so he can't, but he is a smart cat and he senses things. They know their names now."

"Do they like them?" Sylas shook his head. Of all the things running through his head right now, questions regarding his pets were the last thing that he knew he should be asking. Really, they didn't matter, not with what he had just been told. But he spoke the question before fully processing what was happening.

"They are satisfied, yes. Cornbread seemed to especially like her name."

"You said that they may come with me to the Celestial Plains."

"Correct."

"What about protecting the village? Never mind my farm, we had an invasion here yesterday." Sylas nodded to the window. "And that's just the start. Everyone is on edge."

"Ah, that. The Hexveil is underfunded at the moment."

"Underfunded?" Sylas grew agitated at this statement. Was that really what all of this was about? The Mana Lumens necessary to keep up the wall that protected their way of life?

"No need to look at me like that. It is something else that we will be able to address once we change public opinion." Wigmund grinned. "Cheer up, old chap!"

"Which public?"

"I don't mean for this to sound offensive, but the one that matters to our overall outcome: the denizens of the Celestial Plains."

"I thought you'd say something like that," Sylas grumbled.

"I agree with your sentiment. Everyone that is here in the Underworld is the same as a person in the Celestial Plains, and if we are being frank, the same as those, like the man you took the farm from—"

"Brom."

"Yes, him. Those who have passed on to the Chasm. They are human as well, at least the ones that aren't demons. Heh."

"I don't see why someone would have to pass from here to there to begin with. How's it their fault that they can't manage their MLus? How does that make them guilty of anything?"

"I appreciate your sentiment, but again, I'm not the one that made those rules. They were made long before the Crafting Laws. They are known as the Rules of Mana Retention. I can summarize them for you rather than let you read them for yourself because the text is quite tedious, but, basically, *in accordance with the stipulations set forth in the Rules of Mana Retention, it is hereby decreed that any denizen of the Underworld who depletes their allocation of Mana Lumens shall be subjected to the automatic, and indiscriminate, transition to the Chasm.* It goes on from there, but basically, it is a law that was implemented to ensure the maintenance of the resources of the Celestial Plains."

"Unbelievable."

"Quite, but we're not going to be able to turn the tide of this war with a discussion on afterlife classes and the distribution of mana wealth." Wigmund yawned again. "Sorry, did I mention I was up late last night waiting for you?"

"Why? Why didn't you just come in the morning?"

"It's fun being a cat sometimes, you should try it. In fact . . ." His whiskers twitched. "Maybe that's something we can explore later. In any event, I will be here tomorrow morning at the same time and perhaps in the same form. You should gather your most loyal and trusted companions to accompany you to the Celestial Plains. And you should know that I do think it's wonderful what you have done here in Ember Hollow. Inspiring, really. This place was a ghost town before you arrived."

"You really know a lot about the Underworld, don't you?"

"Yes. I'm not like the others in the Plains." Wigmund hopped down from the bed. "I lived in the Underworld for a long time. Heard of Draugr?"

Sylas squinted for a moment as he tried to place where he had heard the name. "Maybe."

"It's not so far from here, really. Just past Cinderpeak, a bit farther southeast. Sort of if you were heading to Douro, but you veered off course. I helped revitalize that town. It's what got me into the Plains."

"So people really do make it there by doing good deeds?"

"Yes, but it used to be much easier. These kinds of things change, you know. Sadly. Anyway, tonight, I do hope that you have a blast, Sylas. I hope that everyone in the village enjoys themselves. And when you meet people, which I'm sure you will today, tell them not to worry about the current fluctuation with the system. Hopefully, this is all for the better."

CHAPTER EIGHTEEN

DRAUGR

Mira didn't realize that her Mana Lumens were frozen until she had break-fast with her uncle. She had slept so hard after the night of drinking at the pub that she figured the loan prompt had come and gone, and she just hadn't noticed it.

"You wake up to something new every day," Tiberius said bitterly as he but-tered a piece of toast. "Every day."

She gave the often-bitter man a funny look. "What exactly did you wake up to this morning, Uncle?"

And upon hearing the answer to that question, one asked ironically, Mira stood, excused herself, and headed directly to The Old Lamplighter, where she found Sylas and his friends gathered around the bar, Quinlan shoveling por-ridge into his mouth while Priscilla gave him a shoulder massage.

"That's it, love," Quinlan told the woman as she dug her fingers in deeper. "Feels bloody nice."

"The system is broken, by the way," Raelis said to Mira in lieu of a greeting.

"I saw that. MLus are frozen." Mira took a seat at the bar. "What's going on?"

Azor raced over to her. "What would you like, Mira? Everyone else is having porridge with butter and cinnamon and raisins—"

"And walnuts," Quinlan added. "Don't forget the walnuts. Oi!" he told Pris-cilla. "Go easy on me, yeah?"

"You'll be fine," she told him as she dug in just a bit deeper with her fingers.

"Walnuts too. Does that sound good to you, Mira? Even Cornbread likes my porridge," Azor said as she motioned to the ground, where the farm dog was licking her bowl clean.

"Sure," Mira said.

"I'll be right back!" Azor disappeared in a flash of fire, leaving Mira with Sylas and the others.

"I bet you were surprised when you checked your stats this morning," Quinlan told Mira.

"Actually, it was my uncle who told me."

"Heh. Tibby probably wasn't too happy."

"It's hard to tell with him, but you're right, he likely wasn't too happy. I came over here as soon as I learned of it. What happened?" Mira asked as she focused on Sylas.

Sylas placed his spoon down and grinned at her. "Why are you looking at me?"

"I figured you would know."

"You would have known too if—"

Mira blushed. "Sylas!"

Priscilla laughed. "Ha! I was surprised myself that you didn't stay over last night. You seemed drunk," she told Mira matter-of-factly.

"I was a bit intoxicated, yes, but it had been a terrible day," Mira said. "The village was attacked. I just walked through it now, and was reminded of how terrible that experience was, and *my* home happened to be spared. What I'm saying is that I was flustered. I shouldn't have to explain myself to any of you."

"You might want to rethink where you stay tonight," Quinlan said. "Just saying, things change quickly around here. Might as well act like it's the end of days because that's what it is."

Mira ignored him and peered at Sylas for a moment. "Are you going to tell me what happened to our statuses, or not?"

"Wigmund explained this morning. Everyone's MLus are frozen, and loans are in forbearance. I have a feeling he didn't fully tell me everything, but he spoke to the Council, and he was able to use some mechanism he knew of to hold MLus for the time being through a partial reset. He did this because of what it's going to cost for us to send the messages we need to send."

"Really? And what about the other part of this, Sylas, the MLus he said he had access to?"

"Wigmund can get them, but they will be in exchange for our services. Well, I should clarify: whomever I take with me to the Celestial Plains."

"I'm in," Quinlan said with a belch.

"Quin!" Priscilla smacked him on the back of the head.

"Oi! I have no control over it."

"You most certainly do," she said. "And no burping while I'm massaging you."

"In," Kael told Sylas, "but you already knew that." He elbowed Raelis. "What about you, mate?"

"I thought I said that I was in yesterday," Raelis said, his mouth full of porridge.

"I figured you all would be in. I'm afraid the lord commander will want in," Sylas said as he looked at Mira.

"I'm sure he will," she told Sylas. "And Tilbud?"

"Sure."

"Who else?"

"Me," Azor said as she rushed up the steps with a bowl of porridge. There were three big lumps of butter on it, which were covered in cinnamon, blueberries, walnuts, and even little slices of apple that she had cut so they were semi-submerged by the oats.

"Unfortunately," Sylas said, "Wigmund informed me that bonded spirits can't come. If I were to take the citizenship route, that would be different. But you and Horatio will need to remain here."

"Ah, really?" Azor's flames drooped.

"I'm sorry."

"Priscilla?" Mira asked. "What about you?"

"No, I'm not really the fighter type," the woman said.

"First I'm hearing of it," Quinlan told her. "You fight with me every chance you get!"

She lightly tapped him on the back of the head. "Watch yourself. And really, I need to head back to Geist anyway."

"After tonight though, yeah? The feast, remember?"

"Yes, after tonight, Quin. I promised I would stay."

"Good!"

"Ugh. I have so much to do today," Azor said frantically, her flames whipping left and right.

"Is that your way of asking for help in the kitchen?" Quinlan asked.

"It's not, but it could be . . ."

"I would love to help," Priscilla said. "I know my way around the kitchen."

"Quinlan said you make an amazing stew," Azor told her.

"I've been known to whip up something good every now and then."

Mira returned her focus to Sylas. "What about you? Any additional plans for tonight?"

"Not now, aside from dealing with everyone that comes to the pub. I meant to brew something unique last night, but . . ."

"We were all a little tipsy, weren't we?"

"Correct."

Mira thought back to what had started as a normal night at The Old Lamplighter, how it had quickly morphed into a situation in which everyone seemed to be grieving about the attack together. There were rounds after rounds, and while she normally only drank the light ale, even Mira had finished off a stronger ale.

As to Sylas's suggestion that she should have stayed the night: Mira had been hyperaware of the possibility. She had wanted to, yet her own stubbornness had pushed her away from the pub and out the door, where she drunkenly stumbled home after refusing to let Sylas walk with her. It was the first thing she thought about that morning, with regret, and was likely another reason she hadn't noticed the absence of the loan payment message.

She had no intention of telling Sylas that she planned to stay with him tonight, especially in front of the others, and especially with Quinlan's earlier comment about the end of days. Mira understood that with the way things were about to change, there was no telling how many more nights they had left. But as always, she wanted everything to be on her terms.

"Ever been to Draugr?" Sylas asked her a few minutes later.

"No, why?"

"Wigmund mentioned it. It is the village that he lived in when he was an Underworldian. He said he helped fix it up. I was thinking about checking it out today. Of course, there is plenty to do around Ember Hollow. There's a load that needs to be done. I just thought it would be nice to see, you know, some inspiration."

"Then we'll go there now, after I finish this lovely porridge, and after I drop something off for Miss Barrowsly," Mira said. "And we'll be back in time to help everyone and prepare for tonight's festivities. Plus, the market. It will be open, and the vendors will be showing up later."

"Night Market?" Quinlan asked. "Inaugural, yeah? I'm looking forward to pouring pints."

Sylas smiled at Mira. "Sounds like a plan."

She ate her porridge quickly, her spirits instantly lifted. It had been a shocker to see that the system had frozen in some way, and it was good that this didn't seem like it would become the pressure point that Mira had originally anticipated.

At least she hoped this was the case.

———

After breakfast and as Sylas and Mira cut through the village on their way to Miss Barrowsly's forested home, they ran into Henry, who was with Anders the carpenter, bringing some building materials to his home.

"I'm guessing you already looked at your statuses this morning," Mira told them.

Anders quickly checked his status and gasped. "What the devil? 'Mana Lumens are currently locked.' What is that supposed to mean?"

"I saw it earlier," Henry admitted. "But I have bigger problems at the moment. I just figured the Celestial Plains were up to no good, as always."

"Actually, you're not wrong," Mira said carefully. "The same thing happened during the implementation of the Crafting Laws," she told the two, repeating what Sylas had explained earlier. She had kept expecting him to jump in and add his own explanation but he never did. "So I suppose I should tell you to just sit tight, and not worry about it, but I can understand how it would be worrisome."

"Eh," Henry said, waving her concern away, "it's all madness, all of it. Best we shore up the village for what is to come, just like Tiberius said. Your uncle is on a rampage, and not a bad one. Maybe that's the wrong word for it. He was up all night, patrolling back and forth, and making sure things were in order. Follow me."

Henry led them around his home to an open field in the back that pressed up to the forest. Sure enough, there was the start of the wall, and several of the militiamen were digging.

"A wall around Ember Hollow?" Mira asked. It wasn't unheard of, but the way that the village was designed, it would be hard to completely protect. Not only that, the creatures of the Hexveil were known to go around objects in other ways, such as tunneling beneath them. She also wasn't certain a wall would be able to stop a Taurigraith, or any of the other nastier flying demons her uncle had spoken of.

"What's that look?" Henry asked her. "You don't trust your uncle?"

"No, I'm just concerned it won't be enough."

"He said there will be watchtowers too."

Sylas groaned. "I get what the lord commander is trying to do, but we still don't know the result of our other plan yet. All of these things would need to be dismantled if we're successful."

"Eh, I don't know." Henry motioned to some of the militiamen who were working on the wall. "And these lads agree with me. Maybe it's something we keep up. Keep Ember Hollow secure."

Mira didn't say anything, but she could tell by the look in Sylas's eyes that he was thinking the same thing. Likely not the exact same thing, but his own version of it, something she confirmed later as they left Henry and Anders.

"You don't like it, do you?" she asked as they exited the village. "What my uncle is doing."

"Walls are helpful. Walls are good. Walls keep *them* out and *us* in. But I don't personally think it will help much in Ember Hollow if the main wall, the Hexveil, is down. Maybe I'm being selfish, but I always liked the open nature of the village. I know we have our issues, but if we all start walling in our places, well it will look like . . ."

"It will look like what?" Mira asked after he trailed off. He had that look in his eyes again, like he was reliving something that only Sylas understood. She reached out and took his hand. "Like what?"

"Like my kingdom, the Aurum Kingdom. Everything, especially near the border, was walled off. I remember missing the interior of the kingdom, all the open space. There were still walls, but they were mainly for sheep and other livestock, not the kind that you would put around an outpost, which is what I think Tiberius would prefer. I guess I'm saying I don't want Ember Hollow to look like that, but at the same time, especially if what we do fails, I could see how it would help."

Mira took his hand. "I know what you're saying. If things don't change soon, if we don't have a viable solution, people are going to do crazy things. And we really can't blame them, can we? In a way, it is in our nature. When we are threatened, we make rash choices for our own safety. That's what my uncle is doing, and he is forcing his choice on all of us, whether we would like it or not. Personally, I don't think it's a battle worth fighting."

"Which one?"

"I mean with my uncle. We're not going to be able to stop him. In fact, this may be a good way to distract him, unless you are planning on bringing him to the Celestial Plains."

"I wanted to ask you about that, what you thought. I know he'll want to go, but I probably operate better with my friends; Tilbud, if he is willing; and you."

"And our pets," Mira said.

"Them too. They will probably all come, but who are we kidding? We do have to remember that even if they have magical powers, they need to be taken care of to some extent. I also don't know what this campaign will look like, nor do I know where it will take place. I don't know anything really about the Plains aside from the main city, Galataport."

"Should my uncle go or should he not go? I don't know. But I do know this. I met you on the cusp of hell and if we're being honest," she said as she turned to him, "I don't want to lose you. I don't know if I can technically lose you to the Plains, or what would happen if the worst took place in the sky above. I don't know. Because I don't know, like my uncle, I'm making a rash decision to join you and whomever you decide."

"We probably should bring Tiberius, shouldn't we?"

"Yes, we probably should, but that doesn't mean I want to, and that doesn't mean that there shouldn't be some rules in place. Because my uncle will want to lead everything, you know that. It is in his nature. But we don't know what we're up against yet, and if we arrive there and it's not exactly what he planned, he has a way of short-circuiting."

"And that's where my men come in handy. They are good at adapting on the fly."

"So in a way, everyone is bringing something to the table."

"I suppose in a way, that's true. And that is what a core crew, my old mates, should be able to do. But I can do that too. I have led thousands before."

"You don't give yourself enough credit, Sylas. Maybe this is the perfect opportunity to show what you're capable of to yourself and leave my uncle behind."

"So he can continue to turn the village into something it maybe shouldn't be? I guess that's a tough choice I'm going to have to make. Do I want to come back and potentially come to blows with him about what he's done to my home? Do I trust him not to push things to the extreme? Or do I bring him with us, and run the potential of Tiberius disrupting the progress of our mission in heaven, whatever that mission may be?"

"I can always stay behind to watch my uncle."

"I thought you said you had to come with me, something about being so close to hell . . ."

"I did say that, didn't I?" she said as they reached a home in the woods that Sylas had noticed once before. "Let me just drop this off, then we can continue this conversation."

"Let's finish the conversation now and then I will drop it off with you. I've always wanted to meet Miss Barrowsly."

"Why?"

"I think you told me before that she's one of the oldest residents here. Maybe she knows something. Maybe I should invite her to the Feast tonight."

Mira imagined what this would look like. "Miss Barrowsly doesn't really get around. She can hardly walk."

"We can send someone around, can't we? Your uncle has horses. Surely, he has a carriage somewhere tucked away."

"Actually, he does. How did you know that?"

"I've been in your backyard, I've seen it."

"Right. So what are you thinking regarding the trip to the Plains? My uncle, yes or no?"

Sylas brought his hand to his chin, which made Mira laugh. "What?"

"Look at you, so deep in thought."

He smiled. "I suppose I am, yeah?"

"You really don't have to make a decision now. You can mull it over in Draugr."

"Maybe I can."

"We can sit at a café there, if there is a café, and weigh out the pros and cons. How's that? And then we will return to Ember Hollow and deal with everything from there, back to our lives. But before we do that, Miss Barrowsly. She won't be expecting another visitor, so maybe let me speak to her first."

———

Miss Barrowsly was just about the oldest-looking person Sylas had encountered in the Underworld. The woman was hunched forward and she had to use a walker to move. Because of her posture, it seemed like she wouldn't be able to make eye contact with Sylas, yet she looked up at him with big, curious eyes when he approached.

"Mira," she said as she gripped the apothecary's arms. "He's cute. Just like you said."

"Sylas, Miss Barrowsly; Miss Barrowsly, Sylas," Mira said with a flash of embarrassment.

"Hi," Sylas told the older woman as he approached. He thought of offering her his hand, but decided against it when he saw just how frail she was and the way she trembled. "It's nice to finally meet you. I've heard good things."

She released a hoarse laugh. "Please. What's nice to say about me? I've been here for as long as I can remember and I can't take care of myself. Not good enough to join my sister up there," she said, squinting at the Celestial Plains, "and not bad enough to take a one-way trip to the Chasm."

"You have a sister?" Mira asked. "This is the first I've heard of her."

"I do. We got in a fight, one that ended in a fatal way. What I'm saying is that I accidently killed her, but, as I said, it was by accident. I'm no murderer."

"How did you kill your sister?" Sylas asked after looking at Mira to confirm that this was a line of questioning she was also interested in pursuing.

"Oh, that. I'll admit it was my fault. We always argued about one of our mother's recipes. You see, we worked in a kitchen together in King Nova's summer home."

"King Nova?" Sylas asked, recalling the statues he had seen dedicated to the man who had united the Aurum Kingdom hundreds of years ago. King Nova was a legend, and thinking of him made Sylas wonder where he could be now. While the king had done a load of good for the Aurum Kingdom, in the eyes of a Shadowthornian, he would have been a villain.

"Yes, you've heard of him."

"I have," Sylas told the older woman.

"He was a bit of a prick," she said, "but from my experience, that's normal for a king. Hopefully he's burning in the Chasm."

"Right," Mira said as she bit her lip. "So what happened in the kitchen, Miss Barrowsly?"

"We were arguing about our mother's recipe. I had a bucket of dishes in my hand and set them down. They were soapy, you know, and we continued arguing until I slammed my fist on the table. This caused the bucket to fall, the dishes scattering. My sister went to pick up the dishes and slipped. She hit her head on the corner of the butcher's table and it killed her."

"That's terrible," Sylas said.

"It gets worse. King Nova had me executed thinking it was foul play. I ended up here, as you can see, and my sister found her way up there." She pointed a shaky finger at the sky.

"Do you know her name?"

"Of course I know my sister's name," Miss Barrowsly told Sylas. "It's Vaire. She's up there. Last I remember hearing, she was in Izalith."

Sylas's eyes went wide. Vaire of Izalith, also known as the high seraph, who sat on the Celestial Council. What were the odds that she was related to Miss Barrowsly? Mira gave him a funny look, not sure of why he had reacted in such a way.

The older woman coughed. "So, that's what happened, and that's why I'm here."

"Have you tried contacting her?"

"Why bother?" Miss Barrowsly asked. "I know the recipe was right. I was older. I spent more time with our mother. If Vaire can't admit that she was wrong, why should I apologize for what happened?" The woman started coughing again. "Drat, all this talk has triggered my cough. Mira, dear, I need to rest. It was nice for you to bring your boyfriend around, but his questions have flustered me. I should probably lie down."

"Sure," Mira said, "let's get you inside."

———

The village of Draugr resembled Ember Hollow in numerous ways. There was the main road that everything branched from, and it was quaint, manageable. Unlike Ember Hollow, the tree at the town center was alive and thriving, streamers hanging from its branches. Sylas spotted a pub, a general store, an outdoor market, and everything from a lumberyard to a butchery.

Set in a valley and surrounded by mountains with flat tops, Draugr had a feature that Ember Hollow did not, one Sylas and Mira had continued to discuss.

"Maybe it's not that bad," Sylas said as he examined one of the watchtowers. A portion of the village, the side that faced the Hexveil, also had a wall. "It does seem like the wall isn't quite serving its purpose, but perhaps it acts as a deterrent."

"Perhaps," Mira said. "What do you think Wigmund wanted you to see here?"

"I don't think he wanted me to see anything. It was my idea to come. I just think it's good to know how Ember Hollow could look if everything works out the way we'd like it to."

"I suppose it could look like this. There is still a lot that needs to be done, and I don't know what to do with the tree in the town square," Mira said as she gestured to Draugr's magnificent tree.

"Maybe an arborist? Is there an arborist class?"

"It could be one of those classes that was affected by the Crafting Laws, although I don't know why they would go after it. Come," Mira said as she turned to a small restaurant with outdoor seating. "Let's have a bite and then head back."

"The porridge wasn't enough for you?" Sylas teased.

"I've never been to Draugr. I figured there would be a local delicacy here," she told him with a playful harrumph.

They found a table. Sylas looked across the road to see that the pub, one called Draugr's Twenty Casks, which also had outdoor seating. It wasn't something he had considered for The Old Lamplighter, but it was certainly something he could get behind.

"What happened back there?" Mira asked. "At Miss Barrowsly's? You never told me why you were surprised by her answer."

"Ah, that—"

A waitress appeared. "Hello," the woman said with a pleasant grin. "We have a special today, sauced apples with cinnamon bread. It comes with a special Draugr tea." She produced a menu. "We have other options as well, but people usually get the special."

"The special it is," Mira said.

The waitress smiled and left.

"Miss Barrowsly's sister," Sylas said, "she was one of the people on the Celestial Council. I'm certain of it. Vaire, the high seraph of Izalith. Which just so happens to be directly above Ember Hollow from what I recall, meaning Vaire is able to look down at her sister."

"Huh. That would explain the shocked look on your face."

"She is definitely a person we should convince to send a letter. Do you think you have that much influence with her?"

"Me?" Mira considered this until the tea came. The waitress made a show of pouring their glasses, smiled, and left again. "I don't usually have personal conversations with her and that would be personal."

"It could be exactly what needs to happen, too, as part of the overall plan. She seemed to have some influence, Vaire."

"Maybe *you* should speak to her."

"Why me? She's your client."

"I think Miss Barrowsly likes you, Sylas."

"What makes you think that? She basically shooed me away."

"Believe me. I could tell. I've brought other people around before—"

"You've had more boyfriends in the Underworld?" he teased.

"No, my uncle. And I also brought Cody and Duncan to help move something."

"Well, I get it with your uncle. Cody and Duncan are harmless, though."

"Agreed. And she was nasty to all of them. So for some reason, she seemed to like you."

Sylas touched his shoe against her boot under the table. "Could it be for the same reason you like me?"

"I don't know," Mira said as the special came, which consisted of apples that had been fermented into mush and warm slices of cinnamon toast. "But let's cross that bridge when we get there. Besides, we still have the issue of my uncle's involvement."

"Yes, pros and cons. The pros of bringing Tiberius with us is that our dear lord commander is battle-hardened, even if he doesn't look it on the surface. He is patriotic in a way that would be to our advantage. He won't go down without a fight, and by bringing him, he won't funnel his paranoia into making things worse in Ember Hollow."

"And the cons?" Mira asked as she spooned some of the apple onto her cinnamon bread.

"If we bring him, Tiberius will want to take charge. If things do not go the way he likes, he will react poorly. He is, for lack of a better term, the adult version of a brat. He barely gets along with Quinlan and Raelis will snap at him, I'm sure of it, if we give him the chance. Because Tiberius insists on leading, it might create issues for us that I've yet to see. He is also ornery and wants to be the hero, which will cause issues within our ranks."

"So what do you think, then?" Mira asked after she ate her first bite. "This is very good, by the way."

"Tiberius? I think *I* need to let go in some regard." Sylas took a quick look around Draugr. "Let me explain: This place has a wall and watchtowers, and it doesn't seem hostile. I think . . . I think I also need to trust myself more to trust others. My men and I can handle anything the Celestial Plains can throw at us, or at least, we hope that's the case. Tiberius will get in the way of that. He stays behind, and to convince him that it's *his* idea to stay, we commend him on the good work he has done."

"We could also suggest he come check out Draugr. That could work, you know."

"Agreed. It just has to be his idea: he has to find value in it."

"And you will deliver this message?"

"Unless you want to," Sylas said as he took a bite of the local dish, which was much sweeter than he had expected. "But for some reason, the way you're looking at me tells me you'd like me to be the one that speaks to him. In that case, I'll catch up with the lord commander tonight. If he's not at the feast, he'll be about."

"Good. Do that. And remember, the more you appease his ego, the easier this will go."

"I hope not all men are like that."

Mira took another bite and shrugged.

CHAPTER NINETEEN

A PUB QUIZ FOR THE AGES

The pub filled with people, many of them curious about what had transpired that morning. Yet word got out quickly, especially after Tilbud took center stage.

"First, my good men, my good ladies, my good everyone, we will feast until we can feast no longer! That delicious smell?" The archlumen took a dramatic sniff of the air. "Ah, yes, *that* smell. That savory bouquet, my dears, that enticing scent, that divine odor, that simply exquisite aroma, *that* is the result of Azor's and Quinlan's and Priscilla's hard work. I am told that the starting dish will be a hearty Geistian stew, the main dish will be beef and ale pie, and this will be followed by dessert, which I'm told is a pastry stuffed with fermented Geistian redberries glazed in caramel." He brought a hand to his heart. "I might have snuck one in earlier. So enjoy, and before you do, is everyone at the table they would like to sit at for the quiz?"

There was murmuring among the crowd as Sylas poured up more pints.

"We're going to be the Ember Maces again," Duncan told Tilbud. He was joined by the militiamen Gary, Henry, and Cody.

Much to Sylas's surprise, and a reminder that he needed to speak to him later, Tiberius begrudgingly sat at the militiamen's table as well.

"Fine, the Ember Maces," Tiberius grunted as he waved Tilbud away.

"Cornbreads for us," Mira said excitedly. She sat at a table with Nelly, Karn, and Catia, Cornbread currently in her lap.

"Ember Maces, Cornbreads . . ." Tilbud moved on to the Seedlands farmers. Rather than go with the name the Good Seeds like they had at the last pub quiz, Edgar, Lucille, Trampus, and the often quiet pepper farmer, Sterling, went with Bountiful Harvest.

Iron Rose was there with friends from Cinderpeak, the brewer already a few pints in. "What were we last time?" she asked as Tilbud came around. "Troll-eyed Tricksters? This time we're going to be the Celestial Stompers, as in, if they bring the fight, we'll bring it right back!"

There was some nervous laughter as Priscilla brought out bowls of stew.

"And your table?" Tilbud asked a mixture of people from Douro and Cinderpeak, including Constable Leowin who seemed to be friends with one of the women seated there.

Leowin cleared his throat. "Long Arm of the Underworld." He laughed at his own joke when no one else did.

"Let me guess," Tilbud said as his eyes fell to the table with Godric, Bart, Mary, Anders, and a woman with her shaved head wrapped in a scarf. "The Lava Boys?"

"The Lava *Loves*," Mary told him with a wink.

"Lava Loves. Or Lava Lovers? And careful who you wink at," Tilbud said as he winked back at her in an exaggerated way.

"Loves," Bart said. "No lovers at this table, not to my knowledge."

"Wonderful," Tilbud told him. "Absolutely wonderful. I love it."

"Heh. This looks like it'll be more fun than I thought it would," said Raelis, who sat at the bar with Kael, both of whom planned to leave during the quiz, to the market, make sure the vendors were all ready to go, and open The Petticoat Lamplighter.

"It's always a good time," Sylas told him. "And you learn something too."

"Suddenly I'm less interested," Raelis joked.

Quinlan came up from the basement with another cask as Tilbud stopped at the last table, which consisted of Shamus, the Brassmeres, John, and making his pub quiz debut appearance, Malcolm the grain supplier.

"Last, but not least, what name are we going with tonight?" Tilbud asked them.

Shamus spoke for the table: "The Chasm's Worst Enemies. Hear! Hear!" he said as he lifted his pint glass.

There were a few replies, but Sylas could also sense the nervousness in the room, especially with everyone's MLus frozen.

"Good, let me see here," Tilbud said as he quit writing the names in air using his Quill power. "Ember Maces, Cornbreads, Bountiful Harvest, Celestial Stompers, Long Arm of the Underworld, Lava Loves, and The Chasm's Worst Enemies. Did I miss any? No? Good. Lovely, really. A host couldn't ask for better names. Or a better crowd. Or better food. But enough from me. Enjoy your meals. I will be back shortly to start the quiz. Until then, you can find me at the bar, or perhaps at the absolutely divine Catia's table, where I assure you that

I have not—and would never have—shared any answers, or for that matter, questions, with the beautiful, mysterious, alluring lumengineer."

The archlumen took a seat at the bar and Quinlan gave him a bowl of stew. "Eat up," he told Tilbud. "It's Priscilla's best yet."

Tilbud took a bite of the stew. "My word. This is bloody marvelous! Even better than I expected." He glanced over to Priscilla, who was now distributing stew with Azor. "Marvelous!" he shouted over to her in his typical charismatic way.

The second course came and everyone dug into the hearty beef and ale pies. Raelis and Kael left to open The Petticoat Lamplighter, the two bidding Sylas farewell.

"This is a meal fitting for a rare Thornsday pub quiz, truly," Tilbud said as he continued to pick at his pie.

Sylas used the rag tucked into the front of his apron to wipe up a small spill from the counter as he spoke to Tilbud: "I've been meaning to talk to you about tomorrow."

"Yes? Mira already mentioned that Wigmund visited. I spoke to her on my way in. She is doing a wonderful job running the market, you know. It will be most profitable once our MLus are reactivated."

"She is. So you're interested?"

"In being the spiritual guide, caretaker, and resident archlumen of a roving pack of warriors set to take on Celestial Beasts? By the jilted heavens, Sylas, you bet your MLus—not that we can right now—I am in. Bloody excited, if we are being honest. Nervous? Not as much as I should be. I look forward to the challenge, really, and who wouldn't? Who wouldn't want to go where no Underworldian has gone before in pursuit of an incredible quest. Or really, just a chance to preserve our way of life here. That is what this is all about, yes?" He ate more of his pie. "Yes?"

"Indeed."

"Indeed. But, I will silence myself now," Tilbud said as he made a gesture like he was locking his lips, "to mentally prepare for the quiz. It will be, I assure you, a pub quiz for the ages."

After dessert, Tilbud took his place in front of the teams. He cleared his throat, the archlumen's sound magically amplified, overpowering Bart's humming and Mary's song.

"*Fine, fine,*" Bart sang in key. "*The quiz begins!*"

Mary played a few more closing strokes on her lute and they took their seats with the rest of the Lava Loves as the audience clapped.

"You know the rules," Tilbud told everyone, "but do you know the prize? First, a refresher: write down your answers, no cheating, no looking at your neighbor's table, no whispering the answer out loud, no answer sharing via magical means, and no barking out the answer, Cornbread. I will repeat the question once, but only after I've given everyone a chance to write down what they know. There will be three rounds, and I'm feeling a little loosey-goosey tonight, likely because of the great food, ale, and a short visit with Gertrude earlier, so there will be no pattern to the questions, no themes, if you will. Is everyone ready?"

"You said something about the prize," Tiberius reminded him. "But you never said what that prize was, wizard. Instead, you told us we knew the rules, yet you then repeated them."

"That prize? Yes, the prize. I was going to offer up a magical tuning fork able to produce a goose's honk, but I'm saving that one for myself. Thank you, Nelly," he told the woman, who was currently holding the enchanted object. "So then, the question is, what will you win? Everything is free tonight, MLus no longer mean anything, at least for now. And as we have already discussed, there is nothing to worry about. This has happened before. If you have questions, ask someone else, now's not the time," he said to Cody, who had raised his hand.

Cornbread barked.

"Yes, I'm getting on with it. That prize, the prize that your table will win, will be a custom lesson with me. Ta-da!" The air sparked with Mana Lumens. "Yes, I will teach you a spell, which I will choose, or give you limited options to pick from, for free. A Lumen Ability for free! Do you know how to fly? If not, I will show you the way. Perhaps there is something else you may like to do, like write a message to a special someone," he said as he traced a heart in the air and flicked it toward Catia, who turned away bashfully. "I will show you how to do just that. There are caveats, because there always are, but rest assured that everyone at your table will learn how to do something they didn't know how to do before. How am I so sure? I'm not. If you already know how to do everything I can show you, then congratulations. You are an archlumen. You don't need me. Shall we begin?"

"Yes," Tiberius said with his usual grumpiness. "You talk too much, quiz master."

"I would say something like 'words are what separate us from the animals and the beasts,' but I'm sure that they speak as well, and I happen to like Sylas's and Mira's pets. Now, on to the first question, if I may be so bold: Who is the enigmatic figure known for leading the Rebellion of Solyphia, at the onset of the Crafting Laws, which was later crushed by Celestial forces?"

"Boo," Iron Rose said before she leaned forward to the person on her team responsible for writing the answers and whispered something into his ear.

"Boo, indeed." Tilbud told the crowd.

As he stood behind the bar, Sylas got distracted by a conversation in the basement. He headed down to find Quinlan and Priscilla arguing about something.

"Just go up there and have a good time, love," she said in a thin voice. "I can handle this."

"You should go up there and have fun. You said his quizzes were legendary. Just let me and Azor take care of everything else."

"Why are you arguing with me about this?"

"Why are you arguing with *me* about this?" Quinlan asked Priscilla. "This is a ridiculous thing to argue about. I'm literally telling you to go have a good time, love, and you're telling me to go have a good time. I don't want to have a good time. I want something to focus on. I have . . . I have a lot happening tomorrow. I don't want to think about it."

"That's why I'm telling you to go out and have a good time!" Priscilla told Quinlan as she stomped her foot.

"Hey, hey, hey," Sylas told them. "Quin. I need you up at the bar."

"Understood," he said in a very soldierly way. He followed Sylas up the stairs.

"Sit," Sylas told him. "And take it easy, yeah?"

"Yeah."

"Let me get you a pint, just relax a bit. Don't think about things too much. You don't want to start fighting with her."

"No, I don't."

As he poured Quinlan a pint, Sylas tuned in to Tilbud's next question: "This particular spectral beast roams the forgotten corners of the Chasm, a creature known for its terrifying wails said to drive even the bravest demon hunter to the brink of madness. What is its name?"

"Easy." Tiberius tapped his finger on their answer sheet and mumbled something to Cody.

"Final one," Tilbud said after a few more questions, none of which Sylas knew the answer to. "A crystal-encrusted spire once said to be a gift from the Celestial Plains now lays in ruins in what Underworldian city? For a bonus, what is the name of the famous root in this region said to cure sadness."

Mira's eyes lit up at this question as she told Catia the answer.

Tilbud collected the answers. Rather than have the tables check each other's papers, he sat down and quickly scanned through them all. Once he was ready, he announced the answers.

"Morgath the Unyielding was the leader of the rebellion," he told them, which brought groans from some of the patrons. Tilbud continued through more answers until he got to the other questions Sylas had heard. "The creature of the Chasm known for its chilling wails? That would be the Phantom Howler. *Yeeeo-yee-yee!* Ahem, I heard it sounded something like that."

"Knew it!" Tiberius chortled. "And it sounds exactly like that."

"That's easy," Quinlan said as he stared down into his ale.

"Encountered one before?" Sylas asked his old friend.

"Twice. If you make yourself an earplug out of fabric, you can tune it out. Pretty easy, really."

Sylas caught the answer to the last question he'd heard from Tilbud: "New Albion is the name of the city with the crystal-encrusted spire and the root? Well, Mira should know that one."

"Albion root," she said.

"Yes, indeed. Now, in the lead with eight correct answers are the Cornbreads," Tilbud said as he checked his tally. "Next up with six points are the Ember Maces, Long Arm of the Underworld, and Lava Loves. Yes, a tie for second place at the moment. But rest assured, there are two more rounds, and I also have a bonus question if there is a need for a tiebreaker. Azor?"

"Who needs another pint?" the fire spirit asked as she rushed forward. She was joined by Horatio the water spirit, who also carried a tray.

A few people asked for more, and once the pints were handed out, Tilbud began the second round.

This second round of questions flew by because Sylas had to keep going up and down the stairs handling various things, from taking dishes down to replenishing his casks, not to mention brief discussions with Priscilla, who insisted on speaking to him about Quinlan every time he came down.

By the time he was back behind the bar, pouring pints again, Tilbud had tallied the answers to the second round.

Sylas only caught a few of these answers:

"The lake known for its eerie fog that never leaves? That would be Wraithswater Lake," Tilbud said. "Which brings our final question, the rumored artifact, which in fact, doesn't exist, yet is said to rest at the depth of a labyrinth in a forgotten corridor of the Grace Academy? Anyone?"

Catia raised her hand. "Chrono Shard of the Abyss?"

"Yes! Really? No one else knew it?" Tilbud asked.

Tiberius moaned. "How are we supposed to bloody know that, wizard?"

"I haven't been here long enough to know something like that," Bart said, which had Godric laughing.

"Mate, you act like you *haven't* been around since the Crafting Laws," Godric teased.

"Oi!" The two playfully wrestled with each other and calmed once Tilbud silenced the room with a loud clap that seemed more amplified than it should have been.

"On to the third round! After tallying up the numbers, it appears that the Cornbreads remain in the lead with sixteen points, followed by the Ember Maces who have moved up to fifteen points. Congrats," he told Tiberius's table, several of whom cheered one another and hooted. "And in third place is The Chasm's Worst Enemies with thirteen points. It is still anyone's game, well, some of you might find it hard to win, but you never know what will happen now, once everyone is locked in and ready to be quizzed. We will begin the third round with an easy question that has ten answers," Tilbud said. "The only way to get the point is to get all ten answers right."

"It should be worth more than that," Tiberius grunted.

Quinlan overheard the remark since the Ember Maces were seated close to the bar and scoffed. "Thorny Thornian," he said under his breath, a big smile on his face.

Tilbud continued: "For your first question, I want you to write down ten Underworld cities, villages, towns. However you see fit. Ten locations. Surely, all of you will get this right."

Taking a break, Sylas counted out ten places he knew. There was Ember Hollow, Duskhaven, Cinderpeak, Battersea, Douro, Draugr, Geist, Gloombra, Lilihammer, and Wraithwick. He noticed Quinlan counting out on his fingers as well.

"Get to ten?" Sylas asked.

"I think so."

Once everyone was finished writing, Tilbud continued: "What is the name of the ancient fortress outside Gloombra that once housed representatives from the Celestial Plains and was later abandoned?"

"Ah," Tiberius said as he tapped on the table. "I know that one!"

"Then write it down, and don't say it out loud. I will add, for those seeking to do a little wanderlusting, this ancient fortress is quite a nice place to visit if you ever go to Gloombra and decide to go on a little excursion."

"I'll keep that in mind," Quinlan told Sylas. "Could use a vacation after all this."

Tilbud waited another minute and moved on to the next question. "They claim that there is a giant, bioluminescent creature that lives in a deep cave somewhere in the Chasm. What is this creature called? And if you know the local name for it, that will be a bonus point for your team as well."

Tiberius grew excited as he whispered the answer. Sylas shot a look over to Mira, who glanced at her uncle, squinted, and told Catia to write something down.

"Next up, and I expect those of you who have been here for more than a few months to know the answer to this one," Tilbud said. "What is a Celestial event that happens once in a millennia when the golden skies above us turn dark for a single night?"

A few people nodded, others glanced around the room, and several just sat there drinking their pints as they gave up on the answer.

Tilbud's next question involved architecture: "There was an ancient bridge that used to connect the Underworld to the Chasm. Many of you do not know it, considering it was destroyed long ago, but you might know its sister bridge in Battersea. Name the bridge in Battersea and the ancient channel of trade between the Underworld and the Chasm."

Blank stares. The room turned so quiet that Quinlan swiveled around to see what had happened. Patches hopped down from his perch on the window and made his rounds, moving between people's legs, his tail gently tapping them.

Tilbud chuckled to himself. "Yes, I thought that might stump some of you. Onward and upward! There is an herb that one can find in the Gloomflower Meadow, and I'm not talking about the ghostly luminescent flowers that grow while there. This herb, white in color, is said to cure insomnia. Name that herb."

"Azor," Sylas said as a few people finished their pints. "Horatio?"

The two spirits, who had been in the basement with Priscilla, raced up and started distributing ale, Azor with a hurried look on her face.

"Do I detect a little steam?" Quinlan whispered to Sylas.

Sylas winked at his old friend. "Perhaps."

"Really, I don't blame them. I don't blame anyone." Quinlan listened to the next question, which was about a famous bard from Geist. "Heh. I actually know the answer to that one. That bloody fool was all the rage for a while until he up and disappeared. Chasm or Plains, no one knows."

The quiz continued until Tilbud reached round three's final question: "They say that there is a rare artifact located in Battersea, a mystical chalice, one filled with a liquid that grants visions of hidden truths. Yet for those who have actually tasted it, it just makes you feel a bit randy. Ahem. Believe me, I know." He jokingly adjusted his collar. "In any event, what is the agreed-upon name of this chalice? Bonus point if you know the actual name."

"Now hold on," Tiberius told the archlumen. "There's a fake name *and* an actual name?"

"Yes, and if you know what it is, you likely know its public name. So write it down. If you know its actual name, write that down for a bonus point. I told you, this can be anyone's game. When you're ready, slide your papers to the front and I will collect them."

The teams finished writing their answers and handed the papers up to Tilbud. He graded them quickly, his eyebrows rising every now and then as he came across an answer that made him laugh.

"Great, first, as always, I will go over the correct answers," Tilbud announced once he had finished. "Luckily for all of you, everything has been tallied, so listen carefully and you may learn something here. As to the fortress outside of Gloombra, that would be the Fortress of Eternal Sun. I spent a few days there and I can tell you, it is quite a marvelous place. Visit if you get a chance."

"I knew it," Bart told Godric. "There was a song about it."

Godric cast a glare in Bart's direction. "Well, you should have told Mary."

"I did, you told her—"

"And on we move," Tilbud said. "The bioluminescent creature that lives in a deep cave of the Chasm is a Gloamserpent. The locals call it Phantomboil due to a boil on the back of its head."

Tiberius rubbed his hands together at this; Mira gave him a dirty look.

Tilbud moved on to the next question, which was about a Celestial event. "That would be Shadowfire Night, the night that the Plains go dark." All the color drained from Tilbud's face.

"What is it, man?" Tiberius barked as the crowd started murmuring.

"I can't believe . . ." Tilbud's eyes settled. "Ahem. We will address that later," he said with a tight grin aimed at Sylas. "Next, the question about the bridges. The bridge that once cut through the Hexveil and linked to the Chasm was the Bridge of Chanced Return, not too far from Geist, in the Cloud Forest. It's sister bridge in Battersea you know as the Bridge of Echoing Stones."

A few of the people grumbled about this answer. "How is anyone supposed to know that?" Nelly asked.

"The herb from the Gloomflower Meadow said to cure insomnia is known as a moonroot," Tilbud said as several tables moaned.

Sylas headed downstairs to bring up some clean pint glasses, where he once again got caught in a conversation with Priscilla, who was laughing about Azor and Horatio. "Those two are something," she said as Sylas finally broke away.

Sylas returned to hear Tilbud read the answer to the last question. "The mystical chalice has two names. The answer that most of you know is the Chalice of Lurid Revelations. However, its real name would be the Chalice of Salacious Fornications." He laughed. "And now you know. Careful if you seek it. Ahem. Ahem, ahem, and a final, ahem. Everything has been tallied, as previously announced, I will go ahead and come out to say that in first place are the Cornbreads. Congratulations!"

"What?" Tiberius threw his hands up into the air as Mira's table clapped. "It can't be—"

"Yes, lord commander," Tilbud said, "not only can it be, it was. Better luck next time. Your team did come in second place, though." He waved his hand and their scores appeared, the Cornbreads with twenty-seven points; the Ember Maces with twenty-five; The Chasm's Worst Enemies with twenty-four; both the Long Arms of the Underworld and the Lava Loves with twenty-two; the Bountiful Harvest with twenty-one; and finally, Iron Rose's Celestial Stompers with a measly fourteen.

"Is there a prize for last place?" Iron Rose asked to the laughter of many.

"Yes, I believe—"

Before Tilbud could finish, Tiberius pushed away from his table and marched out the door. Sylas looked from Quinlan to Mira, and back to the front door of The Old Lamplighter as it slammed shut. "Now is as good of a time as any," he told Quinlan. "Hold the fort down until I'm back. I believe I will check on the market while I am out as well."

———

Sylas caught up with Tiberius in the street outside. The lord commander had turned cold, the shorter man hunched over, his arms tensed.

"Lord commander," Sylas called ahead. "Slow down for a moment."

"You don't need to come after me!"

"Clearly, I do. What happened back there? Everyone was having fun." Sylas gestured toward The Old Lamplighter.

"We were so close," Tiberius said, his voice cracking. He turned away from Sylas. "So bloody close."

"You can't win every time."

"I know that! I was a lord commander; not every engagement was a successful one. I just wanted to beat . . . I just wanted to beat Mira's team," Tiberius said with an exasperated breath out. "She is so smart. And we were so close." He kept his back to Sylas. "And now, I've made a fool of myself. I'm mad at that as well, mad at myself, if we're being honest."

Sylas had the urge to come forward and pat him on the back. He resisted this at first, but then he remembered what they were up against and how everything could soon change.

So he did it.

Sylas stepped forward and patted Tiberius on the back. At first, the lord commander flinched, but then he eased up once Sylas stepped aside.

"I was meaning to talk to you about something," Sylas said after a moment of silence.

"Yes?"

"Tomorrow, me and a few of the lads will be heading up to placate the demands from the Celestial Plains, the hunt I was telling you about. I thought you might want to go, but then I realized that, knowing you, you would be more interested in making sure Ember Hollow was cared for in our absence. With the invasion and everything that's recently happened, and the chance that we may fail, I figured you would've already made plans to do what you need to do here."

"Yes, someone should stay in Ember Hollow and continue to shore up the village's defenses." Tiberius brought his hand to his chin as he considered it.

"I honestly think that would be an excellent usage of your military capabilities and planning. You already have the militia. Related, have you been to Draugr?"

"I can't say that I have, but I did hear that they have a rich history. Why? What does that have to do with defending Ember Hollow?"

"It has a lot to do with it, actually. I found out recently that Draugr used to be about the same size as Ember Hollow. They've built defenses over the last few years and it is quite protected now."

"Is it? Huh. Maybe it would be a good idea to see how other villages do it," said Tiberius, who seemed just drunk enough to think of this as his own idea. "Before the boys begin in the morning, I could head there. Yes. Maybe stop in Battersea and visit a sauna before I go. Unwind a little before it all gets serious. They do have the best ones there in Battersea, you know. I believe I told you that."

"You have. I like that idea of yours," Sylas said. "No sense in reinventing the wheel. It's a different location, set in a valley. But I liked the way that they erected the walls. They were mostly on one side of the village, the side facing the Chasm. My thought was that it would be easier for things to get around it, but I think it's more of a preventative measure. With the watchtowers they have, it allows them to guard more efficiently. But you would know better than I."

"Yes, I would," Tiberius said as he continued stroking his chin. "In that case, I will handle the village while you are gone. Ha. I don't know why I'm telling you like that, it's not like I don't already handle it. But you know what I mean. And really, I wish you luck. I am also aware that you and your men are fully capable of handling something like this. Will you by chance be bringing Mira with you?"

"Only if you think it's a good idea."

"Yes, I like that for you all. She will act as a good support unit. And I'm assuming that there is at least one kooky archlumen coming as well."

"Certainly, and . . ." Sylas said as he bent down and picked up an invisible Patches. He hadn't been fully certain Patches had been there until he felt the cat's tail brush against his leg. "I'm assuming Patches will be joining me."

Tiberius jumped back as he saw the pub cat take shape. "Where did he come from? Right, right, the cat can turn invisible. Such a spooky cat," Tiberius said as he extended a hand to Patches's head. "May I?"

"By all means."

While Sylas held Patches, Tiberius scratched the cat's head. Patches immediately purred.

"He's friendly—" Tiberius shot his hand down by his side, as if he realized he was being vulnerable. "Anyway. Good talk. I think it is best that you and your lads go to the Plains and I stay here to make sure the village is ready for the invasion, if it comes to that." He started to walk away and stopped. "One more thing."

"Yes?"

"Two more things, actually. Good luck if I didn't already say it. And thank you, Sylas." The lord commander jutted his chin out and moved on without another word. "Good luck and good night."

"You just have to learn how to deal with people," Sylas told Patches once Tiberius was gone. He nuzzled his head against the cat. "Let's go check out the market."

———

Sylas spent about twenty minutes at the market making his rounds. Kael and Raelis were doing a great job running The Petticoat Lamplighter, and everyone seemed to be having a good time there. Even though there was no sun to set in the Underworld, they had placed lights out, a way of letting visitors know that this was a special event. Aside from talking to Florence and Percy, he also spoke to Esta, and assured all of the other vendors that Mira would be by later.

By the time Sylas got back to The Old Lamplighter most of the people cleared out, some on their way to the market, and others on their way home. There were still a few regulars, however, and more importantly, there was Tilbud, who seemed absolutely ecstatic to see Sylas.

"There he is, the man of the hour. Join us," he called from the booth he was sharing with Mira and Catia.

"Want anything?" Azor asked.

"No, I'm fine. I'll be back behind the bar in a minute."

"Don't worry, I've got it. Quinlan, Priscilla, and Horatio are downstairs tidying up, so it will be a quick close tonight."

"Good," Sylas told her as he took the seat in front of Tilbud, next to Mira. "Let me guess: This is about some epiphany you had during the pub quiz?"

"Indeed, it is," Tilbud said.

"And, he hasn't told us anything about his epiphany," Mira said. "He simply teases it out."

"I have been known to be somewhat of a tease." The archlumen snorted. "Somewhat." In typical Tilbud fashion, he moved from humorous to serious in a flash. "It has been a while, Catia."

She turned to him. "What has?"

"Come out with it already," Mira told him. "You have been dancing around this since Sylas left. Also, Sylas, my uncle. All is in order?"

"I'll tell you later," he assured her. "Tilbud? Enough with the mysteries. What's going on?"

"The Shadowfire Night. I was here during the last one, you know."

"You said that was a millennia ago," Mira said. "Unless I heard you wrong. You've been here that long?"

"Do I look it?" Tilbud asked with dismay. "And yes, I have been here for a lot longer than I care to admit. But I was here at that time, and it was quite the experience, I must say."

"You never told me you were *that* old," Catia said.

"You never asked. And last I checked, a good archlumen never kisses and tells."

"Eww. She probably assumed because of your playboy ways that you died young and simply stumbled upon all your magical abilities," Mira teased. "But now that you say it, it does make sense with your unique command of Underworldian knowledge."

"Are you calling me unique? I'm flattered." Tilbud took a pink handkerchief from his pocket and wiped his forehead. "Very flattered, actually."

Mira rolled her eyes. "Are you ever going to tell us what you are trying to tell us?"

"The suspense, can't you feel it? Doesn't it make you feel alive? It certainly makes me feel alive, or it's the wonderful food I had earlier and the two strong ales talking. What can I say? I'm a bit nervous about the trip tomorrow, even though I'm also looking forward to it. We will discuss that in the morning. First, Shadowfire Night. I wonder if this very strange celestial event has anything to do with what the Celestial Plains are planning."

"Shadowfire Night," Catia said. "Why would it have anything to do with that? Wait." Her eyes lit up. "It takes a lot of Mana Lumens, doesn't it? I remember learning about it at the guild, but they mostly glossed over it."

"It doesn't just take a lot of energy, it is a redistribution of Mana Lumens," Tilbud explained, "a cycling, if you will. Perhaps that is also one of the reasons they are looking to close the gap, and by gap I mean the Underworld. It would explain quite a lot. They would cycle the mana out, and it would come back stronger than ever."

"Why do they need it?" Sylas asked. "And why didn't Wigmund mention any of this. He seems to be on our side."

"I've only met him twice," Tilbud said. "Is that your impression of him?"

"Yes."

"My impression wavers between that and some self-interest that I can't quite identify yet. Perhaps it truly is the preservation of the Underworld, perhaps it truly is that simple." Tilbud took a drink from his pint glass. "But I have my doubts."

"It's certainly something we can ask him tomorrow," Mira said.

"Yes, we can. And we should. Maybe your doomsday message is in relation to Shadowfire Night, Sylas. Crazier things have happened, yes? The last one was quite some time ago, so people tend to forget about it. You know who would know about it, though. Manaseers."

"Nuno should have mentioned it, then," Mira added.

"Yes, but he might not have been here at that time. I do not know how old he is. And until you experience it, and let me tell you all, it is an experience, it is hard to understand how truly terrifying and marvelous it is at the same time."

"Why terrifying?" Sylas asked the archlumen.

"The Underworld goes dark. The only thing that you can see is the Hexveil, and if you live far away from it, there is no light. None at all. This is unsettling to many people, you know. If you know a Lumen Ability, and I happen to know several, it doesn't work during this time. So you are left in the dark. It is truly terrifying."

————

Sylas thought about Tilbud's revelation as he brewed later that night in the cellar, the pub quiet aside from a little chatter at the bar between Azor and Mira. If the fire spirit thought it was strange that Mira was planning to spend the night, she didn't say anything about it. When he returned to the main floor, she blew Sylas a fiery kiss before turning downstairs with a tray she planned to clean.

By this point, Quinlan and Priscilla had gone to Sylas's farmhouse with Kael. Tilbud and Catia had left to stay at Nelly's. Raelis was already asleep in the spare bedroom and Cornbread had joined him. This left only Patches, who trailed up the stairs after Sylas and Mira.

"I can't believe I'm staying at your pub," Mira said as she looked around his room.

"Cozy, right? I swear, a while back, I heard someone call this place 'the cozy abyss.' I tend to agree." Sylas took off his boots and got comfortable on the bed.

Patches hopped up and joined Sylas. The cat stared at Mira with curiosity in his eyes as he purred.

Mira removed the jacket she was wearing, folded it, and placed it on a chair. She approached the bed and sat near Sylas.

"Get comfortable," he told her.

"I am," she said as she leaned back, her shoulder now against his. "You never told me what happened with my uncle earlier."

"Ah, that. Your uncle. The good news is, he's not going with us. He isn't the first superior officer I've had the pleasure of manipulating in subtle ways. I got used to doing that over the years. When I first came here, I didn't want to play the game. But sometimes it helps."

"You aren't exactly explaining what you told him."

"I just tried to make Tiberius feel as if he were the one who came up with the idea of staying. I suggested he check out Draugr, and he's going to do that for some ideas."

"He is?"

"Indeed. He said he would go to Battersea first to visit a sauna."

"That sounds more like him."

"He actually gave me his blessings, if you can imagine that. He looked like he was going to cry there for a moment because he lost to you."

"Really? That's why he stormed off?"

"You didn't know? You really couldn't tell?" Sylas playfully elbowed her. "You had to have known."

"I didn't, honest." She started laughing.

"You two are quite different, but you do share a competitive streak."

"I'm not competitive." Mira lifted Patches and kissed his cheek. "Isn't that right?"

He mewed in response.

"Sure, keep telling yourself that."

"I think I might," Mira told Sylas. "But you did good with my uncle." She placed Patches down and leaned forward to kiss Sylas on the cheek. "I don't know how you did it, I don't know how you work your magic sometimes, but you're a good man. You really are, Sylas."

"And you're an even better woman." He slipped his arm around her and brought Mira in closer. "The best."

"Are you trying to turn this into a competition?"

"No, you've already won."

"Please don't tell me that you're my prize."

"You took the words right out of my mouth."

CHAPTER TWENTY

THE THREE REALMS RENEWED

Patches paced back and forth at the foot of the stairs. *Really?* he said as he looked up to the big man's room. *How long will she be here?*

What are you so worried about? Cornbread asked as she took a seat next to the pub cat. She nudged him with her snout.

I just don't understand why she's staying here. That is the largest bed in the Tavernly Realm, you know. Where am I supposed to sleep?

I was going to stay in the other man's room, but then he started snoring. Cornbread squinted up the stairs. *I didn't like that. What was his name again?*

It doesn't matter. The big man and the medicine woman, they're getting too close.

They all have names, you know. That other cat told us.

The question is do you remember them?

Not really.

And please don't bring Wigmund up again. Is he a cat? Is he human? Is that really his name? And what else can he turn into? Patches looked at Cornbread. *Maybe a demon too. Says he's from heaven, but anyone can say that.*

Cornbread did her version of a shrug. *I didn't get that sense.*

You never know.

I meant I didn't smell any demon on him.

The best demons can hide their scent. They're the ones you should be wary of.

Really?

I don't know, Patches said. *Stop asking me questions.*

We could run up there and surprise them? Would that make you happy? Cornbread beat his tail back and forth. *That would make me happy!*

What do you mean?

I mean run up the stairs and jump on the bed. That would surprise me if I were them, if I were human. They are probably asleep by now.

What's the point of sleeping next to someone anyway?

You sleep next to me all the time, Cornbread said as she licked Patches's face. *And the big man.* She licked his face again.

Hey! What did I tell you about doing that?

Maybe they're just like us. Just trying to stay warm.

Patches didn't say anything. He sat there for another moment, and eventually moved to licking his paw.

We could check on the goose. I believe her name is Gertrude. Humans have strange names. Cornbread laughed. *Like me. My name is strange. Your name makes sense because you do indeed have patches of black and white fur.*

And?

And nothing. Just an observation. Come on, Cornbread said as her tail beat back and forth. *Let's see about the goose.*

Fine. But I'm leading the way. Patches took off toward the cat door. He carefully let himself out and waited on the stoop for Cornbread to join him, the dog as clumsy as ever with her movements. She licked his face again, but this time he didn't say anything.

Cornbread followed him, the two weaving their way through Ember Hollow, parts of which were still under construction. They reached the market, where they heard a discussion taking place.

Not you again, Patches said as they came around a couple of crates to find Wigmund the orange tabby talking to Gertrude.

You're back! Gertrude let out a little honk. *You two missed it. The market was great. There are some new humans here, and they were all so friendly with me. I really like the two medicine people.*

"That would be Percy and Florence," Wigmund told her. "They were rescued, you know, from the Cloud Forest by Sylas, Mira, and the other soldiers."

You're really just going to tell us everyone's name and expect us to remember them? Patches asked as his tail flicked at the ground.

Wigmund laughed. "I always liked cats, which is why I became one. Easy to go around this way."

That's not what I asked you.

If I could become any other animal, I don't know what I would change into, Cornbread said as one of her ears flopped over.

Gertrude laughed. *That certainly is a conundrum.*

I'm serious. I haven't really thought about what kind of animal I would become. I like eating meat. I like barking. Cornbread woofed to illustrate her point. *I also like sleeping, running, hearing, and sniffing.*

You just described most animals, Patches said as he finally sat. He returned his focus to Wigmund. *Why are you here exactly?*

"I'm just waiting for Sylas and Mira to wake up."

Don't you live up in heaven? Gertrude asked as she gestured toward the sky with her beak. *Why would you come here when you could stay there?*

"I've always been a fan of this place, that's why. It is nice to prowl about. More interesting here than up there. At least to me. I suppose some of my colleagues wouldn't see it that way, but they're not here and, really, who cares what they think?" Wigmund licked his paw as well, which caused Patches to stop.

You mock me?

"Absolutely not, I'm just trying to get better at being a cat."

And you can't become one up there?

"I can, but that is a different kind of cat. But enough of that talk for now. Tomorrow," Wigmund said, growing serious, "tomorrow, Sylas and several of the others will go to the Celestial Plains, to a place known as the Celestial Sea. There will be Celestial Beasts there, and they will hunt them."

Cornbread barked. *Then we are going with them!*

A sea? Patches asked. *Will there be swimming?*

I love swimming, Cornbread said.

"I suspect that might be the case. Your powers will work there, but there will be changes. The Celestial Sea is a sacred part of the Plains, but the mana there can do strange things. I will give the same warning to Sylas and Mira in the morning. But you should be ready for the unexpected."

Cornbread woofed. *Anything to help the big man!*

"I appreciate your enthusiasm. And I want you all to do well. A lot is riding on how you perform. I can't say for certain that this will even work."

I don't understand, Patches said.

"You don't need to understand fully. But stranger things have happened." Wigmund smiled at them. "Now, if you excuse me, I have some prowling to do."

———

[You have 27 days until the invasion.]

Name: Sylas Runewulf
Mana Lumens are currently locked.
Class: Brewer
Secondary Class: Farmer
Tertiary Class: Landlord

Sylas swiped the information away and brought Mira in closer.

She yawned. "I hate reading that. 'Mana Lumens are currently locked.' But you know what? Maybe we deserve it."

"Ha. You mean we deserve not to have powers?"

"I don't know. I really don't know. And apparently, that's not for me to decide. Who . . . ?" Mira sat up and pulled the blanket over her chest as her eyes fell upon an orange cat seated at the edge of the bed.

"Good morning," Wigmund said. "I thought this would be a surprising way to wake you up."

Sylas fought the urge to kick at the cat. "Will you meet us downstairs?" he asked Wigmund as he massaged his temples with his hand.

"Certainly."

"He's worse than Tilbud," Mira moaned once the orange cat was gone.

"They do share a trait, that's for sure. I'm surprised Azor didn't warn us."

"I wanted to," the fire spirit said as she rushed into the room, once again startling Mira, who brought her blanket to her chest. "I'm sorry, Mira! Happy Fireday, if Wigmund didn't say anything. I wanted you both to sleep in. You deserve it!" She saw Mira's look and slumped to a degree. "I should go, shouldn't I?"

"Please," Mira said, and once Azor was gone, she spoke under her breath: "Remind me never to sleep at the pub again."

Sylas laughed. "Come on, it's nice being greeted in the morning."

"By the divine arbiter of the Celestial Plains or a frantic fire spirit?"

"It beats waking up to Tiberius and his grumblings."

"You may have a point there. In any event, let's head down. Had I known . . ." She shook her head. "It doesn't matter. Besides, I can smell breakfast."

"Another benefit of spending a night at the pub. It's nice on the farm too. We could have stayed there, but Quinlan claimed it."

"Another time, then." Mira leaned forward and kissed him on the cheek. "Let's seize the day, shall we?"

After dressing, Sylas and Mira headed downstairs, where they found Wigmund seated at the bar in human form. Quinlan, Raelis, and Kael sat with Priscilla in one of the booths, while Tilbud and Catia stood outside speaking, Cornbread circling around them. As always, Azor moved frantically about to make sure everyone was comfortable. But it was quite clear with the scene that no one was exactly excited to see Wigmund.

If this bothered the divine arbiter, he didn't show it as he shoveled eggs into his mouth. "Sylas," he said. "Please, join me."

Tilbud, who could see Sylas from outside, said something to Catia and headed in to join Sylas and Wigmund.

"It's time," the archlumen said as he came behind the bar, the first time he had done such a thing. Tilbud, who wore a sky-blue vest and matching pants, as well as a yellow cravat and small hat, smiled faintly at the divine arbiter.

"Time?" Wigmund asked Tilbud. "Go on."

"Time to come clean."

The divine arbiter spread his arms wide and laughed. "Am I not clean enough?"

Mira joined Sylas. "What's going on?" she whispered.

"I don't know just yet," he told her under his breath as Tilbud continued to scrutinize Wigmund.

"I believe I understand what is going on here," Tilbud finally said, his voice loud enough to draw the attention of Quinlan and the others, who instantly stopped speaking. "I might not fully understand it, but I know a few things. One, Shadowfire Night is coming. I was here during the last one, and speaking of it last night reminded me of something that I read years ago about the origins of the phenomenon—that night when Mana Lumens from the Celestial Plains cycle through the Dark Mana Lumens of the Chasm, as once wielded by Fayeth the Raised. She was in that art on the ceiling of the Celestial Chambers."

"I'm aware," Wigmund said carefully. "I do tend to stare up at it from time to time."

"Because it is such an incredible source of energy, it seems like some people would want to tap into it, perhaps steal it for themselves. People like other members of the Celestial Council." Tilbud paused to let that revelation sink in.

"That is quite the allegation. Go on."

"So it got me thinking, why would someone try to close the Underworld? Would it be for Celestial Beasts? Would it be because the Underworld shouldn't exist? Could there really not be enough warriors in the Plains to manage your own problems? A Celestial coup would be much easier to orchestrate in the confusion that follows Shadowfire Night. And it all keeps coming back to this—Shadowfire Night. What I am saying is that Sylas's invasion message is related to Shadowfire Night, that the system placed on us has warned him about this, because it is not only a threat to the Plains, but a threat to the Underworld as well."

"Huh," Wigmund said. "That is quite the hypothesis, and it is similar to the one that I have reached."

Tilbud snapped his fingers. "I knew it! So the question is, who was behind it?"

"Behind it?"

"Behind the coup! It's the Council. Or at least some of the members. They see this phenomenon as an opportunity to seize power. Wait, it was that child one, wasn't it?" Tilbud said. "He was a ripe little—"

"Ah, yes, Nylus. I can't prove anything, but it is his coalition that has been pushing for the closure of the Underworld."

"So that's why I'm getting this message?" Sylas asked. "I'm getting it because this night is coming and Celestians want to take advantage of it? You said you have experienced the Shadowfire Night before, Tilbud."

"I have."

"And?"

"And?" Tilbud asked Sylas.

"I mean, is it safe? If we just allow it to happen, will it just happen? The mana cycled, the three realms renewed?"

"Yes, that is normally how it goes, yes," Wigmund said to Sylas. "But if someone were to manipulate it in certain ways, Tilbud is correct, they could use it to seize power. This would entail the closing of the Underworld which can only be done by bringing down the Hexveil. Do that, and you free up the power necessary to harness the flowing mana of the Shadowfire Night. Hypothesis, of course, but, well? What do you think?" he asked Tilbud.

"I think that is exactly what is happening. It is something I've been discussing with Catia." Tilbud motioned outside, where Catia continued to play with Cornbread. Her absence from the conversation struck Sylas as odd. Maybe the subject was just too much for her to broach at the moment and she needed a moment of reprieve.

"Then we are on the same page."

"A bloody coup?" Quinlan groaned. "All of this stress for a bloody conspiracy? Can't we just root these people out? You're the divine arbiter, yeah? But you have enough power to remove them to prevent this?"

"It doesn't quite work that way," Wigmund said sadly. "But what I can do is provide you with all the Mana Lumens necessary to appeal to the people of the Plains. I can also arrange some things here in your absence. I believe in your cause. I actually think it will work. Believe it or not, the Council is very cautious about Celestial public opinion. If anyone is disliked enough, they will simply be removed from the Council by mana. So if you all do this, and it works as I think it will, then I think the three realms will be safe. There will not be a power grab, it might even expose what some have been plotting, the Shadowfire Night will pass, and things will continue the way that they currently are."

"I still have a few doubts," Sylas said. "First, how can I be the only one receiving this message? If it is a warning about what is to come, who is sending it to me?"

"Yes, that. That is a question indeed," Wigmund said. "And it is not one that I can answer because we do not have, even with our grand power, access to the system necessary to modify it in that way, to see the future. What is your other question?"

"When you first spoke to me, you offered me citizenship. You said the test would be how well we do, and that, if successful, I could open a school for Celestial Beast hunters. Or something to that effect. What did that have to do with anything? And why the test? Why is that necessary?"

"The part about opening a school, yes. I wanted to see how deep you would go with your commitment to the cause. That was all I meant by that. And yes, if you had agreed, I would have lived up to my end of the bargain. The test question is an interesting one. For me to relinquish the funds, I have to have a good reason, and that's what you, and your friends here," he said as he motioned to the others, "are going to provide. I also have to make the test hard enough so the wayward members of the Celestial Council can't quite figure out what I'm up to. Does that answer your question?"

"It does," Sylas told Wigmund.

"It doesn't answer mine," Tilbud said.

"Oh?" Wigmund turned to him. "Then ask away. Now would be the time to do that."

"You still haven't told us the test we will undertake. We were under the assumption that we would be hunting Celestial Beasts. Is that still the case?"

"They may come into play, yes. But I have devised a different task for you. Are you familiar with Luminae?"

"The Beast of Light," Tilbud said, "a dragon once bonded with Fayeth."

"Exactly." Wigmund smiled faintly. "It is said that Luminae still exists beyond the Mana Fields. It is wild there, you know. To bequeath you the number of Mana Lumens I plan to will draw great scrutiny. It has to be warranted. So I thought, rather than go on a beast-hunting mission, I would use your natural abilities to go on a scouting one instead. I want you to find Luminae, and if she doesn't exist, find evidence of her death."

"Wait, you don't happen to mean Luminae, the Dreaming?" Sylas asked.

"Where did you hear that?" Tilbud asked as everyone turned to Sylas.

"It's a song, yeah? Bart the bard was singing it the other day at the market. It was about sleeping. I remember thinking it sounded funny."

"Luminae is sleeping?" Wigmund asked him.

"I don't know. It's just the song that Bart—"

The divine arbiter stretched his hand out and conjured up a portal above him. Bart fell out, the bard still in his light blue nightcap and pajamas.

"What the—" Bart pushed to his feet and lost his nightcap in the process. He grabbed it, and brought it back down onto his head. "What's the bloody meaning of this? Sylas?" The bard motioned to Wigmund. "Who's he?"

"Tell us, good sir," Wigmund began, "what are the lyrics to a song you recently sang about Luminae, the Dreamer."

Bart glanced around again until his eyes settled on Tilbud. "This is some kind of joke? Is this your doing?"

"Not a joke, sadly, because it would be a funny one. The portal? I'm afraid not. Those kinds of abilities are banned by the Crafting Laws. But please, tell us the lyrics so I may write them down." Tilbud's finger glowed. "Go on, Bart."

"Why would you want to do that?"

"Because there may be a clue that we need in the words to find Luminae," Tilbud said.

"I was thinking that as well," said Wigmund.

"I'm surprised you didn't know the song," Tilbud told him.

"I am not privy to every song that the bards sing. And I will admit that this was an oversight on my part. I was going to challenge you with finding Luminae, but now I'm interested in what else we can learn from the song. It is better than the information I had, which is none, aside from a rumor that she may be in the region."

"You were going to send us on a wild goose chase?" Mira shook her head as she realized how strange that sounded, considering her pet.

"Like I said," Wigmund told her, "the challenge had to be adequate for the distribution of immense amounts of Mana Lumens. But go on, Bart, let us hear this song."

"I need to warm up before I sing."

"No need to sing," Tilbud told Bart, "just tell us the lyrics, all that you know, so I can write it down."

"Well, the chorus is 'Oh Luminae, the Dreaming, in your slumber the stars are weeping, rest in twilight's gaze until the time comes for you to wake. Rest now, Dreaming, in the sky, with Fayeth's light that never dies.' I usually just sing that several times because of the complexity of the lute part." He peered up at the ceiling for a moment. "I only actually know one of the verses, and maybe it's not the entire thing. I would be able to find out more had the Crafting Laws not closed the Songweaver Guild. Now, everything is scattered, and it's much harder to learn Underworldian songs."

"That's fine," Tilbud said as he finished writing the lyrics using Quill. "Tell us the verse you know."

"I think it's something like 'In the heart of the Celestial Sea, on a star-kissed isle of rock and scree, a place where auras softly gleam.' Yeah, that's it. But there's probably a part I'm missing." Bart shrugged.

"Does that mean anything to you?" Tilbud asked Wigmund.

The divine arbiter tapped his lip a few times with his finger. "The Celestial Sea is deep in the Mana Fields. It is the source of manastorms, and is generally avoided. There have been excursions, I've been on one, but they are usually just to collect samples and document Celestial Beasts. I can get you all there, though. I can also outfit you. But that's where my assistance must end if we're to later use the Mana Lumens I have available. This information is wonderful, however. It is wonderful because lore from *your* realm may help us solve a great mystery, which will intrigue the Council and the public."

Bart's jaw dropped. "What is this man talking about? Has he gone mad?"

"I assure you, good sir, I went mad long ago," Wigmund said. "Please, rest." He lowered his hand and Bart started to blink. The bard dropped to the ground, and as soon as he was comfortable, a portal appeared beneath him, whisking him away.

"That was easy enough," Tilbud said. "It really is too bad I can't use a spell like that."

"He won't remember a thing, in case any of you were worried." The divine arbiter rubbed his hands together. "This is also exciting. Can you not feel the excitement?"

"I don't know what to think about any of this," Quinlan said to grunts from Kael and Raelis.

"And Luminae needs to be woken?" Tilbud asked Wigmund.

"I believe so, yes."

"In that case, I may have something for that." Tilbud glanced at Catia, who had just stepped in. "I will need to borrow your Amplify ability, love."

CHAPTER TWENTY-ONE

DOING HEAVEN'S DIRTY WORK

I *really have no idea where they are taking us, but I certainly don't mind being carried,* Patches told Cornbread, the pub cat now in the big man's arms.

Cornbread ran around excitedly. *I can't believe we're going somewhere. I love going places! But everyone seems so serious.* She woofed. *What's there to be serious about?*

Oh, bother.

Gertrude, who was held in the medicine woman's hands, let out a little honk. *We're coming to a stop. Look alive!*

The group, which also contained the humans and the strange red-haired man named Wigmund, reached the woods outside of Ember Hollow. It was here that Wigmund placed his hands in front of him and created a pillar of light. He gestured for the big man to step in.

What's that? Cornbread barked.

*Where—*Patches yowled as they shot to the sky, the two landing in an area covered in a thick mist. The others appeared around them, the wizard and the warrior men, as well as the medicine woman and Gertrude. Cornbread and Wigmund were the last to take shape.

Look at all the fog! Is that water? Where are we?

"You're going to need to be quiet now," Wigmund told Cornbread, who beat her tail excitedly.

Patches struggled to get out of the big man's arms. He managed to free himself, and once he reached the ground, Patches gazed up at the sky above. It was dark, filled with a scattering of stars. His eyes grew wider as he took in the sight, which looked like the swirl of galaxies, nothing like the golden clouds that normally sat above the Tavernly Realm.

"You are in the Celestial Plains," Wigmund said to the humans and the animals, his voice clear. "You will notice my mouth is moving in a strange way. That's because I'm speaking both of your tongues at different times, yet you're hearing it through your own ears. But do not mind that. First, the animals. You have been brought here to assist them in reaching Luminae, a dragon of mana, who may or may not exist. But we do have a lead, and that lead points us to the Celestial Sea, the primordial soup of our three realms, if you will."

A sea is a lot of water, right? Cornbread asked.

That's right! Gertrude told him.

Patches scoffed at Wigmund's statement. *Are you not all-powerful wizard?*

"I am, yes."

Then wouldn't you know if the dragon exists or not?

"Not necessarily. Mana here is much more abstract." Wigmund cast his hand at the sea beyond, one filled with glittering water that was soon obscured by a thick mist. "The closer you get to it, the harder it is to see."

And will you journey with us? Patches asked.

"I'm forbidden from doing so if I am to reward the one whom you call the big man."

Cornbread barked. *I'm not scared. What about you, Patches?*

I've never been scared a day in my life. And my name isn't Patches.

"Of course, it isn't," Wigmund told him knowingly.

Then what are we waiting for? Gertrude waddled toward the shoreline. The medicine woman came and scooped her up again. *Let's get out there!*

————

"We need to be careful," Mira told Gertrude as she held her tight in her arms. "We can't just go wandering off. Not with the fog like that."

The fog was indeed thick, to the point that it was difficult to see more than a few feet ahead.

Near her, Tilbud produced the lyrics to the song using Quill and examined them. "'On a star-kissed isle of rock and scree, a place where auras softly gleam.'" He shrugged. "I daresay this is the easiest riddle I have come across. Oh no, I've done it, haven't I?" He winked at Mira.

"Why are you winking at me like that?"

"What could possibly go wrong, eh?" Quinlan asked, intuiting the question that Tilbud was referring to.

Kael, who sat on the shoreline with his legs crossed, lowered his head. He took a deep breath in through his nostrils. "It is strong here, the mana."

"Yes, you can certainly feel it," Wigmund said. "A bit stuffy, if you ask me. But that is what you get when you get this close to void mana. I know none of you are here for a manaphysical science lesson, but what you're looking at, the mist, is part of a manastorm that can appear at any moment. It is created from Mana Lumens and Dark Mana Lumens, and, in that way, it is unaspected. Ripe for the molding. You can sense it," he told Kael, "and I'm assuming you can as well, Tilbud."

"Indeed."

Quinlan grunted. "It just looks like a dreary fog to me."

"A fog before a battle," Raelis added.

"Yes, it could be that," Wigmund said, "but do not be so certain. What you may encounter out there will be very curious, perhaps aggressive, and certainly dangerous. And, as Patches has already discovered," he said as he pointed at the cat, who now stood on *top* of the water, "you will be able to walk across the sea. You won't be the only thing."

"We walk across the sea and try to find Luminae," Mira said, still processing everything. She couldn't shake the uncertainty she felt. The sound had settled, but when they had first arrived, there were howling winds. It very much felt like the calm before an incredible storm.

"I believe that is what will happen, yes," Wigmund said. "Continue across until you find Luminae."

"Of all the people in the Underworld, you've chosen us," Quinlan told the divine arbiter. "I still find that part hard to believe."

"I didn't choose you, Sylas did. But I can see now that you all are chosen in your own ways, and if you are able to find Luminae, which I'm certain you will be, you will be champions in your own right. Even if we can't fix the Underworld." He showed them the palms of his hands. "I'm not saying that to tear your hopes down. I wouldn't be here if I didn't believe this would work. And I wouldn't be giving you the tools you need to make this mission a success."

A golden orb appeared in front of them. It floated over to Tilbud as a silver light twisted around it.

"Do you know what this is?" Wigmund asked the archlumen.

"I've read about it. It's known as a Manaporter, I believe."

"Correct. It will bring you back here," Wigmund explained. "If a storm starts, or you encounter something that you cannot defeat, you may return. But note there is a delay here. And if you did something like use it right before a Celestial Beast took a swipe at you, it would likely land its attempt. You don't want that. You don't want Mana Lumens stripped away from you."

"Understood." Tilbud touched the orb, which shrank until it completely vanished.

Wigmund sent his hands behind his back. "Now, your armor."

Mira gasped as plated armor made of a golden metal took shape over her body. She looked down at her arm and noticed the intricate engravings that traced up toward her elbow, the golden metal lightweight and polished to a bright sheen that looked magical.

She wasn't the only one who now wore the armor. Sylas and his soldier friends all had something similar on, though theirs was much bulkier, with thick gorgets that covered their chins. Much to his delight, Tilbud's armor was more formfitting like Mira's, without the gorget and with a stylish cape attached to it.

"Would you look at that?" Quinlan said as Cornbread barked, the farm dog also in golden armor that ran down her back.

"Gertrude?" Mira asked as she glanced at her goose, who wore armor that extended all the way up her neck and formed into a little helmet over her head. Even Patches had armor, which Sylas was already commenting on as he scooped the cat into his arms.

"An armored cat," he said as Patches's whiskers twitched. "I do believe I've seen everything now."

"And there's more," Wigmund told them. "You're going to need weapons, and I think it would be best if you select them yourselves. Hold tight." They flashed away from the Celestial Sea and appeared in an armory, one set in a room with a painting on the ceiling that resembled a great battle, the corners splattered with blood. There was a long sword rack against the wall and a table full of magical instruments. "Go on now, choose something."

Sylas and the other soldiers approached the sword rack. Quinlan went for a great sword that was nearly as long as he was tall. He nodded and rested it against the armor on his shoulder. "Wouldn't be able to hoist something like this back in our world," he said with a grin.

"In that case, let me get two." Raelis went ahead and selected a pair of expertly crafted swords. He found a sheath that would allow him to keep them secure on his back, while Kael eventually settled on a halberd, and Sylas went for a long blade that almost resembled the thickness of a butcher's knife.

"This'll do," he said as he turned to Mira and Tilbud, who were now examining a table of wands.

"I don't need a wand; I certainly don't," Tilbud was telling Wigmund, "but if you are certain that it is a better conduit for mana, then that should work for me."

"It certainly is that." Wigmund picked up a wand made of bone. "This one. It's made from a Taurigraith's collarbone. I had it engraved," he said as he showed Tilbud some of the detailing, "years ago, by a woman who lived in Draugr. Take it."

Mira selected a small black wand. "I like this one. Perhaps I should have something else as well."

"Huh." Sylas eyed a dagger with a gleaming silver hilt and a black leather sheath. "That should do."

"Great," Wigmund told them as armored Cornbread sniffed at one of the swords still on the rack. "Then we head back."

"But we take this first," Mira said as she produced the Silver Thread pills she had made from the herbs she and Sylas had collected in Lilihammer. "The pills will help with focus, and they have other properties." She distributed two to each of them. "We should find a way to give them to our pets as well."

"If only we had a bit of meat, yeah?" Quinlan said as he turned to Wigmund. "If only there was someone who could make things magically appear."

"Ah, yes," Wigmund said, "a bit of meat coming right up. A quick meal and then we go!"

———

Sylas wasn't surprised to see that Raelis was the first to push ahead into the fog. He was quickly joined by Kael, the pair scouting ahead as Tilbud, Sylas, and Mira joined them, with Quinlan at the rear.

The last thing Sylas had asked Wigmund before they ventured into the mist was to relay a message to their pets. "Remind them to stay close. We don't want to lose them here, wherever here is," he had said as he peered off into the mist.

Patches and Gertrude did just that, the cat staying near Sylas and the goose just a few paces ahead of Mira. Cornbread moved back and forth from the front of the party to the back, the dog unable to contain her excitement.

"At least she isn't barking," Tilbud said as Cornbread continued to charge back and forth, back and forth.

They continued on top of the Celestial Sea, which Sylas would have taken as impossible had he not grown used to the otherworldly physics of the three realms, from the water that he had discovered he could swim in indefinitely to his power to magically fill a cask of ale without many resources.

Even if he was familiar this sort of misty and foreign environment, Sylas didn't particularly enjoy the feeling it gave him, the sense that he was no longer in control of his own movement. It felt like a wave could come at any time and sweep them away.

Darkness. Like the Cloud Forest, it was odd to not be able to see what was directly in front of him, to not know what lay in the beyond. All he could see were Realis and Kael; that, and the occasional flash of light beneath his feet.

Quinlan snorted. "Bloody wild to think of it, really, a handful of blokes, a couple of pets, and a beautiful apothecary heading off into the unknown. Doing heaven's dirty work."

"That is certainly one way to put it," Tilbud said as he again produced the lyrics of the song. "Let's stop here," he told Raelis and Kael. The two naturally moved into a protective position, while Sylas and Quinlan did the same on the other side of Tilbud and Mira.

"What are you thinking?" Sylas asked Quinlan.

"I'm thinking that it won't be long now until we come across a nasty bugger. That's what my gut is telling me, anyway." His gaze hardened as he stared into the fog, which was occasionally accented by trailing flashes of light, like they were in the eye of a hurricane.

This thought had Sylas looking back to Tilbud and Mira in a matter of seconds. "Let's keep moving."

"We can always get back to the shore," Tilbud assured them as he refocused on the text. "'In your slumber the stars are weeping,'" he read, repeating the words under his breath. "'Rest in twilight's gaze until the time comes for you to wake.' There is nothing bloody helpful in the chorus, which gives us, as I said, Mira—"

"I didn't say that the chorus had the key."

"No, but you did imply it. All we really have here is that Luminae is in the Celestial Sea, on a star-kissed isle of rock and scree. We can already see the softly gleaming auras." Tilbud motion into the fog ahead.

"What's scree exactly?" Quinlan asked.

"Rocks," Kael called over to him.

"What if we just look for rocks under the water and start following them?"

"Can we . . . ?" Sylas crouched. He pressed his hand through the surface of the sea and noticed a strange sensation on his fingertips as if it were being sucked down. "Back in Lilihammer, I was able to swim without needing to breathe. Maybe if we found the rocks below, we could follow them on their natural path to this star-kissed isle."

Tilbud raised an eyebrow at him. "Huh. Huh, huh, huh. Actually, that's a brilliant idea. Who wants to test that? No one?"

"We are all wearing armor," Raelis reminded him.

"I'll do it," Sylas told the group. "Someone hold on to my foot."

"I've got you," Quinlan told Sylas as he crouched beside him. Sylas set his sword down on top of the water. It floated slightly as the calm waves rolled by, but it never moved beneath the surface.

Once he was ready, Sylas pushed his hand in deeper. He glanced at Quinlan, nodded, and pushed the other hand in. "Here goes," he said as he forced his face in. Sylas opened his eyes underwater and noticed that he didn't need to breathe here, or that he was already breathing and there were no bubbles associated with it.

He felt a flash of apprehension but let that fall aside as he moved all the way into the water, aside from foot that Quinlan was holding. To make sure that he would be able to free himself, he resurfaced on his own. He was surprisingly light, even with the armor.

"It will work," Tilbud said with delight. "How wonderful. It's too bad I didn't bring a set of swim trunks, but I suppose that is fine."

Sylas stood and flicked some of the water away. "It's the same as it was in Lilihammer," he told Mira.

"I see. In that case, I guess we just jump in the water and go from there." She laughed. "If it wasn't already crazy enough, we're now adding a new degree of it to this adventure."

"We certainly are," Tilbud told her. "But I think now we will be able to find this Luminae and the star-kissed isle she calls home. All we need to do is follow the rocks and, call this an archlumen's intuition, the *light*. Was it more visible under the surface?" he asked Sylas.

"It was coming out of it, I think."

"Interesting, but not all that surprising. We may just save ourselves a lot of trouble, mates." Tilbud cracked his knuckles. "Grab your favorite pet, and let's go for a swim."

––––––––

What is the meaning of this? Patches yowled as the big man held him in one arm and swam with the other.

He's holding you because you won't swim on your own, Cornbread told him.

I do not want to be underwater, especially in this dreadful armor!

This is the best, Gertude said as she twisted ahead. *Come on, Patches, scaredy-cat!*

Don't you dare call me that!

It's your name!

My name is not Patches. I do not have a name. Everything doesn't need a name, he said as the big man held him even tighter. *Oh, bother. Let me go. I can swim myself!*

Patches pushed away from the big man and started to swim on his own.

So you can swim? Cornbread asked. See?

I told you I could swim.

Just try to keep up. And remember what the Wig Guy said.

Wigmund is his name.

See? Cornbread laughed at the armored pub cat. Things can have names. I'm Cornbread; that's Gertrude; and you are Patches.

I will deal with you later.

I'm sure we'll cuddle later.

Just pay attention. I'm not cuddling you, Patches told Cornbread.

I'll cuddle you, Cornbread! Gertrude volunteered.

You are soft, like a pillow, Cornbread told the goose.

I take offense to that!

Both of you, pay attention, Patches scolded the other animals. *This is supposed to be serious. What did Wigmund say, something about a primordial soup?*

I would love some soup right now, Cornbread told Patches as he swam ahead.

Just try to behave yourself! Patches looked up as something massive moved over the waves. It resembled an enormous fish, yet it was made of chunky blips of mana that all twisted in its belly.

Cornbread stopped to look up at it, as did the humans. Gertrude only stopped when she realized that she was at the front of the pack now.

The goose returned. *I don't know what that is up there. But I'm glad we are down here. I don't know how we would fight that thing. Let alone kill it.*

———

While they could *breathe* underwater, they couldn't speak. Yet all of them stared in silence as the massive beast, one that was celestial in nature, passed overhead. Sylas watched it with awe. The creature was larger than a ship, blips of light emitting from its belly. It looked like it could have been friendly, but he saw the tendrils that the Celestial Beast dragged against the top of the waves, the way they were hooked and covered in barbs.

They moved on.

He didn't know how they could have been more cautious considering their precarious situation, yet now, walking the floor of the Celestial Sea, he felt like they had reached a new level of caution. Tilbud was at the front, tracking lights.

Patches swam next to Sylas, the cat finally taking the initiative. When they had first gone under, the cat had fought Sylas so much that he had been forced to hold Patches to his chest and swim with one arm, which wasn't easy, considering he still gripped the sword.

But he had grown used to it. And it wasn't exactly like swimming anyway, it was more like flying, which allowed Sylas to easily manage the sword while he moved ahead.

Swimming toward some unknown destination, through the murk, their way lit by Celestial Beasts swimming above and a glimmering pattern that Tilbud had discovered was coming from the seafloor—Sylas swallowed his sense of wonder and focused on what lay ahead.

His focus was so intense that he could hardly think of anything else. Any thought that came seemed to filter away, vanishing into the water behind him. He found himself intently examining the rocks ahead, gauging everything about them, noticing that they didn't have any plants growing from their crevices, so there was nowhere for something to hide.

Just like with the Celestial Plains in the Underworld, the light emitted from above was doing whatever it could to reach below. Yet that which was above corresponded to that which was below. And this turned out to be true even in death for Sylas Runewulf.

But he was fine with his death. As long as he had his pub, his farm, his friends, the market, and, most importantly, Mira.

He pushed on and caught up with the apothecary. Sylas reached a hand out to her and she took his, the two swimming ahead, Cornbread at his left, Patches just behind him. He shot Mira a smile as Gertrude twisted through the water again, the goose in her element.

Ahead, the rocks started to grow larger and more jagged. This forced them to swim closer to the surface. They had to be cautious since there were still Celestial Beasts above, enormous ones, even larger than the first they had seen earlier.

Kael and Raelis were the closest to the surface, the two former soldiers tracking the movement above. Sylas felt a hint of pride in knowing them. The group would be almost impossible to defend from their current positions, but he knew they would try. This begged another question, one that he realized he probably should have asked Wigmund: What happens if they died in heaven?

There was no telling. All he knew was that he wasn't going to let it happen.

After swimming a bit longer, the rocks started to shift upward again. They prepared for this by getting into a formation, Kael, Raelis, and Quinlan, followed by Sylas, Mira, and Tilbud. It was useless to try to wrangle the pets, so they didn't focus on that. The group was intent on reaching what appeared to be a rocky beach.

The soldiers moved ahead first, then Sylas.

As soon as he was out of the water, his feet on solid rock, Sylas turned back to the sea. The Celestial Beasts were close, but they hadn't spotted the group of Underworldians. He waited there for Mira and Tilbud to emerge, and Sylas was not at all surprised to hear her gasp.

"I would have never imagined something like this," she said in a soft voice.

"If only there were a way to capture this moment," Tilbud said, shock writ large on his face. "Try as I might, I don't think I will ever be able to describe the beauty."

The Celestial Beasts lit up the fog like lightning, so bright that they were actually able to cut through the mist. They didn't seem demonic in nature, but as Sylas had noticed beneath the surface of the water, they were clearly armed and ready for combat.

He scooped Patches into his arms. While the cat didn't like being wet, he did like being held and immediately started purring as Sylas remained focused on the enormous monsters in the distance.

"Well?" Quinlan said. "We reached an island. It seems… What was the word?"

"Star-kissed," Tilbud said as he swept his hand toward the rocks beyond, which all glittered in the fog. They couldn't see through the fog to see what was at the center of the island, but it seemed as good a direction to go as any.

"Star-kissed, right. Is everyone accounted for?" Quinlan asked.

"Present," Raelis said. "I found your brother too." Raelis jutted his chin to Kael, who stood on the outer perimeter of the group, silent as always.

"What about the pets?" Quinlan asked.

"All accounted for," Sylas told him as he placed Patches on the beach. The cat took a moment to glare at the sea before finally joining Cornbread, who sat near Gertrude, the goose adjusting her armor with her beak.

"In that case," Tilbud said. "Let's go where no Underworldian—or for that matter, Celestian—has gone before. You get my point. Onward, ladies, gents, and pets, and don't stop until we find Luminae!" Tilbud brought up his wand and disappeared into the fog.

CHAPTER TWENTY-TWO

LUMINAE'S AWAKENING

Sylas and his group pressed deeper into the mist. He kept his sword drawn, prepared to strike anything that made an attempt to attack them. At least with what they'd seen below the sea with the Celestial Beasts, the monsters would be accompanied by light, perhaps making it easier to see them coming.

This would be nothing like the campaigns he had been on back in his world, or even the Underworld, where ambushes were something of which to be wary. But they still moved like an ambush was a possibility, Sylas yet again swallowing the sense of pride he felt in being with his men, armored, ready for anything.

"Just like old times," Quinlan said as if he could read Sylas's mind.

Raelis disagreed. "Old times? When was the last time we were venturing into the fog in pursuit of a dragon made of mana? In your wildest dreams, mate."

"Or nightmares," Mira said.

"Hold." Kael put a hand up and everyone bristled.

Sylas squinted into the fog ahead, trying to see the thing coming their way. And whatever it was, it was moving quickly, the light growing brighter around the incoming monster. Sylas and Quinlan jumped left while the others moved to the right.

The Celestial Beast, a creature with the body of an elk and a magnificent set of horns, each with a bulb hanging from them, skidded to a halt.

"Not today," Tilbud said as he hit it with a burst of mana.

This didn't have the intended effect as the creature opened its mouth and absorbed the mana, the light rushing into its throat and illuminating part of its chest. It returned fire through the tips of its tendril-like antlers. The beast's attack would have hit Tilbud had it not been for Kael, who grabbed him just in time to protect the archlumen.

Quinlan rushed in with his big sword and struck the Celestial Beast down. The creature hit the ground; before Quinlan could strike it again, Gertrude went for her dive-bomb attack, the goose thrusting into the air and coming down to pierce the Celestial Beast with her beak.

She remained there for a moment stuck in the beast's chest until Mira helped her out.

"You need to be careful with that," Mira told Gertrude.

"My word," Tilbud said as he approached the dead Celestial Beast, which twisted as veins of light started to spread through its body. "I may be less helpful than I thought. Although there are other abilities I could have used . . ."

Cornbread sniffed at the creature as it faded, the mana from its body filtering away.

"Things aren't going to be what we expect," Sylas said. "Wigmund should have reiterated that point a little further, but going forward."

Quinlan grunted. "Going forward."

"It feels like we are heading up a hill," Raelis said as he looked ahead. "Maybe Luminae is at the top."

"It would be good if we could trigger any other potential enemies," Kael said.

"Trigger other enemies, you say? I think I may actually have an idea for that," Tilbud told him. He approached the Celestial Beast and pointed at a portion of its antler, the tip, which was fashioned into a prong. "Mira, you have a dagger, don't you?"

"Yes. And?"

"I need this. I don't really have anything else that would serve its purpose in the same way," he said as he examined the antler.

"I'll get it for you," Quinlan said as he opened his palm to Mira. She gave him the dagger and he went about trying to cut the antler. Sylas knew it shouldn't have cut through, but as he had noticed earlier, there was something tendril-like about the antlers, and Quinlan was able to smoothly cut a small piece off.

"Perfect." Tilbud tapped his wand against the portion of the antler and placed it on the ground. The piece of antler righted itself on the two prongs, which it used as legs to limp ahead.

"Ah, like you did at the Grace Academy with the paper goose," Mira said.

"Precisely. If anything else comes our way, it will have to meet this little pretty first," Tilbud said as he examined his creation, "which may give us extra warning. I'm not certain, but I figured he could help."

"No, that's good," Kael said. "I would scout ahead but we need to stick together."

Cornbread stared at the piece of antler that Tilbud had animated. She looked like she was trying to stop herself from barking, but the pressure became too much. She finally started up, barking loudly as Tilbud's animated antler took off. She was quickly shushed by everyone, including Patches, who bolted over to the dog and swiped at her with his paw.

"By the gods, Patches," Quinlan said with a cackle. "You run a tight ship."

It seemed like they would be able to continue, but then Sylas noticed a shift in the fog directly behind them. It was as if the sun were coming out from behind a dark cloud, the light bright enough that he had to bring his hand over his brow.

"It's a big one," Kael said. "This was the fight we were dreading. Tilbud, Mira, move ahead and stay low."

"Now hold on," Tilbud said as he lifted his wand, the archlumen having to look away as he pointed it at the incoming light. "I haven't tried this one before, but mana doesn't work here the same way it should, so let's—"

He fired his wand at the approaching monster and the light shrank until it was no brighter than a firefly. The Celestial Beast, which resembled the enormous one they had seen earlier with tentacles, was now about an inch long, zipping around them as it tried to figure out what had happened to it.

Cornbread jumped, caught the beast in her mouth, and swallowed it. She looked like she was going to bark, but didn't this time, wagging her tail instead.

"Did you just *Shrink* a Celestial Beast?" Mira asked.

"Did Cornbread just bloody eat one?" asked Quinlan.

Tilbud pumped a fist in the air. "Whew! I'm so glad that worked. I had to save face, you know? Especially after my performance just now against the one with antlers. But that apparently works. Shrink. Ha. I didn't think it would. In fact, now that I see that Shrink can be used on Celestial Beasts, it makes me wonder if we could use them on monsters from the Chasm. Imagine a bunch of mite-sized monsters roaming around."

"Mite-sized or bite-sized?" Quinlan asked.

"Good god, man! That is hilarious." Tilbud laughed nervously at Quinlan's pun. "This is all going smashingly well, I would say. All we have to do now is find Luminae. Everyone, stay on your toes, and that goes for you as well," he told Gertrude. "The day is still young, or the night, if we are being honest, is still young. We will reach the end of it yet!"

"Just stay focused," Sylas reminded all of them. "We're getting closer."

———

Tilbud's animated antler worked as the archlumen had intended, stirring up anything along the path and giving them advance notice. At the front of the group, Kael and Raelis often responded the quickest. They were assisted by Patches and Cornbread, who were starting to get the hang of what they were doing. Gertrude intervened a few times with feathered daggers and her beak drilling power.

While Sylas wanted to join the fray, he was too busy keeping guard alongside Quinlan.

"If only we knew what Luminae smelled like," Quinlan said. "Then we could use Cornbread to our advantage."

"What would a dragon made of mana smell like?" Tilbud asked. "I'm not being facetious either, I'm genuinely curious."

"We just need to keep moving ahead until we find it. If it is made of mana, then perhaps it is something we will be able to see, even with the fog," Sylas said.

"Maybe we are going about this the wrong way," Mira said. "If we were louder, we could bring Luminae to us."

"We certainly could, but only if the dragon were actually awake," Tilbud reminded her.

"Should we be looking for a den of sorts, or maybe a—" Quinlan wasn't able to finish his question as a flash of light ahead caught their attention.

A Celestial Beast shaped into the form of a blob sludged forward, where it attempted to strike Kael, only to be repelled by Raelis. Mira pointed her wand at the Celestial slime and zapped it with a burst of mana, which it absorbed. But it froze long enough for Kael to finish the beast.

The Celestial slime let out a terrifying shriek as it expired.

"Oh, great," Quinlan said once they heard similar shrieks in the distance. "All his friends will be here shortly."

"Slimes made of light." Mira lowered her wand as she considered this. "Actually, I may have a solution."

The shrieks grew louder, the noise made scarier due to the fog obscuring everything around them.

"At this point I'll try anything," Tilbud told her. "What are you thinking?"

"There are slimes not far from the Shadowstone Mountains. Silver Thread shares a property with Bronze Silver Thread, which I've used before to stop the slimes from bothering me when I gather herbs."

"How does that work exactly?" Tilbud asked hurriedly. "I have not encountered these slimes."

"You haven't? I'm surprised to hear that. To get them to go away, I usually swat at them with leaves from the plant, which I have affixed to a stick. What I'm saying here is that we just need them to touch it. So, I don't know, throw the pills I have at them?"

"Throw. Yes, this is good, this is very good, Mira. I can handle something like that with a variation of my flying skill. The Silver Thread pills please," Tilbud said, "and everyone prepare for an onslaught of Celestial slimes. My, how I've always wanted to say something like that!"

Mira opened a satchel and dumped the remaining pills she had made into his hand. As lights began to coalesce all around them, signaling that the slimes were moving in, Tilbud tossed the Silver Thread pills into the air.

The pills hovered above their heads like a swarm of bees. As soon as the slimes appeared out of the fog, a pill would slam into its body.

"It's bloody working!" Quinlan said as one of the slimes froze in place. The others reacted in the same way, hissing and popping as they solidified.

Cornbread approached one of the hardened slimes, sniffed it, and made a disgusted face.

"Before we move on, let me be the first to say brilliant work, Mira," Tilbud told her as he pushed deeper into the fog ahead.

————

I didn't know a slime could smell so bad, Cornbread said as she rejoined Patches at the front.

You shouldn't go sticking your nose where it doesn't belong. Haven't you heard that before?

We couldn't smell it before when it was made of energy. But after the medicine lady froze it, I could. What was her name again?

It doesn't matter. Hey! Patches said as Cornbread licked his face.

We're supposed to find a big monster named Luminae. That's what Wigmund said. I wonder what it smells like. If it's made of energy, it wouldn't have a smell, but if it's solid like the slimes . . .

Patches stopped trotting along.

Why did you stop? Cornbread asked as she circled around to join the cat.

Gertrude sidled up next to him as well. *What's going on? Why are we stopping? The humans are continuing on. Slowly, I'll add.*

Patches turned to Cornbread. *Use your nose.*

I already did. What do you mean? the dog asked the cat.

I'm not exactly giving you a compliment here, but pay attention. You have the strongest sense of smell of all of us. I want you to stick your nose up in the air and take a big whiff of the air. Do you smell anything that resembles the slimes? Do you smell anything that resembles a creature made of energy that has taken on a form like ours? You know, one that you could touch. That you could bite? Think of it like that.

The big man said something to the pets. When they didn't respond, he approached them and was about to scoop Patches up into his arms when he stopped. He returned his focus to the other humans as the farm dog stuck her nose into the air, her eyes clenched closed.

You can do it, Gertrude told Cornbread. *Find what we're looking for.*

I can do it, Cornbread said as she canceled out the scents she was already familiar with.

She let them drop away: the smell of the big man, the medicine woman, the wizard, the other soldiers, the smell of the slimes, of Patches and Gertrude. Cornbread knew she needed to sniff beyond them, and she knew that the scent would resemble, if Patches's theory was correct, the petrified slimes.

Everyone grew quiet around her. As if she were starting to howl, Cornbread adjusted her throat and aimed her snout even higher.

Finally, she found it. She grew excited. Cornbread jumped ahead, her tail wagging as she took off running. *Follow me!*

Good! Patches called after her. *We'll catch up!*

Sylas slowed once Cornbread reached an enormous mound of crumpled rocks. She stopped barking and sniffed at it excitedly. "Finally . . ." he said.

"That was some run," Quinlan said as he crouched to catch his breath.

They had chased the farm dog for thirty minutes through craters, up hills, around odd stone formations, and past the occasional Celestial Beast, which the group quickly handled.

"Yes," Tilbud said as he approached one of the large rocks. He placed his hand on it and closed his eyes. "Quite the run indeed."

"Am I the only one who is thinking we're looking at a big pile of stones here?" Quinlan asked.

"Maybe Cornbread found a bone or something beneath it," Raelis quipped.

"No," Kael said as he continued to examine the mound. "There is something here."

"I know that. I was making a joke, mate," Raelis told him.

"All jokes aside," Mira said, "I don't think Cornbread would lead us on a—"

"Wild goose chase?" Quinlan couldn't help but laugh at his own joke. "I know, it's *corny*."

"You should take what we are doing more seriously," she said, but there was a hint of humor to her voice, one that indicated she too was ready to let the sheer anxiety of what they were doing roll away for a moment.

Tilbud pressed his ear to the rock. "Just as I expected," he said as he turned back to the others. "This, my dear friends, my dear pets, is, if I'm correct, Luminae. Cornbread, you are a very good girl, yes, yes, you are."

The dog wagged her tail and barked.

Quinlan gave the rock formation a skeptical look. "Are you sure about that, mate?"

"Are you unfamiliar with the concept of hardened mana? It is a real thing, you know, especially once it has gone dormant. What I'm saying here," Tilbud said as he carefully knocked a fist against the stone, "is that this, my dearies, is a sleeping dragon of mana, currently in stone form."

"Why don't you go ahead and tap it a little harder, then," Raelis said. "Or Kael and I can beat it with our swords."

"Let's not and say we did, yes? No, we do not want to be here when Luminae awakens. I mean that sincerely." Tilbud glanced up to the top of the mound, which was obscured by the fog. "But luckily, we have had a plan since our discussion back in the pub." He produced the tuning fork, the one with the goose honk trapped within. "As you know, I am currently dampening this using an ability called Amplify."

"I still don't understand how that works," Quinlan said.

"Were you listening back at the pub?"

"Maybe."

"Casting Amplify once is similar to what Cornbread is able to do with her barks," Tilbud told Quinlan as he gestured at the dog. Cornbread, who had been sitting and panting, realized that people were paying attention to her. She stood and let out a quick woof.

"Easy," Sylas said as he got down on his knees and hugged her. He kissed the dog. "You did good. You're a very good girl." Patches approached and rubbed his tail against Sylas's arm. Gertrude joined him, the goose wagging her tail feathers as Tilbud spoke again:

"If you cast once, Amplify amplifies. If you cast it twice, Amplify dampens, but only at its highest level, which is why I borrowed Catia's spell; or rather, we traded to satisfy system requirements. In any event, the reason we aren't hearing Gertrude's captured honks is because currently, I have dampened the sound. If I cast the spell again, thrice, if I may, it will remove the dampening, and we will once again be left with the loud honks of an agitated goose. That, my friends, is what we are going to use to wake Luminae."

"A goose's honk?" Quinlan asked.

"Precisely."

"And what if it doesn't work?" Mira asked.

"Well, we'll try something else. You weren't planning to give up now, were you?"

"Of course not."

"I would hope not." Tilbud examined the tuning fork for a moment. "But I think this will work. And if not, I'm sure we have a plethora of Plan Bs, including using brute force until it finally awakens. But I don't think it will come to that. I have read a treatise, you know, on hardened mana. If there is a being within, it can be disturbed. So let's disturb it. First, all of you need to stand there, together. Grab your pets."

Sylas took Patches, Raelis scooped up Cornbread, and Mira grabbed Gertrude. They joined Kael and Quinlan in the place Tilbud had indicated.

"How's this?" Raelis asked.

"Good. Yes, stay there. I will take care of the sound and once we are certain that Luminae is awake—and before you ask, Quinlan, I am nearly certain we will know—once we are certain, we will portal back to Wigmund. Yes? Are there any concerns? Any doubts?"

Sylas exchanged glances with Mira. The apothecary said, "I have numerous doubts, but I don't think airing them will lead to better results."

"Likely not," Tilbud told her. "And do be sure to hold on to the pets. This is going to get loud."

Raelis shifted Cornbread in his arms so that he could cup her ears. Sylas tried to do the same with Patches, but the pub cat wasn't having it until Kael came to help.

"Right, good. Here goes nothing," Tilbud said as he raised the tuning fork. He pointed his wand at it. One golden bolt of mana later, the tuning fork started vibrating.

As carefully as ever, Tilbud placed the tuning fork in a crevice of the rocks, deep enough that it wouldn't dislodge itself. He joined Sylas and the others.

"That is intense," Quinlan said after the first honk, which made Sylas feel like something had popped in his eardrums. The sound was much louder than even he had expected.

"I told you it would be," Tilbud told him, the archlumen now holding his fingers over his ears. "Keep an eye on the stone. If it starts moving, or if you see light peeking out, that means it's time to go!"

Another honk.

"It's okay," Sylas told Patches. "You'll be okay." The cat was squirming now, yet Kael was gentle enough and was holding his head so that Patches couldn't full-on attack Sylas or him.

Cornbread started the whine.

"We have to be certain," Tilbud told the farm dog, even though she couldn't understand him.

Another two phantom honks and finally, there was some activity. At first it felt like an earthquake as the ground moved, but then an arc of light exploded out of the side of the mound of rocks.

"Tilbud," Mira said, alarmed.

"We have to be certain." He had his hand around the Manaporter, holding it to his chest.

Another honk and more energy blazed out of the rock, lighting up the fog.

"Tilbud . . ." Quinlan growled.

"We just need one more sign," Tilbud said as the ground shook even more, the mound of stone coming to life. The sign Tilbud needed came after the next honk as a pillar of light bloomed from the other side of the rock mound, so bright that all of them jumped back.

Sylas never saw the archlumen activate the Manaporter.

One second, he stood there with Patches in his arms, Kael helping him control the pub cat. The next he was on the shore of the Celestial Sea, where this had all started.

———

"Right," Tilbud said, a wild look in his eyes as he turned back to the fog, which now strobed with light. "This should be interesting to watch."

"Do you think it's dangerous?" Mira asked Tilbud as Gertrude struggled in her arms. "Easy, girl. Easy," she said as she stroked the goose's head.

"Is it dangerous? Why, of course it is, but I believe we are safe here. Isn't that right, Wigmund?"

"Indeed," the divine arbiter said as his form appeared into existence next to Tilbud. It was only after he stood there for a second that Sylas realized Wigmund's robes had been on the shoreline the entire time, and that he had simply retaken them. "We are safe," Wigmund said as a near-translucent shield of golden mana encapsulated them. "We could head back, but I figure you would like to watch what happens next."

"Most certainly," Tilbud said.

"And the rest of you?" Wigmund asked.

"As long as it doesn't kill us, sure, why not?" Quinlan said.

"We're already dead, remember," Raelis told him.

"Yeah, that. Heh. Well, in that case, what do we have to lose?"

"And what did you do exactly?" Wigmund asked as the fog beyond started to roll away. Bolts of mana flashed through it before retracting toward some glowing beacon in the distance. "Was it what you had planned?"

"It was. Almost down to the letter. We amplified an enchanted goose honk that I had trapped in a tuning fork," Tilbud said matter-of-factly. "This seemed to awaken Luminae."

"Ah, yes," Wigmund said, excitement in his eyes. "Waking a dragon with an enchanted goose honk. Ingenious, really. I await the songs the bards will one day sing of this."

"Is it safe here?" Mira asked again, nervous.

"Once we see Luminae's first flight, we will leave and make plans from there. We are lucky, you know. What we are set to witness will be studied for years."

"Shouldn't there be others here to see it?" Sylas asked as the sky beyond filled with more golden bolts of light.

"They will be able to see this from Galataport and they will be here shortly after, another reason we should go soon. As your friend Kael can attest, they will be able to feel it as well."

Sylas glanced at Kael, who now sat, his head bowed as he inhaled deeply.

"Ah, there!" Wigmund motioned to the distance just as a great flare lit the sky.

It was brief, but Sylas saw the dragon of mana twist through the fog, its body illuminated in the same way as the other Celestial Beasts, yet much brighter. Painfully bright. Luminae brought her head back and roared, the massive Celestial Beast releasing so much light that Sylas had to look away.

It was a sight he would never forget.

————

Wigmund and the others appeared in what Sylas recognized as the divine arbiter's study.

"We are still in the Plains, it seems," Kael said as he approached the window, which overlooked what Sylas assumed was Galataport. Wigmund certainly had a view, one that saw numerous buildings, a sparkling body of water, and round hills in the distance covered in trees with golden leaves. It reminded him of Battersea in certain ways.

"Yes, you are," Wigmund said. "I wanted to brief you before you head back. But that's not going to do," he said as he looked at the stool where Sylas had sat on his last visit. "How's this?" One of the bookshelves that Tilbud had just started to examine disappeared, replaced with a long sofa covered in gold and velvet. "And you won't be needing that anymore," he said with a quick grin as their armor and weapons disappeared. "Please, sit."

The three soldiers sat, as did Mira, Gertrude still in her arms. Sylas remained on his feet, and Tilbud, now standing near another bookshelf, stayed in place. It was clear by the way his eyes darted to another bookshelf that he wanted to peruse the titles.

"We lived up to our end of the bargain," Quinlan began as Patches started to explore, the cat hopping up on one of the bookshelves.

"Yes, you will certainly be able to fund your MLu expenditure now. Do not worry about that part," Wigmund said. "I've also made it easier by setting up centers in every town, village, and city of the Underworld for people to send their messages from. They are aware, and many of the messages have already been recorded. You will simply use the MLus to make an announcement that the dispatch campaign shall begin."

"Are you serious?" Sylas asked.

"How long do you think you have been gone?" Wigmund asked.

"A few hours?" But then Sylas realized what the divine arbiter was suggesting. "Time passes differently here, doesn't it? Is that what you are saying?"

"Like in the Chasm?" Mira asked.

"Yes, exactly like that. You may remember your trip to the Chasm and how when you returned, the days had flown by," Wigmund said. "It is very much like that. Only faster."

"How many days have passed?" Kael asked.

"Twenty-five."

Sylas did the math in his head. The morning of their trip, there had been twenty-seven days until the invasion. "So you're saying there are only two days left?" he asked, his voice filling with both shock and anger. "Two days?"

"Yes, and people are beginning to go to sleep there, so one day, really." The grin remained on Wigmund's face. "I was getting worried, if we're being honest."

"Why didn't you tell us that time would accelerate like that?" Mira asked him.

"I thought it would put additional pressure on you."

"Bloody hell," Quinlan said as he threw his hands in the air. "We basically have a single day for this message to spread, and for your people to take action. That's what you're saying?"

"Indeed. But now that you're back, I do not think it is cause for concern. That is enough time to make changes."

"What about the Hexveil, its funding, or however you put it?" Sylas asked.

"Ah, that. I was able to do something there as well by tapping into some emergency funding that the Council has access to. The wall will remain intact, for at least the next two days. There have been a few breaches, but all have been handled successfully and none were near Ember Hollow. I would like you all to relax for a moment and understand, truly, what you have done. By completing my request, you've allowed me to legally free up the funds you will need to broadcast the message. The dispatch itself is already handled because I was able to tap a clause regarding Celestial Liaisons."

"I don't understand how you are able to set up the centers," Raelis said.

"Not a center, a Celestial Liaison. Most places have a building that was formerly a Celestial Liaison. For example, Tree Spire in Geist. Some have been demolished, but there are still ruins, even in a place like Ember Hollow—"

"Ember Hollow has something like that?" Mira asked Wigmund.

"At the city center, yes, the big tree there. Surely you've seen it. The Celestial Liaison. Didn't you ever wonder why it was so large?"

"I just accepted it was there," she said. "And dead. The tree is dead."

"It is, but its core is not. I was able to use it, and others like it, to get the message across. You'll see what I mean when you return. If this doesn't work, it will certainly be one of my last acts as divine arbiter. There are already some saying I have abused my seat. But I believe those accusations will be dropped once the results of the dispatch are known. So those are things that you should be aware of. You don't have much time, nearly a month has passed, things will be different, and you have all done incredibly well. Any questions?"

Cornbread barked.

"Yes, you are a good girl," Wigmund told her.

"I guess let's get back and see what we can do," Sylas said.

"I will portal you there now."

"One last question," Kael said to Wigmund. "How will we know if it has worked or not?"

"Besides the obvious—the Hexveil *not* coming down—you will know. Sylas will know. Tilbud?"

"Yes?" he asked the divine arbiter.

"Here." Wigmund pressed his hands into a prayer position. He pulled his palms apart, producing a solid brick of golden mana. "These are the Mana Lumens you will need to fund the announcement. That part will be easy. As soon as someone records their message it is saved and ready to be sent. All stored messages will be sent tomorrow morning, so be sure to get the message out today, I'd say before you decide to call it a night. That would be the best time because most have already recorded messages out of sheer curiosity."

"Understood," Tilbud said as the brick of shimmering mana faded. "Not to worry. These MLus are in good hands."

CHAPTER TWENTY-THREE

THE GREAT DISPATCH

You're back!" Azor said as Sylas and his companions all appeared inside the pub. The fire spirit was joined by Horatio, who wore a similar fireweave apron to hers, even if he didn't need it.

"You must be hungry," the water spirit said. "Hi, Tilbud."

"And hello to you, good sir. I hope you had—"

"Actually, yeah, that would be nice," Quinlan told the two as he took a quick look around. "We could use a bite." He moved to the door and opened it. "Just as I expected regarding the lord commander," he called to Sylas. "Come take a look."

Sylas and the other soldiers joined Quinlan to see what Tiberius had done. There were barricades and palisades, a roadblock, a wall facing the direction of the Chasm and watchtowers surrounding it. He also noticed trenches, but the biggest change was the one that Wigmund had hinted at.

"What about that?" Sylas said as he motioned toward the center of town, to the once-dead tree that was now covered in shining golden leaves.

"I was getting to that," Quinlan said as Tilbud and Mira joined them.

"By the jovial gods and all their debauchery," Tilbud said. "It's bloody beautiful!"

Azor spoke from the back of the group. "The gold tree is crazy! If you approach it, leaves fall and they tell you to prepare a message for a loved one in the Celestial Plains by holding the leaf and thinking of the message."

"Really?" Tilbud asked. "That's brilliant."

"Should we try?" Quinlan asked Kael.

"Let's. Sylas?"

"I'll try," he said. "I'd love to send something along to my mother, even though I've never met her. I wonder if I could send one to my father as well, considering he's in the Chasm."

"No telling," Tilbud said, "but it's worth a shot. Then, I must go to Catia so we can get our message out to the Underworld."

"I should come with you," Sylas said.

"All of you need to eat something and relax for a moment," Azor said. "When was the last time you ate?"

Quinlan couldn't help but laugh. "About twenty-five days ago."

Azor tried not to snort at his comment and failed. "And Priscilla told me to tell you to fetch her as soon as you return. So there's that."

"Then we're all going to Battersea after a meal, it seems," Quinlan said. "Yeah?"

"Works for me," Sylas said to the grunts of Kael and Raelis. "Mira?"

"That's perfectly fine by me."

"In that case, let's send some messages," Tilbud said. "To the tree then back for a meal, yes?" He swept the ends of his jacket aside and strutted toward the tree and its golden leaves. As the archlumen approached, a leaf fell into his hand. "Interesting." Tilbud closed his eyes for a moment and then the leaf vanished. "Good. That's easy enough." He wiped his hands together. "Who's next? And remember, you don't have to say your message out loud. The system will know what you're thinking."

They all gathered around the tree that used to be a Celestial Liaison as golden leaves fell. Sylas caught one of the leaves and a prompt appeared.

[Would you like to send a message to a loved one in the Celestial Plains? Y/N?]

"Yes," he whispered.

[Your message will be sent to the Celestial Plains. Unfortunately, if this loved one is in the Chasm on a Celestial Campaign, it will be held until they return.]

Sylas thought of the message that he wanted to send.

Dear Mother,
I am here now in the Underworld running a successful pub called The Old Lamplighter in a village called Ember Hollow. I also own a farm in the Seedlands.

And I'm the co-owner of the Petticoat Lane Market, also in Ember Hollow. I'm sending you this message to let you know of my presence here, and that I am thriving in the afterlife. If the Underworld folds into the Chasm, all that will be gone. I'm not the only one who has reinvented themselves here, so I ask you to send a message to the Celestial Council and let them know that my world is worth protecting.

I do hope you are well. And I hope, once Father returns from the Chasm, that you share this message with him. You are always welcome to visit me here in Ember Hollow. I'm usually at the pub, the market, or my farm.

Your son,

Sylas Runewulf

[Have you finished with your message? Y/N?]

Sylas nodded, unsure what else he could say. His leaf faded away.

He looked right and saw Mira finishing up, a tear in her eyes. Sylas waited until her leaf had vanished and then placed an arm around her shoulder. "You good?"

"Good," she said.

Raelis caught another leaf and sent a second message. "What?" he asked once Quinlan gave him a funny look. "I've been with several angels in my day. If they're up there, they'll want to hear from me."

Quinlan nearly fell over laughing. Even Kael, who was normally quiet, burst out in a cackle. Quinlan finally got control of himself. "You can't be serious, mate!"

"I'm dead serious," Raelis informed the two brothers. "We're sending messages to loved ones, yeah? Well, I had a couple of loved ones at brothels and whatnot—"

"You know, that's not a bad idea," Tilbud said. "I didn't think about sending one to former lovers."

"Maybe that's not the best idea," Mira told them, a pained expression on her face. "We want people to advocate for us, not be reminded of the potential trouble we caused them."

"No trouble on my end," Raelis assured her. "But maybe Tilbud should tread carefully."

"Perhaps you are right," Tilbud said as he looked over to see Duncan and Henry approaching, the two militiamen in new armor.

"You're back," Duncan said. "I'll tell Tiberius."

"Not necessary," Mira said. "We still have things we need to do. But we will return later, and I will speak to him then. You have done a lot in the village."

"We have some walls around the market too, and a gate," Duncan told her. "I hope you don't mind, but we kept the market open while you were gone. Cody and I managed it. Having people around and enjoying themselves kind of gave everyone hope."

"That's fine." Mira glanced back to Sylas and Tilbud. "Shall we? Food and then Battersea. The day is still young, even though it's almost night. I think. It is almost night, right?" she asked the two militiamen.

"By my reckoning, that's right," Henry said as he tapped his club against the toe of his boot. "We'll keep guard. You all do whatever needs to be done."

Their group was just turning back to the pub when Mira spotted something. "Is that . . . ?"

"Miss Barrowsly?" Sylas asked for her as the older woman shuffled toward the tree, Cody assisting her.

"Ah, I sent Cody to her house to check on her," Duncan explained to Mira, "just like you asked. Since you weren't here to give her medicines, Percy and Florence have been making them, and Cody and I alternated between delivering the stuff and checking she was okay. I guess he told her about the tree."

"I really can't believe it," Miss Barrowsly said as her eyes traced over the golden leaves. She could barely shift her body in a way that would let her look to the top of the tree, yet using Cody as leverage, her hand on his arm, the old woman was able to see most of it. Her eyes then fell onto Mira. "You're back?"

"I am. Are you here to send a message?"

Miss Barrowsly looked indignant for a moment. She held her chin up as she tilted her head to the sky. "I suppose it's time to admit that maybe I didn't know the recipe after all."

"What's she going on about?" Quinlan whispered to Sylas.

"Her sister is on the Celestial Council. They had a falling out years ago about a recipe, during the time of King Nova, if you can believe that."

"King Nova?" Raelis grunted. "Now there is a name I haven't heard in a long time."

Mira had moved to help Miss Barrowsly, who continued speaking to her: "They told me you went away on a grand adventure."

"You could say that, yes."

"I'm so glad you're back."

"I'm glad I'm back as well."

"An adventure with your handsome boyfriend. Must have been nice."

Mira smiled. "It was something, all right."

"How do I do this?" Miss Barrowsly asked as she squinted toward the tree. A golden leaf fell in her direction, and she reached a shaky hand to it. "Oh, that's how. Makes sense. Let me just think about what I want to say to Vaire. She . . ." The older woman teared up. "She didn't deserve to go that way. But I could never tell her that then. Things change. I've changed. And who knows what

Vaire has been up to, now that she's in heaven." She squeezed the leaf, closed her eyes, and it disappeared. "There, I said my piece."

———

I'm so happy to be back! Cornbread barked several times as she rushed around the pub.

Patches, who had already taken his perch on the windowsill, watched her with his big eyes. He agreed with her sentiment. *I'll admit, it is nice to be home in the Tavernly Realm.*

It's more than nice!

The big man and the others were gathered around the bar, eating and drinking. Gertrude was there as well, the goose standing on the bar as the medicine woman smoothed out some of her feathers.

The fire spirit and the water spirit came up from the basement with more food, which they quickly distributed to everyone.

It should have been a celebration. *After what we just went through, we should all be celebrating,* Patches thought. But no one was cheering and clapping, there were no songs, and while everyone seemed to enjoy the food and drinks, it was clear that there was tension in the air.

I wonder what they're planning next, Cornbread told the pub cat.

Patches's whiskers twitched. *There's no telling.*

———

After the meal, Sylas, Mira, Tilbud, and Quinlan traveled to Battersea, from which Quinlan continued to Geist so he could fetch Priscilla.

"Right," Tilbud said as he cracked his knuckles, the archlumen now in a deep maroon blazer, blue collared shirt, and maroon trousers. "Let's get Catia."

"To the guildhall?" Mira asked.

"No, her home. She won't have the same hours since she's been demoted. And it goes without saying, but it's best if we keep a low profile." As soon as these words left his lips, the archlumen grimaced. "Oh, my."

"What is it?" Sylas asked.

"Take a look above."

Sylas peered up at the sky. It was golden as usual, but then he noticed bits of shadowy black spreading rhizomatically across the horizon like smoke. They were multiplying quickly.

"Shadowfire Night," Tilbud said.

"Is that how it looks?" Mira asked him. "That's terrifying."

"The day before, yes. Which would coincide with how many days we have until the invasion," Tilbud told Sylas.

"So not a lot of time."

"No, not a lot we can do, aside from send out the message that triggers the trees. What I'm saying here is that it is time to get the message out." Tilbud pointed a finger in the air and took off toward the Brenham District.

"He always has to be dramatic, doesn't he?" Mira asked.

"Always."

As they moved through Battersea, the three traveling up and down hills as they cut through alleys that Tilbud deemed shortcuts, Sylas saw that most people had yet to notice the change in the sky. Only a few of them had observed the phenomenon and, as far as he could tell, no one knew what it was.

They reached the district where Catia lived and Sylas took Mira's hand as they landed. The three traveled up a small hill, one lined with quaint homes, many of which had tiled roofs. "Ah, here," Tilbud said as they stopped in front of a home with two doors. Tilbud knocked at the door on the right, looked to the door on the left, and then knocked again. "I'm sure of it. Last time I visited I was in the throes of passion, you know."

"Oh, please," Mira said.

Catia opened the door and gasped upon seeing the archlumen. She rushed forward and hugged him. "I was wondering when you'd return," she said as she tightened her black robes. "You were gone for too long!" She looked almost angry. "I was worried sick."

"Yes, about that, my love, apparently, time moves differently there than it does here, which is something Wigmund failed to tell us. But nothing to worry about. We did what needed to be done, and I'll catch you up on that later. Well, I suppose I should tell you what you need to know about already, the actions Wigmund has already taken."

"I saw. There are golden trees all over Battersea. Didn't you see them?" she asked Tilbud.

"I guess we took the one route that didn't pass near any of these trees. So, no, no I have not seen them. Most unfortunate, really. As I would have liked that."

Catia gestured toward the city as she spoke with her hands, the woman much more animated than she normally was. "They are all the rage. People have been preparing all sorts of messages. No one quite understands what happens to the messages after the leaves disappear. It's not like they explode toward the sky, or anything. They simply fade away. Of course, Sir Gregor and others at the guild have tried figuring it out, but they don't know anything, not really. And any connections the manaseers might have with the Plains haven't provided any information, from what I've been told. Although, we could ask Nuno."

"No, that's unnecessary. I believe Nuno's portion of this story might be over," Tilbud said, "but good on him for helping us with Article 6196A and not being a shifty, shady, no-good manaseer like his peers. Once all is over, maybe I will find him and buy the young-old boy an ale. I will also see what I can do to clip the wings of future manaseers, if I may be so bold."

"Tilbud," Sylas said, hurrying him along.

"Right, revenge later, important tasks now. Catia, dear Catia, as you can see"—he motioned to the sky—"things are changing relatively quickly."

She brought her hand to her mouth as she took in the sight. "I was wondering what it would look like. Shadowfire Night?"

"Precisely," Tilbud said, "and there is still work to be done. You don't happen to have a back patio, do you? I can't say I remember the layout of your house—"

"You should, you've been here six times," she said sharply.

"Heh. Well, in that case, all I can remember is your bedroom. Did I just say that? Of course, I did, because right now, I have a lot on my mind and I'm letting the words flow as they come. But, never mind me, dear, beautiful Catia, let's just focus on what we need to do next, which is announcing that the dispatch will begin shortly."

"So we are not sending it to people anymore?"

"Yes, we still are, in a way. The dispatch shall take place in the morning. We're simply telling everyone that it is their final chance to write their message if they hope for it to be delivered to the Plains. And we are doing so, I believe, *without* mentioning the potential doom that is to follow. I'd rather these messages be genuine, not desperate. So . . . what about something like this? Wait, let's head inside first. Or better yet, the back patio."

"The patio. Follow me."

Once they were outside of Catia's home again, Sylas spotted one of the golden trees nearly half a mile away. It glimmered just like the Celestial Plains, impossible to miss.

"How about something like this?" Tilbud said after he had traced up some words in the air with Quill. "And please, make comments, Mira, Catia, Sylas, if you will."

"Looks good to me," Sylas said after he read the text.

"Actually, I would change this part," Mira told him she pointed out a different way to phrase the opening line.

"I like that," Tilbud told her after he made the adjustment. "Catia?"

"Works for me."

"Sylas?"

"Same," he said, unsure of what to expect next.

Tilbud explained the process as he touched his chest, producing the brick of Mana Lumens that Wigmund had given him. "Use this," he told Catia, "Clairvoice will do the trick—"

"No, Lorewave. It's better. I have been spending time in the Groundwing Archives, you know, and this is what they have used to quickly spread information in the past. Clairvoice is better in a concentrated area. Lorewave and really," she told Tilbud," you do it."

"In that case, Lorewave it is. You will all receive the prompt shortly," Tilbud said as the brick fizzled away.

Mana rushed into the air, swirling like primordial dust in the wind as it spread over the city to the hills beyond, past Lake Seraphina, into what Sylas assumed were the far reaches of the Underworld.

The prompt came to Sylas a few seconds later:

[This is your final opportunity to send a free message to a loved one or a friend in the Celestial Plain. The golden trees will cease collecting messages in the next few hours, so get your message in now. To express your feelings and update those you care about who reside above, simply approach one of the trees and follow the instructions. There is no cost associated with sending a message this way. Thank you for using this chance to connect with those in the Celestial Plains.]

CHAPTER TWENTY-FOUR

CAKES AND PINTS

The prompt that came to Sylas the next morning was the most unsettling thing he had seen in life or death. He stared at it blankly for a moment, Mira asleep next to him, Patches tucked somewhere beneath the covers, and was unsure of how he should react. It was the moment he had dreaded.

[**You have 1 day until the invasion.**]

Yet even with the tension he felt in seeing the prompt, there was also an overwhelming sense of acceptance, of knowledge that he had done everything he could to try to prevent the inevitable.

Sylas turned to Mira and moved just a bit of her hair aside. The apothecary blinked her eyes open. She gasped as she took in his face.

"What is it?" he asked her.

But by this point, Mira was on the move, straight over to the window, where she peered out. "Look!"

Sylas joined her as golden motes of mana shot from the tree at the center of Ember Hollow into the darkened clouds above. They traveled skyward in waves, some brighter than others. "That's it?" he asked. "The dispatch?"

"I believe so."

Azor burst into the room. "Happy Wraithsday!" she said with her typical flare. She saw what was going on outside and rushed over to the window to join them. "Are those the messages? They are! By the gods! This is wonderful!" She did a fiery somersault.

"They have to be," Mira said as more waves trailed up into the darkened sky. "They're not just coming from here, either."

"They must be pooled from all the golden trees in the Underworld," said Azor.

"I'm more concerned about the color of the sky," Sylas told the two. There was still some golden light shining down onto the Underworld, but it was patchy now, like a thunderstorm was rolling in.

"Everyone is downstairs," Azor said. "We wanted to give you all some time, you know to—"

"Thank you, Azor," Mira said. "We will be down shortly."

Patches popped his head out of the blanket as Cornbread came rushing in. The cat glared at the dog as she jumped onto the bed and immediately started licking his face. Eventually, Patches gave in and actually nuzzled up next to Cornbread. Surprising all of them was Gertrude, who waddled into the room and also jumped onto the bed.

"Is it okay for the goose to be on the bed?" Azor asked.

"I don't think it matters anymore, at least not today," Mira said. "We will join you downstairs in a moment. If possible, can you take our pets with you?"

"Sure!" Azor floated over to the animals and formed a wall of wispy purple and blue fire that had the three racing to the exit in a matter of moments.

"That's certainly one way to do it," Sylas said with a chuckle after they were gone.

"I didn't mean for her to traumatize them."

"Patches is sort of used to her antics by now, so Azor has to really make it seem like she's going to do something or he won't listen."

"Next time, I believe I'll just grab Gertrude and walk her down myself. Cornbread would join us," Mira said. She pointed out more messages firing up into the foreboding clouds like reverse droplets of rain. "It really is so beautiful, especially against something so dark. Or I should say, it would be beautiful, if those golden flecks didn't hold such important messages."

Sylas slipped a hand around her waist, the two still looking out the window. "Even if this is the last day of peace for us, it was worth it. It was worth every moment." He kissed her neck.

"We opened a market," she said, growing a bit emotional.

"What a wonderful market it is."

"And you helped turn Ember Hollow from a ghost town to a bustling little village. Your pub has brought a lot of good moments to a lot of people. Your farm has inspired others to do something with their lives, people like Duncan and Cody." She stopped speaking and took a deep breath. "I guess I'm just trying to say that you are right, Sylas, it has been a good run, worth every moment." Mira squinted out the window. "It looks like my uncle and his men are making their rounds." She did a double take. "Are there more militiamen now? Women too."

"It looks like it."

"I haven't spoken to my uncle since we returned. I should probably stop by."

"I wouldn't be surprised if he was able to get more people to join, and you're right, you should. Although, Tiberius must see the activity at the pub by now and know that we're back. So maybe he will come by here. But back to what you were saying about people living their lives."

"Yes?"

"Imagine what it would be like if all of us knew the day that we were going to die, or the day before some imminent disaster, one that is unavoidable."

"What do you mean, Sylas?"

"I mean if we actually *knew*. That is what today feels like. We know that we're not going to die, but we know that something catastrophic could start tomorrow that could change everything. So it's sort of like that, knowing that something is coming rather than being surprised by it. We should live today like it is our last day, our actual deathday. That's what I'm saying, Mira. Deathday. You know, I always found that phrase that people use here kind of funny."

"Yes, it is a strange thing to celebrate, but I see what you're saying. Do you think we should have a cake?"

"Actually," Sylas said as he scratched his beard. "That's not a bad idea. We could turn it into a real celebration. We have the ale, we have the friends, we have great chefs in Azor, Priscilla, and Quinlan, and we have Tilbud to entertain us. Yes. Let's do it. Cake and pints. This is brilliant. It will be dark later and we won't be able to see anyway."

"You'll have Azor."

"That's right! I didn't even think of that, although her power comes from a bank of shared MLus so she might be quite dim."

"We'd better hurry."

Once he was ready, Sylas headed downstairs to find a spread of food. There were pastries and fried eggs and bacon, the smells all hitting him at once. He'd been so distracted upstairs that he had hardly noticed how busy the pub was. He spotted Kael and Raelis at the table closest to the back door, Tilbud and Catia, Nelly and Karn, and some of the regulars he was accustomed to seeing, from the people who lived around Cinderpeak's volcano, to some of the Seed-lands farmers.

He looked out over the people who were gathered one last time, a few filling their plates, and grabbed a pint glass.

Sylas tapped a fork against it.

Ding, ding, ding.

"As everyone knows," he said as he offered Tilbud a quick nod, "today is the last day before the invasion, at least according to the messages that I have been receiving every morning. Now, we have to be ready for tomorrow, that is a given. Luckily for Ember Hollow, I already saw Tiberius out there with his men, and I've been told that he has done a good job of shoring up the village. We should certainly bring them food as well."

"I can make more," Azor volunteered.

"Actually, yes, but I thought we would make something else today. Not just breakfast food. We're going to treat today like we should, with reverence, but at the same time we should celebrate all that we've built here, both in the village and in our own afterlives. And as childish as this may sound, I think we should do so with cake."

"A cake?" Quinlan asked as he glanced at Priscilla. "What kind of cake?"

"A big one. Imagine the biggest wedding cake you've ever seen. Something like that. Something that everyone can get a slice of," Sylas said. "And something that we can bake relatively quickly. It will become dark this afternoon, so dark that we might not be able to see anything even with the fire spirit among us. So until then, let's celebrate like it's all of our deathdays with one caveat in mind: we cannot be afraid of what is to come."

"I love cake," Quinlan said.

Beside him, Raelis laughed. "Yeah, you do."

"Hey! Is that supposed to be some sort of fat joke—"

"I have everything to make a cake," Azor announced.

"You most certainly do," Priscilla told her. "I used some of it to make the tarts this morning."

"I stocked up while you were gone," Azor told Sylas. "While everyone could have been buying everything up due to the lack of MLu tracking, most people have only been doing so within their means, strangely enough. Well, not all people. I personally stocked up. Horatio and I did. But we're not people."

"No, we are not," the water spirit chimed in.

"So we could do it, then. A late lunch, with cake," Sylas said. "We'll make a day of it. And later, tonight, I'll crack open some casks and then all of you can get to bed early, ready for whatever tomorrow brings."

———

The potential final day of the Underworld progressed as even more people came by The Old Lamplighter. Each person grabbed a plate of food, an ale, and joined in the conversations. The patrons and friends played games led by Tilbud, who seemed especially charismatic as he performed numerous magic tricks, from animated origami to a speed-dating game using the Quill power that had everyone laughing. They tried to not to be afraid of what was to come. That was the only ground rule that Sylas had set out.

As the day pressed on and the cake cooled in the basement, Sylas and Mira brought food to the militiamen. Kael and Raelis joined their patrol, while Quinlan and Priscilla continued to serve drinks and food at the pub.

Sylas spotted Tiberius, who had just finished giving out orders for a pair to move to the northern side of the village. He approached the lord commander with his hand extended. Tiberius shook it, his grip less firm than it normally was. "Now, we wait," Tiberius said with all the poise of someone who had said something similar before and meant it.

"That's all we can do," Sylas told him.

The gold above them was now nonexistent, the day darkening by the hour. Sylas could still see everything, almost as if it were bathed in a strange twilight, but he could tell that this would end soon.

"It seems like a lot of people are going in and out of the pub," Tiberius pointed out.

"We're having a bit of a celebration for all we've done, all we've strived for. Actually, I came out here not only to give food to your men, but also to invite you in," Sylas told him. "The cake should be ready soon."

This seemed to pique the lord commander's interest. "Cake, you say?"

"Come on, your men have it from here. You've trained them well."

Tiberius held his head high as he considered Sylas's compliment. "I have, yes."

"Then you can afford a small break before everything goes dark."

"I've prepared for that as well." Tiberius motioned to torches that he had piled up on a cart. "I asked around in Draugr and other places. Everything indeed goes dark, and fire is much less powerful than it normally is. Maybe that's not the right word, but you know what I'm saying. I was told that the darkness seems to extinguish the fire after a while, so I trained my men to stay in a formation around the village that allows two of them to continually light the torches."

"Smart."

"There won't be a lot of light, but there will be some. Azor and I actually did a test run with it as well, but we don't know how strong she will be."

"No, we don't," Sylas said as they were about to enter the pub.

"Wait."

Sylas turned back to Tiberius. "Yes?"

"Don't worry about patrols or anything tonight. Just relax. You and Mira earned it," he said. "My men and I have it from here."

"Are you certain?"

He puffed his chest out. "I am."

Cornbread barked once Sylas opened the door to The Old Lamplighter. She rushed over to Tiberius and the lord commander bent over to pet her.

"It's cake time!" Priscilla called up from the cellar, which had everyone in the pub murmuring with excitement.

"Yes, cake!" Tilbud said as he pressed a green orb into his hands, one that fizzled out with a pop. He joined Catia at one of the booths, and she placed her head on his shoulder.

Soon, and only after a small argument with Quinlan to remind him that he'd be unable to carry the cake himself, Priscilla brought up a three-tiered chocolate cake, which she set on the bar. She helped Azor and Horatio distribute slices, the fire spirit lightly toasting some sugar-glazed nuts on top of each slice.

They were all just finishing their cake when the Underworld went completely dark.

"Ah yes," Tilbud said as the glow of mana dissipated all around them, "Shadowfire Night has officially begun."

———

We have to stay vigilant, Patches told Cornbread and Gertrude. The fire spirit had faded to the point that she was just a flicker, and many of the humans in the pub sat as close as they could to one another, clearly afraid for what was to come.

But Patches wasn't scared. As usual, he patrolled with full confidence, knowing that he could defeat anything that threatened his realm.

I feel like I've seen something like this before, Gertrude said as she peered often into the dark.

As do I, Patches told her.

I don't remember a time when everything was dark, Cornbread said. *But I can see well enough. Not as good as you,* she told Patches.

No, no you cannot. But that's fine. We need to continue our rounds. Patches moved to the cat door and the other two followed. Someone said something to them, but the three ignored the human as they moved on.

They circled around the village, starting with the market, all the way to the medicine woman's home. The militiamen guarding the village continually refueled their torches, yet they provided little light in the overwhelming darkness.

Soon, it became clear that there was nothing for Patches, Cornbread, and Gertrude to guard against. Patches assumed there would be demons, but none ever came. There were no signs of trouble, nothing to indicate that they would need to do any fighting that night. While everything around them was black, Patches could actually see the glow of the big wall in the distance, the one that protected his world from the hell beyond.

This isn't as bad as I thought, Cornbread told the cat.

No, it is not.

Does that mean we should go back to the pub?

Patches didn't answer. Instead, he started on another round of patrolling. *There has to be something out here. What about Wigmund?*

We haven't seen him since we got back, Gertrude told him.

Maybe that's a good thing.

Patches sat and licked his paw by the roadside. He scanned the surrounding area once again. Everything was secure. The Tavernly Realm and the Marketly Realm were safe. *But what about the Farmly Realm?* he wondered.

You look concerned, Gertrude told him. *That, or you're deep in thought.*

Should we check the Farmly Realm? he asked Cornbread.

No, I don't think we should. I think the humans have it this time. Cornbread relaxed onto her belly. *For once.*

Maybe . . . Patches considered his next words carefully. *You know what? Maybe you're right. Our watch hasn't ended, but for now, everything seems to be in its right place. Let's get back to the pub.*

Are we going to sleep with Sylas and Mira?

The big man and the medicine woman? Patches asked her.

Correct!

You think they will let a goose join them? Gertrude asked.

I think so, Patches said. *But if we ever see Wigmund again, I'm going to tell him to pass along a message to the two of them.*

What message is that? Gertrude asked the pub cat.

No more new pets. He smirked at Cornbread and Patches, hiked his tail up, and headed behind the pub.

———

Sylas sat up the next morning and immediately noticed the golden glow that illuminated his bedroom. For a moment he thought he was dreaming. He placed his hand on Mira, still asleep next to him, the apothecary curled to one side. Gertrude and Cornbread were at the foot of the bed, and Patches was under the covers to his left, the pub cat warm as ever.

The prompt appeared:

[Your loan payment has been postponed until tomorrow. Your total loan balance is 20238 Mana Lumens.]

"It worked?" Sylas whispered as he adjusted to the light in the room. He rubbed his eyes as the message about his loan payment trickled away. "No invasion." Just saying the words caused his heart to pulse. "No invasion," he whispered again, quieter, as if stating the obvious would somehow turn the world dark again.

Not wanting to wake Mira, Sylas slipped out of the bed and moved to the window. He spotted the militiamen in the streets below all standing in a line before Tiberius, who paced, the lord commander saying something excitedly.

The men and women in the militia erupted into cheers. This had Cornbread barking in a matter of moments, Gertrude honking, and Patches scrambling to get out from beneath the covers as Mira woke up.

"Sylas?" she said, her eyes filling with joy upon seeing the golden light in the room. "Wait. We actually did it?" She pushed herself up. "The sky is golden again. The Underworld is here, the Hexveil—"

"If the Hexveil had fallen, your uncle and his men would be fighting by now." He ran his hand through his hair and turned back to her, excitement in his eyes.

"Then we did it."

"I think we did," he finally said.

"Happy Thornsday!" Azor burst into the room, the fire spirit accompanied by Quinlan, who had a pan and a big wooden stick.

Quinlan beat it excitedly, the sound echoing to the far corners of the small room. "We did it! We did it! The heavens be damned!"

"Quinlan!" Mira shouted as he fell over laughing.

"It was Azor's idea, honest." He got hold of himself. "It's celebration time—"

Cornbread continued to bark wildly at all the excitement.

"The whole village will be up shortly," Quinlan said as he tried for a serious face.

"But we're out of ale here." Azor glanced at Sylas. "You didn't brew last night, remember?"

"That's fine. There's always the stock at The Petticoat Lamplighter," he suggested.

"I forgot about that," she said. "There's also leftover cake."

"Are you thinking what I'm thinking?" Quinlan asked as both Kael and Raelis peeked their heads into Sylas's bedroom.

"Oi, mate!" Raelis said. "We survived without having to fight a thing. Imagine that. You're not going to believe who is downstairs—"

"I'm still trying to wrap my head around it," Sylas told him hurriedly as he returned to Quinlan's question. "Cake and pints, yeah?"

"Sounds like a bloody good way to get the day started to me," Quinlan said.

"Cake and pints," Mira said. "Now, and I mean this with the utmost sincerity, would everyone please get out of *our* room. We'll be down shortly. And Azor? Leave the pets here. I think we all deserve to sleep in today."

"Normally, I'd say that's fine," Azor told Mira, as her flames dimmed, "but there are Celestial visitors downstairs."

"Wigmund?" Sylas asked her.

"Yes, but he brought someone else as well. Tilbud is speaking to them now."

"Who did Wigmund bring?" Sylas asked, assuming it would be a Council member.

"A woman."

"Vaire?" Mira asked. "Miss Barrowsly's sister?"

"Not exactly. The woman claims she is your mother," Azor told Sylas, "and she'd like to meet you."

Sylas straightened up. "Why didn't you lead with that?"

"Because Quinlan came in beating his pan and I got distracted."

"Heh," Quinlan said as he gritted his teeth. "Maybe not the best way to break the news, yeah?"

"I tried to tell you," Raelis called over to Sylas.

"It's fine," Sylas finally told everyone. "I'll be down in a moment. Kael, grab one of the casks from the market, would you? I know we're not supposed to, but I don't think the Pub Alliance will care. Azor?"

"Yes?"

"Prepare the cake and some breakfast, if you don't mind."

"I'll help her," Quinlan said. "Priscilla is already down in the kitchen anyway."

Everyone shuffled out, leaving Sylas and Mira alone with their pets. "Are you ready to meet your mother?" she asked carefully.

Sylas shrugged. "After what we just went through, what's the worst that could happen?"

The two laughed, Cornbread woofed, Gertrude honked, and Patches scurried out of the room.

ABOUT THE AUTHOR

Harmon Cooper is a bestselling author of LitRPG and progression fantasy, including the Pilgrim, Sacred Cat Island, Cowboy Necromancer, and War Priest series. Born and raised in Austin, Texas, he lived in Asia for five years before moving to New England and then finally settling in Portugal.

Podium

DISCOVER MORE

STORIES UNBOUND

PodiumEntertainment.com